THE DROWNING MARY

LA MARIE SE NOYANT

Tony Boucher

Published in Great Britain in 2019
by AGB Publishing

ISBN 978-0-9928737-8-3

For Lynda
my rock

With special thanks to
Tony McGuire

Also by the same author

The Unfortunate Basil Albright
driver boy
The Tukul with the Blue Door

The Drowning Mary
is the sequel to
The Tukul with the Blue Door

Francois Degarmo had created so many paintings it was difficult to remember them all. But there is one he will never forget...

Friday 21st May 1953
École Supérieure des Beaux-arts,
Marseille,
France

Francois Degarmo knew when to stop meddling. He had learnt long ago how that one last stroke could have disastrous consequences, how that one mark too many would shout at him every time he looked at it.

He also knew this painting would be different, although he must keep it in his style, for him that was important: that manic spontaneity, those frantic brushstrokes, that thick swirl of frenzied movement. Always from the heart, impulsive, chaotic, the journey unchartered, the destination unknown, that Degarmo uniqueness which could never be replicated. This painting more so than usual.

Most of his paintings were completed in a matter of minutes, some longer, never more than a day. Even then they gave the appearance of having been finished within the blink of an eye.

The first stroke was red, the colour of blood. A thickly smeared protracted teardrop five centimetres long and one centimetre wide, about two-thirds up and a quarter way in from the left side of the canvas. He knew from experience never to start from the centre, that would be far too perceptible, like giving your intentions away from the start, a whirlpool which every other colour would flow into. A quick glance down, another stab of the brush onto the palette, quickly followed by another. Each action becoming more frantic, each rise and fall faster, transferring brushes from hand to mouth to fingers, all without caution, like a juggler leaving no time for deliberation. Sometimes he would wait, adding and waiting, waiting and adding, knowing something would appear at any moment. It always did, sometimes early on, sometimes later, sometimes he would have to wait for hours. Many couldn't see when it happened, but Francois Degarmo did, he could see nothing else.

This time an eye appeared, then another, wide, staring, frozen in time. Followed by a mouth which he circled with emerald green straight from the tube, dragging a dry brush over the small blob and smudging it out of recognition. A woman's features gradually grew out of the paint, her head facing upward, as though she was laid out on the ground: she looked serene, angelic, like an apparition under a translucent green. With a palette knife he dragged a thick ball of black away from the face, then a quick swipe of burnt sienna. He encircled his thumb around her head in cobalt blue, the perfect colour. Then like a conductor holding a baton he pinched the end of a brush, stroking turquoise over the canvas, as though the thin wooden handle had become liquid between his two fingers, adding more and more of it in a circle, as if he was creating ripples in water.

Francois Degarmo knew his was a style that attracted much criticism, mostly from his tutors, but also from fellow students, one mockingly accused him of having no more talent than a demented chimpanzee. '*True art will bare your soul to the world,*' he told him in return.

Raising his brush once more, Francois paused before the paint touched the canvas, knowing that one last stroke would be the one too many. He took a step back and stared at the finished work, something he had done many times before. It was only now he could see the mastery, the boldness of his brushstrokes, the earthiness of some colours, the vibrancy of others. This was beauty at its finest, ugliness at its most repulsive.

He would call it *La Marie se Noyant* — The Drowning Mary.

Francois Degarmo was a true artist.

Monday 14th June 2010
La Provence Newspaper,
Marseille,
France

Lucile Billet had spent the last fifteen minutes explaining to her editor why she had spent so much time away from the office, beginning with the story about Norris Kinley finding his father, even if he happened to be buried six feet under a broken slab of stone at Saint Pierre Cemetery. Secondly how Helaine Bonard came to be reunited with her son, informing him of Madam Veronique's involvement — a name not unknown to the ageing and work-beaten editor. Lucile knew neither story would make headline news or even a single column between the ads on an inside page. An Englishman walking out on his family and a reformed prostitute unable to care for her son twenty-seven years earlier was not exactly going to excite the gossip hungry residents of Marseille. More importantly for the tough-minded editor, neither was it going to increase the lagging sales of his newspaper.

"*The Markovic affair,*" she said in French. Lucile had planned her timing to perfection, she knew exactly what impact those three words would have on him. She hadn't honed a reputation as a serious investigative journalist without picking up a few tips along the way.

"*The Markovic affair?*" he repeated with an eagerness that had him pulling up a chair and leaning wide-eyed over her desk. "*Explain.*" The hard-nosed editor was a man of few words and even less patience.

"*I think Madam Veronique was the prostitute in the photographs.*"

His chin dropped, leaving his mouth agape, his body like a limp rag as if all the air had been sucked from it. "*You think Madam...*" Forgetting himself and the reputation of his newspaper — or more to the truth, the lawsuit that could follow. He straightened up. "*Evidence?*"

The editor had taken Lucile by surprise when he suddenly turned up and asked about her whereabouts a minute earlier. Laid on her desk like a loaded gun was the notebook Matthieu had stolen from the Madam, with its gold Eiffel Tower embossed into a rich brown leather it would be hard not to miss. Lucile managed to avoid looking down, holding the editor's gaze. "*Give me a month and I will get it.*"

"*One week.*"

Lucile softened her eyes and returned a flowery smile, "*Henri, one week will not...*"

"*Tell me what you've got after one week,*" he said as he rose from his chair. Henri liked nothing more than to stamp his authority, but deep down he knew any fresh information on the infamous scandal would double the circulation of any newspaper. He also knew one false move, one comment written without verification, could mean the paper drawn into an expensive libel case, especially with Alain Delon involved and the Pompidou family still wielding some power. Then there was Madam Veronique herself, he knew she still had influence in Marseille, though greatly depleted since her days running the brothel. Luckily for Lucile the editor still remained ignorant of the notebook laying only centimetres from his fingers, and

Lucile was going to keep it that way — for the time being.

She watched his pear-shaped frame disappear into his office. Stretching her neck up she yelled out one word, and in no particular direction. "*Julien!*" The loud clamour coming from the bustling office continued as if she had just whispered it. She took a deep breath and shouted again. "*Julien!*" Lucile waited.

After several seconds, a man appeared in front of her. He was distinguished looking, smartly dressed, with a full head of grey, bordering on white hair. Julien had an intelligent face with a road map of creases on his soft and permanently tanned skin. He was in his mid-seventies but had the stature of a man half his age. After working as a jobbing reporter on a Paris newspaper the confirmed bachelor retired to the South of France for a quiet life, carrying all intentions of writing a bestselling crime thriller. Failing miserably he soon became bored of finding ways to fill his days and secured a part-time job on the La Provence as a researcher. Having a reputation as a man with unlimited knowledge and more contacts than a corrupt gendarme he became well sought after amongst the newspaper's reporters, especially on the annual Christmas quiz night.

"*Sit down Julien.*"

He had seen the same determined expression on Lucile's face many times before. "*I have an unfaithful footballer Angelique is hoping...*"

Lucile interrupted. "*She can wait. Henri says you must drop everything and work for me,*" she lied.

"*Then I will have to speak...*"

"*What do you know about the The Markovic affair?*"

Julien's lips stretched to a half grin, his head drifted forward. "*Are you kidding me?*"

The Markovic affair? The Markovic affair rocked the very foundations of the French Establishment in the late sixties. It had everything an ambitious thirty-two year old Paris reporter like Julien could ever have wished for at the time: sex orgies, a famous film star, a top politician campaigning for presidency, the same politician's wife involved in explicit lesbian photographs, blackmail, the French Mafia, the French Intelligence Agency, the murder of the famous actor's bodyguard. Add them all together and you have the Markovic Affair. What's more, even to this day the murder of Stevan Markovic remains unsolved.

Julien's grin quickly receded as he saw the serious expression on Lucile's face. "*What do you want to know?*" he asked.

"*To start with Julien, where are the photographs?*"

Photographs? After Markovic's bullet-ridden head was found in a public dump, explicit photographs were discovered in the glove compartment of his car. Rumours spread that some were of Claude Jacqueline Pompidou (her husband, ex-Prime Minister Georges Pompidou was campaigning to become President at the time), the pictures were said to show her in a compromising position with another woman, an attempt to destroy her husband's bid for the highest office in France.

Stevan Markovic was known for throwing lavish parties catering for 'specialist tastes.' Rumours also spread that these parties were frequented by the Pompidous. Unknown to Markovic's guests, hidden cameras had been planted in the bedrooms from which he used the pictures for blackmail. Who the two women were in the photographs also remain unsolved.

Julien gazed down at her, interested to know where this might be going. "*If it was Madame Pompidou in the photographs then her husband would have destroyed them immediately after becoming President.*" He perched himself on her desk with one leg stretched out on the floor, sitting up with a straight back, his delicate fingers resting on one knee, as always his nails were perfectly manicured. Julien loved nothing better than to strike a pose, especially in close proximity to the more attractive employees of the newspaper: this had Lucile wondering why he did it next to her since compared to Angelique and most the women in the room, she didn't feel particularly attractive. "*You know he accused Louis Wallon and Henri Capitant...*" he said.

"*Who?*" Lucile interrupted.

"*Louis Wallon and Henri Capitant were head of the French Secret Police. Pompidou accused them of setting up the photograph with the prostitute. Along with Luicien Aimé-Blanc...*"

"*Lucien Aimé-Blanc,*" she said, like she had heard of the name.

"*The very same...Pompidou accused all three of having a hand in it.*"

"*Why them?*"

"*He had made it clear that he was going to reform the police, throw out the baggage, stop the corruption. You wouldn't believe how much of it there was in those days.*"

Lucile recalled how Madam Veronique hinted about the policemen visiting her brothel, most of them high ranking.

He continued. "*No proof could be found though.*" The words tailing away as Julien's gaze began skating over the papers littering her desk.

Lucile slipped a sheet over the notebook, hoping he hadn't noticed — he had. It was his job to notice everything. "*So it appears as if they were prostitutes in the photograph,*" she said, not wanting to tell Julien about her suspicions over Madam Veronique. Not yet anyhow, for him, just stick to the facts. She needed him to find out for himself, confirm her suspicions.

"*If George Pompidou could prove it was a prostitute then he would probably have kept the photographs safe. And if he lost the campaign to become President.*" He paused for a second. "*Who knows, he probably would have insisted they bring back the guillotine.*"

"*But he won the Presidency.*"

"*Louis Wallon and Henri Capitant got to keep their*

heads...he sacked them instead. He appointed Alexandre de Marenches, probably on the condition that he gave him the photographs. Either way I think they ended up in the President's hands." He paused for a second. "*Where they are now?*" As if he was asking himself the question. He dropped his bottom lip and raised his shoulders with an overstated French shrug.

A shriek came from the other side of the office. "*Julien!*" A woman's voice — Angelique's.

Julien stared at Lucile with large eyes. She picked up the desk phone and tapped in three numbers. "*Good Morning Angelique.*" The words sprinkled with sugar. After a short wait. "*A footballer playing away. Oh Angelique, I could find you an entire team who can't keep their cocks...*" Lucile held the receiver away from her ear, keeping the phone hanging for several seconds. She put it back on the base and peered around the side of her monitor, watching as Angelique stormed into the editor's office.

She returned her attention to Julien as though nothing had happened. "*So who killed Stevan Markovic?*"

"*Ah yes, who killed Stevan Markovic?*" he replied, like he was treading the boards in an Agatha Christie play. "*That was the problem, lots of people wanted him dead. Far too many.*"

"*Alain Delon?*"

Alain Delon? Alain Delon was a famous French actor and sex symbol, someone who mixed in dubious circles. In the early sixties he hired two Belgrade streetfighters as bodyguards, Milos Milosevic and his friend Stevan Markovic. With Markovic's reputation as a card cheat, along with his involvement in various illegal activities, he and Alain Delon parted company. Delon also suspected Markovic had photographs of him.

"*He was taken in for questioning because of a letter Stevan Markovic had sent to his brother. Delon was filming in St Tropez at the time. Delon's agent and chauffeur were also questioned. But it was his friend Francois Marcantoni who got arrested.*"

"*Tell me about Francois Marcantoni.*"

Julien began answering in short, snappy sentences. "*Corsican gangster. Bank robber. War hero. Close friend to Alain Delon. Not a man to be crossed.*"

"*You said Delon was questioned about a letter Stevan Markovic sent to his brother.*"

"*Ah yes, it was Markovic's brother who poked the hornets nest. He received a letter from Stevan before he was murdered. It said if he ever got killed then it would be at the hands of Alain Delon and Francois Marcantoni.*"

"*Psychic.*"

"*Concerned.*" Julien rocked his head from side to side. "*Scared.*"

"*Delon and Marcantoni could have killed Markovic and planted the photographs knowing it would put the heat on the Pompidous,*" Lucile said, her words tailing away as her eyes turned away from Julien, watching Angelique storm out of the editor's office and return to her desk. "*What happened to Marcantoni?*" Her words slow.

"*Lack of evidence. He was released after a short spell in custody and went back to live in Corsica. He is still alive, the last I heard. He'll be an old man now, probably in his nineties. He may even be back in Paris. I can find out for you.*"

"*Please Julien.*"

He thought for a moment. "*Unfortunately I have no contact in Corsica.*"

Lucile remembered Norris mentioning he knew someone living in Calvi. She would have to think about that one.

"*Le Parisian did a large piece on the murder. I know someone there, I'll get him to tell me what he knows. Probably want something in return though.*"

"*Great, thanks Julien. Tell him about Angelique's footballer.*" Lucile widened her eyes. "*What are the chances of finding out who the prostitute was?*"

"*Obviously zero if it was Claude Pompidou. Also probably zero if it was a prostitute.*"

"*Probably is not a no Julien.*"

"*It will be difficult. Louis Wallon and Henri Capitant are both dead. Luicien Aimé-Blanc...I don't know, he was a young chief of police, maybe alive. Alain Delon, he is...*"

Lucile interrupted. "*Alive, I know. Still not bad either.*"

"*Not my type,*" remarked Julien with a smirk. "*It's common knowledge that he won't speak about it, not to anyone, especially a journalist. I'll see what I can find out about Lucien Aimé-Blanc.*"

"*Thank you.*" Lucile began tapping her fingers on the sheet covering the notebook. "*And Madam Veronique?*"

"*You mean Susanne Dennel.*"

"*Susanne Dennel?*" Lucile sounded surprised. "*I never knew that.*"

"*Not many people do. No one can keep a secret from Julien Caron though.*" He glared long and hard at Lucile. "*Not even Lucile Billet.*"

Lucile decided to come right out and say it. "*I think Madam Veronique is the prostitute in the photographs,*" she said abruptly, then sat back and waited for his reaction.

None came, Julien remained in the same position, appearing to be unaffected by her revelation, staring at her with his signature half-grin, half-smirk. "*Why?*" he said after several seconds.

Just as she was about to answer Henri appeared beside her desk again. Neither Lucile or Julien could work out how this lumbering bear of an editor could suddenly surface as if he came out of nowhere.

"*Footballers and their sordid affairs are what sell this newspaper!*" he said abruptly.

"*Hello Henri.*"

"*Hello Julien...Them and that two-faced thieving politician*

Flament."

Lucile felt she had no choice but to nod in agreement.

"*I'm relying on you Lucile, remember one week, show me something worthwhile or Julien goes back to Angelique.*"

The editor stood for a couple of seconds, gave her a sharp nod and quickly departed.

"*Was that a threat?*" remarked Lucile.

"*Returning to Angelique?*" Julien said through a smile. "*Is there worse?*"

"*You said why Julien...Why what?*"

He thought for a moment. "*Ah yes. Why do you think Madam Veronique was the prostitute?*"

"*Do you remember when I asked you to find Helaine Bonard for me, that her working name was Heloise.*"

"*She had a son...*"

"*His name is Matthieu.*"

"*Ah yes, Matthieu.*" The words protracted. "*You said it was about the spread you wrote on working girls a few months back. I assumed you were following it up. Nice work by the way.*"

"*Thank you Julien, but in fact it was about something else. Helaine was a witness to a murder.*" She paused for a second. "*Okay...It wasn't exactly a murder.*" She bobbed her head from side to side. "*It's complicated...I was helping an Englishman.*" Lucile didn't want to go into the details. She needed Julien to focus on telling her about Markovic. "*We were trying to find the murderer of...*"

"*Which wasn't a murder.*"

Lucile sighed. "*His father. I thought there was a story there. Helaine worked for Madam Veronique many years ago. The Englishman and myself went to see the Madam. To cut a long story short she has lots of photographs on her wall. Most taken around the sixties and seventies. One has Georges Pompidou with Claude on one side and Madam Veronique on the other. She told me she knew them. She said she knew many famous people.*"

"Alain Delon?"

"No. I didn't see him. Neither did she like it when I mentioned his name."

"Stevan Markovic?"

Lucile remained quiet, feeling awkward for not knowing the answer.

"How does this photograph prove that Madam Veronique was the prostitute in the Markovic photograph?"

"She told me it wasn't Claude Pompidou, as though she knew who it was. It felt as though she was trying to tell me something."

"Ah yes. And did you ask if it was her?"

"I wanted to. Maybe I just didn't want to hear her say no. Like I said, it's complicated. You weren't there Julien. She wasn't actually throwing her arms round me in a display of friendship. What I did see in the picture was that Madam Veronique had a very close similarity to Claude Pompidou, maybe a younger, more attractive version, like she would be the obvious choice if you wanted someone to be her in a photograph."

Julien thought she was trying to convince herself. "*When was the picture with the Pompidous taken?*" he asked.

"*I don't know. After the Markovic affair I think...*" She rolled her eyes skyward and shook her head. "*Maybe before. It was difficult...*"

Julien's gaze remained on Lucile. "*I don't understand, if she is friends with the Pompidous then why would she want to ruin them?*"

"*I've asked myself that. Maybe they weren't friends. There is a lot we have to find out Julien.*" Now it was her turn to outstare Julien. "*There is something else.*" Lucile slid the sheet of paper from the notebook and pushed it towards Julien. For a minute it looked as if he was going to ignore it, he just gazed down at the tiny, worn label, as if it was taking ages for him to read the two dates, 1968-1993. He moved his hand slowly towards the book and pinched the cover between two fingers, gently lifting it like he was opening an ancient parchment. He read the first line on the first page.

12 Novembre 1968 Dominique (Renard) Clémentine 100 FRF

His eyes scanned downward, carefully studying each line in turn. Each one had a date, a name — two names, one a man's, the other a girl's, then an amount of money. Julien turned several more pages as gently as he did the first, each one looked the same, occasionally there would be a block of handwritten notes, like a writer's comments scrawled in the margins, most about the client's preferences. On one line he noticed a woman's name where normally the man's name was. Sometimes he saw a repeat of a girl's name. As he went further in the amount of francs increased. There were hundreds of lines — thousands.

Lucile remained silent, watching Julien's eyes move from side to side, her gaze flicking from the notebook to his face, wondering what was going through his mind.

He closed the book, wanting to ask where she got it, but knew too well a journalist would never give up their source, not even to a trusted colleague. He knew who it belonged to though. Lucile knew he knew. Julien waited, his face impassive.

Lucile continued. "*I was told many of the names are false, made up by the clients themselves. Sometimes the Madam would give them a nickname. The thing is Julien, if she knew their real name she would use it.*"

Julien sat motionless, keeping his silence.

Lucile wanted to force the point. "*If there were famous people she would have used their actual names, their real names Julien. Think about it, their actual names.*" Lucile stared at Julien. "*Film stars, politicians, pop stars.*" She paused for a second. "*Married film stars, married politicians...*" She stopped and waited again. "*I'm sure there is something in there about the Pompidou's. Something about the Markovic affair.*"

Julien finally spoke. "*Who knows it exists?*"

"*There was a rumour amongst the girls. Also Matthieu and...*"

Julien interrupted. "*Matthieu...Helaine Bonard's son?*"

"*Yes, it's a long story...it was him who gave it to the Englishman.*"

"*The Englishman?*"

"*Yes. Norris Kinley is his name.*"

"*Norris Kinley?*"

"*Yes.*"

"*And Henri, does he know?*" Julien asked.

"*No. Not yet. Not until I have to tell him.*"

"*Who knows it is you that has it?*"

"*The Englishman.*"

"*The Englishman, Monsieur Kinley.*"

"*Yes.*" Lucile puffed the word out.

Friday 1st April 1983
Parc de la Vauquelin,
Marseille,
France

The park gates should have been locked every night before dusk; but they never were. The authorities knew this, the police knew it, the men prowling the paths knew it, the working girls and rent boys knew it. Francois Degarmo especially knew it.

For the people in power it was a way to keep 'those types' off the streets. Out of sight and out of mind they would tell themselves. Only these same people in power didn't have to look much further than their nose to see who 'those types' were. Maybe these same people in power had good reason to keep it off the streets, away from the view of any passing stranger or reporter. What happened in the park, stayed in the park. Apart from this night. Those gates would not stay open for much longer.

No one knew exactly how the park got to what it had become, it just seemed to evolve over the decades. The rumour was that it started with one randy park attendant wanting a secluded place to satisfy his sleazy cravings. Word of this had got around the working girls — word always got around the working girls. Anyway, the park attendant's marital home was located, a threat of blackmail was made, a gate was left unlocked one night, then the following night, then all four gates soon after. The word is that they have never been locked since. The strangest thing, it was why the gates had been put there in the first place, to keep this type of sordid activity away.

The park happened to fit the bill perfectly, as if someone had specifically designed it that way. About twelve football pitches in size, oval in shape. A narrow concrete path encircled a large grassy area with the odd tree dotted around. The path was about ten metres in from a two metre high fence. In some places it was closer, other places further, nearly thirty metres. It was what was between the path and the fence at these spots that made this park ideal. A dense mixture of shrubs, bushes and trees — but not too dense. It wouldn't be unusual to see a man and a girl disappear into the undergrowth, or in some cases a pretty boy with a far less attractive man.

The only lights were from the lamp posts, all perfectly spaced apart, enough for the girls to parade their wares, like birds of paradise trying to attract a mate, yet far enough so they could vanish unseen after a successful coupling had been made. No one ever questioned why a park that was meant to be locked up at dusk needed lights in the first place. It was said the girls had complained it was too dark, that on some moonless nights they couldn't see a hand or whatever else was in front of their face.

Occasionally a girl would take a leave of absence, usually for a stint in prison. '*She is on holiday*,' they would say to anyone who asked. Sometimes the departure would be permanent, mostly after a fatal drug overdose or a falling out with their pimp. Other times it was age, very rarely was it willingly. This would leave a space for a new arrival. These comings and goings saw prime territories contested and claimed, strongly defended by the girls, or failing that, their pimps. Cat fights were always violent, faces clawed, clumps of hair yanked out. Most of the time they were friendly towards each other, always watching each others backs.

The boys had their own place in the park, a small area of path near the western gate.

During the day the park took on a whole new personality. This is when the path would be used by joggers, when young children could be heard screeching as they played on the grass, the wind carrying their screams into the far corners of the park. Maybe a group of teenagers sat in a circle with a cloud of smoke drifting above their heads, a joint being passed from one to another. Where sunbathers lay soaking up the sun, workers breaking for lunch, dog walkers, old people sitting on a bench waiting for God, mothers with push-chairs. Apart from the odd discarded condom laid out like a dead jellyfish in the bushes, and the abundance of cigarette butts littered around the lampposts, no one would ever guess what had been happening only hours before. This was a park with two souls.

Francois Degarmo pushed the gate open and stepped in. An excited nervousness had crept though his body, as it always did, as though he had walked into another world, a world of seediness and secrecy, a place where you could remain unseen, where no one was there to judge you, where people were there for only two reasons — buying and selling sex. A market for bare flesh that was only open at night.

He could feel the adrenalin pumping through his body, heightening and honing his thought process, sensing people without actually seeing them, a place where you could smell sex. Then after, when he had finished, he would return to his apartment, pull the cork from a bottle, sit back in his chair, wallow in the last seedy hour, sometimes begin a painting, sometimes masturbate from the memory. But not this night.

Francois Degarmo continued to wait at the southern gate, the highest point in the park, twenty metres to his left it gradually sloped downward, causing much of the park to be hidden from where he stood, not that he could see much in the dark, just the distant yellow glow from the lamp posts. It was quiet, eerily silent, just the rustle of leaves from a slight breeze. He moved away, stepping off the path and into the shadows, trying to see into the distance. Only two lamp posts were visible from where he stood, their balls of light turning everything they captured into ghostly shapes. It was there he saw a movement, the silhouette of a girl prowling around under one light. She stopped, a spark as a cigarette was lit, highlighting her face; he could see she was black skinned, a mop of tight curly hair bristling for that split second. Another girl came into view, much taller, long straight hair, a short skirt displaying long legs. Francois thought he could remember her from a previous visit. She was cold, skillful, got the business over with quickly — too quickly. He watched as she strolled past the other girl, her steps were clipped, slow, one foot crossing in front of the other, overemphasised, like a model on a catwalk. She continued, disappearing into the darkness. He saw an outline of a person approach the black girl, his sweat polished baldness shining as he stepped under the light. Even from where he stood Francois could see he was pot bellied, a baggy suit dripping from his body. Probably a salesman visiting the city — his wife would never know. For a few seconds the man and girl faced each other, something was passed between them, the contents carefully scrutinised by the girl. They walked away together, Francois followed the pinpoint red from the cigarette light as it floated into the shadows, vanishing a few seconds later.

Francois Degarmo stepped onto the path and began making his way down the slope, towards the western gate, here the area between the path and the fence was free of undergrowth, where he could see the railings and through to the road on the other side. Here he knew there would be no activity. Francois had time, he was in no rush, he liked to soak up the atmosphere, although he knew once he had finished the deed he would leave the park immediately, his step would be quicker, his head down, a man in retreat. Once he had left the park he would return to normality, or as close to normality as Francois Degarmo could get.

It was dark, the only illumination came from the house lights on the other side of the road. He knew a face would only appear when it was just a metre away. A car drove by. For that split second he was exposed in their headlamps, maybe the occupants had seen him, maybe someone in the house opposite had, probably frowning with disgust, maybe laughing at him.

He continued on. The silhouetted outline of someone ahead was approaching, getting closer with each step. It was darker, virtually pitch black after leaving the glimmer from the houses. Whoever it is was only a few metres in front of him. A man appeared, short, chubby, drooping shoulders, he looked like a loner, Francois recognised the type, after all he was one himself. His thick glasses glinted from the lens as he took a quick glance his way. They both turned away. The man continued on with quick, terse steps, Francois recognised the escape, that desperation to get away, not to be seen. He was probably ashamed, needing to return to normality as soon as possible after jettisoning his seed, knowing he had spent money on something most normal people would get for free, probably having spent more than he wanted. She was there to feed a drug addiction, strip him of as much cash as possible. The girls have a saying. '*When you are unzipping a man's trousers you are also opening his wallet.*' All that man had done was help her achieve that aim, one harmless fuck, that was it, one fuck that would stop her from shoplifting or robbing someone's house. Maybe she had young children to feed, maybe he had taken advantage of a vulnerable woman. Vulnerable! Francois chuckled to himself, there was nothing vulnerable about these girls, they knew exactly what they were doing.

Francois passed under the first lamp post. Approaching the western gate, he saw a smartly dressed boy in his early twenties, wearing light coloured baggy slacks and a crisp shirt with sleeves rolled up to his armpits. The boy was roaming between the gate and the lamp post, trying to snare his first punter. Francois could feel his eyes on him, he continued to look down. The boy took a step back. The language of the park understood.

Francois had finally arrived at the western gate. Two boys were talking to each other under the light. Both as smartly dressed as the first, the blonde one wore white tennis shorts and a polo shirt. Francois thought he was trying to create a theme, maybe role-play — a punter pretending to have picked-up the young sporty type, the foreplay would be a discussion about his game. '*Maybe I could help you with your stroke. Maybe we could go somewhere quieter and I could show you my fore-hand,*' he would say. The two boys gave Francois a quick glance before continuing with their conversation; they knew he wasn't there for them, it was like they had a sixth sense.

Several steps later and directly in front of him he saw the contours of two people disappear into the bushes, two black phantoms slinking away. He heard a sharp "shh", followed by whispered voices and the brushing of leaves. Francois was becoming excited, feeling part of the night, like a nocturnal animal.

The next lamp post was ahead of him. Two girls were under the light, about three metres either side of the post, both prowling back and forth, neither intruding into each others territory, managing to keep visible under the light. The one closer to Francois had a long red coat, she stepped towards him, a bare leg poked out between the front flaps, presenting itself up to the top of her thigh, he wondered if she was naked underneath. He glanced at her face, he thought she looked around fifty, maybe more, but was probably younger. She was gaunt looking with bleached hair, her thick make-up failing to hide a heavily lined face. She smiled at him, a smile that wasn't a smile, she stared at him through two soulless eyes. He returned a curt shake of his head and continued on, quickening his step, feeling exposed as he passed under the light. The next girl came into view, short skirt with fishnet tights, sharp stilettos and plump legs, far too plump for the length of her skirt; someone should speak to her about that he thought. A metallic blue puffer jacket covered her body, brown hair tied tightly in a pony tail, like it had been plastered back. A man in a dark jacket with a baseball cap pulled down over his eyes walked past him, he heard the girl speak, then the man's voice. Passing her he saw another girl, just catching the edge of the light. She looked young, in her teens, long fair hair, dressed in cut-down jeans, so short the white cloth of her inside pockets poked out from under the denim, tucked into them was a black netted leotard, teenage girl meets seedy nightclub singer he said to himself. Francois thought she had an air of desperation about her, like she needed a quick fix — or her pimp did. When she saw Francois she beamed out a white toothed smile, like she knew him, like she wanted to be his friend. Another year and those teeth will have turned black he thought, or even gone altogether. He wasn't sure about her and continued.

Francois Degarmo walked on, he heard noises as loud talking becoming raucous laughter. Three silhouettes were ahead of him, getting closer, animated, looking like they were staggering, bumping into each other. They had short, slight bodies, clutching each others shoulders and shoving each other around, laughing as they did. Their chuckling stopped as soon as they saw him, their noise becoming spluttered squeaks as they suppressed laughter. Three boys in their early-teens passed by, their laughter bursting out when they were a safe distance.

Another girl was facing away from him, her blonde hair just catching the light from the next lamp post, she was speaking to a man. Francois heard him speak, just one word, "*Heloise.*" Like he had repeated what she had just said. He stopped and turned.

The young girl with the cut-down jeans wasn't where he had seen her last, although he could just make her out in the distance, closer to the lamp post, under the full light. She had taken the place of the plump girl, he knew she would have to relinquish it as soon as she returned. He began walking towards her. He thought she looked even younger and prettier than before, not yet ravaged by the life she had chosen, or more than likely, forced onto her, he knew that would come though. She turned her back on him and began strolling away, towards the lamp post. Francois wondered if she had rejected him, he wouldn't be surprised. He stopped as she turned at the lamp post, spotting him immediately, her mouth widened, giving the same beaming smile as before, as if she had nothing between that and a grin. He felt relief. She began walking towards him, stopping only centimetres away, her body virtually touching his.

"*You could not resist me Monsieur?*" Her voice sounded sweet, slightly derisive, the words spontaneous though, not the customary text spoken by most of the girls. Francois couldn't decide if it was a statement or question. She was still beaming out the same wide smile, he thought it looked false close up, frozen in the same shape, held too long, as was her stare. It was then he realised the innocence, the naivety, that quality that drew him to her in the first place had been misplaced. This was a girl very much in control of the situation.

"*My name is Nicole.*" Like she was trying to make him welcome. She had still yet to receive the money.

"*Hello,*" was all he said.

"*It is three hundred francs Monsieur.*"

He had never paid more than two.

"*Two hundred and fifty.*"

"*Goodbye Monsieur.*" She swung around and began walking away.

Before she even took one step. "*What do I get for that?*"

She turned back."*You get to fuck me,*" she said with a mischievous tilt of her head, as though it would be a privilege. The smile held strong. She waited, her playful glare hanging on him.

He paused for a moment. He knew this was just a business

deal, they were going through the motions, words kept to a minimum. The merchandise settled, the price fixed, seemingly unnegotiable. "*Okay.*"

She sprung out a hand, holding it out flat, her eyes still fixed on his, the smile remaining. "*Then that will be three hundred francs Monsieur.*"

He paused for a second. "*Yes, of course,*" before delving into his pocket and pulling out his wallet, counting the notes one by one, he returned the rest. Nicole's glare had remained on him the entire time, not blinking once, not until he had finished. She looked down, the first time she had, flicking through the notes, counting as she did.

Her smile fell away. "*Follow me Monsieur.*"

She quickly stepped off the path and onto the grass, then followed the dark fringe of the undergrowth for about ten paces. Without any hesitation she disappeared into a space between two bushes, looking as if she had done it a thousand times before. He followed her, finding himself in a clear shapeless area of about four metres in diameter, surrounded by various sizes of shrubbery, just a carpet of dry earth underfoot. He was surprised how well his eyes had adjusted to the dark, managing to see a large dense bush in front of them, and beyond that the trunk of a tree rising into the night sky.

Nicole led him around the bush, stopping beside the tree. She turned. "*Are you hard Monsieur?*" she said coldly. The words sounded mechanical, clinical, like a nurse had asked him.

"*No, not yet.*"

"*Take it out.*"

Francois undid his buttons and fumbled around inside, he pulled out his penis, allowing it to flop into the outside world, the air stoked it, it felt free. He encircled his hand around it, rubbing it slowly. Little progress had been made. She was standing quite close, he stared down at her mouth and lowered his head towards her, he needed to feel that intimacy.

She jerked her head back, as though in disgust. "*No*

Monsieur, no kissy kissy."

He raised a cupped hand towards her breast, only to see her quickly drop down to a crouching position. Her face was only centimetres from him. She looked up and sighed. "*It is still too soft.*" The words remained cold. She patted his hand away and wrapped her own hand around it. "*You will need help.*" Holding it, loosely at first, she then spat on it, sliding her hand over it, concentrating on that one sensitive area, a skill taught to her by another girl and honed to perfection.

He stared down at her, wanting it desperately to happen, too desperate.

He saw her take something out of her pocket, a small silver packet. He knew what it was. She flicked the button of her cut-down jeans, followed by the sound of her zip. She would be ready once he was. Time was money.

"*You are still too soft Monsieur.*" She looked up at him, loosening her grip. "*Would you like me to use my mouth?*"

She wouldn't kiss him, she avoided him touching her breast — but she was prepared to put his penis in her mouth. "*That would be helpful,*" he said.

"*It is one hundred francs for a suck.*"

A moment's pause. "*I have already paid you three hundred.*"

"*No Monsieur, that was for a fuck, this is for a suck,*" she said before closing her hand around him again and giving his penis a gentle squeeze, quickly releasing it, as though in irritation. "*It would help,*" she said, then waited, looking up at him. Her eyes were soft, large — impatient. "*It would help Monsieur?*" she repeated forcefully.

He stared down at her. "*Okay.*" He pulled out his wallet again, holding the notes close to his face, carefully studying each one in turn, they all looked the same in the dark. He managed to see two with the number fifty in the corner: peeling them away he handed them down to her. She looked at them closely before stuffing both into her pocket. Her fingers returned around him, further down. He thought he heard a noise. "*What was that?*"

He heard rumours that voyeurs used the park, men lurking furtively in the bushes, getting to know the popular places of business. One hand always occupied.

She froze for a second and listened. "*Probably a fox.*" Was all she said.

He felt a soft warmth slide over him, continuing for several seconds, the sensation becoming more intense with each movement, he felt her hand tighten again, he could feel himself becoming harder. She pulled away, within a flash the silver packet was torn open and the condom rolled over him, all in a matter of seconds. She stood up, at the same time pulling her cut-down jeans to just above her knees. Turning to face the tree she leant over, one hand pressed flat against the trunk, the other behind her, like a sprinter in a relay waiting to be handed the baton. Further she leant, her body nearly at right angles to her legs, her knees slightly bent, pushing herself back. She tried to guide him in. He was still too soft. She rubbed him over her opening for several seconds before trying again — without success.

She turned and slowly pulled up her cut-down jeans. "*I am sorry Monsieur but you have gone over your time.*"

"*No. It will happen. I just need time.*"

"*You can pay me another three hundred francs if you like. Then I can give you time.*"

"*I have paid you already.*"

"*You paid me for twenty minutes.*"

"*Twenty minutes, that was never...It hasn't been twenty minutes.*"

"*It has...I even let you go over...Another three hundred will get you another twenty minutes.*"

Francois glared long and hard at her. "*I haven't got another three hundred,*" he lied.

She turned. "*Goodbye Monsieur.*"

"*No wait. I will give you another hundred.*" Francois put his hand into his pocket. He froze. His wallet had gone. He remembered one of her hands was pressing on that same area. "*You have taken my wallet.*"

"*I have not... Why would I ask for more...*"

Francois grabbed her arm and pulled her towards him. "*You whores are all the same.*"

"*Get off me or I will scream.*"

Before her lips could part a large hand was slapped over her mouth, at the same time spinning her around so the back of her head was pushed hard against his shoulder.

She tried to shout, the sound hitting the air with just a whimper, falling into a muffled hum. She shook her head, trying to free herself, his hand remained strong. She could feel his other arm wrapped tightly around her, trapping her body. She tried struggling, attempting to free herself, writhing in all directions like a fish gasping out of water, all to no avail. She soon realised it made his grip tighter, containing any movement to a bare minimum. She tried looking at him, her eyes were round, angry, determined, glaring at him with such hatred he could feel it burning into him.

Francois knew he couldn't let her go, not at that time, she would run away screaming. He could feel the vibration under his palm, she was trying to force some semblance of sound out. He had no choice but to keep his hand hard over her mouth, his arms clamped around her, trapping her to his own body. The more she struggled the tighter his hold became. He was forcing her head back into his shoulder, the other hand around her chest. All he wanted was for her to stop, remain quiet, just return his wallet, that was all, just stop, then he would let her go. He suddenly felt a sharp pain on his leg, a clipped "*Ah!*" Stopping the sound before it become too loud. He lifted his foot, he felt her struggle again, even more determined, they lost balance and fell. She tried to kick back again, her shoe glancing off his shin, making him yelp again. She felt herself forcibly being swung around and thrown onto the ground, he fell on top of her, slamming into her body, one of her arms trapped underneath. She felt a searing pain as the air was forced from her lungs. His hand had slipped from her mouth. A gasp, followed by a scream, again it was quickly stifled. She wondered if one of the other girls had heard, knowing she would summon others, come to her rescue. She wasn't fast enough, his hand had slapped back on her, covering her nose and mouth, the only noise she could make was like a pig's squeal, now his fingers were pressing hard into her cheeks, like he was about to snap her jaw in half. Then she felt a hand slide down her body, towards her crutch. This wasn't about him wanting his wallet, this was a pervert at work, she had heard about these types of men.

He slid a hand downward, continuing over the softness of one breast. All he wanted was to slide it into her pocket, retrieve his wallet, that was all he wanted, nothing more. Once he had it he would tell her she could go, as long as she remained silent he would say no more about the theft. All he wanted was to go back to his apartment. He would never return to the park. As long as she remained quiet, that would be the deal, the only deal, there was no plan B. Another sharp pain, this time in his chest.

She let his hand slide down to the top of her leg, until her arm was free, then slammed an elbow hard into his rib-cage. Trying to break free at the same time.

He could feel her struggling. His arm quickly returned to where it was before, trapping her once again.

She tried making a noise, any noise, even if it was a stifled hum at the back of her throat, the loudest hum she could muster. She felt his grip tighten. Then the pain came with a vengeance, in her lungs at first, like they were burning. Then her head, as if it was about to explode. Her heart was trying to pound through her chest, attempting to force the nonexistent oxygen around her body. Still his hand remained clamped over her, harder than ever. Her head being forced back even more over his shoulder. She thought her neck was about to break. She tried to force her mouth wider, bite the flesh of his palm.

He could feel a movement under his hand, she was trying to open her mouth, maybe take a bite out of him. He squeezed even tighter. His fingers pushing hard into her cheeks.

The pain was now unbearable, she thought her teeth were being forced from their gums, her trapped arm felt as if it was being torn from its socket. She tried sucking air into her lungs, any tiny amount, all that followed were spasms of airless gulps. She began fighting back again, only to feel herself becoming more exhausted, feeling his grip become even tighter, unbearably tight; she thought her skull was about to be crushed. Her muscles began losing all strength. She was giving up.

He felt relief, she was relaxing. That is all he wanted, for her to stop. It would be over soon and they could go back to their own lives. He would hold on for a while longer.

It must have been minutes since she had taken a breath. A hazy veil had been drawn over her eyes. She could feel herself loosing consciousness, her life ebbing away. One last pitiful effort to force herself free but his grip was too strong. All strength had now deserted her.

He could feel her still trying to fight. Why? He just wanted her to stop. Then he would let go.

She was helpless. Her eyes began to fill with tears, streaming from her eyes. She wanted to tell him that he was taking her life away. She wanted to plead with him, tell him she needed to live. Did he realise what he was doing? That he would spend the rest of his life in prison. That she wouldn't say anything to anyone if he just let her go. She tried to turn her head, to look at him, speak to him with her eyes. She tried to nod, to say she understood, he had won, now he could let go.

He felt her head turn, trying to force his hand away. He couldn't hold her any tighter and he wasn't about to loosen his grip — not now.

She wanted to cry out for mother, the only person that had ever loved her, the only person she had loved. She wanted to shout for the father she never knew. She needed to tell them their daughter was being murdered, that she needed help, she had never asked for much before. If he wanted to compensate for his desertion. If her mother wanted to compensate for her drinking, for having her taken into care as a young and naive girl, leaving her to be abused by the people who were meant to look after her, then the time would be now. Her tears had started to sting her eyes, her mouth trembling under his grip.

He could feel her trying to scream, he could feel a dampness run under his fingers, his grip began slipping on her skin. Why won't she just give up?

She had never done anything bad, nothing you could say was terrible, just petty thieving, that is all. Nothing to deserve this. She was happy before, only seeing the good in life, the good in people, everyone she met seemed to warm to her, all the other girls liked her. Why was God punishing her this way? Why was He allowing her to die for something she didn't do?

He felt her neck muscles relax. Maybe she has learnt her lesson. He would give her several more seconds, then let go.

She could feel the pain beginning to fade away. Death would soon be upon her, only moments away. His mouth was right against her ear. She could feel his hot breath, his knees either side of her, gripping her legs, his elbow clamping an arm in, the other arm trapped underneath her own body. This would be her last experience of life. She felt herself ebbing away.

"*Stop struggling,*" Francois whispered.

She had stopped.

"*Good,*" he breathed, still holding onto her, remaining in the same position for several seconds after. "*I'm going to let go now.*" Slowly he let his grip slide away. "*Good.*" He released her.

Her head fell back onto the ground. Her eyes open, soulless, staring up into an empty void.

He put a hand on her chest, there was no rise and fall. He gave her shoulder a shake, only resulting in her head flopping to one side. He put his head over her mouth, hoping to feel the warmth of her breath on his cheek, there was nothing. He stood, pulling her arm up as he did, wanting her to rise with him, it remained limp, lifeless. He let go, it fell like it belonged to a rag doll.

At first his mind wouldn't accept what had happened. It couldn't possibly have been him. All he did was hold her, prevent her from running away, stopped her from screaming. It must have been a heart attack. She was probably a drug addict, maybe she had taken something without him seeing, maybe fixed herself before they met. That was it, an overdose.

Francois Degarmo looked down in shock. His penis was erect.

He stared at her, like a shadow laid out on a dark blanket, as if she had fallen asleep in the late evening gloom. Even then she had a serenity about her, an innocent beauty. He felt like a prince that could wake her with a kiss. He looked down at himself again, he was still erect, a cool breeze brushing his bare flesh. He looked around, studying what little he could see. Nothing, they were alone.

No one would know, He knelt down and undid her zip, grabbing her cut-down jeans he yanked them over her feet. He slid a hand over her breast, just below her neck, slowly slipping it under the leotard, feeling the softness of her nipple. He bent further down, kissing her on the lips; they were still warm, but had lost their pinkness, turned to grey, the skin surrounding them a discoloured purple. He raised his head — this prince's kiss hadn't woken her. He wrapped his fingers around her thigh, pulling it towards him, parting her legs. She was now visible. Francois Degarmo was going to get what he had paid for after all.

He was startled by a rustle in the leaves and rose to a half standing position, frozen like a statue, his knees bent, his arms held wide, like a surfer riding a wave. He listened, his head motionless, his eyes flicking from side to side, searching the area where he had heard the noise. He could see nothing. Maybe a fox he thought, maybe not. He had to get away quickly. A girl might come with a customer. He had forgotten about the voyeurs, he could be seen, he may have been seen, they could have already gone to get the police, but that meant they would have to own up to their dirty little habit. He tried to think, nothing tied her to him. That was the nature of this business, two strangers meeting and having sex, then going their own way, neither knowing who the other was. He also knew Nicole was not her real name, only she would know what that was. And she didn't know his, not that it mattered if she did.

A panic surged through him. His wallet! He crouched down again, searching her pockets, they were empty. She must have thrown it somewhere, ready to be picked up later. The ground was a dark brown, virtually black, the same colour as his wallet. He brushed the area with a flat hand, sweeping it around the dry earth, walking on all fours, reaching further out. It could be anywhere. He stopped, he had to think, wondering if there was anything in it that could identify him. He never used credit cards, not now. There was the cash, notes, also coins in a zip-up compartment and a small sketch pad, but no writing in it. That was it, nothing that had his name or address, not that he could recall. They would have his fingerprints on them though. So what, they didn't spell out his name, they could belong to anyone, any punter. So could the wallet, that also could have been dropped at anytime, maybe days ago. He had convinced himself. He stopped searching.

He gazed down at her again. Her body was too much in the open, she may even be visible in daylight. He dragged her further into the undergrowth, dropping her behind a thick bush. He scooped up some loose earth and threw it over her, soon realising it was a futile exercise, it would take too long to cover her entirely. There was no more he could do. He went to leave, stopping himself before he had even taken a single step. He was going to exit the way they had entered, someone might see him, identify him later; that was probably Nicole's own way in, her entrance, her space, it would be obvious he was the killer. There was only one thing he could do, make his way through the undergrowth, in the direction of the western gate, get as far as he could, emerge from the bushes when he had got there. Hopefully the two boys he saw earlier would have gone.

He also knew trudging through the undergrowth wouldn't be easy, it was dark, some places dense, and there was also the chance he may inadvertently bump into someone. He knew these bushes had a life of there own at night, like a Brothers Grimm fairy tale. He would have to go carefully. He thought about following the fence. There was a pavement, a road, then houses. Someone could be walking on the other side, they would see him. It would be too risky.

Francois Degarmo took one last look at her before he began walking away.

His shoes crunched noisily over the dry earth. Feeling his shirt cling to his back from the sweat, he could smell the stench of his own body odour. His mouth was dry, he wanted to swallow but couldn't. It was dark at the beginning, darker than he had ever known it, he couldn't see more than a metre in front of his face. A bush or tree would appear without warning, as though it had jumped out, he had to negotiate his way around, sometimes by feel, sometimes having to backtrack, like he was in a maze. It wasn't until he got level with a lamp post that a meagre light penetrated through the undergrowth, dappling the shrubbery, creating leafy outlines with black spaces in between for him to travel through. There he could pick up speed slightly, until he too left that behind, entering into the dark once again.

As he rounded a large shrub a sudden movement startled him, he could see the silhouettes of two people, one a man, he was crouching, he quickly straightened, his back to a tree, rummaging around at groin level. A girl stood up, her posture defiant, as if she was going to hold her ground, confront the strange man who had suddenly appeared out of nowhere.

Francois recognised the contours of the woman immediately, it was the plump girl. "*Sorry,*" he said, quickly turning away, taking a step to the side. He had no choice, he would have to get back on the path, and quickly.

With an undignified lurch he stumbled out of the undergrowth between two thick bushes, their branches intertwined, his arms held high to make himself as narrow as possible, without checking who might have seen him he hurried back onto the path. A swift glance back, he had made little progress. The lamp post where he had spoken to Nicole was just behind him. He cut across the grass, at least he would be in the dark until he arrived at the western gate. With his head down and his stride lengthened he hurried along, soon he would be out of the park. Francois Degarmo was desperate. He was a killer in retreat.

Monday 14th June 2010
Breidjing Refugee Camp,
Ouaddai,
Chad

"*You can see she is not here,"* Crystal said through gritted teeth. "*You are frightening the children.*" Glancing down at them clinging onto their mother's robe.

The captain ignored her, continuing to bark his orders at the soldiers as they searched Arafa's tukul, anything that might give him a clue as to where the assassin was. He knew while she roamed free his life would always be in danger.

Breidjing Refugee Camp had been swarming with government soldiers since Major Marius Guerrette was shot. But as many as Captain Neo Nkusi tried to summon, it would still not be enough. There were thousands of the brown tents in the camp, all identical, far too many to count and far too many to search.

The Chadian officer had been standing only centimetres from the Major when the shot was fired, when he heard the crack of the explosion, that flash of light, the crunching thud as the Major crumpled on the dusty ground, seeing the white-washed wall behind him splattered in blood. Although this wasn't what had shocked him. The Captain had seen many a man die in horrific and bloody circumstances, many at his own hands, and not even batted an eyelid. This was different though, this bullet was meant for him, he knew it should have been his own blood on that wall. This was a revenge for a revenge for a revenge, a wheel that wouldn't stop turning until he was dead — or the assassin was.

He knew the killer was young, just a girl, he didn't know her name at that time, nor her exact age, only that she was tall and thin. Out of the corner of his eye he caught a glimpse of her blue patterned headscarf as he turned to make a hasty retreat into the security office, only to save his own skin, expecting a bullet in his back at any moment. What he didn't know was what she looked like.

It was only after that Captain Nkusi realised she must be same girl who helped her brother escape from the hospital: a notorious rebel fighter, whose face had been severely burnt at the Captain's own hands. The escape was also aided by another brother, during which one of Captain Nkusi's own guards was killed and a policeman badly wounded. He also knew these same two brothers, along with their father were killed in a bloody skirmish at Scorpion Rock, he knew this because their killings were under his orders. But she was not amongst them at the Rock. She was with them earlier, but where she vanished to was unknown — until now. He also knew she must still be in the camp.

Crystal knew Arafa would never talk. She was a proud Tama mother who had already been through so much. A woman who only knew the hardships in life, who lived a hand to mouth existence with only one objective, to keep her three children free from starvation and disease, she had lost two already. She didn't know whether her husband was dead or alive, she guessed he was dead, six years without a word — although Crystal could see some hope still remained in her heart. Arafa also knew her husband could have even been killed by this same man ransacking her home, smashing her table, ripping her bed linen. The hatred of Tama people by this government soldier was well known.

"*She is not here, you can see she is not here. There is nowhere to hide, surely you can see that.*"

Again the officer ignored her. The reputation of this Chadian officer was well known, a man with an evil and bloody reputation. Only now it was worse, he was like a trapped animal, his life would be under continuous threat. He knew anyone who was capable of such a cold-blooded murder would be capable of anything, that they would never give up.

Crystal refused to move, standing her ground, even when the soldiers blatantly knocked into her.

She would not put it past him to beat Arafa to an inch of her life, let his men rape her, even hold a gun to her children's heads, threatening to shoot them if she didn't talk. While Crystal was there, Arafa and her family were safe. Crystal was the camp manager, a lawyer with close ties to Amnesty International. She had only heard about his atrocities, never witnessed them first hand, he was always careful about that. Since the peace treaty had been signed in January he was more than aware that the International Criminal Courts were compiling lists of people wanted for war crimes.

"*Do you honestly think she would come here knowing this would be the first place you would look?*" Finally she had caught the attention of the captain.

He took one step towards her and pointed at Arafa. There was something in the tone of his voice that told her he was capable of anything. This was a desperate man. "*She says thin, a headscarf, two eyes, two ears, a nose and a mouth, that she is as black as night. This describes every girl in the camp. What do you propose, I slaughter them all like the pharaoh did to get at Moses. Because if that's what it takes...*"

"*Moses survived,*" Crystal interrupted.

The officer took another step towards her. "*You also knew this girl.*"

Crystal gritted her teeth. "*You lay one finger on me sweetie...*" She stopped talking, glaring long and hard at the officer. "*This family is under the protection of the United Nations. If you lay one finger on them I'll pay for you to go to The Hague myself,*" she said in Arabic so Arafa could understand.

Captain Nkusi looked Crystal up and down with such indignation it made her feel as if she was just a worthless inconvenience, something he would swat away like an irritating fly. He barked more orders at the soldiers and waited while two left the tukul, their weapons at the ready, their eyes scanning the immediate area as soon as they stepped outside. The officer waited, a shout through the door, "*Clear.*" He too departed, the third soldier followed, his eyes hanging menacingly on the two women as he did.

Crystal looked at Arafa. "*I'll help you clear up.*"

"*No, you must go. I will be safe.*"

Crystal stepped outside and into the courtyard, her eyes searching in every direction, she had to be suspicious of everyone; the Captain would have her followed, probably for the next days, maybe weeks if he couldn't find Jamia. Crystal was now a marked woman. As she stood at the courtyard entrance she thought about Jamia, how alone she must feel, how her life and Ali's would now be in the hands of others. Then she thought about how unwell Ali was, that he was going to need expert medical help as soon as possible. Crystal wanted to tell her that she hadn't deserted them, that if she were to see them it would mean certain capture, even to smuggle a note to them would be dangerous. From now on Crystal could trust no one.

The Chief at Guereda had arranged everything before the shooting, Jamia's transport to Breidjing, the identification of the target, where she would stay. He found a safe tent for her to hide in after she had undertook the deadly deed. He also thought it was highly unlikely she would make it that far — she had. The chief would now have to arrange her escape from the camp. He also thought she would be on her own.

After the shooting, Crystal had taken Jamia to Arafa's tukul, only so she could be reunited with her youngest brother Ali. The Major had taken him there, away from the evil clutches of Captain Nkusi. It was at that time Jamia learnt she had shot the wrong man, she had put a bullet in the same person who had saved her brother's life. The intended target, the Chadian officer who killed her brothers and father was still free, she was told that he was the man standing next to the Major at the time. If it wasn't for Ali she would have gone out and killed him too. Now nothing else mattered. Now she had something to live for, she would have to stay alive for Ali.

At the safe tent she was told to wait until one of the chief's people came to collect her, when he thought it was safe to do so. But he also knew the longer she stayed there the more danger she was in. The rescue would have to be soon, within days; he knew the soldiers would be searching for her, it would only be a matter of time. She would have to go back to Guereda but only for a short while; even with the town remaining a rebel stronghold, the Captain had eyes everywhere, eventually word would get out.

Ali was in his mid teens — the time he had spent on this earth that is — intellectually, emotionally, he was less than half that age, the reason he was known as the boy who never grew up. The bloody events at Scorpion Rock had left him severely traumatised, not being able to process the atrocities he witnessed had shut his mind down. Ali was now in a deep, dark place, a place from where he would never escape without expert help and the love only his sister could give him, as she had done for her entire life. No one knew this more than Jamia herself.

The chief had two of his people at the camp, an old man and woman, the tent had to look occupied. They had hung out clothes, cooked the meagre aid rations on fires in the courtyard, but most of all they were there to warn the two occupants if the soldiers were getting close. A small, shallow hole had been dug behind the tent where Jamia and Ali would climb into if they were under threat — although it was only made for one both would have to squeeze in. A millet stalk cover with a fake fire on top had been built ready to be slid over the hole once the occupants were inside.

For three days Jamia never left the tent. Day and night had begun to merge into one. She hardly slept, and when she did it was filled with the same nightmare. One where she saw goats and cattle feeding in lush green pastures, rivers with cool clear water, villagers going about their daily chores, everyone seemingly content with life. Then she sees the sky turn black, feeling as if it is closing in on her. She tries to run but it shrinks around her, until she feels she can touch it. Only when the sky is about to engulf her does she wake in a cold sweat. Then she would see her brother laying next to her, his face only a few centimetres from hers. Jamia was too afraid to go back to sleep again, spending the rest of the night staring at Ali. Even though his eyes were shut she never knew if he was asleep or awake. Ali was all she had.

It was on the evening of the fourth day when Jamia had scurried to the back of tent, pulling Ali with her, huddled in the corner, both arms wrapped around him, as she always did when she heard someone approaching. Waiting for that command from the old man or woman to quickly climb into the hole, or worse, be dragged out by soldiers. She watched nervously as the flap opened, it was neither the old man or woman — nor was it a soldier. A girl stepped in, just shy of her twenties. A feeling of relief surged through Jamia when she spoke in Tama. "*We always seem to meet in unfortunate circumstances,*" the girl said. The flap hadn't closed properly, leaving a slither of light to penetrate the tent, catching the white of her teeth as she beamed out a friendly smile. Jamia could see the outline of a woman much shorter than herself, a round face under her headscarf, her plump cheek bones. Jamia knew this girl wasn't from the camp. The girl stepped forward and knelt in front of them, tucking her feet under herself. She stared at Jamia. "*It is Nya.*" She drew her head forward and pulled her headscarf back. "*Nya remember?*" She waited for recognition, none came.

Jamia pulled Ali closer.

"*I am Nya. My mother works for the Chief. You stayed with us in Guereda...remember?*"

Several sharp nods were returned. Nya moved to give her a hug only to have Jamia draw back.

"*Who is the boy?*" Nya asked.

"*He is my brother.*"

Nya angled her head to look at Ali's face. He remained inanimate, two soulless eyes gazing blankly towards the ground.

"*The boy who never grew up. Papa told me...*" She paused. "*The Chief told me about him.*"

"*His name is Ali,*" Jamia said forcefully. "*He has a name!*"

"*Sorry. Is he...?*" Nya stopped. "*We haven't allowed...*" A friendliness returned to her eyes. "*Then I shall call him Ali,*" she said with a half smile, knowing his presence in the escape would make the risk of capture much greater.

"*I killed the wrong man.*" Jamia spat out. "*The picture the Chief showed me, it was the wrong man.*"

Nya fixed a stare on her. "*You did not kill the man you saw on the camera?*"

"*The man on the camera was the wrong man.*"

"*No Jamia. If you have killed the man we showed you, then he is the right man.*" Her voice became assertive. "*Then you have killed the evil one.*"

"*The man who killed my brothers and father is still alive.*" The words tailed away. "*The man you showed me on the camera was not that man,*" Jamia repeated softly, the enormity of what she had done still haunted her.

"*But there were pictures of him...*" Nya paused for a second. "*There was a picture of his brother.*"

Their attention was broken by Ali shuffling in his sister's arms. "*Have you come to take me to the Chief?*" Jamia asked softly.

Nya wanted to continue the conversation, find the truth, discover the true identity of the man Jamia had shot. Realising there was no more to be said she turned her attention towards Ali, her eyes darting around his face. "*You will leave your brother with someone?*"

Jamia wondered if it was more statement than question. To her it didn't matter, the reply would have been the same. "*My brother will come with me.*"

"*It would be too dangerous.*"

"*Then I will stay here.*"

"*The soldiers will find you. If what you say is true and that monster is alive...*" Nya paused for a moment. "*Your life will be in Allah's hands.*"

"*As are all our lives. Only God will know when it is our time to die.*"

"*We can come back for your brother.*"

Jamia looked down at Ali, her chin cradled over his head. "*Then I will wait with him.*"

"*If I leave you here you will die. You both will...*" Nya stopped, she had no choice. She had already made the decision.

Nya was glad she didn't have to confide in the Chief. He would have put her own welfare as his priority. Although she was the daughter of his housekeeper, he had raised her like his own child, even having her call him Papa. He was the kindest and wisest man she had ever known but Nya knew he would leave Jamia and Ali here rather than put her life at risk — like any father would.

She wouldn't mention he was responsible for the death of an innocent man. He would find that out sooner or later, punish himself for that mistake, she thought it might even break him. He knew it was really his finger around the trigger on that gun when Jamia fired it. Throughout her entire life Nya had never argued with him, not once, she had always obeyed him like a dutiful pet — not that he asked much from her. Living on the fringes of the war the Chief had always wrapped her in cotton wool, kept her away from the fighting and killing.

Nya would still have to face the music when she returned to Guereda. She was not meant to be in Breidjing, arriving there without the Chief's permission, the first time she had violated his trust. It was a young man the Chief had chosen for the task of rescuing Jamia, one of his bodyguards, a fearsome and trusted warrior from the same tribe as Nya. She knew the young bodyguard had feelings for her, managing to persuade him to take her with him, telling him the chief wanted them to travel as a couple, it would be less conspicuous. She had added that no one should know about it, there were spies everywhere, he was not to tell a soul, not even mention it to the Chief.

"*I fear Allah has not finished with either of you,*" Nya said.

"*When will we leave?*" Jamia asked.

"*Tomorrow morning.*"

"*It will be daylight!*"

"*The soldiers will be watching the roads at night.*"

"*They will be watching the roads in the day.*"

"*They will least expect it then.*"

Jamia thought back to the day she had helped Assim escape with Djamel. She had done it then, she could do it again. "*What is the plan?*"

Tuesday 15th June 2010
La Provence Newspaper,
Marseille,
France

Julien sat with his back as straight as a rod, his hands clutched together in a ball, resting them on the front edge of the desk, his head angled downward, facing the open notebook, not believing what he was looking at.

Instead of studying the book from the beginning, page by page, line by line, Julien decided to prioritise by dates. Stevan Markovic's body had been found on the 1st October 1968, he would work a week back from that date, then a week forward, and so forth. Methodically and clinically analysing each line, each individual word, looking for any name he might recognise, note connections, clients whose names had been repeated, girls names, the reason for a particular nickname, special requests, even looking for anagrams, no stone was left unturned. This was Julien in his prime, this was what he was good at, this was the culmination of all those years solving puzzles, how that rook could checkmate in five moves, tackling the most difficult crosswords, always timing himself, like an athlete trying to beat his personal best.

He realised there was no analysing needed for what he was looking at, it was as clear as daylight, as if it was shouting out at him. Julien thought it was impossible for that name to be there, anyone else, maybe — but not this name. He had to think. For the time being he would keep it to himself.

Lucile had not long arrived at the office and was already on her second cup of strong coffee, no milk, no sugar, looking down at her mug like she was staring into a black hole.

Julien was far away in the corner of the office, as far from her as anyone could be — not by choice. The editor had done it on purpose so she couldn't commandeer him all to herself, as she did on a regular basis — not that it ever stopped her.

Lucile leant over, stretching herself to the limit. This was the only way she could see Julien, to sit at the extreme right of her desk, look through all the bodies and screens into the distance. He was sitting in his usual straight back position, gazing down at something on his desk, hopefully the notebook. He looked up at his monitor and tapped something into his keyboard. Then he stared straight ahead, but not at anything in particular. Lucile knew he would have already been sat there for ages, for someone who was meant to be part-time he seemed to spend more time in the office than anyone else, not that Lucile was complaining, he had a lot of work to do. From the corner of her eye she saw Angelique stand up behind her desk, probably hoping people would look at her. There was nothing more Angelique liked than to be the centre of attention, she had the looks and she knew it. She was speaking on the phone in an over-animated conversation, displaying her fake smile, as though butter wouldn't melt in her mouth, probably talking to the footballer's wife — or even the footballer himself. Lucile turned to look at the editor's door, it was shut; she scanned the immediate area, expecting him to sneak up on her in that furtive way he has, thankfully he was nowhere to be seen. She saw Angelique slam the phone down, probably for effect, she had always been a drama queen. She then looked back to Julien who was still staring into space, deep in thought, lightly tapping the front edge of his desk.

Lucile opened her own notebook, flicking back and forth through several pages, having trouble finding the one she needed. She wished she could be more like Julien, organised, a human filing system. Eventually she found the page and flattened the fold with a clenched fist. She took her phone from her bag and punched in some numbers. The dialing tone stopped.

A heavy breath was followed by an abrupt, "*Yes.*"

"*Monsieur Bret?*"

A short silence. "*Who wants to know?*"

"*My name is Lucile Billet.*" Lucile waited.

"*And?*"

"*Are you Victor Bret?*"

"*I do not know a Lucile Billet.*"

"*Are you the Victor Bret who worked for the police force when...*"

The phone went dead.

Lucile paused for a second before punching in the numbers again. The dialing tone stopped, followed by silence.

"*Hello.*" Lucile waited. "*Hello,*" she repeated before waiting again. "*Please do not hang-up. I have news that will clear your name.*" She knew the person at the other end must be interested in what she had to say, otherwise they would have not answered again.

A short silence. "*Who are you?*" A woman's voice.

"*Oh...May I speak with Monsieur Bret?*"

"*I am Madame Bret and you didn't answer my question.*"

"*My name is Lucile Billet.*"

"*You are a reporter?*" The words sounded tetchy.

Lucile spoke quickly. "*Yes, but please do not hang-up. I work for La Provence in Marseille. Please do not hang-up. It is about the Stevan Markovic murder. I have news that may help your husband clear his name. You may get compensation. I know a good lawyer that specialises...*"

The woman interrupted. "*How did you get our telephone number?*"

"*Be reassured Madame Bret, it wasn't easy.*"

Lucile could sense someone else listening in, heavy breaths on top of the womans, a mans, sounding like a heavy smoker. She raised her voice. "*Tell your husband I might be able to prove it wasn't Madame Pompidou in the photographs.*" Lucile said, then heard muffled voices in the background.

"*How?*" It was the man's voice again.

"*Because I believe I know who the woman was.*"

"*Who?*"

"*Until I know for certain...*"

"*So you don't know?*"

Lucile forgot the man she was talking to was once a policeman, she would have to be more careful. "*This is why I am talking to you Monsieur Bret. May I call you Victor.*"

An abrupt. "*No.*"

"*May I ask you some questions?*"

"*You may ask them. If I choose to answer them will be a different...*"

"*Victor, if you help me, I can help you.*" Lucile waited. Silence. "*You told Le Parisian newspaper it wasn't Madame Pompidou in the photographs.*"

"*Because it wasn't. I was surprised when I heard there was a rumour saying it was.*"

"*Who started the rumour?*"

A short silence. "*I do not know...maybe the SDECE.*" He said it as though he knew it was them. "*The Counter-Espionage department to be exact.*"

She was pleased, at least it was something, at least he was talking.

Lucile turned to another page in her notebook and ran a finger downward, stopping halfway. "*Louis Wallon?*"

Silence.

Her finger dropped to the line below. "*Henri Capitant?*"

More silence.

The line below that one. "*Luicien Aimé-Blanc?*"

"*Someone wanted me to say it was Claude Pompidou in the picture.*"

"*Who?*" She waited.

No answer.

"*You were dismissed from the force?*"

"*You have done your homework Mademoiselle Billet. But it was not for that.*" After a deep sigh. "*It was for something else.*"

Lucile thought she heard the woman in the background, sounding angry, just catching the end of what she was saying. "*...fool, we lost...*" then it faded away again.

She kept looking over to Julien, catching him glancing towards her once, like he had a sixth sense. She thought he looked concerned about something.

"*You said it was for something else?*" Lucile asked.

Victor blew out a sharp sigh. "*Yes,*" he repeated softly. "*It had nothing to do with the Markovic affair. So if you do prove it wasn't Claude Pompidou in the photographs it still won't clear my name.*"

"*Did this have something to do with you being the first policeman on the scene.*"

When Julien was giving Lucile the information about Victor Bret he mentioned that it was strange an ordinary Gendarme was first at a murder scene.

He continued. "*Yes. I was the Gendarme in the town of Elancourt at the time. A scrap dealer was searching around the local dump.*" The phone went silent for several seconds. Lucile could hear more angry words in the background. When Victor began speaking again he sounded weary. "*He was a friend of mine.*" Appearing to put more emphasis on the was. "*It was him who found Markovic's body.*"

"*So he contacted you direct?*"

"He shouldn't have been there, I mean taking metal and anything else he could sell. It belongs to the council, they would see it as stealing. Money earned from the dump should go back to the community."

"You got a cut?"

Silence.

"You were dismissed for turning a blind eye to someone stealing rubbish?" Lucile wanted her tone to sound sympathetic.

"I was dismissed for not saying it was Madame Pompidou in the photographs. Everything else was just an excuse."

"So you told them you were first at the dump. You said it was you who found Markovic."

"No, that would have been a lie. I was a policeman, we are meant to believe in the truth." His voice dripping with sarcasm. *"It was too early. What would a policeman be doing at a dump at six o'clock in the morning, it would have been far too suspicious. I had to tell the truth, say it was my friend who found the body. That was my first mistake. It was him who told the police everything. You asked me if I got a cut of my friend's earnings. I didn't. But the police told him he would go to jail if he didn't say I did, if he didn't say I was corrupt. So my friend incriminated me."*

"Then they threatened you with dismissal if you wouldn't say it was Claude Pompidou?"

"They asked me if I had seen the photographs. I said I had. That was my second mistake. I didn't know at that point what it was all about." There was a long pause. *"I lost my pension, my reputation, everything."*

Through the clattering of pans Lucile thought she heard the woman's voice again, this time from a distance but still sounding hostile.

"Tell me what happened when you arrived at the dump?"

"I went straight to the victim's body. The killer tried to hide it in a sack, but it had got torn down one side, half of him was hanging out. That is when I saw the skull had been bashed in."

"*The newspapers say he was shot.*" Lucile sounded surprised.

"*Whoever the murderer was, wanted to hide the bullet hole.*"

"*And you didn't know who the victim was at that time?*"

"*No.*"

"*When did you find the photographs?*"

"*There was a car, the only one there. I searched inside. That was when I found the photographs, they were in the glove compartment. It looked as if it had been left open on purpose, like they were meant to be found. And how did Markovic's car get there. I mean a dead man can't drive. Something wasn't right.*"

"*You looked at the photographs?*"

"*Yes. At first I thought the victim was one of those voyeurs, someone who got a kick out of those sort of things. The dump has a reputation. That was my immediate thought. He was just a pervert who went a step too far, who got a bit too nosey with the wrong person.*"

"*Would you describe them?*"

"*The photographs?*" he asked.

"*Yes.*"

"*Two women.*" There was a long pause. "*On a bed, naked, touching each other. One was young with long black hair. The other was blonde, older looking.*"

"*In her late fifties?*"

"*No, younger. If you're asking me if it was Madame Pompidou...it wasn't. I would have recognised her immediately, which I didn't. This woman was heavily made-up. It may have fooled the man on the street but not me.*"

"*What did she look like?*"

A short pause. "*Not like Madame Pompidou.*"

Lucile felt stupid for asking the question. She was trying to picture Madam Veronique from the photographs on her wall. "*How old did she look?*"

"Mid-Forties."

"If I was to show you a photograph of a woman do you think you could identify her as the woman in the photographs?"

"Maybe. I don't know. It was a long time ago. Like I said she was heavily made-up."

Lucile didn't have any pictures of Madam Veronique, but she knew where some were. She knew the one with her standing next to the Pompidou's was probably taken around that time. Maybe there were more. How to get them? That was the problem. She might have to speak to Matthieu, maybe Norris.

"It may take a few days to get them. Then I can post..."

"No! Not in the post."

"I can email jpegs if you..."

"No, please, we will have to meet."

"But it would..."

"I can't help you otherwise."

"But..."

"No," he barked, like that was the end of it.

Lucile was surprised by his insistence. This was wasting time. The editor had only given her a week. *"Okay. Where?"*

Same day
Breidjing Refugee Camp,
Ouaddai,
Chad

Jamia had remained inside the tent with Ali, huddled together in the shadows, her long fingers wrapped around one of his hands, the palm of her other hand resting on his shoulder, stroking the back of his neck, trying to comfort him. For the past few hours she had been staring nervously at the entrance flaps.

It was early morning at the Breidjing Refugee Camp and Nya had told them she needed to step outside for a short while. She had already been gone for what seemed hours. They hadn't seen the old man and woman since they had brought them their breakfast. Jamia began to fear the worst, she thought they had been caught. Now the tent had become their coffin. She and Ali woud be left to die on their own, of thirst and starvation. The alternative was just as bad, she waited for the soldiers to come.

Jamia thought back to two weeks before, when she had been left alone in the desert, when there appeared to have been one outcome only: she had prepared herself for the inevitable. For her at that time it wasn't difficult to accept her fate, with her family gone there was nothing else left to live for. Now it was different, Ali was alive.

She recalled the tense standoff with a government soldier when she helped her brother Assim escape. How her weapon was aimed at him, wondering if she had the courage to fire it. His rifle was ready to be raised, for him there would be no hesitation, he would have taken her life without batting an eyelid. It ended with Djamel thudding the metal blade of a letter opener into the soldier's neck, nearly decapitating him — only to save her life.

She remembered walking in the barren wasteland of the Wadi Fira with her two brothers and the old Shaman woman. How the old woman had given them leaves to chew, stopping the energy from being sapped from their bodies — until it began to sap Jamia's sanity; her brothers telling her she was slowing them down, that she should wait with the old woman under the shade of a tree, telling her they would return with their father. She remembered insisting Assim and Djamel leave her the pistol before they departed for Scorpion Rock, knowing suicide would have been the preferred option if the Janjaweed were to find them. The weapon only had one bullet, she would use it on the old woman.

Jamia would never see Assim and Djamel again or her Papa. She also thought Ali had been taken from her. Four martyrs taken by Allah.

She recalled waking and seeing the grey corpse of the old woman laid next to her, as if she had been given to her by Allah just so Jamia could survive; that God had decided the old woman's job had been done and it was time for her to return to Him.

She remembered trying to make it to the rebel stronghold of Guereda, how a trapper had found her staggering in the wrong direction, heading towards Darfur and Janjaweed territory, being told later that she was as close to death as anyone could be. Then in Guereda the Chief took her into his own home where she could regain her strength with Nya's help. The Chief having pictures of the Chadian officer on a camera, the same man responsible for killing her brothers and father in cold blood, including many more from her tribe, She thought how easy it was for him to persuade her to execute him, how easy it was for her to accept the probability of being gunned down herself.

For Jamia in the past few weeks, death had never been that far away. The thought of living didn't bring her freedom from the nightmare either, but all that had to be left in the past, now she had something to live for. Her brother Ali would not survive without her.

Jamia was jolted out of her dream when the flap was flung open, allowing the tent to be bathed in bright sunlight. Silhouetted in the opening was Nya.

"*We leave now,*" Nya said immediately, a look of urgency etched into her face.

Jamia quickly stood, lifting Ali at the same time, her long arms enclosed his thin body. She drew her headscarf over her head and did the same to Ali. He had already been clothed in a girl's robe and headscarf; with his soft skin and boyish face they hoped it wouldn't draw attention. They all knew if there was one person the Chadian officer would recognise — it was him.

Nya looked at Ali, she would try one more time. "*He won't make it. He will bring us all down.*"

Jamia ignored her.

Nya nodded sharply, she had no choice. "*Then we had better go.*"

Nya held the flap open, allowing Jamia and Ali to enter the outside world for the first time in four days. The old man and woman were stood at the courtyard entrance. Jamia thought they had begun to look more like refugees as the days passed, as if they were beginning to melt into Breidjing itself. Jamia sensed someone else behind her, she spun her head around, a young man was standing at some distance to her left. At first she didn't recognise him until she saw it was the Chief's young bodyguard from Guereda. Gone was his dusty vest and bullet belt, the automatic rifle, the camouflage trousers, the appearance of being born with a weapon in his hand: now he was wearing dark trousers and a clean white polo shirt with the blue UNHCR logo, a light blue baseball cap on his head.

Nya spoke in Tama, her words business like. "*The old woman and man will lead the way. We will follow ten paces behind. Ali will walk between us. Mahamat will follow, he will keep his distance.*"

"*Where are we going?*"

"*We must not rush. We are just three girls minding our own business. When we get to our transport we will all become one family. We are sisters with our grandparents moving to the Kounoungo Refugee Camp, our parents are there. Mahamat is our driver. Remember one thing, anything unusual will give us away.*" Nya handed Jamia a water container. "*Here, carry this.*"

"*Where are we going?*"

"*Pull the boy's headscarf forward. Your brother's name is Luiza until we get to Guereda.*" She bent down and stared directly into Ali's face. "*Your name is Luiza until we get to Guereda. When we want you to do something we will call you Luiza. Do you understand?*" She held the stare for several seconds, soon realising he was looking straight through her.

"*Where are we going?*" Jamia asked again.

Nya nodded to the old woman and man. They disappeared through the entrance. "*To the distribution tents, then Guereda.*" she finally replied.

Jamia shot a hard glare at Nya. "*The security office is opposite the distribution tents!*"

"*So is our transport, come on.*"

Jamia looked to her left again, Mahamat had gone. She took a step forward, holding Ali's hand. Nya followed slightly behind. They stepped through the courtyard entrance and onto a narrow track, no more than two metres wide. Every day for the past six years Jamia had walked out of her own courtyard and onto a track not dissimilar to this one and thought nothing of it, now it felt like she was walking into a river of fire. On each side were millet stalk fences enclosing courtyards behind them, all with the same brown tents. A swirl of wind caught the ground in front of them, causing a dusty tan mist to rise in the air, hanging there for several seconds before it slowly drifted back down. As it settled, Jamia could see the old woman and man waiting in the distance.

"*Do not look behind, Mahamat is with us, just continue walking,*" Nya said.

For the two days she had been at Breidjing, Nya had been watching the camp, discovering when it was at its busiest, when they would blend in with the crowd.. That was why she had purposely chosen this time, just after the people had eaten their first meal — if they had one. There would be mostly women around at that time, mothers and daughters going about their morning chores, wearing the same long robes and headscarfs as them.

A woman passed them, balancing a plastic washing-up bowl on her head, piled high with laundry, a young child on her hip. She was making her way to one of the wells dug in the wadi near to the camp, where yellow water lay at the bottom of the ditch, poisonous to drink — but some still did. There were older children, all boys, about Ali's age, walking to one of the makeshift schools, where they would sit under a tarpaulin tied between two trees. A group of younger children skittered around, running past them, a punctured football tucked under one of their arms. Jamia negotiated herself around a child standing like a statue in the centre of the track, having to manoeuvre Ali to one side so as to not knock into him. The boy was wearing a threadbare oversized shirt and shorts, staring at the children running past him. Normally Jamia would have approached him, talked to him, scolded the others for not letting him play. She continued on, staring straight ahead, her hand tugging at Ali's arm. Two men in prayer caps and long white abayas overtook them, their robes flapping gently in the breeze. Then a man with a blue short sleeve shirt and light trousers walked by in the opposite direction. More children with their mothers. From the recently lit fires, smoke rose into the air, caught in a slight breeze, drifting away in the same direction, merging into one thin mist, as it did every morning. Breidjing had become a tented city in the throes of waking.

At the end of the track they turned a corner, there they saw the white roofs of three huge distribution marquees looming high above the brown tents, like cathedrals dominating the skyline of a city. Nya knew their transport and freedom would be behind them.

They turned another corner. Jamia glanced over to where her brother Djamel had worked, she suddenly stalled, her entire body had stuttered to a halt. When she began walking again she felt as if all coordination had deserted her, thinking she could stumble at any moment. Her body began to feel cold, the blood draining from her head, she felt nauseous, as though she could faint at any time. She stopped again, gripping Ali's hand tightly as if he was giving her some kind of balance. She took a deep breath and regained her composure.

Jamia glanced over again. There he was, standing in the entrance of the security office, only a few metres from the place where she had shot Major Guerrette: the same man he had been exchanging angry words with when she fired the pistol, who like a coward had retreated back into the office, the same man who had killed her brothers and father. Around him stood three soldiers, all with semi-automatic weapons, forever vigilant to anyone who got close — until Jamia's capture that is. To their right, at head height, less than two metres away was a smeared brown patch on the whitewashed wall — Major Guerrette's blood. If she still had the pistol Jamia might have put right what she had failed to do four days ago. She also knew there would be no escape this time — she looked at Ali and continued walking. In her peripheral vision she could just make out the officer's posture, he was still looking away. She pulled her headscarf further forward and tried to put her body between him and her brother. But when she slowed, so did Ali, always staying that two arms length behind her. She gradually pulled his arm in and tucked it into her side, drawing him beside her.

Nya had seen everything. She noticed when Jamia had come to a halt, saw her shudder like a ghost had passed through her, the weakness in her legs, the quick glances towards the officer. At that exact time she knew exactly who he was, the first time she had seen this monster.

Two young hearts were beating hard.

"*Continue as normal,*" Nya breathed. She stepped next to Jamia, blocking the officer's view of Ali, trying to make it not look obvious. She also wanted to look the officer in the eye, only to see what evil looked like, to see the man who had caused so much pain to her own people. Her eyes shot a glance his way, hoping he was still looking in the opposite direction — he wasn't. Did he see her? Her eyes shot forward again, wondering if she had drawn attention to them. That one stupid mistake could mean death for everyone involved.

To their left a white woman appeared, one with an immaculate hair style and wearing a white lab coat over a thin summer dress, looking much like a pharmacist stepping out onto a street in St. Tropez. "*We need to speak Captain,*" She yelled in French as she strode towards the officer.

Jamia recognised the voice immediately. "*It is Crystal,*" she mumbled through a closed mouth.

"*Do not stop,*" Nya whispered.

Both girls continued walking, Ali's arm still tucked into his sister's body.

Crystal spoke again, now only feet from the officer, her voice firm. "*Food has gone missing from the aid tents?*"

Nya, Jamia and Ali were now only metres from the officer, the two girls looking straight ahead, failing not to look suspicious. Jamia took a quick glance down at Ali, he was still walking, gazing blankly towards the ground, his headscarf had slipped back, his face in full view, Nya stepped in front of him. Everything felt as if it was happening in slow motion.

Crystal spoke again, her voice becoming more angry. "*That food is for the refugees, not your soldiers Captain.*"

Nya, Jamia and Ali had now passed them. Behind her she heard Crystal speak again, her voice becoming even louder. "*I will report you to the United Nations if any more food goes missing.*"

They heard Captain Nkusi laugh, sounding like it was a weapon firing.

Nya guided Jamia and Ali down the side of one of the distribution tents. A long fence of intertwined branches was to their right, it surrounded three tukuls inside a large courtyard, like they had been there before the camp existed, as if it was the reason this land was chosen in the first place. Nya had tested this same walk several times over, repeating it many times in the last days, even this morning, the reason she had been missing, waiting for Mahamat to arrive in the land cruiser.

The track opened out, following a long, one storey, whitewashed building to the left. Ten metres in front of them was an iron grey rock breaking through the ground, like a whale had surfaced for air. They turned left, now they were at the back of the marquee, a large flat expanse of canvas rising high above them like they were beside a chalk cliff face. Several vehicles were parked in the distance. Two huge troop carriers were furthest away, beside them an old rusty tractor, then a blue wagon, a Land Rover with a red cross. But it was a dirt splattered white Land Cruiser Nya led them towards. On it were the large blue letters UN, just distinguishable on the driver's door. Several boys were kicking a ball around only metres away; it landed at Ali's feet. He picked the ball up and threw it back, his headscarf sliding from his head. The boys looked at him in confusion, the eldest began laughing.

Mahamat was sat at the steering wheel, the old couple next

to him sharing the front passenger seat. He watched them approach, his face masked in relief.

Nya, Jamia and Ali reached the vehicle less than a minute later. They climbed into the back, keeping Ali in the centre.

Mahamat fired up the engine and the Land Cruiser moved off, moving slowly at first, only speeding up a few minutes later as they exited the camp and onto a narrow dirt track.

Nya leant forward and looked at Jamia, "*They only stopped searching the vehicles yesterday. We were told soldiers were needed at the eastern border. This is why we had to wait.*" She sat back and crossed her arms.

Ten minutes later they passed through a small abandoned village, it looked as if no one had lived there for years. The thatched tukul roofs were missing and most of the millet stalk fencing had been pulled down, anything that could have been used for a fire. Bones of cattle lay around, marking the spot where they had dropped. The entire village had fallen into ruin. They drove on, ahead of them lay a vast flat area of sandy ground and low lying red rocks. They arrived at a wide wadi, already having passed over several narrow ones, but this was by far the widest, at least four car lengths in width. Without stopping Mahamat guided the vehicle over the riverbed, a sandy motorway disappeared into the distance either side of them. After that the track followed a line of acacia trees, narrowing virtually to a goat's trail in places. Mahamat continued, skillfully negotiating the potholes and deep trenches gauged out by the heavy rains from a few years back. No one had seen a drop since.

"*Why are we travelling east?*" Jamia asked, concerned.

"*It is...*" Nya began.

Mahamat interrupted her. "*North west will take us towards Abeche. If we go on to Guereda from there we will be stopped at Am Zoer.*"

It was the first time Jamia had heard him speak.

"*But east will take us to the Sudanese border. There will*

also be government soldiers there. If not them, then the Janjaweed," she said.

"*We will join the main road at Biske then travel north on the track to Guereda. Under the circumstances it is the safest route.*"

"*Under the circumstances?*"

"*If we are stopped by government soldiers then I am taking you and your grandparents to be with your Mama and Papa at Kounoungo Refugee Camp. That is the story. The Janjaweed will not touch us. The Chief has made sure of that.*"

"*My Mama and Papa are dead,*" Jamia snapped. "*As are my two brothers.*"

Nya spoke without looking at Jamia. "*It is just a story. The Chief...everyone in this vehicle has gone out of their way to rescue you.*" She paused for a second. "*And your brother.*"

"*The Chief wants me alive because the Chadian officer is not dead.*"

"*The Chief has other...*"

It was the old woman who interrupted Nya this time. "*Everyone is tired, we are all nervous. This kind of talk will not help. Allah will guide us.*"

They continued in silence, sometimes slowly as Mahamat avoided the potholes and rises, other times they managed to pick up speed as the ground flattened. An hour later they passed through the deserted village of Biske. Even though the war had ended, its inhabitants still hadn't returned, not to more suffering, not to more death, opting for the safety of the camps.

Mahamat turned onto the main road. A minute later two large wheeled army trucks passed in the opposite direction, then a convoy of UN buses carrying refugees away from Darfur, the first driver honked the horn, holding up a large flat hand to the windscreen, like he knew Mahamat.

Ten minutes later and to their left was a large group of trees, it appeared as if there were hundreds of them, many growing out of the bed of a small dried-up lake, others bordering its sides. This was the sign for Mahamat to turn left, leaving the main road behind them. They drove onto another dirt track, hardly noticeable, the moving sand had covered much of it, only the channels made by previous vehicles gave any indication that it was there at all.

Jamia thought she saw a tan mist in the far distance, maybe a dust spiral, appearing to move along the ground. It wasn't a vehicle though, looking to be many smaller clouds, like a herd of stampeding animals. She noticed Mahamat looking more and more in his rear view mirror, just swift glances at first, then longer stares. She also felt their vehicle speed up slightly, the swerves becoming more pronounced, sometimes driving through the potholes rather than avoiding them. At times the clunks were so loud she thought the wheels would be torn off their axles. Their bodies were being flung in every direction. Jamia put her arm around Ali and pulled him close. As Mahamat's foot pressed harder on the throttle Nya turned her head to look behind, not able to see anything through the thick dust cloud left in their wake. She turned back and leant forward, clutching the back of Mahamat's seat.

The old man also glanced behind. "*I will tell you when to stop,*" he said.

Mahamat nodded.

For another five minutes they drove on, Mahamat continuing to zigzag violently along the path, their own dust cloud becoming even thicker.

The Land Cruiser became filled with the sound of huge engines. Nya turned back, holding her headscarf against her neck, just making out the outline of a large vehicle. The truck was nearly on them, only a couple of metres away. Jamia also looked behind. Towering above the back window was a huge troop carrier, only the battle green of the grill visible. Jamia looked through the windscreen, the smaller dust clouds ahead of them had gone. It was a trap, she was sure of it, their enemy would be in front and behind of them, they would have nowhere to run. This was it she thought, she would suffer the same fate her brother Assim had at the hands of this monster. She knew there was no escape.

"*Slow down,*" The old man said.

Mahamat brought the Land Cruiser to a near walking pace.

"*Pull off the track, see if they just want to pass.*"

Mahamat drove on for another few seconds before he pulled the vehicle over, manoeuvring it in a crescent so he was facing back onto the road — just in case. He was sure the Land Cruiser could easily outrun a troop carrier if need be. He wound down the window, stuck his arm out and waved them on, only to watch them slow to a halt. The roaring of the engines fading to a rhythmic chug.

Mahamat turned towards the old man. "*It is them,*" he said, keeping the engine turning over.

A soldier appeared, his weapon at the ready, then another, more decamped out the back, one from the cabin. Jamia took a fearful glance behind, expecting to see Captain Nkusi. She turned back, holding Ali's head to her shoulder, not wanting him to see the flash of a gun as it was fired.

"*Stay in the vehicle,*" The old woman said.

The sound of a loud crack came from high up on the other side of the track. A gun had been fired. The first soldier fell. More cracks, soon merging into an explosion of sound. The noise was coming from behind a rust coloured rock. Two more soldiers fell. Mahamat slammed the Land Cruiser into gear, the vehicle shot back onto the track and sped off. Several seconds later there was a flash, followed by a whistling noise, then an explosion. The troop carrier was engulfed in a ball of flames. Soldiers fled.

The Land Cruiser travelled on for several more uneventful hours, leaving the Ouaddai district and into Wadi Fira. A few hours later they passed the village of Gindo, children ran out to greet them. Mahamat ignored them and drove on.

Sometimes the track would be more accessible, allowing

them to make good time, other times it became rough and barely passable, occasionally it would disappear altogether. Mahamat would always find it again, driving with the confidence of a person who appeared to have had made this same journey many times before.

Seven hours after leaving Breidjing Refugee Camp, tired and hungry but alive, they arrived at their destination, the town of Guereda.

A Land Rover was waiting for them on the outskirts. Mahamat stopped in the road and allowed them to pull up beside. Windows were wound down, enthusiastic handshakes and friendly smiles were exchanged, Allah repeatedly thanked. They were escorted into the town of Guereda.

Wednesday 16th June 2010
Rue Sainte-Ascelina,
Marseille,
France

Both Lucile and Norris remained in their seats, staring through the windscreen of her Citroen 2CV — named Claude. "When you spoke to your mother on the phone did you ask her about the time she came to Marseille?" Lucile asked.

Norris took a few seconds to answer. "She said she couldn't remember."

Lucile turned to look at him, trying to read his face. "You sound skeptical."

"You don't know my mother. She's a law unto herself. One minute you think she has the IQ of a genius, the next she has the mentality of a young child."

"She sounds interesting."

Norris turned so they were eye to eye. "Interesting is one way you could put it. I'll get to the truth. I might have done so already if an overexcited French journalist hadn't insisted I stay in Marseille. Especially when she wouldn't take no for an answer." At the time Norris hoped Lucile wanted him there for other reasons, namely himself. He breathed a heavy sigh as if he had conceded defeat. “You said you were in urgent need of my help?”

“Madam Veronique,” she said, raising her eyebrows, waiting to see his reaction.

He rolled his eyes. “I should have guessed.”

“We are parked in her road Norris.” Greatly emphasising the word ‘are.’ “Only this time it is me that needs your help,” Lucile said, taking on the expression of an abandoned puppy. “My editor has only given me a week...and that was two days ago. And I have to meet someone. I take it you have your phone at hand Norris?”

“Yes.”

“Is it charged?”

“Yes!” He sighed. “Just like you said.”

“Take it out.”

“What the phone?” Norris asked with a mischievous grin.

Lucile angled her head and raised her eyebrows.

Norris’s smile quickly faded as he took out his phone. She held up her palm. “Take a photograph of it.”

“Your hand?”

“Yes!”

He held the phone up so it was directly in front of his face and prodded the screen.

“Let me see.” Lucile looked at the picture. “No Norris! You must get closer so you are filling the screen.” She sighed with frustration. “And remember, she did say you could have the painting. That is why we are here.”

“She did,” he replied unconvincingly.

“I need an excuse to get into her apartment again. This is the only way...I take it you do want the painting?”

“To tell you the truth...”

“My God Norris, you English are so obliging. It was part of the deal that she didn’t keep it, remember? And she offered to give it back to you...remember? You must sound more convincing.”

Norris opened his door, hearing the bottom of it scrape against the frame, as if it didn't fit properly, like the car might snap in half just by this one small act. Norris was sure he felt Claude nudge down slightly. He quickly stepped out before it was too late.

They walked to the front door of 139 Rue Sainte-Ascelina and for the third time in nearly two weeks Norris pushed the apartment 7 button. A crackling noise came from behind a small round grill set in a metal plate, quickly followed by a delicate metallic French voice. "*Yes?*"

Norris spoke in French. "*Hello Madam Veronique. It is Norris Kinley, if you remember...?*"

"Of course I remember you Monsieur Kinley, who else speaks such awful French." Madam Veronique replied in perfect English, her words carrying a playful sarcasm.

"I have Lucile Billet with me."

The reply was immediate. "Yes I know."

Lucile looked for a camera, not seeing one. "How did she know?" she mouthed.

"May way we come in?"

"Don't you think you two have done enough damage already."

An uncomfortable silence followed.

"*We will help you see Matthieu,*" Lucile lied, finding it ironic that only a few days ago she was trying her hardest to get him away from her.

Madam Veronique ignored Lucile. "Why are you here Monsieur Kinley?"

Norris waited. Lucile whipped the back of her fingers against the top of his arm.

"Oh...On my last visit you said I could have that painting. The one by Francois..."

She interrupted. "Yes I remember."

"I wondered if we might discuss exactly that." His words sounded false.

Lucile rolled her eyes.

"But it is worth a great deal of money," Madam Veronique replied.

"I am willing to pay you half of its value." Norris remarked, not thinking of anything else to say, nor the implications.

Lucile swung around in disgust.

Norris continued. "You told me once that discussing money is so vulgar. It is even more vulgar when it is done out here on the street, is it not?" He waited again. "May we come in?"

Madam Veronique reverted to French. "*I believe you have something of mine Mademoiselle Billet.*"

Lucile, surprised at hearing her name, held her hands out as though in prayer, then opened them up. "The notebook," she mouthed to Norris before clearing her throat. "What would that be Madam Veronique?"

"How do you English say Monsieur Kinley, maybe we can exchange gifts?"

Lucile stepped closer to the grill. "I think that could be an option, maybe we can discuss the details over a cup of your delicious coffee."

A long wait, then a buzz and a click from the door. Lucile and Norris stepped in.

Madam Veronique was already waiting at her door as they finished climbing the seemingly endless flights of steps, Norris gasping for breath. Lucile thought she looked exactly as she did before, an old whore trying to hide her age.

Madam Veronique turned and disappeared into her apartment as soon as she saw them.

Lucile and Norris followed her, entering the large drawing room, him sitting in the same chair he had occupied on the last two visits, he had the feeling it was all beginning to feel far too familiar. He turned and stared at The Drowning Mary. Although he had missed noticing it before, it now seemed to fill the entire room. "You said I could have it the last time I saw you."

"But why Monsieur?"

He turned back. "Why what?"

"Why do you want it?" Before he could answer. "You told me you were no art expert, and my guess is Francois Degarmo is not exactly to your taste. I would say you are more a Monet's Poppy Field in Argenteuil man."

Lucile glared long and hard at Norris.

"The Drowning Mary belonged to my father. A lasting memory you could say." Norris just realised. "You don't know do you? My father did die, but not..."

Madam Veronique's voice softened. "Yes Monsieur Kinley, I heard." She straightened her back and clutched her hands together.

He wondered how she knew. "That is why I want the painting."

"Ah yes. The memory." Her tone turned derogatory. "He has two sons. Is that still in your memory?"

Norris wished he had come more prepared. "I...it is my mother who has the receipt though. Matthieu is not her son."

"Then maybe your mother should come and collect it."

"Maybe I am speaking on her behalf. Maybe..."

Madam Veronique interrupted. "Or have you come to take it from me?" She turned her attention towards Lucile. "Like someone else once took something from me."

Lucile was becoming impatient, she needed to get her out of the room. "I think this would be better discussed over a cup of coffee."

"Think about it Monsieur Kinley," Madam Veronique said. "We both want things returned." She glanced up at the painting, like she was stamping her ownership on it. Lucile and Norris watched as she left the room, vanishing out of sight. Lucile gave Norris a sharp nod. He rose from his chair, stepped over to where the photographs hung on the wall and took out his phone. Keeping one eye on the door to the kitchen he held it in front of one of the photographs, the one with Georges Pompidou standing between his wife and Madam Veronique, he tapped the screen, the fake noise of a shutter. Lucile frowned. Norris turned the sound down. He then held the phone in front of the photograph with her and Charles Aznavour. Followed by another with an ageing Maurice Chevalier.

A soft, "Pssst."

Thinking the old lady was returning, Norris turned towards Lucile in panic. Instead he saw her hold up a flat hand and nudge it forward. Norris drew down his lips and crumpled his eyebrows in confusion. 'Oh,' he mouthed in realisation and moved the phone closer. Without even looking at the screen he began taking shots of as many photos on the wall as he could.

He heard the clinking of cups and quickly slipped the phone into his pocket, remaining where he stood, concentrating on one photograph without actually seeing it.

"*Ah yes Monsieur Kinley.* I remember you like old photographs. Would you like to have them also?"

"People should only have what belongs to them," he replied, relieved that she appeared not to have suspected anything. He returned to his chair.

'Job well done,' Lucile's eyes told him.

Madam Veronique poured out two coffees. "One sugar if I remember correctly Monsieur Kinley?"

Norris returned a single nod.

As the coffee was handed out in silence, Lucile took the opportunity to talk. "*I was thinking of writing an article about the Markovic affair,*" she said bluntly. "*I remember on our last visit you said you knew one of the women in the photographs.*"

Madam Veronique opened the door to a cabinet and took out a brandy glass along with a bottle of cognac, filling it to half way. "*I remember.*" She sat down and took an extra large sip from the glass, keeping it in her mouth before gulping it down, like she wanted to dispel the sour taste of Lucile's words.

"*Who was it?*"

Madam Veronique ignored her, keeping her attention on Norris. "We have not finished discussing the painting Monsieur

Kinley."

"*Was it you? Were you one of them?*" Lucile blurted out.

Madam Veronique sighed. "You mentioned about paying me half of its current worth."

Lucile continued. "*Did you know Luicien Aimé-Blanc?*"

"Or we could discuss the other matter. About something that was taken from me...from this very room."

"*What about Louis Wallon and Henri Capitant. Did they pay you to be in the photographs?*"

"Or you could go to the courts, try and get it back that way Monsieur."

"*How about Alain Delon and Francois Marcantoni. Did you know either of them? You know Markovic's brother accused them of the murder.*"

"But you would have to explain why it is in my hands Monsieur Kinley, how your father tried to blackmail me with it."

Norris tried to speak. "It wasn't blackmail..." Not being allowed to finish the words.

"*I know you know something Madam Veronique,*" snapped Lucile. "*It would be better if you told me everything. You know how sensationalist we reporters can get when we only know half the truth. Or should I call you Susanne Dennel?*"

For several seconds it was like a lead weight had dropped into the room. In the past Norris had found Lucile to be endearing, drawn towards her in a beguiling sort of way. Now he felt he had seen another side of her, the reporter's side, a side he didn't like. He discovered from the first visit why women in Madam Veronique's profession changed their names, like Helaine to Heloise, using it only for professional needs, keeping their two lives separate. He found out their real name was personal to them, only known by a select few. He also wondered if she was known only as Veronique at one time.

Madam Veronique smiled at Norris, as if she had dismissed Lucile. "I will take half of its current worth."

Lucile began to speak, "*Was Susanne Dennel the woman in...?*"

The old woman closed her eyes and took a long breath, wanting to make Lucile feel inferior. "Plus the return of what is mine. Also I would like to speak to Matthieu... alone. Then I will give you the painting Monsieur Kinley."

Lucile snapped her head towards Norris, wondering how he was going to respond.

"I am afraid I only have the authority for one of those conditions."

"Then that is a shame Monsieur Kinley."

This time Norris looked long and hard at Lucile. She remained silent.

Madam Veronique noticed the unspoken exchange between them. "You appear to have nothing to say about the matter Mademoiselle Billet." She then spoke in French, the words assertive, like she was not to be disobeyed. "*I believe you have something of mine. I would like it back.*" Her eyes were fixed. "*Do not underestimate me Mademoiselle Billet. Your newspaper is La Provence, is it not?*" She didn't wait for an answer. "*I believe it is owned by Bernard Tapie.*"

Lucile remained silent. She took it as a threat; as it was meant to be.

"Mademoiselle Billet's silence says so much Monsieur Kinley."

"My silence means nothing." Lucile also reverted to French. "*If I didn't have whatever belongs to you then there would be no need for me to explain myself. And if I have what you say I have I wouldn't exactly admit it to you, would I? Like I said, my silence tells you nothing.*"

"We are all at the mercy of time Monsieur. Maybe I should give the painting to the Pompidou Centre. A painting like this should be owned by everyone, should it not? One day, when we are no longer here The Drowning Mary will neither be yours or mine. "

Lucile turned to look at the painting, thinking a child could have done better.

Madam Veronique saw her gaze up. "Some paintings are there just to be looked at. Some become part of you. Tell me Mademoiselle Billet, what does The Drowning Mary do to you?"

"It is not my thing Madam."

"And you Monsieur Kinley?"

Norris thought for a while. "The painting is part of my father. I am part of my father. Therefore the painting is part of me. Does that answer your question?"

Madam Veronique took another large sip of cognac.

"So what is it to you?" Norris asked as he watched her tip the glass up and gulp the liquid down.

"You want me to say I am captivated by its energy, that the colour dances on the canvas. No Monsieur. It is paint on canvas. The canvas was white, now it is dark. It is like life is it not? It was a gift, that is all, just a gift."

"Is that why you keep it on that wall, between the windows, left in shadow, in permanent darkness?"

"With many admirers come many gifts Monsieur. Some I like more than others. Some I like more for different reasons. When Remi Cochet gave it to me he told me that in a few years it would double in money. That was in 1983 Monsieur. What must it be worth now, one hundred thousand euros?...More? You said you would give me half. Would you give me more than fifty thousand euros...more than fifty thousand of your Great British pounds?"

Norris still had his inheritance: a lot more than fifty thousand euros, a lot more than fifty thousand pounds. But it wasn't a bottomless pit. He also knew that as and when his mother departs this world he would have the house, which will be worth a tidy sum, maybe in the millions; he could buy a small flat somewhere, live of the proceeds. But she was a strong old bird and would probably last for many more years, ten, maybe more.

"*And were you given a gift to appear in a photograph as Claude Pompidou?*" Lucile threw in.

Norris was only there as a favour to Lucile, to take pictures of the photographs on the wall. That he had done already. The painting was only an excuse to enter the apartment. Now he felt they were crossing unacceptable boundaries.

Madam Veronique answered Lucile with another long, hard stare. She then turned her attention back to Norris. "If I can see Matthieu and have back what rightfully belongs to me, then you..." She emphasised the word once more. "You...Monsieur Kinley can have the painting for...shall we say the princely sum of one euro."

Lucile knew exactly what the Madam was up to.

"One euro." Norris said softly, as if the two words had slid off his tongue.

"That is all it is worth Monsieur." She blew out a sharp breath. "One hundred thousand euros, only a fool would pay that. It is not even worth a tiny fraction of that. It is worthless Monsieur. Look at it."

Norris looked up. He remembered doing some research on Francois Degarmo when trying to find his father. He could find nothing out about the artist, only about the time The Pompidou Centre hung The Foundering of Death, and that was just a small column in a newspaper criticising the purchase. Now it seems his father had paid well over the top; and then he never had it in his possession.

Madam Veronique wanted to see Matthieu, but that was up to Matthieu himself, Norris would have no control over that. She wanted the notebook back as well, to him it was worthless, like the painting is to Madam Veronique. But that was also out of his hands and he knew Lucile would never give it up. He looked at Lucile, her return glare felt as if it was tattooing the word 'no' onto his head. The conversation they were about to have was not going to be an easy one.

Norris and Lucile were sat in the same position, staring through Claude's windscreen, along the length of Rue Sainte-Ascelina. Norris tried to imagine it in its heyday, the huge cars pulling up outside Madam Veronique's establishment, the expensive jewelers and tailors, the entrepreneurs and artists engaged in amusing conversations outside bustling cafes. Then he saw his father, smartly dressed, swinging his umbrella, puffing on his pipe, disappearing through the door of the brothel. How much it has changed, now rubbish lay in the gutter, bins scattered on the pavement, inept graffiti daubed on the walls.

"Pass me your phone," Lucile demanded.

Norris obeyed, he felt he had no choice.

Her gaze dropped down, her finger whipping over the screen, studying each picture in turn. "Jesus Norris, there's only about two here that are any good."

"Well Jesus Lucile, If you had asked me I would have brought my Nikon along and set it up on a tripod." He noticed a newspaper kiosk in the far distance, an urge came over him to storm over there and buy a packet of cigarettes: he remained seated.

"Sorry Norris, these are great." She said falsely before prodding frantically at his phone.

"What are you doing now?"

"I'm emailing some..." Her eyes wide in concentration. "I'm emailing them to someone." Her finger manically tapping away. "I need to get prints..." she said slowly until the words tailed away altogether. "I need to get prints made." One last prod. She looked up. "There...I need to get prints made. I need to show them to someone. Prints would be easier, they are more permanent. Your phone could get stolen, you could lose it, what if you fall out with me?"

"I don't think..."

"When the prints are made I want you to delete them."

"Who?"

"Who what?...Oh. I'm sending them to Antoine, our dark room guy." She looked down again, her finger began frantically tapping the screen again, she held it up to her ear.

"No, I mean who have you to show them to?"

Lucile appeared not to have heard. "*Come on,*" she mumbled to herself, gazing upward, tapping Norris's phone on her ear. "*Ah! Antoine. I have just emailed you some jpegs. I need you to... When!...No first thing in the morning.*" Her face tightened. "*Sod Angelique's footballer and his fucking tart...Mine are priority. Speak to Henri...Listen Antoine, keep them hidden and don't show anyone, mostly Henri...So in fact don't speak to Henri...I don't know how, you work it out...Yes, okay. The usual...goodbye.*" She pulled a notepad from her bag, flicking swiftly through the pages she stopped at one. Then began prodding the screen again, she glanced at the page once more, tapped it a couple more times and waited. She spoke, her tone became calm and measured, friendly. "*Ah! Monsieur Bret, it is Lucile Billet. We spoke yesterday...Yes...How about. Oh..Is that Madame Bret again, how nice.*" Lucile rolled her eyes. "*Yes I have...Tomorrow...Good. Where?*"

Norris saw the white of Lucile's knuckles as she clenched tightly onto his phone, any harder he thought she might even crush it.

"*Beaune! That's over four...Oh, Is that Madame Bret again...Okay. Yes, in the afternoon sometime. I'll ring when I get there.*" Lucile gave the phone one last hard prod as if she had stabbed it with a knife. She then leant forward and began stroking the top of Claude's dashboard. "We have got a long journey tomorrow *my little cabbage*, we had better give you a good night's rest."

"Don't you have a phone of your own?"

"Yes, it's in my bag somewhere. Oh! sorry." With a drop of her wrist and an impish grin she handed it back to him.

"So you have to show the prints to this man Monsieur Bret?"

"He was the policeman who found Markovic's body, he also found the photographs."

"Oh." Norris nodded slowly, recognising the importance of the meeting. "How far is Beaune."

"In Claude, five hours, maybe six. If we get there at all." Lucile leant forward and turned the key, the engine popped loudly, followed by a rattle from the exhaust, it then fell into an erratic groan.

Just as she was about to manoeuvre out of the space. "That painting could reach double what she thinks. All we have to do is persuade Matthieu to see her."

"My God Norris! Couldn't you see she was playing with you. That painting isn't worth the canvas it is painted on."

He sighed deeply, knowing the truth behind her response. "And give her back the notebook," he said.

"You've got more chance of seeing God!" Lucile nudged Claude forward. "I'm not discussing it anymore."

"I'll give you a cut."

"You weren't even going to come back and get it."

"It's a matter of principal. Now I've seen it again I realise it reminds me of my father."

"Without the notebook you wouldn't have found out about your father."

"Two hundred thousand euros Lucile...maybe pounds. I'll give you half."

There were a few seconds of thought before Lucile spoke again. "Didn't you hear her, it is worth nothing! I'm not going to discuss it anymore Norris. If you want the painting you will have to do it without the notebook."

"But that is what she really wants if..."

"No more Norris! I'm not going to give you the notebook, even for a million euros." Lucile snapped. With a glass shattering crunch she slammed Claude in reverse and rolled the car back a little. "The French people have a right to know what their politicians have been up to." After several attempts at coaxing Claude into first gear, she shot out of the space and sped off.

Norris turned to look at her, strangely thinking how soft her skin is, how full her lips are, how large her eyes seemed. He tried to lighten the mood. “We?” Is all he said.

“What!?” Lucile snapped.

“You said if we get there.”

“What!?”

“Tomorrow. When you go to Beaune.”

“Yes...Claude and I.”

“Oh...Well...I can tell you now Claude wouldn’t even make it out of Marseille. I’ll hire a car, we can go together.”

Lucile thought for a moment. “Okay, on one condition. You don’t mention the notebook.”

“I’ll try not to.”

“No. I want you to promise.”

“I promise.”

“Or the painting.”

“I promise.” Several minutes had passed before one of them spoke again. “So her name was Susanne Dennel?” Norris announced.

“Yes, very few know it. It seems she was telling the truth when she said her father was a war hero.”

“I never doubted her.”

Lucile smiled. “Julien will find out more...”

“No!” Norris interrupted “Leave her be.” He calmed down. “Just let her private life be hers. If you want to find out Madam Veronique’s involvement with this Markovic fellow so be it, but at least let her keep something that is hers.” He realised she had only done what she thought was best for Matthieu when she raised him, trying to protect him, give him a better life. One she never had herself. In a strange way during the times he had met Madam Veronique he realised she had been through so much. In some ways he had grown to have a lot of respect for her. He felt the notebook was about revenge, retribution for the people of Marseille for taking what belonged to her and her family.

"I'll try, but sometimes they're connected. Remember Norris, she told us about her father sending her to Switzerland with her sister and mother. She told me to write how the people of Marseille had plundered everything they owned. And I might do just that, the public hate hearing the truth about their ancestors screwing over their own people. Probably why she wants me to write about it. I don't trust her though, she's a crafty old mare."

"Screwing over...A crafty old mare. Any more quotes from EastEnders?"

Lucile laughed. "I gotta lot to fank Kat Slater for."

"Doesn't quite work with a French accent."

Lucile laughed again, it made Norris feel good.

She pulled up outside the Cozy Hotel. "I'll see you here in the morning, ten o'clock."

"I'll have the hire car...Oh, what did you mean by the usual?"

"Sorry?"

"You said to Antoine, the dark room guy...Okay, the usual. What is the usual?"

Lucile looked at Norris and smiled.

"We have mad passionate sex."

There was a short silence. "That's alright then."

With a teeth grating creak he opened Claude's passenger door and stepped onto the pavement, glad to have survived another journey.

Thursday 17th June 2010
Parc Bouzaise,
Beaune,
France

Norris had parked the Peugeot on a piece of dusty wasteground just off the Allee du Dr Bouley. Not because it was away from the busy tourist centre, although that was a good enough reason in itself, but because Lucile insisted they meet in a park. She preferred these clandestine rendezvous to be in open spaces, where they could talk freely, where she wouldn't have to look over her shoulder all the time, concerned about people listening in on their conversation.

It was Monsieur Bret who chose Parc Bouzaise — or his wife did.

"The Gods are looking down on us," Norris remarked as they decamped the car, the meaning of which he had to explain to Lucile. He wasn't wrong, it was a lovely warm day with a clear baby-blue sky. In the distance, through the gaps between the trees they could just see the sunlight glinting like jewels on the lake's surface, their sparkle guiding them to their destination.

A few minutes later they arrived at the park, about the size of two football pitches, a boating lake at its centre, long and narrow, surrounded by tall trees perfectly equidistant. Everything from the close mown grass to the flowers and the ball shaped bushes were all impeccably manicured. Several small rowing boats crewed by young couples and families with small children drifted aimlessly over the calm water. Altogether it had an ambience that gave the visitor the peace of a library and the tranquility of a Buddhist temple.

"It was nearly worth the four hour drive," Norris remarked.

"There is only one thing that would make that drive worthwhile and that is Monsieur Bret recognising Madam Veronique in the photographs," Lucile replied.

Once they had reached the lake they crossed the narrow wooden bridge to the other side, just as Lucile had been instructed to do. Norris stopped to study a plaque nailed to the handrail. On it was a picture of a fish with pink fins, there were other plaques, some with birds, so faded by the sunlight it was difficult to distinguish them apart. It was then, in the corner of his eye he saw Lucile raise a tentative hand to shoulder height, as if the acknowledgment wouldn't be an embarrassment if it wasn't them. Norris looked up to see an old couple sat on a bench behind the trees, catching sight of the man just as he returned his hand to his lap.

They were aged about eighty, although she looked older than him. He was round, flabby, turkey necked. The woman was the opposite, small, spiky features, everyone's grandmother, a kindly face which took Lucile by surprise. She was expecting the opposite, the matronly type, large and overbearing. Both shared that sun-dried provincial look. Very French thought Norris.

Introductions were made and limp handshakes exchanged. The old couple eyed Norris with uncertainty. Lucile had introduced him as her driver, she told them he was English and spoke very little French; which they seemed to accept with suspicion. All four sat on the bench, the old couple in the middle, Lucile next to Monsieur Bret. Madame Bret sat on the edge with her back towards Norris, virtually blocking him out. He sat back, having to look in from behind the old woman.

Lucile delved straight into her bag and pulled out a large brown envelope. "*If I show you some photographs could you tell me if the woman in them is the same one in the Markovic photographs.*"

"Yes," Monsieur Bret puffed out with a sharp nod.

Lucile slid out the prints Norris had taken on his phone at Madam Veronique's apartment, seven in total. She separated the one with the Pompidous and handed half of the others to the old man, the better ones.

Monsieur Bret held it with both hands, like he was reading from a speech. "*It was over forty years ago,*" he said.

Madame Bret spoke. "*Why do you want him to stir all this nonsense up again? It has brought us nothing but misery.*"

Lucile ignored her. "*You can't change the past Monsieur Bret...May I call you Victor?*"

Monsieur Bret thought for a while. "*Ah yes, of course.*"

Lucile waited for Madame Bret to offer up her first name. She didn't.

"*Please call me Lucile and this gentleman is...*" Lucile leant forward, then back, having trouble seeing him. "*This is Norris.*"

Neither turned to look at him.

Lucile thought Victor needed some incentive. "*You can't change the past Victor. But you can put right what was wrong and by the sound of it you have been terribly wronged. If we can find out who this woman is then maybe we can find out who killed Stevan Markovic. We can use it to change the future Victor, your future. If we can prove they tried to blackmail you into saying it was Claude Pompidou then we can say you were wrongfully dismissed. Hounded out of the police force. The compensation money could be huge.*"

Norris thought it sounded rehearsed, even if he did only understand a small part of it.

Lucile continued. "*It was not your fault. You were a victim of circumstances. My God Victor, it wasn't even you in the wrong place at the wrong time. It was your friend.*"

Madam Bret sighed loudly. "*And if he does recognise her? What then? More hatred. You don't know what we went through. Police tearing the house apart, harassing and threatening us, stopping us in the car for any little excuse. Only because we would not tell a lie.*"

Lucile noticed she had used the word 'we,' realising she must have gone through as much of the trauma as her husband. "*I will try and keep your name out of it,*" she said, knowing there was little hope.

Victor looked down again, although this time he seemed to be staring through the photograph, like it was transparent.

"*I have more,*" Lucile said as she began handing them over one by one, leaving the one with the Pompidous until last. "*I am sorry they are only photographs of photographs.*" She became worried that he was taking the quickest of glances before accepting another.

"*Show her it,*" Madame Bret said.

Lucile studied the old woman's face, it had the look of hard, cold stone.

"*Show me what?*" Lucile said, her eyes darting between Victor and his wife. No one replied. "*Show me what!?*" she repeated.

"*Show her it!*" Madame Bret repeated with equal force, switching her glare towards her husband.

Victor remained motionless.

"*What?*" Lucile asked again.

"*Show her the photograph Victor,*" the old woman said, her tone more conciliatory.

Victor slid his hand into his inside pocket. He pulled out a photograph and handed it to Lucile, avoiding all eye contact. As soon as she set eyes on it, an overwhelming wave of excitement surged through her from head to toe. She knew that in her hands was one of the most notorious photographs from one of the most infamous scandals ever to hit modern day French politics.

Shot in colour, it was of two women, both naked, both sitting in the middle of a large bed, their legs apart, one pair over the top of the other. Their arms wrapped around each other in a tight embrace. They were kissing, not a friendly peck, this was an open mouthed kiss, a tongue searching out a tongue kiss. Lucile noticed the bedsheets were still relatively neat, as if it was just the start of what was about to happen. Also the picture was fuzzy on either side, like it was vignetted, as if the camera had been hidden. One of the women had long black hair and was facing the camera, her features mostly obscured by the other woman's head, even so, by the tone of her muscles Lucile could tell she was just entering middle-age, forty would be her guess, but she still had a good figure. Although she couldn't see her face properly Lucile felt intuitively that she would be attractive. Her hand was round the back of the other woman's head, her fingers intertwined in shoulder length blonde hair. Only a small part of the woman's cheek was visible but Lucile could tell she was quite a bit older. She was slim, but her waist had flesh rolls, especially where she leant into the other woman, also the legs, the lower muscles were floppy, gravity forcing them to hang down, leaving bony thighs. Lucile guessed she was at least fifty, maybe more. "*Where did you get this?*" she finally asked.

"*It is from Markovic's car,*" Victor replied.

"*You have had this all this time?*"

"*Yes,*" he answered slowly.

"*There are more,*" Madame Bret said.

Lucile's eyes widened. "*More?*" An eagerness entered into her voice. "*May I see them? It will...*" Her words tailing away as she understood what this was about, she smirked with realisation. "*How much?*"

"*You tell us,*" said Madame Bret.

Lucile stared down to the ground, this was an opportunity she couldn't throw away. She knew La Provence paid for photos all the time, on a daily basis. Mostly from freelance photographers, occasionally from picture libraries, but also from the public, as long as they didn't try to fleece the paper; the editor despised greed. There was a going rate for buying such pictures and Henri would rarely deviate from that set price, although Lucile knew these were different, very different. These photographs were in a league of their own. "*How many more?*" she asked.

Victor answered. "*Two.*"

"*But they are much better than the one you have in your hand,*" Madame Bret added.

"*I would have to see them.*"

"*How much?*" The old woman repeated.

"*If we pay for them they would become our property.*"

"*Of course. But you must tell no one who gave them to you. If you do, we will deny it. Once you have them you will have no need for my husband to be involved any more.*"

Lucile looked down at the photograph once again, biting her top lip, deciding her next move. She rose from the bench with her phone in hand. "*Wait here,*" she said and began punching numbers into the screen, strolling down to the lake as she did. When she got to the water she prowled up and down its edge, at one time stopping and kicking a twig into the lake. Several times she raised her hand and sliced it through the air. Norris thought it was probably out of frustration, he had seen it before. Other times her head would bob from side to side, not once did she look behind her at the three on the bench. A few minutes later she prodded the phone. For several seconds she remained standing in the same spot, gazing out into the water. She returned and sat on the bench.

"*How come you have them?*" Lucile asked, the insinuation was plain to hear; that they were in fact stolen.

"*I was keeping them for national security,*" he replied.

"*How come you have them?*" Lucile repeated.

There was a long silence. The old woman glared at her husband, waiting for him to answer.

"*For my own entertainment,*" he said sheepishly before glancing towards Norris, hoping for some man-to-man support. "*Sometimes...*"

Norris interrupted, speaking in English. "Sometimes us men like to do things alone. Sometimes we need a bit of incentive."

Lucile smiled, then translated.

Madame Bret turned and stared judgingly at the Englishman.

Lucile continued. "*My editor is an old guard journalist, you know, set in his ways, hasn't accepted things have changed, doesn't know the world is moving on.*" Lucile couldn't bring herself to repeat his offer. "*The modern...*"

"*How much?*" Madame Bret interrupted.

"*If the two are acceptable...five hundred euros each. One hundred for this one.*"

Madame Bret puffed out a cynical breath and looked away in disgust. She turned back. "*Ten thousand euros for the three.*"

"*I'll come clean with you. It was my editor who told me to offer five hundred first, then one thousand each if you didn't accept, throwing this one in for nothing. He told me to go no higher.*" Lucile turned towards Victor. "*Monsieur Bret, if you want your name to be kept out of it then we lose our provenance. We need proof of where they came from, who had them last, why they had them, that is why I asked. My editor is worried the paper will be accused of setting it up ourselves, that we will be taken to court. Without your good name they are worthless.*"

"*Then we will sell them to another newspaper,*" said Madam Bret.

"*Let me use your name as the source then I can persuade my editor to go higher, maybe quite a bit higher. You might be able to sue the police for loss of earnings or...*"

"*No!*" Madame Bret said flatly. "*If we allow you to use our names then we will be accused of withholding evidence. I...We do not trust the police, they are all corrupt. My husband will go to prison.*"

Lucile drew down her lips and nodded empathetically. "*That is what my editor said you would say.*"

"*They are worth a lot of money.*"

"*Not without Victor's name. Other newspapers will say the same. I am sorry but two thousand is...*"

"Five thousand for the three." Norris threw in, just like that, as if it were an auction. Sitting back on the bench with his legs stretched out and his arms folded over his chest, his gaze fixed on a single spot on the lake. He slowly turned his head towards Madame Bret, then Victor, then Lucile. "Please translate."

Lucile cleared her throat. She repeated what Norris said word for word.

Madame Bret remained silent.

Norris continued. "Cash...I will get it tomorrow."

"Tomorrow!..." Lucile managed to stop herself. She knew it meant an overnight stay, time was running out, another precious day would be lost.

Norris raised his voice slightly. "If the photographs are acceptable to Mademoiselle Billet then she will pay you five thousand euros. We will have to find another provenance elsewhere, your names will not be mentioned. I promise you that, and an Englishman's word is his bond."

Lucile translated, having to explain the last sentence.

More silence.

"*Ten thousand is our...*" Madame Bret began unconvincingly before her husband quickly intervened.

"We will take it," Victor said in English through a strong accent. "After all, I have no use for them now." His lips falling short of a smile. "Old age," he added.

"Good. We have a deal," Norris said, looking pleased with himself. "Have you got them with you now?"

Lucile translated.

"*No,*" Madam Bret snapped.

"*Yes,*" Victor countered.

"In that case may we see them," asked Norris. "We are not going to waste money on a hotel room and go to the trouble of drawing five thousand euros from a bank if they are not acceptable."

Lucile translated, pluralising the word 'room'.

"*How do we know you will not run off with them?*" Madame Bret said.

Norris raised his hand to say he understood. "I promise. And as I said, an Englishman's word is his bond."

"*Yes yes,*" Madame Bret said with a dismissive wave of her hand.

Victor delved into the inside pocket of his jacket. He pulled out two more photographs, Lucile went to take them. "*No.*" The word like a dog's bark. He held them out for her to see, only for the briefest moment though.

"May I see?" asked Norris. "After all I'm paying for them."

Victor leant forward and held one in each of his hands. Madame Bret turned her head to the side, overplaying her disgust. Again, Norris was only allowed a brief look before Victor whipped them away. "And you must never say who gave them to you."

"I promise." Norris looked at Lucile, both were satisfied the content was an improvement on the first. "Tomorrow morning then." He raised his eyebrows and waited, the slightest of nods was returned. "Shall we say ten o'clock, same place."

Lucile translated.

As they stood at the hotel reception desk Norris let Lucile do the talking, only managing to catch some of the conversation. He did understand. "*Two doubles,*" although he had no idea what the word adjoining was in French, he only hoped with some small miracle it was in there somewhere.

"*We only have them on different floors,*" the hotel receptionist replied.

Norris didn't understand all of what Lucile said when having to explain to the mousy, waistcoated young girl why they had no luggage, but he did hear the irritation in her voice when she felt she had to account for why not, like she was wanting to tell her that this was not some sordid impromptu affair — or an affair at all, hence the separate rooms. The way Lucile said the last words in plain and simple French made Norris wonder if they were actually meant for his ears.

"A freshen up, then dinner in the restaurant. I'll give you a knock," Lucile said it like an announcement.

Facing her at the dinner table felt very intimate for Norris, they had been through so much over the past weeks. He felt their relationship had gone past that of being just friends, the way her eyes hung on him, the way she would laugh playfully at his jokes. This was when he felt transported to another place, one he had never been to before. A place that made him feel warm and content, sensations he hadn't experienced before, feelings he couldn't put into words, or maybe just one — love. How would he know? Unlike the long car journey to Beaune, when periods of silence could be ignored while Lucile took in the view, it was different in the restaurant. There they were facing each other, no escape, staring at each other like lovers – – or not, that was the choice. Loosening their tongues with a bottle of Clos des Mouches managed to break most of the ice. It started with Lucile telling Norris everything she knew about the Markovic affair, how there were so many missing pieces in the jigsaw puzzle. Norris nearly scuppered the conversation by remarking that three of the pieces had cost him five thousand euros.

"Three thousand." Lucile corrected him. "Two will come from the newspaper. And you didn't have to do it."

"Yes I did," he replied, wanting to tell her he did it for her.

Lucile's expression softened. "Thank you Norris."

She went on to tell him that gossip was rife in France at the time of the murder. All the perpetrators had to do was spread word of the existence of the photographs and their subject matter, the French public would fuel the rest themselves.

After the Markovic affair they spoke briefly about Norris's search for his father; prompting him to talk about the painting. "There is more to The Drowning Mary than meets the eye," he told her, and that was it. It was obvious Lucile had no interest in discussing it, reminding Norris he had promised not to talk about it. They had managed to get back into Madame Veronique's apartment and take the photographs, as far as Lucile was concerned the painting had no more use.

They briefly mentioned Helaine's reunion with Matthieu, then wondered if she knew about the death of Major Guerrette. A long silence followed.

They spoke about Lucile's holidays in the Isle of Wight, she told Norris that was where she had acquired her obsession with EastEnders, which continued to this day. "Thank God for iPlayer," she remarked. "The other day I watched six episodes back to back; if you don't believe me." She threw her arm out wide, nearly taking out a passing waiter. "Then ge' ou' my restaurant." Followed by an embarrassed wine induced cackle.

Norris suggested it was probably why she spoke English with an East London accent. "Mixed in with that sexy French accent," he added, wondering if he should have.

The conversation moved on to English politics, Norris telling her how old Etonians are trying to rule the country and hoped the public wouldn't notice.

"How old are these old Etonians?"

Norris chuckled. "No it has nothing to do with age. It's a school for boys who want to run the country."

"You have a school for boys who want to run the country?"

"Don't you in France?" Norris was enjoying himself.

"No." Lucile said, sitting back in astonishment.

Talking about Eton led to him telling her about his own

time spent at boarding school. She realised his was clearly not a school for boys who wanted to rule the country, not lawfully anyhow, not if they wanted it run by men with a penchant for mental and sometimes physical abuse. He saw the surprise on Lucile's face when he mentioned the word fag, from watching EastEnders she always thought it meant cigarette. She also got the impression Norris must have had a lonely childhood.

They soon changed to French politics, which was predominantly Lucile being obsessed with Carla Bruni — not in a good way either. Describing her as a power hungry, attention seeking, gutter rat, drunk on pond water. "And she sings like onc," she added. Norris got the feeling they had crossed paths at one time.

Sometimes they became quite philosophical, talking about life in general; how the slightest change in fate can change the direction of a life, which is why they were sitting together in a restaurant discussing why they were sitting at a restaurant table discussing why they were sitting in a restaurant. It made them laugh out loud.

Norris couldn't remember the last time he had had such an enjoyable time. With Lucile he felt like time had stopped, something he wanted to last forever. He had even lost the urge to have a cigarette, something that always crept up on him after a meal.

One hour later Lucile opened her bedroom door. "Norris! It's eleven oclock," she said.

"I know. I've been thinking about that photograph."

She remained at the entrance. "What photograph?" Her words spoken through a weary sigh, which Norris couldn't deduce whether it was the two bottles of wine or just tiredness.

"The one Monsieur Bret gave you to look at."

She perked up slightly. "What about it?"

He looked both ways along the corridor. "We can't discuss it here."

Lucile stepped aside. "I was going to have a nightcap

anyway. There's a half bottle of plonk in the minibar."

Lucile sat on the bed, barefoot, her toes poking through the bottom of her jeans, her back resting on the headboard. "What about this photograph?"

"I was thinking."

"Is that wise?" Even through the slurring he thought the accent still remained sexy.

Not wanting to disappoint he blew out a laugh. "If these photographs were meant to be a setup, then why that one? Why one where you can't see her face? I mean if they wanted people to think it was Madame Pompidou why have one with her facing away."

"Is that it Norris?"

Norris handed her a plastic tumbler of wine. "I think it's a fair point though."

Lucile took a sip and grimaced. "Ugh, I could run Claude on this stuff...Okay, what would you do if you wanted photos of the future president's wife to look like she was a having a lesbian romp?"

Norris perched himself on the edge of the bed, his face changing to an expression of realisation. "Of course, make them look like the real thing."

"Exactly. And if it wasn't Madame Pompidou you wouldn't want a full facial shot with all that wonderful detail, would you? Like I said in the restaurant Norris, it wasn't that the photographs existed, it was the rumour they existed. Whoever murdered Markovic just needed something tangible to hide in the car."

"Yes," Norris said in agreement. "Did you see Victor's hands? They looked as if they had the grip of a vice. I mean if I did want to snatch the pictures, you know, like his wife thought we would." He stopped, their laughter faded away. Norris leant back onto the headboard, close to Lucile, leaving his legs dangling over the side, just managing to keep his tumbler upright. "I'd like to see them around the neck of his wife. My

God, does that woman need to take a happy pill."

Their laughter vanished altogether, replaced by an awkward pause.

"Anyway, that woman in the photographs, the one with black hair, she reminded me of someone," he added.

Lucile slid down the headboard and turned to look at him, nestling her cheek into the pillow.

Norris looked at her, he wanted to stroke the hair away from her face, kiss her forehead, kiss her on the lips. He did neither.

"Yes, it reminded you of Madam Veronique," she said.

Norris raised his legs so his whole body was now stretched out on the bed. He wanted to slide down the headboard, nestle his head into the pillow as she had done, so they could be face to face, eye to eye, lips to lips. Realising that would be impossible while holding the tumbler and too obvious if he was to put it down, as if he was announcing his plan of attack. He knew he was over thinking the situation, as he always did, even as a young boy. He remained where he was. "No, not her."

She stared up at him. "You only had a quick look Norris. It was Madam Veronique, believe me." Her words had remained soft.

This wasn't a time to argue. "I don't know. Maybe."

Lucile raised her head off the pillow. "When you have been a journalist for as long as I have Norris you get an insight into people's minds. Madam Veronique is the woman in those photos. I knew it before and I know it now."

"Maybe we will know for certain tomorrow."

"And there is something else I am sure of. Madame Bret would have accepted the two thousand euros."

"Maybe." Norris repeated for the third time, like his mind was saying something else. He moved onto his side, perching his head in his palm, resting the tumbler of wine on his hip with the other hand. He leant slightly closer. "If you have an insight into people's minds then what am I thinking now."

"What you are thinking? Probably what an idiot you are for paying five thousand euros."

He leant in slightly closer. "That is not..."

"Jesus Norris what are you doing?!" She yelled out, leaping off the bed.

"Sorry, I lost balance."

"There was no need to throw the wine..."

"No, I didn't mean it, I just fell forward, it was an accident."

"You pay five thousand euros for some photographs and you think you can..."

"No I lost balance," he pleaded. All hope vanished.

"I'm not Helaine, Norris."

They both froze.

Lucile closed her eyes in shame. "I didn't mean that."

A moment's thought. "I know," Norris replied, his tone sympathetic.

Lucile looked down. "Jesus Norris, look what you've done. It looks like you've tried to murder me." She began laughing.

In front of him, on the white duvet was a large splatter of red from the wine.

"Oh...Sorry."

Her laugh died down to a chuckle. "I can't sleep under that now."

Norris slid off the bed, pulling the duvet with him, rolling it up under his arm. "Wait here," he said and left the room.

He returned several minutes later with another duvet. "Its okay, I haven't used it." Spreading it neatly over the bed and flattening it with a sweep of his arm. "Good night." Was all he said before turning and stepping towards the door.

"Norris."

He stopped. "What?"

"You can stay if you want."

Same day
The Chief's home,
Guereda,
Chad

Nya walked into the room holding a tray filled with flat breads, cakes and biscuits. As she placed it in front of Jamia and Ali, shards of ice clinked noisily inside two glasses of cool water, not once did she make eye contact with them. She then walked over to the other side of the room and began removing ornaments from a low, small round table, cleaning each one in turn, placing them carefully onto the shiny tiled floor, her movements slow and methodical.

"*Why are you cleaning?*" asked Jamia. She knew from the time Nya helped her recover after her ordeal in the desert that manual work was below someone in her position, the daughter of a Chief — even if she wasn't really his daughter, even if her mother was the cook and housekeeper.

It took a while for her to answer. "*I am no longer his daughter. I have disobeyed him.*"

Nya's voice was so cracked and thin Jamia thought she was about to burst into tears. "*Who?*"

"*Papa. The Chief.*"

"*Why? What did you do?*"

"*It is nothing.*"

"*It is something. What did you do? Tell me.*"

Again, she took time to reply. "*I tricked Mahamat into taking me with him to the refugee camp.*" Her gaze dropped to the floor. "*I did not have Papa's permission. Mahamat is also being punished. He will blame me like Papa does. He will no longer like me.*"

Jamia thought she sounded more upset about getting Mahamat into trouble than being punished by the Chief. She thought back to how strict her own Papa had been with her, also remembering how headstrong she was, thinking she might have done the same as Nya. "*You should obey your Papa at all times,*" she said.

"*I just wanted him to respect me. I wanted to earn his...*"

Before Nya could finish, the door was flung open and in walked one of his bodyguards — not Mahamat. The Chief followed close behind, determined, striding out as he passed the bodyguard, he stopped. The room fell into silence.

Jamia looked up at him. She thought he had changed, even from just a week ago. Gone was that kind and friendly expression, that considered intelligence. Now his face was tight, intense, uncompromising in thought, as if he had just been given bad news, much worse than knowing his daughter had disobeyed him.

He turned to give Nya a sideways glance, then a flick of his finger, a silent command for her to leave the room. He waited for the door to shut. "*How is the boy?*" His words businesslike, like he didn't want to know the answer.

Jamia stared coldly up at him, sliding closer to her brother. "*He has my love and the love of Allah. That is all he needs,*" she answered as though it should not be questioned, even by a Chief.

"*Good. The love of family is important, but you know yourself the boy is not well, he needs help, help that your love alone cannot provide. Nor the love of God.*" He paused, as if waiting to study Jamia's reaction. "*It is not safe for you here in Guereda.*"

Jamia stood up, wanting to look the Chief eye to eye. The bodyguard tensed up and took a step forward. The chief raised a finger, the bodyguard stopped.

Holding her brother's hand Jamia spoke firmly. "*That monster is still alive because you showed me a picture of the wrong man. It was your fault I killed an innocent man. It is your fault that I have not avenged the death of my brothers and Papa.*"

"*People you love will never die.*"

"*Nor does it seem the people you want dead.*"

The Chief could hear the hatred in her voice. "*I was too hasty in thinking it was him. It was not you who killed the wrong man, It was me. But I did it for you to be free. For the people of Guereda to be free. I did it for Dar Tama to be free.*" The Chief glared long and hard at Jamia. "*He is fuelled by the same as you...revenge. He will not stop until he has that revenge. It is your father he blames for the death of his family, as you blame him for the death of your family. Now his revenge is your death, your brother's death. It is a matter of honour. While you are alive he will never be free. It is you or him.*" He paused. "*We have already tried to free you.*"

Jamia's eyes became wide. "*You tricked us didn't you! You knew the Chadian officer would come after us. Those trucks! You had someone tell them which route we would travelling.*"

"*We had to draw him away from the camp.*"

"*That is why you are punishing Nya, because if it failed she may also have been killed. What about the old woman and man. What about Mahamat, were you going to sacrifice them along with me and my brother?*"

"*You were not in danger, you were never in danger. People were watching you all the way. Allah was with you. Mahamat and the old couple knew everything. Would I risk my own brother and his wife?*"

Jamia stared up at him, digesting what he had just said. "*Did Nya know?*" she asked softly.

He paused for a moment. "*No.*"

"*She doesn't know now, does she?*"

The silence was answer itself.

The Chief had read the intent behind Jamia's words. At that moment he knew the young woman before him had lost none of her will, none of her intellect.

"*He wasn't amongst them, was he? You did not kill that monster, did you?*"

"*He is a shrewd man. He probably guessed it was a trap.*" The Chief looked uncomfortable. "*Now it is worse, now he knows you are in Guereda.*"

"*That is the true reason why you want me out of this town. It has nothing to do with helping Ali. While I am here, Guereda will be at risk. You will be at risk.*"

He looked towards his bodyguard and nodded with a movement so slight it might not have been there at all. The guard left the room.

Jamia sat back down on the cushion, her arm around Ali, huddled together as if they had become one. The Chief stepped back to where Nya had been cleaning and began picking up the ornaments, placing them attentively back on the table, gently touching each one so they were nudged back in the exact position as before.

He turned to face Jamia. "*Her punishment will only be for one week...If her mother Fatimah had her way it would be forever. It took all my skills of persuasion to keep Fatimah and our daughter here, that woman is as stubborn as a mule.*" He paused for a moment, a humbleness entered into his eyes. "*I remember you when you were a young girl, when your father used to bring you to Guereda on market day, because it was only you that could control your brother's tantrums. I could tell then you were headstrong, smarter than your age, smarter than all the boys. Sometimes I looked at you and saw a mature woman in that small body of yours.*" There was a moments pause as the hint of a grin appeared. "*You and Nya are alike, you are like sisters.*"

Jamia felt he was trying to tell her something.

The door opened again, sliding slowly over the floor. A woman entered wearing a long green robe, a blue headscarf coiled around her head, sunglasses covered her eyes, there was no flesh on display whatsoever, even her hands and feet were hidden under the robe. The same bodyguard as before followed her in, then another: it was Mahamat. Jamia wondered who she was, shc looked different from a Tama woman, her posture, those large black glasses, Jamia thought she was one of the Chief's rich friends, someone important, maybe a friend of the Sultan. But all that was forgotten as she saw Mahamat step closer. The Chief could see Jamia's expression change, her chin raised, her eyes wide, gazing up at him.

"*The guilt of being responsible for someone elses disgrace is double your own,*" the Chief said, glancing towards Mahamat with a wry smile. "*Double again if it is someone you have feelings for.*"

Mahamat gazed down at Jamia. His face never seemed to change, dark, hard, like stone, as if he had been born with hatred in his body. For the split second Jamia looked at him she could see something else behind those cold eyes, in that fleeting moment she knew he was trying to tell her that he felt the same for Nya as she did for him.

Jamia jolted her head to the side, she had not seen the woman approach, removing her sunglasses as she stepped forward. Jamia saw two beautiful emerald eyes, the skin surrounding them pale and soft, the eyebrows fair and perfect. The woman began uncoiling the headscarf, leaving the soft blonde hair to drop to her shoulders.

Jamia had known hardship for most of her seventeen years on this planet. She had seen children perish from disease and hunger, some under the worst suffering possible. Having to look helplessly into the eyes of a young child minutes from death was something that would haunt her forever. She herself was no stranger to drought and war, knowing death could be just around the corner. So far she had managed to avoid turning that corner, but she knew she could easily fall to one of those same diseases, to a bullet or gang-raped and killed by lawless soldiers. It was a life where Jamia had learnt to suppress her emotions, to hide her anguish. As she looked up at the woman all that disappeared, she wanted to cry, stand up and fling her arms around her. Jamia heard words instead, her own words, but it was as if someone else spoke them. "*It is too dangerous here,*" she said.

"*That is my problem sweetie,*" Crystal replied, her attention held on Ali. She knelt down and placed her palm gently on his cheek, sliding it under his chin, stroking her fingers through his hair. She kissed his forehead. Ali remained quiet, his gaze in a faraway place. Gone was the carefree boy she remembered back at the camp.

She turned to look at Jamia, her voice gentle. "*We need to get him some help honey.*"

The Chief spoke. "*We have to get both of you away from here. To a place where you will be safe.*"

The Chief waited for Jamia to answer.

Crystal spoke again. "*I will take you to France. A place called Marseille. It is by the sea, you will see many wonderful things. From there we will go to my home in Canada. I remember when I first came to Breidjing camp, when Djamel...*" She paused for a second, lowering her eyes. Her voice became assertive as she raised her gaze again. "*When your brother Djamel introduced you to me I remember the first thing you said was that you wanted to become a doctor. You also said you wanted to see the world...Do this in Djamel's name honey.*" Crystal held one of Jamia's hands. "*This is only the start of your dreams. Don't think about what has been, think about what is to come.*"

Jamia shook her head. It felt as if a wind had taken hold of her, that she had lost control of her own words. "*No! I cannot leave Chad. This is my home. I have to avenge the killing of my...*"

"*Oh sweetie, you must think of Ali first. He is your priority now. He will get help from doctors in my country.*" Crystal spoke to Jamia as if she was talking to the young and innocent eleven year old girl she first met back in the camp. "*Sometimes honey, the world is not as we wish it. People can do bad things to others.*"

"*I want that man to die a horrible death. I want him to suffer like he made...*" Jamia stopped abruptly, she pulled Ali closer, her words became less forceful. "*Like he has made us suffer.*"

The Chief spoke. "*We will finish what we started, we will avenge the death of your brothers and father, I promise. Then you will be free to return.*"

Crystal picked up a biscuit and took a bite out of it. "Mmm." Her voice became matter-of-fact, as if Jamia had no choice. "*It is all arranged sweetie. We will leave tomorrow.*" She stood.

The Chief spoke again "*Afterwards, when your brother is better, if you still want to, both of you will come back here to live with Nya, with Fatimah, with me. We will become one family.*"

Jamia glared at Crystal, she was finding it hard to speak. "*We will not get to France. It is too dangerous!*"

"*If you stay here you will be in worse danger, your brother will be in danger,*" said the Chief.

"*I will be travelling with you,*" Crystal said "*You will both be under the protection of Amnesty International. We have managed to get you Refugee Travel Documents. Someone is meeting us at N'Djemena airport, she will have them with her.*" Her voice softened. "*She has gone to a lot of trouble honey, we cannot let her down.*"

Sunday 20th June 2010
Cozy Hotel,
Marseille,
France

Lucile inhaled deeply. "I am also unemployed Norris," she suddenly announced mid-conversation, then waited while it sunk in, surprised by how unfazed he appeared. "You know this means you won't get the two thousand euros from the paper," she added.

Norris straightened his back and shrugged. "But I am now the proud owner of three of the most notorious photographs in French political history," he replied with a mischievous grin.

"Without any provenance they are worthless, and we can't prove they are genuine unless we can get someone else to endorse them."

"Like Madam Veronique?"

"*Yes,*" Lucile replied in French like a puff of air.

"You've got more chance of seeing God, and that's coming from an atheist."

"I am not convinced."

"What, about me being an atheist?"

"No. I know a way she will verify it."

“Ah.” Norris stretched the word. “The notebook. I’m still not convinced it is her,” he said for the umpteenth time. “And she definitely won’t verify it if it is not her, even with the notebook. Anyway it was meant to be part of The Drowning Mary deal.”

“What is that saying you English have?”

“Which one? We have many.”

“The two birds one.”

“Kill two birds with one stone.”

Both fell into a thoughtful silence.

“It would still warm the hearts of many of my fellow countrymen though, I mean knowing I have something over the French Establishment,” he joked again, still purring from the memory of their night of passion, although he could clearly see she wasn’t on the same heady cloud as him. “Sorry,” he said, noticing her unease.

“My God Norris, why do you English have to apologise for everything?”

“I wasn’t. Not for everything anyway. So tell me how come you are no longer a bona fide employee of La Provence?”

“What?”

“Why do you no longer work for the newspaper?”

“Oh.” Lucile described what had happened...

She was sitting in front of Henri’s desk, staring long and hard at the editor, her smile gradually dissolving as she realised what he had just said was in all seriousness. Henri had never been much of a joker and no one knew that more than Lucile. “*Say that again Henri.*”

“*I want you to stop investigating the Markovic affair,*” he repeated, then looked at her, waiting for the inevitable storm to hit.

Lucile’s smile had completely dispersed, her mouth now agape with disbelief. “*Is it because the person who gave us the photographs will not give us permission to use his name?*”

"*No,*" he said abruptly.

The realisation suddenly hit her. Lucile drew down her lips and nodded, her gaze finding empty space. She had recalled what Madam Veronique said, '*Do not underestimate me Mademoiselle Billet. Your newspaper is La Provence, is it not? I believe it is owned by Bernard Tapie.*' Lucile knew the old woman still had contacts in high places.

Henri continued. "*But the paper will still buy the photographs.*"

"*The paper will still want to buy the photographs,*" she repeated. "*Why does the paper still want to buy them if they are not running the story?*" She was managing to stay calm.

Henri had prepared the answer. "*To show goodwill. We will even pay more than the two thousand.*"

Lucile thought he looked embarrassed. She knew something was not quite adding up.

"*Maybe a lot more,*" Henri added, his stare hanging on her as if his eyes were saying something else.

Lucile had to think quick. "*You are too late Henri. Monsieur.*" She suddenly stopped herself. "*My source insisted on ten thousand euros,*" she said with a smirk. "*When we refused to pay it he burnt all three of them right in front of my eyes,*" she said with a deep sigh while raising her hands in fake despair. "*They no longer exist Henri.*" She knew Henri didn't believe her.

"*I'm sorry Lucile but it is not my decision,*" he said, shuffling a sheet of paper as if it was the end of the matter.

"*I know why,*" Lucile said.

Henri sighed with impatience. "*I argued your case.*"

A sharp. "*Why?*"

"*Why did I argue?*"

"*No Henri. Why has he stopped the story?*"

"*He said it had already been investigated to the...*"

"*No!*" She snapped, stopping him dead. "*The truth Henri...Why has he stopped the story?*" Her voice was becoming angry.

"*He said it is too risky if we...*"

"*No Henri, the fucking truth.*" She was shouting.

Henri shrugged. "*I don't know...Please stay calm Lucile.*"

"*No! I won't stay fucking calm. And why does he want to buy the photographs?*"

Henri remained silent, not wanting to poke the bear anymore than he had to.

Lucile's mouth fell open, slowly breaking into a smile — another realisation. One word had come to mind, 'notebook.' His name must be in the notebook she thought — and the owner of the newspaper knew it. She would have to get it back from Julien.

Her voice became calm and measured. "*Why don't you tell him I have ten thousand euros worth of ash if he wants to buy the photographs?*"

Henri took a deep gulp, his body stiffened. "*There is something else.*"

Lucile glared at him, waiting.

"*Angelique's footballer is turning into quite a story.*" Henri stalled for a moment, he could see Lucile's eyes narrow, her face turning from red to purple.

"*So?*" she said.

"*He wants you to assist her.*"

"*Who? Angelique?*"

"*She's getting out of her depth. Julien is also off the Markovic story, he's back with Angelique.*"

"*You want me to assist...*" Lucile started to yell before the words tailed away into silence, her glare boring into the editor. A smile of realisation slowly stretched across her face. "*Who does this footballer play for?*"

"*Actually it's footballers, three so far. They go to these parties with...After that article you did on working girls I thought this would...*"

"*Who do these footballers play for?*" she repeated. "*It*

wouldn't be Olympique de Marseille would it?"

Henri didn't answer, his silence was louder than any words.

"*The owner has unfinished business there, doesn't he?*" She nearly broke into laughter. "*He pays your wages so he pulls your strings. My God Henri where is that great investigative reporter we all used to look up to.*"

Henri remained silent.

"*Well Henri.*" Her smile became wider. "*At least I'm not under any deadline now.*"

Henri's face brightened. "*I'm glad you see my side...*"

Lucile rose to her feet and leant forward with her arms splayed out, her body half over his desk. Her words came out cool and calculated. "*Henri, you can go to hell, and while you're about it you can stuff Angelique's footballer...sorry, footballers, up her arse. In fact she would probably enjoy it. And you can tell the owner of this fucking rag there is an English saying my grandmother used to say...It is better the devil you know.*" Just as she got to his door Lucile turned, prodding her chest. "*This is one devil you should have kept knowing.*"

"And that was it Norris. Before he could say anything else I walked out."

Norris wasn't sure how to react.

"Henri is just a puppet though."

Feeling he should be doing something, Norris picked up one of the photos, studying it for the umpteenth time, his eyes darting around the picture.

"You seem to like them Norris." The sarcasm obvious.

There were two women, both naked. The older, blonde haired one was lying face up with her lower back arched, her shoulder blades pressed into the crumpled sheets, her body slightly angled towards the camera, but not looking at it, she wasn't looking at anything, her eyes were half-shut, appearing lost in the moment, her mouth open, round, in the shape of an O. Her breasts had drooped downwards, her nipples erect, one pointing accusingly at the camera. Her head was raised, as if she had been looking at the black haired woman only seconds before, holding it there, waiting. The other woman was otherwise occupied, her face buried between two spreadeagled legs, but not quite in the correct position, the blonde woman's hands hovering above her head, not touching, as if doing so would spoil the moment. For Norris it all looked far too fake.

The camera's position appeared to be quite high, aimed downwards towards one side of the bed. The photograph was dark and fuzzy on the edges, the same as the first picture they had seen, like two curtains ready to be drawn. Norris could see the room was plain, the two pieces of furniture visible were old, worn, cheap, provincial. A narrow area covering the width of the photo at the bottom was made up of heavily scuffed floor boards, a glimpse of a tasseled rug edge to the right. The walls plain, painted in a neutral colour, virtually grey. Unlike the first picture they had seen in the park, the blue sheets had now become ruffled, like a choppy sea. The photo reminded Norris of a still from a film.

Lucile saw Norris had begun to frown, his gaze becoming a lot more intense. "If you ask me I would say the black haired woman looks more like her, " He drew his head back. "But look at the nose. Madam Veronique's nose is different, and her jaw...It's difficult to tell."

"Maybe she's had a nose job."

"No. Madam Veronique's nose is more feminine, and her jaw is...Bloody hell!" Norris suddenly froze, stretching the two words in one long breath.

"What?"

"Look!"

Lucile leant over.

His finger was aimed at a dressing table set back in the far right corner, part of it hidden by the photograph's dark edges. On it was a three piece mirror, a larger section sitting in-between two narrower ones, slightly angled inward. It was what was reflected in the mirror on the right one that he was pointing at. "Look!"

Lucile nudged closer to Norris, staring down, looking directly at what was at the end of his fingertip. In a small section of the mirror, bleeding off at the top and the left, encroaching on the central mirror was a reflection of something rectangular, partly concealed by a vase of wilting flowers. But to him it was unmistakeable."

As she leant foward Norris nervously slid his arm around her and placed a hesitant hand on her shoulder, slowly stroking it. She remained silent, motionless, showing no reaction to his show of affection.

"It is isn't it?" he said.

"You wouldn't have a magnifying glass on you, " she said sarcastically.

"Tell me what you see?" he asked.

Lucile wrapped her fingers around Norris's wrist and pulled the picture closer to her. "Is that the painting we saw at Madam Veronique's apartment?

"It's The Drowning Mary. Although this one is the other way around. We need another mirror to see it..."

Lucile interrupted. "She must have had it in her bedroom before she hung it in the main room. If I was her I would have kept it there."

Norris gently prodded the picture. "That is never Madam Veronique's bedroom."

"We don't know that."

"No Lucile, I do. I can tell you Madam Veronique's bedroom would not look like that in a million years. She might be a Madam but she is a Madam with taste."

Norris picked up the other photographs. The dressing table and the reflection of the painting in the mirror were exactly the same, everything in the room was. The only difference were the two women, they had changed positions, the black haired one had moved up, a tongue close to one nipple. The blonde woman's arms wrapped around her, two hands flat against her back, her fingers splayed out, her cheek nestled into the top of her head, this time her face was full on into the camera, although her eyes were closed. He thought he recognised her but couldn't quite put his finger on it, again it all looked far too staged.

"There is only one way we could find out if it was her bedroom," Lucile said.

"No way! Taking photos of photos was bad enough but getting into her bedroom is another..."

"I think she likes you. You could seduce her," Lucile joked as she peeled herself away from him. "Or we could just ask Matthieu, he must have been in there at sometime in his life.

"They were taken over forty years ago."

"Maybe Helaine would know. I will go and see her." She gazed at him for several seconds. "Either way Norris, I will have to take the photographs with me."

"They'd be safer with me, especially if your editor didn't believe you burnt them and he's told the owner. I can come with you. After all Matthieu is my brother."

"I thought you bought them for me." She raised her eyebrows and glanced down at his groin. "Or do you want to keep them for yourself?"

Norris searched for a reply, none came.

"So I can have them?"

"I feel this is now a joint venture," he finally said. "I'll keep one, you take the others. For diplomatic relations I'll let you choose."

Lucile breathed a heavy sigh and took one of the photographs, the first one Norris had been studying.

He looked down at the one left in his hand. Norris had seen pictures of Madame Pompidou on the internet. Although she was an attractive woman, he thought she had a strong, almost masculine face, 'horsey' as his mother would say, but a nice mouth with full lips. He always felt she looked intelligent and cultured. Her hair was fair in every image, almost white, maybe a tiny tinge of gold, always the same length, hanging down to what he thought was not a particularly feminine neck, just falling short of her shoulders. But it was her nose, prominent, protruding, the slightest of bumps at the top; not like the woman in the photograph.

He also knew all three photographs were of poor quality, grainy, the older woman's face no bigger than a thumbnail. He needed to compare them closely to be absolutely sure it wasn't Claude Pompidou, and if it wasn't, which he was nearly one hundred percent sure, then who was it?

But for him, there was something far more important; he needed to find out why The Drowning Mary was in the room.

Monday 21st June 2010,
Guereda Airport,
Guereda,
Chad

The name Guereda Airport was a slight overstatement, in truth it was just a long, thin strip of smooth, dusty land cleared of all rocks, vegetation and trees, as if someone had just waxed hairs from a leg. There were no buildings whatsoever, nothing that you would expect to find at an airport, no terminal, no control tower, no air traffic control, just a few trails for the aircraft to taxi away from the so-called runway. And the one dirt track leading all the way to the town of Guereda.

The greatest danger for any incoming aircraft were roaming animals. Being given prior warning of an aircraft's arrival, a truck would often be seen twisting and turning down the runway, scaring away the wayward beasts. If no warning was given, then the pilot would be left to his own devices, having to make several low sweeps to frighten them away, followed by a sharp death-defying turn to land before any of the beasts returned. Today, because of the prolonged drought, most of the animals were dead anyway.

It was only a fifteen minute drive from Guereda to the

airport, the shortest part of their journey for the three travelling, but it would be by far the most dangerous.

Captain Nkusi had not yet entered the town, he knew the chances of finding Jamia would be near-on impossible. Apart from upsetting the recently signed peace agreement, Guereda still had the reputation of being a Sudanese rebel stronghold, any incursion could prompt another battle, and the Chadian officer knew that. His best strategy would be to send in a spy, establish Jamia's whereabouts, at the same time keeping track of the comings and goings from the town.

The Chief at Guereda had two choices, send the UN Land Cruiser out alone, not an uncommon sight, hopefully its lack of protection would deter any suspicion. Or send it surrounded by a heavily armed convoy. He chose the latter, the Chief also had spies. He just hoped the Chadian officer wouldn't be able to raise enough soldiers in the short journey to the airport.

Word had been sent back to the Chief. The Humanitarian Air Service aircraft had landed on time. The bowser had arrived at the airport and had already started refueling.

The Chief began assembling his small army of fighters into several automatic machine gun wagons in full view of everyone. Two women and a boy climbed into the UN Land Cruiser positioned between two vehicles. For the time being they would remain where they were.

The bowser's cabin stunk of aircraft fuel, leaving a taste inside Crystal's mouth like a rotting almond. Her worst fear was from a misplaced spark or even a bullet, or spontaneously combusting from the blistering heat, if that was possible — either way it would mean curtains for all of them, including the nervous sweat-sodden driver who hadn't spoken a single word during the entire journey. Her only compensation was that he must have passed middle age many years ago and if he had had the good fortune to survive this long — well, she just hoped his God was still looking down on him this day.

Crystal was relieved to hear the engine fade sluggishly to idle and the bowser draw to a halt. They would soon be able step out into the relative comfort of the outside air.

For the fifteen minute journey Crystal, Jamia and Ali had been squashed out of sight in the passenger side footwell, amongst all the dirt trodden dust, empty water bottles and rotting remains of the driver's many lunches. Their backpacks laid out in comfort on the seat in front of them. Every pothole, every mound, every turn on the dirt track tossed them around like they were in a tiny rowing boat during a heavy storm. It was the scorching heat that was the worst though, unbearable, crushing down on them like a heavy weight. Crystal was also blind to the direction they were travelling. At that moment in time, the bowser could have stopped anywhere, they could decamp the vehicle directly in front of Captain Nkusi.

Travelling to the airport in the fuel bowser had been the Chief's idea. He knew the arrival of a Humanitarian Air Service aircraft, then having to be refueled was not uncommon; in fact, in most cases, a necessity.

At the same time the bowser had left the depot, the Chief began assembling his small army of fighters on to several machine gun wagons in full view of everyone.

Two women, one black, she was taller than the other and was wearing a long robe and a headscarf. The other was also black, on every other day — but not today. She had been crudely painted in a light flesh colour and wore a blonde wig; also wearing a long robe, but no headscarf. The third was a boy, holding hands with the black woman. All three climbed into the back of a UN Land Cruiser, the same one Crystal, Jamia, Ali, Nya the Chief's brother and his wife had travelled in when they escaped to Guereda from Breidjing camp.

The Chief's command for them to leave would never come.

Without speaking or even looking down, the driver stretched

out a flat hand, showing them his dirt crusted palm, which Crystal annoyingly took as a sign for them to stay. That feeling of being baked alive and the risk of being torched would have to remain with them for the time being. He then opened his door and jumped down from the cabin, vanishing from view. The air entering from the outside gave them some small comfort for a short while. The three were now on their own, huddled together in a space just big enough for one, their knees pulled up to their chests. Ali sat in the middle, his hands wrapped around his sister's arms, his head buried in her shoulder, his eyes vacant, his thoughts locked in — as they had been since Scorpion Rock.

Although neither had said it, not with words, both Crystal and Jamia looked into each other's eyes, realising their lives were in the hands of a man they had only just met, and one that looked like he would sell his own grandmother for a loaf of stale bread. He could walk away from them, allow someone to shoot a bullet into the bowser, knowing no trace of them would ever be seen again. It would be convenient, who would know? What did the Chief say to Jamia before they left. '*A fool who sees a wise man will only see a fool.*' Was he trying to tell her something?

A loud rasping noise came from the back of the bowser, followed by a series of hollow clunks echoing around the fuel hold. Less than a minute later the cabin began to vibrate so violently their bodies also began to tremble. It was so strong Crystal felt that her eyes were going to turn back in their sockets, that her skin would peel from its flesh. This was accompanied by a deafening machine noise, like a continuous drumbeat of thuds filling the entire cabin. On and on it went, as if it would never end. Crystal stretched her arm out so it would reach over both Jamia's and Ali's shoulders, attempting to comfort them, pull them into her, only to feel their vibrations travel up her bones. She knew neither would understand what was happening.

Suddenly the vibrating stopped. Then a moments silence,

before the same noises repeated themselves, this time in reverse, the echo had become more hollow, the scraping moved towards them, until that too stopped. A minute later the driver's door opened and he hauled himself onto the seat, his head even more shiny with sweat, like someone had thrown a tin of varnish into his face, and where he had been wiping himself, tiny tufts of white fluff were caught in his thick stubble. He shoved the grease stained cloth back into his overall's pocket. The stench of the fuel had become more intense, made worse by being mixed with his odorous perspiration, causing him to smell more rank than he had done before, which Crystal thought wasn't possible, just managing to stop herself from gagging. He turned the steering wheel a full rotation and the bowser began creeping forward.

"*Where are you taking us?*" Crystal said in French, her eyes wide with concern.

He ignored her.

"*Where are you taking us,*" she repeated in Arabic.

Again the driver maintained his silence, coaxing the bowser on its slow turn. It stopped again. When he opened his door she heard another sound enter the cabin, one she recognised instantly, the distinctive whirring of a propellor. By its loudness, she guessed it must be close by. The door opened on their side, allowing the light to flood into the footwell. The driver frantically beckoned for them to decamp. Jamia jumped down first, aided by the driver, who seemed to be in a hurry; he then helped lower Ali to the ground. Crystal dropped the backpacks and jumped down after them.

When Ali turned he saw it, less then twenty metres away, waiting, growling, its belly open, like a gaping mouth ready to devour them. It was parked at the end of the runway, a long length of the dirt airstrip stretching away into the far distance in front of it, finally dissolving into a liquid heat haze, like they were about to fly into the ripples of a golden lake.

The door on the side of the fuselage was open, split into

two halves, the bottom flap forming the steps. Someone appeared just inside the open door, waving them in.

The driver of the bowser had already retreated back into the cabin and driven off at speed, as if he couldn't wait to get away; not the orders he was given by the Chief. He had been told to wait, shield the three occupants until they were safely in the aircraft. Instead he left them stranded in the open, perfect for any sniper to pick them off. How would anyone know, the driver had thought? The only people who did know would be far away by the time he got back to town. His problem was he had been owing to the Chief. This job would have paid off his debt; but not if he were to be found out, then it will be increased. Sometime in the near future he will have wished he had waited.

"*Come on.*" Crystal said in Arabic with a forced smile, trying to sound calm, as if what was happening was an everyday occurrence. She took a step forward, looking at Jamia, seeing the fear in her eyes. Crystal also noticed Ali hesitate. She was surprised and glad at the same time, it was the first time he had shown any sign of making a decision by himself. Everything he had done before was always under the direction of his sister.

"*It'll be fine. The first time is always a bit scary.*" Crystal said, having to raise her voice over the noise of the propellor. "*Trust me,*" she added.

Jamia returned a nod, she put an arm around Ali's shoulder and started walking him towards the plane, their robes flapping wildly as they stepped into the dusty backdraft. When they got to the bottom of the steps Ali froze, his body rigid, his eyes wide with fright.

"*We have to climb in,*" Jamia said to him in Tama. Then she repeated the words Crystal had said, "*Trust me.*" She clutched his face, stroking his forehead. "*It is a flying machine my brother. We have seen them before in the sky, remember...I am here. Crystal is here. We will protect you. I will always protect you. Allah will always protect you.*"

Ali raised his eyes, for that split second it looked like he had woken from his torment. She wrapped her arms around him, pulling him into her. She began to weep, but her tears were not in sorrow, this was the first time since Scorpion Rock she had seen Ali — as Ali.

They heard a man speak, his language strange to Jamia, like the words Crystal and the aid workers used sometimes, but his voice was much deeper. "Keep hold of the boy, we don't want him running into the propellor blades" He then bounded down the steps in one stride, stopping beside them. He was tall with thick grey hair and a neatly trimmed beard, not old though, mid-forties, quite handsome thought Crystal. He was wearing sunglasses with a green tinge, someone at the other end of the scale to the bowser driver. The four white striped epaulettes on a crisp white shirt indicated his rank. Jamia thought he smelt of honey.

His mouth stretched into a calming smile as he looked down at Ali. "Is this the boy?" he asked.

Crystal wondered what the captain knew about him. What story did Teresa tell the UN. The truth probably, it would have been enough. "Yes," she replied.

"Poor kid." His concern genuine. He turned his attention back to Crystal. "And you are the lawyer from Amnesty?" Looking at her dusty long African robe and blond hair disheveled from the journey, she had taken her headscarf off in the bowser, a desperate attempt to keep cool.

"Yes I am. My name is Crystal Bullion."

He looked surprised and pleased at the same time. "American?"

"Canadian actually honey." As if she had taken the high ground. "Australian?"

"New Zealand actually," he said with a smile. "Malcolm Kirke. I'm the captain." He waited — as he always did.

"Captain Kirke." Her words no more than a greeting.

He waited for the obligatory 'beam me up Scotty,' none came. He nodded towards Jamia. "And this is the boy's sister?"

"Yes. Her name is Jamia. She is all he has left. He is all she..."

"We have very little time," he interrupted, stretching out a long arm and ushering them into the plane.

Crystal repeated the words in Arabic. Jamia tightened her hold, keeping Ali's head tight against her as she coaxed him up the steps and into the aircraft.

The passenger seats were toward the front, three rows of two on one side, three of one on the other, a narrow aisle between them. The rear was kept for two beds, now an empty space full of hanging straps and metal brackets.

After they sat, Jamia intertwined her fingers into her brother's. Crystal sat on the other side with Ali in the middle, the aisle between her and him.

There was another pilot on the flight deck, this one had two stripes and had remained in the aircraft. He was younger, a native Chadian, seated on the right, busy checking sheets of paper on a clipboard and reading dials. The captain shut the two doors with an echoing thud and walked down the aisle, checking their seat belts. He reached into a small compartment above them and took out three bottles of water, "Mid-flight refreshment," he said before handing them out. Jamia took Ali's bottle. "The dunny is at the back if you need it." The captain slipped away, finally taking his place on the flight deck. Crystal heard the two pilots speak to each other, short snappy questions, one word answers. They stopped talking and looked through the front windows. The captain's hand pushed a lever forward and the propellor noise increased. The aircraft began moving, picking up speed as it bounded down the runway with a series of bumps and jolts. As the noise from the engine increased, so did the loud rattling, everything inside appeared to shake and shudder, as if the entire aircraft was going to fall apart. The nose angled upward, the rattling stopped and the aircraft became smooth. The ground began falling below them. After several minutes the plane banked to the right. Jamia looked through the window. She could see the trees shrinking beneath her, wadis scarring the scorched earth, their narrow tributaries splitting away like branches on a tree, most bordered by lines of bushes. She could see rust and iron coloured rocks breaking through the sandy earth. She could see the circular roofs of tukuls, the fencing enclosing them like someone had drawn a thin line with a pencil. The plane straightened and the earth was replaced with blue sky.

Jamia turned her attention back to Ali. His stare was frozen, his face impassive; she squeezed his hand, afraid he may have slipped back to how he was before. She closed her eyes and rested her head on the seat, listening to the constant drone of the engine, her mind drifted to the events that led to this flying tin can high above the earth. It was something she had always dreamed about, something she had wanted more than anything else. She remembered one of her Papa's sayings. '*Allah doesn't give you what you want when you want it, but gives you what you want when you need it.*' Now she understood what it meant. Maybe this was Allah's way? Her thoughts began to wander back in time.

Jamia's mind was like a sponge when she was a young girl, wanting to know everything about anything. It was on the rare visits to Guereda with her Papa and Ali that she developed this appetite for knowledge.

The only reason she was allowed to go to Guereda was because she was the only one who could control her brother's tantrums. Before it was just Papa and Ali on their own, his desire to drive the small boy out of his youngest son. '*The boy has brought disrespect upon his family.*' he would say after returning from their excursions, cut short because of Ali's outburst. The annoyance still evident on her Papa's face.

She remembered the market more than anything else. A place where she used to take in the many sounds: with each step came a new noise, then the sweet smell of a spice or the sour odour of blood, along with the cries of an animal being slaughtered. Where she heard the people bartering their goods, watched the old men smoking their pipes and drinking tea, talking loudly, the smack of plastic discs hitting wood as they sat on colourful rugs and played their board games. Her favourite trader was hidden between the stalls of mangos and oranges, sacks of millet on one side. On the other, shiny new saucepans and plastic buckets. She remembered the knick-knacks sold there, anything and everything, mostly worthless objects which the stall holder had picked out from rubbish or had just been given by the owner who had no more use for it. She remembered being made by her Papa to walk several steps behind, soon discovering that had its advantages, when she could sneak a quick glimpse at the newspaper or magazine covers fanned out on a rug. Most were years old, not that it mattered. She saw pictures of far away places, ones she never knew existed. Images that may as well have been from a different universe. It was from that stall her appetite to see the world was born, that her hunger for food was replaced with the hunger to travel, an unwavering desire to see those images in all there natural glory. But it could only be the quickest of glimpses. Her Papa wanted to keep her away from knowing such things, corrupting her mind with ideas above her station was not permitted for a young Tama girl, he knew how headstrong and independent a girl she could be. As far as her Papa was concerned her destiny had already been mapped out: to marry a man from her own tribe, probably someone much older than herself, probably someone with a few surplus goats. A contract would be arranged between the two families. If her Papa had ever caught her looking at these images she would have been harshly scolded, banished from ever travelling to Guereda again. He would have said the reputation of her family had been tarnished, that his bargaining powers had been severly reduced, that the dowry she could have earned would have been very much lessened. He never did catch her though — she was far too smart.

Jamia recalled arriving at Breidjing Refugee Camp with Djamel and Ali, she was nearly twelve years old. It was at the start of the civil war, her Papa in his wisdom had seen it coming and had sent them away to avoid the inevitable bloodshed and atrocities. Government soldiers were raping through the villages in Dar Tama. A young girl like Jamia would have made desirable pickings. It was then she lost all hope of seeing the world, she could see no escape from the misery of disease and hunger surrounding her. The desire to travel had been replaced by the need to survive.

Then at the end of March this year Crystal Bullion arrived at the camp. Jamia had never seen anyone like her, she was nothing like the other white women workers at the camp. Crystal had the fairest hair and softest skin, always wore the brightest summer clothes, appeared untarnished by the weather, always looking as fresh as the day she arrived. Someone who spoke Arabic along with several other languages, who wasn't afraid to confront the men, making many enemies in the process but gaining much respect amongst the other aid workers.

She was sent by Amnesty International to speak to the women, old and young. The horrific war crimes in Eastern Chad had filtered through to the outside world, atrocities committed by all sides, and there were many. Crystal was sent there to collate the information, interview as many women as possible. Had they been raped or abused? If so, by who? How many times? Most were too afraid to speak. Some denied anything had happened — but Crystal knew otherwise, she could see it their eyes.

Then Jamia stepped into the field office. This painfully thin, half-starved teenager. A highly intelligent girl, who Crystal discovered spent most of her time caring for her brother Ali. But there was something behind her kindness and her gentle nature, a wisdom well beyond her years. Crystal was concerned about her at first, especially when she displayed a particular hatred towards the Government soldiers. Denying vehemently that anying had happened to her physically, that her hatred was for the Government backed Zaghawa, the people who scourged her own Tama village. Crystal believed her.

Jamia wanted to know everything about Crystal, especially the other countries she had visited. Was it true that people in these places had as much food as they could eat, then threw most of it away? Were there places where there was no disease? Did crops grow all year round? Were there pastures always full of cattle? Were buildings so tall they reached all the way to the clouds? The questions came flying towards Crystal before she had time to answer them.

The aircraft engines continued to growl. Jamia turned again to look at Ali, catching Crystal in the corner of her eye, seeing her head resting on the back of the seat, her eyes closed. How different she looked from the first time she had seen her in that field office. She felt the aircraft bank left, then right again, Jamia turned to look through the window as the wing on her side lowered, watching the earth come into view once more. Everything had become so much smaller than the last time she looked out.

It was the howl that startled Crystal from her nap, her eyes snapped open, the first she saw was the back of Jamia's head, she was looking through the window. Thinking she had had a bad dream and woken with her head against the window Crystal rose to lean over and comfort her. It was then she saw her hand covering her mouth, her brows raised, eyes like pools of water. She placed a hand on her shoulder. "*Are you okay honey?*"

Jamia didn't respond, continuing to stare through the window, tears streaming down her cheeks. Crystal followed her gaze, it was just as the aircraft began to straighten, but that's all it took, just those couple of seconds was enough for her to know what Jamia had seen. She had heard stories about it, about spirits residing in its caves, that it was a dead spirit. In the distance she had glimpsed a huge iron grey rock, virtually black in places. About five kilometres long and two wide. Two long rocks protruded from the front, both in an arc slightly pointing inwards, both long and narrow, one on each side, like pincers. At the back end it rose higher than anywhere else. Tall ridges crossed from one side to the other with narrow gulleys in-between. Although she had never seen it, Crystal knew immediately this was The Scorpion Rock. The place where Jamia's Papa and two older brothers were slaughtered by Captain Nkusi and his men.

Crystal leant over and pulled the window blind down.

"*I should have stayed,*" Jamia mumbled through her hand.

"*For what? Revenge. The Chadian officer has an army behind him. He would eventually catch up with you. It would be you who got killed, not him.*" Crystal spoke with such firmness she felt guilty. She knelt down on one knee in the aisle stretched her arms across Ali's legs and wrapped her hands around Jamia's fingers, her voice softened. "*You must look to what is ahead of you sweetie. It is you and Ali you must think of now, not that monster. His day will come, believe me.*"

A voice came from above. "Is everything okay?"

Crystal looked up and saw Captain Kirke towering above her. She stood, their faces only centimetres apart. "Yes sweetie...and shouldn't you be flying the plane?"

"No worries. This old bird flies itself most of the time. Anyway Alfred is up front looking after the shop." He looked down at Jamia. "What was the shout about?"

"She saw a Scorpion."

The captain took a quick step back, glaring at the floor. "Bugger me! Where?"

Crystal pointed towards the window. "Out there."

He drew his head back with a smile. "I've been told about you Canadians."

"Excuse me honey, we are..." Before Crystal could finish he had slipped back to the flight deck, throwing her a playful wink as he sat down.

Jamia spent the rest of the flight with the blind down.

She closed her eyes again. Seeing the rock had made her think about her family. About Assim, her eldest brother and how he had joined the rebels, fighting the Government forces under the command of her Papa. She then thought about his capture, the torture he had endured at the hands of Captain Nkusi. How she and Djamel helped him escape from the hospital. Her brother Djamel, only a few years older than herself, the most streetwise of boys, always in some kind of trouble. How his wits kept her and Ali alive on the long trek to the camp from their village, giving her the independence she longed for, more than her Papa would ever have done. A dark, heavy cloud hung over her as she thought about her Papa, her protector, strict but always fair. A respected elder within her village who had become a leader of men. He sent word to her in the camp, asking for information about aid convoys, telling her his men were starving, including her brother Assim. Not being able to refuse she agreed to his demands. The reason Assim was caught was that the Captain had tricked her, maybe that was it she thought, it was her fault he was captured and she had suppressed the guilt — until now. She then thought about the mother she never knew, trying to recall any memory of her — none came. She had died giving birth, it was him or her, her mother chose Ali.

Jamia opened her eyes and gazed across at Ali. 'The boy who never grew up' people called him, a name she despised and had many a fight over. Ali, whose mind had shut down after the trauma at Scorpion Rock, at the hands of the same Chadian officer she was sent to kill. Several times she had seen her brother shuffle on his seat, sometimes turning to look at her when she stroked his arm or spoke to him, something he was incapable of a few days ago.

She turned to look at Crystal again; after returning to her seat Crystal had closed her eyes, trying to catch up on the sleep she must have foregone in the last few days. Jamia realised what she must have been through to get to Guereda, and now helping her and Ali to escape.

Jamia stared into empty space and thought about the life she had always longed for. This was the beginning.

Two and a half hours later the Cessna 208 landed at N'Djamena Airport and taxied to the cracked and crumbling concrete bay fifty metres away from the terminal building, the same place Captain Kirke had parked up a hundred times before. He accompanied Crystal, Jamia and Ali as they stepped out of the midday blistering heat and into the relative coolness of the domestic arrivals zone.

An old man was sat behind a desk inside the entrance, staring at them through a burnt-umber face, like an ageing jazz trumpeter with his wrinkled lips and sunken bloodshot eyes. Crystal could tell by the friendly greeting exchanged between him and the Captain that this was far from their first encounter. As they spoke the old man glanced over at Ali several times.

The captain returned. "Wait here," he said. Carrying the self-confidence of someone ignorant to the truth he then strolled over to a uniformed man. Crystal's steps had become hesitant, her body tense, her gaze remained forward, avoiding eye contact with anyone that happened to look their way, trying her hardest not to display the expression of someone that was expecting the worst. She was certain the Chadian army officer had notified security at the airport of their arrival, along with detailed descriptions. She just hoped it hadn't filtered through yet; having experienced first hand the incompetency in Chadian communication and bureaucracy, she just hoped it was the same at this airport as it was everywhere else. She waited.

Crystal wondered what Captain Kirke had said to the uniformed man as he shot a glance their way, feeling relieved when a sheet of paper was signed and returned with a smile. "There, my job is done," he said as he returned, lifting their two backpacks over each shoulder and picking up his own scuffed leather satchel. "Follow me, I'll show you the way."

As they walked the Captain quizzed Crystal about her destination: about the next step in Ali's recovery, how long they were expecting to be away from Chad?

"Where we can get the best help...I'm not a doctor...As long as it takes," were her snappy answers, wanting to give nothing away. Who knows who he would talk to afterwards, especially if he was found to be the pilot who flew them into N'Djamena. She didn't tell him they were running away from a Chadian army officer hell bent on revenge, that their priority was to get away from Chad as soon as humanly possible: to Marseille, then hopefully onto Canada. "It's all in hand honey," was her final comment, not to any question in particular, like it was a firm but polite cue for him to stop the inquisition.

A few more strides and Crystal could see the double doors leading into the main concourse. It was there she had planned to meet up with Teresa. She knew security would be at its most attentive there. While Captain Kirke was beside them in his pilot's uniform she felt it would give some legitimacy to their presence, she also knew if it came to it he would argue their case with the assertiveness of someone ignorant to the truth.

On the flight from Guereda the three had managed to change into clean clothes, discarding the soiled robes contaminated by the stench of aircraft fuel from the bowser. Jamia now wore a clean, long patterned robe with a turquoise headscarf. Ali a fresh, ankle length, white kaftan and embroidered prayer cap, all donated by Nya and the Chief. Crystal wore loose, white linen trousers, a yellow t-shirt with the Amnesty International motif and a lanyard hung round her neck displaying a thumb size photo, also her name and official title of International Human Rights Inspector in bold letters, something she had always worn since arriving in the country. Hoping this rectangle of plastic would get her through many a door — as it had in the past.

As they stepped into the main concourse Crystal remembered it exactly as it was from her arrival earlier in the year, thinking it had the appearance of a tired industrial unit. Between the whirring ceiling fans hung large metallic lights illuminating an abundance of flying bugs zipping aimlessly around in the hot air. Back on her first visit Crystal had become convinced that she was their only target, only to be told afterwards it was probably the deodorant she was wearing.

Crystal was surprised how quiet it was, only a few airport workers and airline staff, just a handful of travellers mingling around, mostly with backpacks: French aid workers she thought, she could recognise them a mile away. With all this space she feared they would stick out like a sore thumb.

Just a few of the check-in counters were manned, the elevated row of screens displayed the long horned orynx logo of Toumaï Air Chad, but it was only the two at the end she was interested in, both had the words Air France. When Crystal looked to the right of one of these she saw Teresa standing there: olive skinned, short, slight build, a pastel pink man's shirt with buttoned-up sleeves and tight faded jeans. Her jet black hair appeared to have grown even longer since the last time she had seen her. It seemed Teresa had spotted her at the exact same time and stretched her arm upward in an exuberant display of welcome. Crystal, trying not to draw attention to herself, acknowledged with a tentative raise of her hand. Half a minute later they were greeting each other with a hug. Crystal pulled back and glanced towards Jamia and Ali, her silence saying more than words ever could. Teresa returned a nod and a smile before looking up at the tall man.

"This is Captain Kirke. He's from New Zealand." Crystal said. "He flew us from Guereda."

The Captain stretched out his arm, his large hand completely swallowing Teresa's.

"Captain Kirke," she said, followed by an exuberant. "Beam me up Scotty."

The Captain's smile was unconvincing.

"Teresa...from The Way for Life charity." She announced before pausing for a second. "Spanish."

"You have them?" Crystal asked.

"I've been here for nearly four hours."

"Yeah, sorry honey, but did you get them?"

Teresa flapped her hands in front of her. "And I have been eaten alive."

"Probably your deodorant."

Teresa plunged her hand into her bag, pulling out the two Refugee Travel Documents. "If you knew what I had to go through to get these," she said, relieved to be handing them over.

"I can guess honey." Crystal peered inside one. Beside a thumbnail size headshot of Ali was a name, Ali Odili, she quickly glanced inside the other, Jamia Odili. Hopefully this was the first step to getting them into Canada.

In the corner of her eye Crystal had seen the screen change. The Air France logo had been replaced with 'Marseille AF805 Check-in, Departure 14.05' under that, Gate 3 and the time, 12.37. She wanted to turn her attention towards Captain Kirke, tell him he no longer had to wait, that he was probably needed elsewhere, that he probably had to fly in some other poor soul in need of help. She didn't though, she selfishly wanted to keep him close to her as long as possible. "I suppose we should check-in," she said, as they joined the end of the queue.

"You know how bad my French is," Teresa commented, handing Crystal her passport and flight sheets. "And I could do with a burger."

Crystal finally stepped up to the counter and handed over the passports and several sheets of paper to a fresh faced young woman in a blue blazer and a patterned scarf billowing out from her neck. The woman glanced unhurriedly at each one in turn before tapping her keyboard and staring at the computer screen. The whole process appeared to take an eternity. "*Bags for hold,*" she finally asked.

"*No,*" Crystal replied.

The woman stretched her neck to look over the counter at their backpacks. "*I hope you have had a pleasant stay in Chad,*" she said like it was automated, then handed back the passports and four boarding cards. "*Security control is that way,*" Glancing towards the end of the aisle.

The words sent a shudder through Crystal.

"*Have a pleasant flight,*" the woman announced, like she was dismissing them.

Crystal gazed up at Captain Kirke, she now knew it was only fair, not wanting him to be involved if anything did go wrong. "Thank you Captain for..."

"No problem," he interrupted, stepping forward, leading them towards security control. He then waited as one by one the four stepped through the open rectangular arch of the metal detector, they emerged at the other side of the baggage x-ray machine and picked up their bags, ahead of them was the glass fronted cubicle of passport control.

It was Crystal who stepped up to the cubicle first, dropping her passport through the opening in the glass, the austere faced man opened it up and looked up at her. He gave her a sharp nod and returned the small booklet, leaving his hand there, expecting the next one to be handed over. Crystal dropped the two Refugee Travel Documents through the space. Lifting her Amnesty International badge she spoke to the man in French before beckoning Jamia and Ali forward. "*These children are travelling under my care.*"

Teresa also stepped forward, much to the man's irritation. All four were now standing in front of the cubicle.

"*And this is Teresa Flores from The Way for Life charity. She has organised the transport for these two children and is also accompanying them.*" Crystal said in the clearest French, like she was speaking to a child, also thinking she was telling him far too much.

The man glared at Teresa and pointed towards a notice

printed in several languages, but not Spanish.

Wait behind line

Only one person at a time.

Teresa nodded with an embarrassed grin and stepped back.

Crystal continued. "*I am a lawyer for Amnesty International.*" She turned, indicating towards Teresa. "*This is my colleague from The Way for Life charity. We are escorting...*" She paused for a second. "*Jamia and Ali Odili...*" Not knowing why she had said their names like that, as if she had been introducing them to him. "*They are travelling to France so they can get medical care. All the necessary documents are...*"

Teresa and Crystal exchanged uneasy looks as the man picked up a phone. He spoke too softly, like a mumble, then replaced the receiver and remained silent. Seconds later the door at the back of the cubicle opened and another man in a similar uniform entered; he looked more official, more superior, he was also followed by a policeman. His gaze travelled around the four in such a relaxed manner it gave Crystal and Teresa some hope that this was just a formality. He then picked up the Travel Documents, occasionally raising his eyes, searching out a face from the group in front of him. Outside the cubicle, another, younger policeman stepped nonchalantly forward and stood just outside the group. Crystal snatched a hesitant glance at him. She also sensed someone else in a dark blue uniform standing behind her. It was then she heard the shout, immediately thinking that this was it, this was the end of the road, they would all be arrested and held up against the wall at gunpoint, only to see Captain Nkusi step out from the shadows. She waited nervously to be grabbed and wrestled to the ground. There was nothing. She looked up, noticing all were looking in another direction.

Captain Kirke had remained just behind the baggage x-ray machine, attentively watching the four as they approached passport control. He then saw Crystal step forward, handing over her passport. He saw her summoning Jamia and Ali, then

Teresa not far behind them, until she stepped back. He saw the controller pick up the telephone and his superior enter the back door with the policeman, then another policeman step over, He saw Crystal glance at him, her face filled with anxiety. Then the other policeman stopping just behind her. By the way Crystal kept scratching her nose and shuffling her feet, the Captain could see she was nervous, well beyond anything he had seen before. She leant on the small counter, staring down at the passports, like she was wishing them back in her hands.

Ever since he had met Crystal at Guereda airport, Captain Kirke sensed something was wrong. Although he could see that it was true, the boy had been deeply traumatised and his sister wasn't in a much better state, he felt he hadn't been told everything, that there was something else other than simply travelling to France to help Ali. When the superior official gazed towards Jamia with a look that lingered more than normal, one that appeared to carry deep suspicion, Captain Kirke knew he had to do something. He couldn't just stand there and watch them being hauled away like criminals.

For some time he had sensed a security guard standing only feet away. Before he could talk himself out of it, before he could weigh up the risk, before he could even think about the consequences, the Captain turned and walked directly into him. "What do you think you're doing mate," he yelled.

Not understanding a word the pilot had said, or even contemplating why he had collided with him, the guard's face had turned to one of confusion. The Captain was taken aback by the lack of reaction. In fact, it was the opposite to what he was expecting, the guard apologetically held up his hands as if to say it was his fault. After a seconds thought and sticking to the same impromptu plan the Captain continued. "Get your hands of me," he shouted, before giving the guard one hard shove back. This time the guard's calm composure changed to a more appropriate response.

The Captain wasn't a small man by any means, a keen

rugby player at good club level back in his home country, used to tackling men to the ground much larger than himself. The guard went to grab the Captain but only found himself being picked up and hurled to the floor with the New Zealander falling on top of him. It was then all hell broke loose. On seeing the ruckus the policeman from the cubicle departed swiftly through the rear door, along with the superior official and the other two policemen. All of them pouncing on the Captain in one chaotic scrum.

The one original passport controller had remained in the cubicle, not knowing whether to desert his post. Realising he had unfinished business with the four in front of him, he quickly handed back the documents and departed through the back door.

Unsure what to do, Crystal stood for a few seconds in front of the empty cubicle. It was then Teresa stepped forward and ushered them towards the gates.

Finding themselves in a long corridor they could see information screens spaced a good distance apart, all turned off except one in the distance, casting a blue light on the wall opposite. On reaching it Crystal could see the large number '3' and below that the word 'Marseille 14.05'. She looked through the glass doors, it was a large room, mainly made up of rows of seats, at least fifty people were sitting or mingling around, some she recognised as aid workers, others, native Chadians.

Crystal immediately walked over to a smart uniformed woman behind the desk and held up her Amnesty lanyard. With a feeling of relief she saw the woman study it with interest. Crystal finally spoke, feeling like she had said the same words a hundred times before. "*I am an employee of Amnesty International,*" she said, turning towards Jamia and Ali. "*We are escorting these two children to Marseille.*" She waited.

"*How may I help you Madame?*" The woman asked as if she hadn't heard.

"*This lady is from The Way for Life charity. She has organised the transport...*"

"*How may I help you Madame?*" she repeated.

Crystal sighed. "*I would like to request immediate priority boarding.*" She softened her voice. "*They will need to be settled in.*" Only to see the woman's eyes slide up Jamia then Ali.

"*Can I see your passports and boarding cards?*" The woman asked. She then picked up a walkie-talkie.

Crystal entered the empty aircraft and sat beside the window, Ali between her and his sister, Teresa in the seat across the aisle.

The Airbus A320 departed N'Djamena Airport at 14.23.

Tuesday 22nd June 2010,
Parc de la Vauquelin,
Marseille,
France

In Lucile's determinate reporter style, she had suggested the meeting take place in a park, but it was Helaine who chose the Parc de la Vauquelin. She chose it for one particular reason and Lucile knew why.

The time agreed was eleven o'clock in the morning, it would be quieter then, children would be at school.

Helaine and Matthieu had entered through the northern gate, the lowest area in the park. Lucile and Norris stepped through the western entrance, leaving Claude parked further up in the road, nursing an over-heated engine.

Helaine had described the exact spot where they should meet, halfway between the two gates, explaining the bench to Lucile in minute detail. '*The one to the right of the lamp post as you're facing the fence,*' she had said, even describing the carvings crudely gouged out by one of the girls. '*Nicole never forgotten,*' she told her. After all she had sat there many times over the years.

Helaine was carrying flowers, a mixture of roses,

carnations and chrysanthemums, an explosion of colour held in one hand. Lucile carried a large dark brown envelope tucked under one arm, not having quite the same impact as the flowers — not yet anyhow. Both she and Norris knew that was still to come.

Cheek to cheek kisses were exchanged, although in true British reserved style Norris greeted Matthieu with a probing glare and a firm handshake. His own sturdy grip was not quite reciprocated, distinctly feeling like he had wrapped his fingers around a dead chicken's foot, he had yet to feel that brotherly bond between them. In appearance they were poles apart: Matthieu was short, overweight, round headed, his dark hair already noticeably receding, whereas he was tall, lanky would be the correct description, a loping walk, and a long face topped with a full head of mousy hair.

The two men sat at either end of the bench, Lucile and Helaine remained standing, staring out towards a lone hawthorn tree surrounded by a green space of freshly mown grass.

Norris tried talking to Matthieu, wanting to thank him for the notebook and his message to look out for The Drowning Mary, even if it was a bit cryptic. Matthieu remained silent, just nodding an acknowledgement before returning to face his mother. 'End of' was the message Norris felt he had been given, halting the one sided conversation in its tracks.

Lucile looked at the tree. "*Is that the spot?*" she asked.

"*That is where they found the body,*" Helaine replied. "*They said she was murdered a few metres closer to us and dragged there. Dumped on the ground like a piece of rubbish. Whoever it was tried to cover her with dirt.*"

"*Would you like me to...*" Lucile didn't finish the sentence.

"*No..Sorry...I would prefer to be by myself. Just while I lay the flowers. If you don't mind.*"

All three watched Helaine approach the tree and place the flowers on the ground, carefully perching them up against the trunk, picking up two bunches of dead ones. She then knelt on one knee, bowed her head, mumbled a few words to herself, crossed her chest, stood and returned to join the other three. As she reached the bench she threw the dead flowers into a bin. Her expression had remained impassive throughout, as it did for everything.

Norris waited, he began patting his body, stopped with his hands held midair and released a long sigh.

Matthieu stared at him in confusion.

"Sorry...I keep forgetting I have given up," Norris said.

Helaine returned and both women were now sat between the men.

"*How long ago was it?*" Lucile asked.

"*Twenty-seven years. She would be in her forties now.*"

Twenty-seven years thought Norris before making a quick calculation, the same year his and Matthieu's father died.

Helaine swept her arm slowly through the air. "*All this was undergrowth back then. That is where I...*" She stopped, her son was sitting next to her, not wanting him to hear the specific details of her trade. "*That is where the girls used to take their clients.*" She pointed over her shoulder. "*And over there, the gate you just came through. That is where the boys hung out.*"

When Lucile and Matthieu turned their heads Norris followed suit, just managing to keep up with conversation, snatching the odd word.

Matthieu knocked a packet of Gauloises against the side of his hand, several of the orange filters popped out, one further than the others, like it was a trick he had perfected over the years. He offered it to his mother, she took it. He encouraged another one out with the same finesse, firstly showing it to Lucile, then to Norris, purposely nudging it forward several times as if he was encouraging him to take one. Norris showed the palm of his hand in an overstated gesture of defiance.

Helaine continued. "*Most of the bushes and trees have been cleared. Enough so they could see all the way to the fence, enough to stop...*" She halted, staring directly ahead. "*The girls insisted that this tree remained, not that anyone listened to us. At first they refused. They said they couldn't have a shrine to a murder in a public park. What they meant was they couldn't have a shrine to a prostitute. That is until Yasmin dropped the name of one of her clients in conversation.*" She waited while they grasped its meaning. "*The tree stayed.*"

Lucile translated to Norris, only enough so he could understand.

Helaine continued. "*Nicole's body lay there for over two days before Fantine discovered her. She said it was the smell. I have never heard someone cry out so loud. Several of us girls came running, thinking it was Fantine being murdered...It was horrible, the insects had already started on her.*" Her head dropped, her stare turned inward. "*Nicole didn't deserve it. She was only eighteen, just a kid, always laughing and joking. Maybe her head was in the clouds but she had a lot to forget. We held an all day vigil in the park. Some of the boys came too. The police had to break it up though. The public began shouting abuse at us, saying we brought it upon ourselves. We gave them as good as we got though...Fucking fascists.*"

Norris shot Helaine a glance when she said the last two words, expecting to see some anger, she had remained deadpan throughout. This was a woman whose life had taught her not to show expression — or just fake it.

Lucile repeated it in English.

"Did they find the murderer?" Norris asked.

Helaine lifted her fingers to stop Lucile from translating.

"*No.*" she said flatly.

"*But you were here on that night?*" Mathieu remarked.

"*Yes.*"

"*So it could have been you murdered.*"

Norris thought Matthieu's tone had a strange bluntness, but not out of concern for her, more for himself. Like he was saying his mother had put herself at risk knowing she had a son. Maybe because it was said in French, maybe because Matthieu still hadn't come to terms with the fact that she was once a prostitute, maybe because he knew that was how he was conceived.

Helaine shrugged. "*Nicole was young, inexperienced. I think that is why she was targeted.*"

"*The other girls saw a man though?*" Lucile asked.

"*The police asked us lots of questions. They asked if there was anyone acting suspiciously.*" Helaine puffed out a fake laugh, one she had practised over the years. "*These men do not want to be seen. It was dark, It is easy not to be seen even if you wanted to be, and these men didn't.*"

"*It was reported other girls saw a man?*" Lucile repeated. She had studied the newspaper articles about the murder when Helaine told her the reason for meeting here. She also remembered her mentioning it the first time she met her at the Parc De La Navale.

"*We don't spend long looking at their faces, if they want us they will make it known. When I spoke to some of the other girls and boys, they also thought they had seen someone walking in Nicole's direction. It was hard for us, we cannot be seen talking to the police. Discretion and trust was important in our...*"

"*Was,*" snapped Mathieu.

"*Was,*" Helaine repeated. "*The police weren't exactly our friends.*"

"*It's still the same,*" added Lucile, thinking back to the article she wrote, as if she was defending Helaine.

Matthieu rolled his eyes. "*But this is a murder,*" he said accusingly.

Helaine remained quiet for a moment, thinking if she spoke again it would attract even more animosity from her son.

Lucile broke the ice. "*But someone did see him?*"

"*Another girl, in the bushes. She thought he was a voyeur at first, we used to get a lot of them. She told him to fuck off. It was only afterwards she realised that she had probably come face to face with the murderer.*"

"*So she could describe him?*"

"No, just the whites of two manic eyes, that was it."

"How was she killed?" Norris asked.

Lucile went to translate, Helaine began to answer before she did.

"She was suffocated. The police said there was no sex involved. In some ways that makes it worse, I mean she was killed just for killing's sake. But her shorts had been pulled down to her ankles and her breasts exposed."

Lucile translated.

"Sounds like a right pervert," said Norris, the sentence tailing away as if he was saying the depravity was worse than the murder itself. "Sorry. I didn't mean to..." He stopped, smelling Helaine's cigarette smoke drifting under his nose. He had the urge to ask Matthieu for one, but didn't.

"Maybe he just wanted to look, you know," said Lucile. *"Like he was in control, like she had become his property, like he could do anything to her he wanted and she wouldn't complain."*

"Maybe." The one word spoken inwardly. *"There is something else."* Helaine paused as if to check herself. *"Something I haven't told anyone until now."* She stopped again. *"I heard something, like a muffled scream. You hear some strange noises in the bushes, animals and things. I think it was Nicole I heard."*

Lucile could hear the guilt in her tone. *"But you weren't to know."*

"I did. It was Nicole. I am sure of it."

Lucile translated to Norris the exchange of words.

"Did you not tell the police?" he asked.

"No," she repied softly.

"They could narrow it down to the exact time she was killed. It could have helped them find the killer."

Lucile translated. Then said "How?"

Norris shrugged.

"The police!" Helaine turned her head, exhaling a long

smoke filled breath. "*Nicole was a prostitute. To the police she may as well have been roadkill.*"

Lucile didn't translate.

Norris got the gist. "Sometimes the smallest piece..."

Helaine interrupted. "*There was something else, a wallet. It was only later we found out about it. We were told it was when they were cutting the undergrowth back...about a month after Nicole was killed. They said a worker had found something. We think the police found it at the time though, kept it to themselves.*"

"*Why?*" asked Lucile.

"*It would give the police more paperwork, use up more of their precious time. To them Nicole was just one more prostitute taken off the streets.*"

"*How near was the wallet to the body?*"

"*A couple of metres, in a thick shrub. I was told it was caught up in some branches. Out of sight. Not a place where somebody could just drop it. It must have been thrown. Sometimes the girls would pick the...*" Helaine stopped herself.

"*But it could have been thrown there at anytime.*"

"*No, it belonged to the murderer. It had Nicole's fingerprints on it.*"

"*Fingerprints?*" Norris asked, not recognising the word.

Lucile translated.

"But that doesn't mean..."

"*There were other prints, all belonging to one person, also on the items inside.*"

Lucile quickly repeated it for Norris.

"*What were the items?*" he asked, again, attempting it in broken French.

"*Money and a small sketchbook.*"

Again Norris had to ask what the last word meant.

"*Yes Monsieur. A small one. Whoever's wallet it was he liked to draw, if that is what you could call it. These were more like scrawled daubings done by a baby.*"

Lucile could see Norris's confusion. "Like they were drawn by a child," she said.

"*You said it belonged to the murderer. How did they know that? It could have been thrown in the bush at anytime by Nicole?*" Lucile was looking for discrepancies. "*I mean if that was Nicole's spot, if she had taken it, it could belong to anyone.*"

"*They found money in her pocket. It had the same prints on them, hers and the murderers.*"

"*A client before...*" Lucile began.

"*No. Sasha said she saw her arrive. She didn't see her go with anyone before.*"

Lucile translated.

"Did Sasha not see who she went into the bushes with?" Norris asked.

Helaine shook her head. "*She was with a client.*"

Lucile spoke. "*How did you find out about the wallet?*"

"*A policeman told us, he was...he was...he was someone we knew. He said he was told it was found when the workmen were cutting down the trees and bushes. He wasn't on the case but also agreed with us, he thought the police had it from the beginning...*"

"*How did you know about the sketchbook though?*" asked Lucile.

"*Once we found out about its existence the police showed us, asked if we recognised it.*"

Lucile shook her head. "*It's no wonder there is so much crime in Marseille.*"

Helaine continued. "*Anyway, that is how I know about the drawings.*" She dropped the cigarette butt on the ground and swivelled her foot on it. "*The scribblings of a madman. I can tell you he was definitely not normal.*"

"I take it the police still have the...*sketchbook?*" Norris tried to revert back to French again.

Helaine shrugged.

Norris puffed out a cynical breath. "A man who draws like a child..." he suddenly froze, his gaze turning towards Lucile, raising his eyebrows and widening his eyes, firstly looking at the envelope, then her. Trying to communicate his thoughts.

Lucile turned to Helaine. "*Do you know any girls that organise parties for footballers...or maybe parties that a few footballers have attended?*" she asked.

Norris breathed out a deflated sigh.

"*Parties?*" Helaine asked.

"*Yes. You know, parties?*"

"*Why?*"

"*A story. Now I'm freelance it would...*"

"*No Lucile...I don't.*" Helaine replied, sounding like she wouldn't admit to it even if she did know. The code of silence still remained.

"*If you hear anything would you let me know?*" There was nothing Lucile would like better than to get one over on Angelique.

Helaine shrugged. Another quietness fell over the four.

Matthieu spoke next, the first time he had for a long time. "*Where was I?*" he asked.

"*Sorry?*" replied Helaine.

"*Where was I when you were in this park?*"

"*A friend looked after you.*"

"*Who? Another prostitute?*"

Helaine looked at him in her customary detached way. "*No. A friend. You were safe,*" she lied.

"Is the park still used at night?" asked Norris, changing the subject. He got the impression Matthieu was like a ticking time bomb.

"*No. Since the murder they lock the gates as soon as it gets dark. They also turn the lights off.*"

"*The girls moved back to the streets,*" Lucile said, repeating it in English for Norris.

Helaine nodded. "*I went to work the docks at Toulon.*

Then...well...you know the rest."

Lucile finally raised the envelope and slid out the three photographs. "*These are them, I'm afraid they are not very clear,*" she said as she handed them to Helaine. She hadn't told either her or Matthieu why she needed them to see the pictures. As a seasoned journalist she knew it was best to let them volunteer any information. From experience, once started they wouldn't stop. She also wanted to watch their expressions, although with Helaine that would be difficult. She especially didn't want them to know they were the photographs from the Markovic affair.

Norris leant forward.

Matthieu's eyes diverted downward.

One by one Helaine stared at each in turn, studying them closely, slipping one underneath the other, repeating it several times. Without saying a word she handed them over to Matthieu. Norris and Lucile waited while he did the same, until he too handed them back. No emotion was shown from either of them.

"*Do you recognise the bedroom?*" Lucile finally asked.

Helaine drew down the corners of her mouth and shook her head. "*No...Why?*"

Lucile leant forward, "*Matthieu?*"

"*No.*"

"*Is it Madam Veronique's bedroom?*"

Helaine stared at Lucile as if she was mad.

"*No,*" Matthieu replied like he had barked the word.

"*Could it be one of the rooms the girls used to entertain their clients?*"

"*No..I know them all. It is not any of them, nothing like them whatsoever,*" replied Helaine.

Lucile picked out the clearest photograph. "*The women, do you recognise either of them?*"

Helaine held the picture between her and her son.

"*What are these photographs?*" asked Matthieu.

Lucile ignored him. "*Do you recognise any of the two*

women?" she repeated.

Matthieu persisted. "*When were they taken?*"

Lucile thought. "*A long time ago.*"

"*You think she is Madam Veronique?*" asked Helaine.

"*Why do you?*"

"*It is difficult to tell. She is a lot younger than when I knew her.*"

"*But you are saying it could be?*"

Helaine thought for a while. "*Yes. The one with black hair, that is what I am saying.*"

Matthieu stared down at it again, pointing to the blonde one. It was then he dropped the bombshell. "*That one could be Claude Pompidou?*"

Lucile kept her excitement hidden. Did he know or did he just think that. She began to laugh, hoping it didn't sound false, leaning over at the same time to study the picture. "*No...Really...Madame Pompidou?*"

Matthieu chuckled with her, it sounded just as false. "*I studied politics in university as my second subject. Most of it was boring. There was this scandal called the Markovic Affair.*" He spoke as if Lucile hadn't heard of it. "*A man called Stevan Markovic was murdered and photographs were found in his car. The rumour was they were of Georges Pompidou's wife and another woman...just like these. They were meant to be fake, a set up, hoping to destroy his chances of becoming President. Alain Delon was...*"

"*Yes, I know the story,*" interrupted Lucile.

Matthieu sighed. "*How old did you say the photographs were?*"

"*I didn't.*"

"*So what are these photographs about?*"

"*I just wanted to know if you recognised the bedroom?*"

"*We don't and you didn't answer my question. You asked if it was Maman's bedroom.*"

"*Maman?*" Lucile was confused. "*Oh.*" Stretching the word

before shooting a glance towards Helaine, the first time she had seen her expression change.

Norris was just managing to keep up with the conversation. "It is because of the painting," he announced, leaving the words hanging in the air, hoping Lucile appreciated the diversion.

"What painting?" asked Matthieu in perfect English.

"The one in the photograph."

Both Helaine and Matthieu's head dropped in unison, searching the photograph.

"*What painting Monsieur?*"

"That is the only reason we asked about Madam Veronique's bedroom." Norris said, watching Matthieu as his eyes darted around the picture.

Lucile remained quiet, relieved that Norris's intrusion had managed to get her out of a sticky situation.

Norris leant over her and pointed towards an area on the photograph. "Do you see the mirror on that dressing table?" He waited.

Helaine pulled the photograph closer.

"Do you recognise what's reflected in it?" He waited again, still leaning over Lucile's legs. "It's facing the other way though, you know, mirror imaged."

"*Would you like me to translate?*" asked Lucile, her words straining as she slid a hand under Norris's body to lift him off her.

"Yes." replied Helaine.

Lucile did and Norris waited.

"*Yes I see it.*" Helaine finally answered. "*Is it the one in Madam Veronique's drawing room?*"

Lucile translated.

"*Can I see?*" asked Matthieu. He took it from his mother and studied it for several seconds before handing it back. "It is by Francois Degarmo," he said in English, just like that, as if discovering it in the picture was no surprise.

"*Do you know when Madam Veronique bought the*

painting?" asked Lucile.

Mathieu chuckled. "*Maman does not buy paintings,*" he said. "*She has wealthy admirers.*"

For a second it made Norris think about his own father...their father. "Who gave it to her?" he asked.

"*I did not ask. Even if I had she does not tell me these things.*"

Lucile repeated it in English. Norris thought about what Helaine had said. The Madam had it in her drawing room, that means it was there when she was there. Maybe it has always been there.

Matthieu continued. "*You haven't told us what this is all about Mademoiselle? You have not told me how old the photographs are?*" he asked.

"*Oh.*" Lucile thought for a while. "*Forty-two years to be exact.*" Knowing the implications of what she had just said.

"*That is nineteen sixty-eight. The Markovic affair was in nineteen sixty-eight,*" Matthieu remarked.

"*That was about the same time Madam Veronique moved to Rue Sainte-Ascelina,*" Helaine added.

"*Where was she living before Rue Sainte-Ascelina?*"

"*Paris, but I do not know the details, it is only what the other girls told me. You know how girls gossip when they get together. And Madam Veronique never spoke about her past. I know she was born in Marseille, lived her childhood there, that she stayed there with her mother and older sister after the war.*"

Norris was just managing to keep up.

"*Yes. I remember her telling us the story about how her father was betrayed.*"

"*Her mother died quite young. Her sister married an artist. That is all we know.*"

"*An artist!*" Norris virtually yelled.

"*Do you know where her sister lived?*" asked Lucile.

"*No.*"

"*Do you know her name?*"

"*No.*"

"*What about her married name?*" Lucile asked.

"*No. She never spoke about her.*"

"*Maman came to Marseille and bought the house at Rue Sainte-Ascelina.*" Matthieu said it like he wanted the conversation to finish.

Lucile turned back to Helaine. "*It couldn't have been cheap. I remember her saying it was an affluent area at one time.*"

"*It was. She made her money in Paris. The people around Rue Sainte-Ascelina were wealthy, had the best of everything. Madam Veronique knew the most important people in Marseille, good and bad, people that were influential. They also knew how to have a good time. They paid good money to have the best.*" Helaine's stare hung on her for several seconds. "*And Madam Veronique's girls were the best.*"

Lucile felt she was recalling it with a fondness. Matthieu also thought the same. He was brought up with these girls, some were like sisters to him, he was like a brother to them. He knew of the lavish parties they had in the house, although he was kept away from them. He remembered watching as the well dressed men entered the house, some even spoke to him. How much he wanted to be like them.

"*Do you know how she made her money in Paris?*" Lucile asked.

"*No.*"

Norris cleared his throat. Lucile took it as a cue to translate.

"*So what about these photographs?*" asked Matthieu, like he was wanting to change the subject. "*You owe me after I gave you the notebook. Remember, I was also the one that told you about The Drowning Mary.*"

Norris detected an animosity to his tone. "We didn't know they came with conditions," he said.

Lucile thought the same. "*You said yourself that they are

fake."

"*But you think the woman in them is Maman.*"

"*Do you?*"

"*What if it is? You will write your article. You will get your fame. Maman is frail, she would not be able to take the publicity, it would kill her.*"

"*Are you saying it is her?*"

Matthieu looked down at the photograph one last time. "*No.*" he said. "*I am not.*" Then stood. "*I have to go.*"

Helaine also stood.

"*No!*" Matthieu glared at her. "*You stay,*" he said flatly. "*Goodbye.*"

Helaine slumped back down on the bench.

"*He will come around,*" Lucile tried to reassure her.

"*No, I don't think he will. He won't let me into his life. I've tried to speak to him, he hardly says a word. I think he's ashamed of me.*"

"*These things take time. He'll be confused. Don't force it, just try and let it happen.*"

"*Yes you're right.*" Helaine replied unconvincingly. She rose again and looked down. "*We will speak soon, yes?*"

Lucile returned a sympathetic grin. "*Of course we will.*"

Norris and Lucile watched as Helaine took a couple of steps towards Nicole's tree, bending her knees like in a curtsy, she then touched the ground and made the sign of the cross. She departed.

"I think she has gone after him," Norris said.

"*Yes,*" Lucile agreed.

"It's like we will never see them again."

"He will come around."

For several seconds both looked towards Nicole's tree.

"I don't understand. I mean if it is The Drowning Mary in the photos then how come Madam Veronique has it now.

Lucile thought. "We have to find her sister," she finally said. "She may know something."

"She's older than the Madam. You do realise she could be dead."

"Maybe, then again, maybe not."

"What about Julien?"

"I don't work for the newspaper anymore, remember. Also finding a woman in Paris with only her maiden name would be like...How do you English say? Like finding a needle in a haystack."

Norris nodded.

"And Henri...the editor will be watching him all the time, asking him what he is doing. There is only one way."

Norris rolled his eyes and blew out a long, slow breath. "Madam Veronique wouldn't give you the time of the day." he said.

"I will tell her that I want to do an article on how her family was treated in the war."

"You have got more chance of seeing God."

"I thought you were an atheist?"

"Exactly!"

Lucile drew down her lips and shrugged.

"There is another way." Norris said.

"How?"

"A trade-in."

"Sorry?"

"There is something she wants back."

She glared at Norris. "*Ah yes, of course.* We can take photocopies of the pages beforehand." The smile soon faded. "It will take time. Then what? We say we will give her the notebook back if she will give us her sister's name. She will want to know why."

"You can tell her about the article you are writing, about Jewish families from Marseille, how badly they were treated in the war. Then hope it works. Don't forget The Drowning Mary is also part of the deal."

"What about Matthieu, she also wanted to see him again...

God knows why, he's a right plonker."

Norris found it endearing the way she tried to mimic an East London accent.

Lucile stretched her arms out. "Ricky!" She yelled in a nail scraping voice. "You are a right plonk..."

"Actually it was Del Boy."

"Who?"

"Never mind."

Lucile continued. "From what I've seen today I don't think her seeing Matthieu again will be a problem. We tell her we have spoken to him..."

Norris interrupted. "Sow the seed so to speak. Maybe that would satisfy her." He paused for a moment. "Before we see Madam Veronique I think we should speak to Remi Cochet, see if he has anything on her."

Thursday 24th June 2010,
Rue de Classerie,
Marseille,
France

Remi Cochet lived on the first floor, in a tired, one bedroom apartment of a three storey house only a stones throw away from the Old Port of Marseille. A place he had lived in for the past forty or so years, one he had chosen on purpose, not because he had friends there, but because at that time it had a blossoming and bustling social scene, although it has to be said that for some time his visits to the bars and cafes had become a lot less frequent, especially since most had had their atmosphere violated with that awful thumping music and those flashing lights that made his head feel as if it was about to implode. The few times he did go out it was to the only bar that still held a more traditional value on social etiquette, where he could have a friendly chat on a cultured and intellectual level, and proudly practice that rare phenomenon he had perfected over the years — artspeak. But most importantly, he chose this apartment because the building had a large space on the ground floor, which also belonged to Remi.

No one visited him now, not that he wanted them to, not

that anyone would want to, including the alcoholic, chain-smoking, sex-starved, middle-aged woman living in the apartment above who seemed to have more men friends than the local bordello.

"I feel I knew your father very well." Remi said, looking at Norris from head to toe. "You are very tall Monsieur," he added, like it was a compliment.

"I get it from my mother's side."

"*Ah yes.*" Remi said in French, fixing his gaze on the Englishman.

Remi was a man that looked after himself, displaying a full head of brown hair, obviously dyed. His body was trim, a chequered shirt tucked under the wide belt wrapped around his beige summer trousers showed no sign of a round tummy, although for the past several years his cravat failed to hide a sagging turkey neck.

"Your father was a true gentleman, dignified I believe the correct word would be in your language. One I would not often use these days Monsieur."

"Thank you, you are very kind Monsieur," Norris replied.

"I can see you are very much like him."

Norris was beginning to enjoy all this flattery. "Thank you," he said, feeling as if he should return at least one compliment. "And you speak very good English Monsieur Cochet."

"*Thank you, in my profession it is a necessity,*" Remi replied in French, repeating it in German, again in Italian, also in Spanish. He reverted back to English. "Please sit Monsieur." Indicating to a worn bright red sofa. "Mademoiselle, please." Sitting on a matching chair himself. The entire room looked as if all the furniture had come from the sixties, like it was stuck in a time warp, as if it hadn't been changed since the day he moved in.

"And how is your father?"

"I'm afraid he passed away." Norris replied. "It was many

years ago."

"Oh, I am sorry." He held his chin high. "Then it is a loss to dignity Monsieur."

"Thank you," Norris repeated for the umpteenth time.

"I had wondered why I never saw him again. We had the good fortune to meet on several occasions. He had a very discerning eye Monsieur Kinley. Very interested in the modern impressionist style. I think he found their intentions were more defined, the relationship of colour more pleasing to the average eye." Remi smiled inwardly, as if he was revving up to his full flow of artspeak. "I remember he used to say if you couldn't afford a Morisot or Sickert then the second tier of Impressionists were a very fine substitute. I also think he liked Marseille, I remember he used to stay for several weeks at a time." He paused for a second, studying Norris's reaction, wondering if he should continue. "I myself Monsieur am drawn to the abstractionists. I find their innocence and childlike spontaneity bewitching. *A tapestry of colour mirroring the complexity of their thoughts*." Remi had only got into first gear, quickly moving up to second. "*Where their object may not be their objectivity but only their objection*." He looked at Norris, noticing he hadn't understood one single word. "It is like the English artist Howard Hodgkin Monsieur, where the paint does not stop at the edge of the canvas but continues over onto the frame...and I'm sure if he could, continue until it covered the entire world."

Lucile sat forward, she was just about to open her mouth, only to find Remi looking at her, as if he was defying her to interrupt him. "*Sorry Monsieur Cochet, please continue.*"

"How is Julien Mademoiselle?"

She was surprised by his change of tack, it reminded her of Madam Veronique. "*Oh! Yes, he is fine.*"

It was only yesterday when Lucile had asked Julien to contact Remi, she remembered him saying he knew him. Julien knew everyone. Everyone knew Julien. He told her that if anyone could help them identify a Francois Degarmo work then Remi Cochet was the man. Lucile never told Julien about the sketchbook. Not yet anyhow.

"There is a..." Lucile stopped, her eyes shot upward. A thumping noise came from above, she thought it was the pipes at first, like there was something wrong with the plumbing. Norris's gaze also rose to the ceiling.

Remi continued as if nothing was happening. "*Have you known Julien long?*"

"Yes I have. Have you?"

"*Ah yes.*" His gaze turned inward, his eyes widened. "*He is fortunate to still be working at his age.*"

Lucile could tell Remi was choosing his words carefully.

The banging continued, settling down to a rhythmic thumping.

"*So you are a reporter?*" Remi asked.

"*Freelance. Julien helps me out occasionally.*"

Remi studied Lucile and Norris, expecting to see a rectangular package tucked under one of their arms. "He told me you have some artwork you would like me to advise you on."

"There is a painting we are interested in Monsieur Cochet." Lucile said. "It is called *La Marie se Noyant.*"

"The Drowning Mary," Added Norris. "I believe it is the last painting my father purchased from you."

Remi looked suspicious. "*Ah Yes*...Although this one was not in the modern impressionist style."

"How long did the gallery have it?" Lucile asked.

"The gallery never did Mademoiselle."

"Oh, I do not understand?"

"We were only acting as agents for the artist. It is not unknown. It was...shall we say on loan."

"To who?" asked Lucile, finding it hard to ignore the noise.

"Oh Mademoiselle Billet, you know I couldn't possibly tell you that."

"Was it Madam Veronique?"

Remi blinked several times. "Who?"

An intermittent woman's howl had joined in harmony with the thumping, becoming louder with each thud.

Lucile tried to mask her awkwardness. "When was it painted?" she asked.

"I believe it was painted in the late sixties. A painting of its time..."

"When in the sixties?"

Remi wondered why this was so important. "I do not know the exact date but I do know it was a painting of its time Mademoiselle, or should I say, ahead of its time. *I believe it brings the viewer face to face with their own preconceived hierarchy of social values. At the same time propelling you forward into a seemingly infinite progression while simultaneously defining cultural acceptabilities.*" Remi said with a long breath of air, as if he was relieved to have finished.

"Sorry, I do not understand?" Norris said, realising his own words were in the same tempo as the thumping from above.

"It questions the possibilities of a forgotten existence."

"It does?"

"It is a reflection of the artist's subconscious."

"It is?"

"Who contacted you?" asked Lucile. "And what is that noise."

"Madame Rousselle, the owner of the gallery. Not the noise Mademoiselle, that is Anna."

"Why?"

"*Sorry, why is Anna making that noise?*"

"*No, that is obvious.* Why did Madame Rousselle contact you?"

The noise suddenly came to an abrupt halt.

Remi paused for a moment as if he was waiting. He breathed a sigh of relief. "Even Anna needs her rest sometimes. Why did Madame Rousselle contact me? Money, it is always money Mademoiselle. Art is like a fashion, you have to know when the time is right. When it is a good time to buy and sell." Remi shuffled forward on his chair, moving closer to the edge, his voice became small, like he wanted to tell them a secret. "Monsieur Degarmo was not a sought after artist until the Pompidou Centre bought The Foundering of Death. Madame Rousselle hoped that would promote him to another level. I believe many showed disdain over the purchase. Francois Degarmo was not a known, or even a popular artist at the time. Personally I think he was underestimated, a painter ahead of his time, very skillful. In fact, a great artist." Remi paused for a moment, appearing to consider his next words. "The Pompidou Centre was really Madame Pompidou's project. She had already bought several paintings, but these were known artists. I think she bought The Foundering of Death as a favour for Madame Rousselle. Madame Pompidou and Madame Rousselle knew each other." Remi paused for a second. "Madame Rousselle had sole rights on all Degarmo's works. She was a very astute woman. Like I said, art is like a fashion, but someone has to create that style, it is not the public, they are like puppets, they have to be told what they like, it is as simple as that. And Madame Rousselle was very good at that. Only the person who Madame Rousselle loaned it to was not willing..." Remi suddenly stopped.

"Madam Veronique." Lucile said.

Silence.

Lucile decided to push it further. "So Madame Rousselle loaned it to Madam Veronique."

Remi ignored her again. "Madame Pompidou was only interested in buying one of Francois Degarmo's paintings. So she chose The Foundering of Death. I believe the gallery in Paris displayed The Drowning Mary for a while. If it wasn't sold, then they would have kept it in storage or returned it to the artist. She hoped after the Pompidou Centre hung The Foundering of Death that The Drowning Mary would...who knows what it would be worth. Only it never did. Madame Rousselle kept it for a while after it wasn't sold, maybe hung it in one of her private rooms. Sometimes she would loan a painting out as a favour, maybe to someone that spent a lot of money in the gallery. Like I said, she was very astute. When she asked for it back, many didn't want to part with it and ended up buying it anyway."

"And Madam Veronique didn't want to give it up or pay for it," Norris said.

Remi remained silent again. That was until the thudding started up again. "Anna is busy this morning."

Lucile released a long breath. "So why did Madame Rousselle loan it to Madam Veronique in the first place?"

Remi raised his gaze up to the ceiling. He finally gave a quick shake of his head. "No reason I can think of," he said.

Lucile had tricked him while his mind was elsewhere.

"She had never been a customer of ours." The words tailed away as he realised.

"Never?"

"Never Mademoiselle. I would know."

"Do you know what happened to Francois Degarmo?" Norris asked.

"We never heard from him again."

"Didn't you find that strange?" asked Lucile.

Remi looked confused. "What was strange?"

"That you never heard from him again."

"Many artists suffer for their art. Vincent Van Gogh was not the only one Monsieur."

"But it was not The Drowning Mary we wanted to discuss with you."

Remi released a surprised. "Oh."

"Would you look at these Monsieur Cochet?" Norris leant forward and pulled four photocopies out of his backpack and handed them over.

As Remi looked down it appeared as if a bolt of lightning

had hit him. "Where did you get these?"

Two days ago...
Commissaire Rougier was just as courteous as he was on their first meeting, inviting the Englishman to sit after a firm handshake. Norris only hoped he would continue to be just as obliging on this visit.

And that is how this meeting started, Commissaire Rougier enquiring whether Norris had spoken to Helaine Bonard, also if he had found out the truth about his father.

After Norris had finished explaining the story of Helaine and his father, Commissaire Rougier looked at him over the top of his glasses. "So your father committed suicide?" he finally said.

"*Yes,*" Norris replied in French.

"Would you prefer to speak French Monsieur Kinley?"

"*No*...Sorry, no."

The Commissaire continued after a short pause. "And you say he was using the name Jean-Paul Karel."

"Yes."

"Why?"

"I think he was in fear of someone."

"Who?"

Norris thought about Madam Veronique, about her contacts in high places. "I don't know."

"And the police investigated it at the time?"

"Yes."

"I don't recall it."

Norris shrugged.

"And your father is now buried at Saint Pierre Cemetery?"

"Yes."

"So he wasn't killed at the Port of Toulon by this..." He looked down at the file again. "Alain Serre."

"His name is now Major Marius Guerrette."

A long silence followed. "Okay," he said, just like that, as if it wasn't important, as if he didn't want to continue the conversation. "Now I have other work." He moved the file to the side. "Thank you for the information."

Norris remained seated. "I'm sorry to ask, but I need another favour."

Commissaire Rougier's glare hung on Norris. "What is it you want this time Monsieur Kinley?"

"In 1983 a prostitute was found dead in a park in Marseille." Norris waited for a reaction — none came. "No one has ever been arrested for the murder."

"You know if you have any new evidence concerning an unsolved case, especially a murder, then you..."

"You will be the first to know." Norris said. "But that is exactly why I need to ask you for something."

Commissaire Rougier remained silent, wanting Norris to determine the direction of the conversation. He raised his eyebrows, which Norris took as a signal to continue.

"The police found a wallet at the murder scene. Inside was some money and a small sketchbook...I wondered if you would allow me to see the sketchbook? Maybe take it away, just for a short while, then I will return it."

"Is that what you wanted to ask me?"

"*Yes*...Yes."

"Why?"

"The murdered girl was a friend of Helaine Bonard. I said I would try and help her."

The Commissaire crossed his arms in front of his chest and sat back. "If you know who this wallet belongs to then you must tell me now?"

"No." Norris realised how blunt it sounded. "No," he repeated softly. "I don't know who it belongs to."

Commissaire Rougier rubbed his fingers over several days of stubble. "You know my colleagues would have had experts look at the sketchbook during the investigation."

"My father was an art dealer. I learnt a lot about art

Commissaire Rougier." Norris lied, he knew nothing. "I may recognise the artist."

"I would be prepared to let you see it here at the station. You will either know who the artist is or you will not."

"I would like to take it. Make comparisons, if it is a little known artist it may take some time."

"That is out of the question." The Commissaire paused for a second. "But I have an alternative."

The shock on Remi's face had not gone unseen. "I'm afraid I cannot tell you where I got them." Norris replied.

Remi wanted to pursue it – but didn't.

"Do you know who the artist is?" Lucile asked.

"No, I do not," he flatly replied.

"Could it be the same artist who painted The Drowning Mary?"

"*No!*" Remi barked out instantly. "Francois Degarmo's touch was more sophisticated, he painted from the soul, from the heart, his is an expression of the human complexity on the inner..."

"You do not feel as if you have to protect him Monsieur."

The thumping from above became faster, the screeching became louder, increasing with each thud.

"I am not Mademoiselle. You asked me if I knew who the artist is? I do not. You asked me if it was Francois Degarmo's work? It is not." Remi suddenly shot out of his chair and grabbed a broom handle with the brush end missing. He thudded it angrily against the ceiling. Lucile and Norris looked up, noticing small dents littered all over the ceiling. The noise stopped.

Lucile took the copies from Norris. "Please take another look, study them more closely," she asked.

She could see they were just scribbles, like a blind man had drawn them, all in pencil.

Remi examined one, then another, then another.

She looked at them again as he passed them back. They looked as if they were drawn from nightmares, like the devil himself had been moving the artist's hand. Each one looked the same but different. Each stroke on the sheet appeared random, unfinished, like the erratic daubings of a madman.

Norris looked directly at Remi. You are the expert Monsieur Cochet. I will ask you again. Do you know who drew these sketches?"

Remi spoke softly. "And I repeat Monsieur. No I do not."

Norris thought for a while. "Do you know where Francois Degarmo is now?"

"Firstly you must tell me what all this is about."

"A young girl was killed in a park..."

"Parc de la Vauquelin." Lucile threw in.

"Around the same time my father purchased The Drowning Mary."

Remi's eyes darted from one to the other, the rest of his body motionless. He remained silent.

"A sketchbook was found at the scene. It was inside a wallet, the copies you have in your hand are taken from that sketchbook."

"But what has this..."

"Money was also found in the wallet...and the murdered girl's pocket. The same fingerprints were found on both. Whoever the sketchbook belonged to was the killer." Norris watched Remi's reaction, outside he looked calm, but inside, Norris felt his thoughts were far from being calm. "Now do you know where Francois Degarmo is?"

A short pause. "No Monsieur." His words shaky. " But why do you keep asking when I have already told you they are not by him."

Lucile took a risk. "But you know the park don't you Remi."

The blood drained from the old gallery manager's fake suntanned face. "I need a drink," he said as he shot up from his seat and scuttled away.

"I think we could all do with one." Lucile yelled after him.

"You haven't answered my question." Norris commented as he returned and handed them each a cognac.

"*No!*" he snapped. "No Monsieur, I do not know where Francois Degarmo is," Remi replied softly, followed by a heavy silence. "If you have your suspicions then you will need to go to the police. But do not ask me to verify the artist."

Lucile knew now would be the best time to show him the photographs, although she was worried he might realise they were the ones from the Markovic Affair, just like Matthieu had done. She was concerned all he would do was verify the painting as The Drowning Mary, which they knew already. But he might recognise the room, maybe the women, either woman. She would have to take the risk, it was too good an opportunity to pass over. Madame Rousselle had The Drowning Mary at one time, Remi knew her, she knew Madame Pompidou. Lucile still had a story that would hopefully rock the French Establishment, she just needed to fit together the pieces in the jigsaw. Remi may have some explanation, something neither she or Norris had thought about. There was no choice. Lucile pulled out two photographs from her bag and handed them over to Remi.

Remi's eyes became large, remaining fixed on one detail at the center of the photograph. His voice had become shaky. "These are interesting pictures Mademoiselle." He took a deep gulp of air. "*Two opposed themes are joined into one static symmetry of passion unifying the female form within a motionless drama,*" he said in one breath, the words forced, unnatural, not up to his usual artspeak virtuosity. He swallowed hard. "I do not deal in photographs or pornography." He stretched out his arm to hand them back.

"These are not for sale," Lucile replied, leaving the pictures in his hand.

Norris leant forward, pointing a nicotine-stained finger at the corner of the photograph. "There, do you see it? Reflected in the mirror on that dressing table."

Remi held them to his face, looking where Norris was pointing, stealing a glance towards the centre several times as he did.

"In your expert opinion Monsieur Cochet, what do you see?" asked Lucile.

"In French or English Mademoiselle?"

"Either."

"*La Marie se Noyant.*" Remi raised his eyes and looked at her. "It is The Drowning Mary. I would recognise it anywhere."

"Do you recognise anything else? One of the women? Maybe the room itself?"

He drew down the corners of his mouth and shook his head. "What are these photographs? Where did they come from?"

"They are just pictures Monsieur."

"Two women are not my thing, neither are smutty photographs."

"Do you know why The Drowning Mary is in the photograph?" Lucile asked.

"*No!*" he barked in French.

"Do you know who either of the women are?"

"*No!*"

"Do you think one may be Madam Veronique?"

"Who?"

Both Lucile and Norris knew he was lying.

Friday 25th June 2010,
Hotel Abella,
Marseille,
France

Crystal tried to unthread the tangle of her thoughts, only to make sense of what was happening. She had just woken and taken several seconds to realise where she was: on a bed, in a hotel, in Marseille, in France. She looked over to the other side of the room, Jamia and Ali were still sleeping off the trauma from their journey.

A feeling of euphoria came over her, they had made it, with the help of others they had achieved the impossible. Not without its difficulties, but she had known beforehand it was never going to be easy. She was alive, Jamia and Ali were alive. It was then she realised how much their lives had been at risk, including hers, very much including hers. That feeling of happiness was swiftly replaced with relief.

More threads began to unfurl, her mind began to wander further back, to the reason Jamia and Ali had escaped Chad in the first place. An innocent girl had killed an innocent man. It was then she knew she had to get her and Ali out of the camp, faraway from Chad, to a place where they would be safe, safe from that monster. She felt a tear run down her face and onto the pillow, her head dropped to the side, the tiny patch of wet felt cold against her cheek. This was a tear of joy.

Crystal had now been awake for well over a minute, those tangled threads were no longer left to roam lawlessly around her head. She had slept, although she wasn't sure for how long. She raised herself up on her elbows and saw the curtains framed with light, it was day. What time? She had no idea. She must have slept all night, maybe ten hours.

She thought about the next step in the journey. About acquiring the necessary visas to allow Jamia and Ali into Canada. She would have to travel to Paris, to the Canadian Embassy, a Permanent Resident Travel Document would be needed and it was her who would have to sponsor them, not an easy task by any means. As a lawyer, no one knew that better than her.

Crystal slid her bare legs over the side of her bed and headed towards the shower, the third one since their arrival in France: this one was to wash the sleep away, she knew it would take many more to wash the dust and dirt away, feeling it had been ingrained into her skin. She needed to do her hair, put some make-up on, return Crystal back to Crystal, someone she hadn't been for a long time.

Ten hours ago Jamia was rooted to the spot, by the hotel window, staring through to the outside, as she had been doing for the past half an hour. But this was a world she didn't recognise.

On the other side was a strange land, one with no trees, no rocks, no scorched sandy ground, no rows of dusty brown tents or millet stalk fencing, no big blue sky. Here there was no earth, no land.

Directly opposite was a building made of something other than mud or canvas, the huge space in front of her was more glass than wall. The windows reflected the clouds and sky, distorting them into small dull squares. Every few seconds her attention was drawn to a noise coming from below. A sound that reminded her of Djamel, when he used to blow through an orynx's horn, proudly informing everyone he had made a kill while on a hunt, but this was not a proud noise, this was the sound of anger, of impatience and frustration. She looked down to the road and heard an assortment of engine noises, she saw vehicles following each other like lines of wildebeest. Either side of them were narrower roads, where only people dare tread, most wearing tight clothes like a second skin. It reminded her of the rows of ants she loved to watch as a small child, scurrying back and forth to wherever they were going. She would listen to her brothers whispering to each other about vast cities with huge buildings, about massive ships crossing the great seas and rivers. How everyone lived in large houses where they could choose the temperature of the air. Where fire for cooking could be lit at the flick of a finger, where they had hot or cold water anytime they needed it. How there was no shortage of food, no drought, no rains that made the land impassable. She had to be careful though, if her Papa ever found out she knew these things then she would be punished, given some ghastly chore, one that would ensure these thoughts were immediately forgotten. Even so, Jamia's dream to see these places never wavered.

Now she was here. Now she had that cool air coming from a grill humming high up on the wall, the flushing toilet, cold water any time she needed it, hot water falling like rain from the ceiling, as if it wanted to wash the country of her birth from her body. It made her think back to the world she had left behind, the great vastness of the land stretching for an infinite distance, the village she would always return to, the tukul she called home. Back to her Papa and brothers, her aunts and cousins, to be with her friends again. She pictured her home, snug in its courtyard, the goats bleating in their pens. She thought about her Papa refusing to accept that his youngest would always remain a boy. How he used to take her and Ali to town on market day, how she was the only one that could deal with her brother's tantrums. She remembered the time when an older boy had picked on Ali, shouting names at him, pushing him to the ground. How Jamia flung herself on the boy like a wild animal, scratching and punching and kicking. How her Papa was the only person that could stop her, angry that he had to leave a meeting of elders. Scolding her for not letting Ali stick up for himself, as if it was her fault. How she met that same boy only days ago, when she was rescued on her journey to Guereda. Now he is the Chief's bodyguard.

Jamia saw faces reflected in the window. Two were her brothers, one her father, one her mother, the other was the man she had shot. Each one felt like a knife stabbing into her thoughts. She turned away.

Her mind returned to the camp, to the time when her Papa had made contact with her. A boy not much younger than herself had blocked her path as she had stepped out of the courtyard. She was startled, having never seen him before. She remembered thinking that he must have been waiting for her. He had the look of a child who had been through so much, that killing was in his skin, that his own death was only a stones throw away, to whom dying was so common it became insignificant. It was what he said that was to change her life so much. The boy said he was fighting under her Papa's command, alongside her brother Assim. He told her they were dying of starvation. That her Papa needed to know the details of aid convoys entering the camp. She had chastised him, telling him children were dying here, not only of starvation but of disease, that it was not only food transported by these trucks but medicine as well. Telling him she was just a simple girl, that she had no knowledge of when the aid would arrive.

"*Djamel.*" the boy said. "*Your Papa said Djamel would know.*"

Crystal stopped before she could reach the bathroom, a noise came from the other side of the door, followed by a click. She watched as it slid inward. "Where have you been?" she asked.

"I had to see someone."

Crystal looked baffled. Their presence in the hotel, even in Marseille was meant to be a secret. "Who?" she asked.

Teresa changed her top and looked for a place to leave the key, eventually laying it on the small table in front of the TV, she then sat on the only chair in the room, finally looking up at Crystal. "You look terrible."

"Thanks honey. Who did you see?"

"Do you remember Norris...Norris Kinley?"

"Ycs of course."

"Then that is who I went to see."

"Why did you go and see Norris sweetie?" Her words sounded weary.

"We need money remember, we are not exactly tourists, hotels and supermarkets are not charities. I rang him and he said he was in Marseille anyway. And guess what?" She waited "He is willing to help."

"Just like that."

"He owes me. I told him the pictures on the camera were the reason that Major Guerrette was killed. That it was his fault the pictures were on there in the first place. That the girl was only a puppet. That her brother is in desperate need of help. He remembered seeing Ali at the camp. I told him about you having to go to the Canadian Embassy in Paris to get the visas. He was buying tickets to fly up there anyway, with a reporter friend, to meet someone. He wanted to know how many more to buy. How many more rooms he needed to book in the hotel."

Crystal returned to sit on her bed. "I don't think Ali should take another journey. He needs to rest, get used to where he is now. And Jamia will have to stay with him. I'll go by myself, you stay with them."

"Will they give you the visas if..."

"I am a lawyer with Amnesty International, they will give

me the world if I ask for it," Crystal announced, not convincing Teresa.

Jamia turned to look at Ali curled up on the bed like a fetus, locked in his own world, not a single sound had left his mouth. She knew Ali was in there somewhere, ready to escape the deep recesses of his mind. When he had shown a reaction boarding the aircraft at Guereda airport, she knew then she would get her brother back. When? With the help that Crystal had promised, soon she hoped. He probably thought the plane was some kind of beast, the sound of the propeller growling at him like a monster, like the spirits his Papa used to scare him with in his stories, when his Papa thought he could purge the boy out of him.

Jamia was jolted out of her reverie by a voice behind her, the words spoken in arabic.

"*Jamia honey, it is Crystal.*"

Jamia hardly recognised the woman standing before her. It was as if Crystal had transformed into someone else. Back at the camp Crystal always looked so different from the other female aid workers. She dressed so immaculately, the sweet smell of flowers that seemed to follow her everywhere, those billowing summer dresses. "This country will never beat me," she would say to anyone that asked.

Jamia's lips widened, Crystal always thought she had the sweetest smile, so innocent, so trusting. She also knew that hidden behind it was a girl that had seen the worst of life.

Standing to the side of Crystal was an olive skinned woman with waist long, black hair shimmering like a raven's feather. The woman Jamia had only ever made eye contact with (Teresa only spoke Spanish and English, Jamia only Tama and Arabic), exchanging the odd acknowledging smile. Teresa never mentioned it, but she had some concerns about the time Crystal would be away in Paris. Especially as it was her that championed getting Jamia and Ali onto the streets of Marseille, to get them used to their new environment, maybe take them to a supermarket, maybe a museum, to see the sea for the first time, to visit the famous Cathedral, or more appropriately, the Mosque. She knew the visas would take time, maybe months. They couldn't stay in the hotel room forever.

Crystal spoke to Jamia in Arabic. "*I have to go to Paris sweetie.*"

"*Paris?*"

"*It is a big city where...where the elders will give us permission to go and live in Canada.*"

"*Canada?*"

"*Remember we discussed it honey. You are coming to live with me in Canada.*" Crystal said, realising the discussion was one-sided, that she hadn't even asked Jamia.

Sunday 27th June 2010
Rue Sainte-Ascelina,
Marseille,
France

Norris opened Claude's passenger door and plonked himself heavily on the canvas seat, "We can't keep on meeting like..." Stopping as he realised how that one forgetful action could have snapped the vehicle in half.

"Where have you been?" Lucile asked abruptly. "I've been trying to contact you."

"I had to see someone."

Lucile waited, wanting to ask who, but didn't.

"It was Teresa Flores."

"Teresa Flores, the Spanish lady? The one who came to the cemetery with Matthieu."

"Yes."

Lucile was intrigued. "About Matthieu?" she said softly.

"No, another matter."

She waited. "Aren't you going to tell me?"

"Yes, but not now. You know Madam Veronique will give us our own parking space soon." Attempting to lighten the mood. "So why are we outside her home again? "

"Julien has been doing some research on the Dennel family."

"I thought he stopped helping you."

Lucile tilted her head and glared at him with raised eyebrows. "You didn't really believe that did you?..Julien has found something interesting. Do you remember how Madam Veronique's real name is Dennel?"

"Vaguely."

Lucile sighed. "Well, her name is Susanne Dennel and her father's name is Nicolas. Remember how she said her father had sent his two daughters and wife to Switzerland and he..."

Norris interrupted. "And he stayed to fight the Nazis. I remember he joined the French Resistance."

"Maybe Nicolas Dennel fought alongside Francois Marcantoni."

"Who is Francois Marcantoni?"

"He was arrested for the murder of Stevan Markovic."

Norris slid his gaze away from the windscreen and held it on Lucile.

"I thought that would get your attention. Before he was murdered, Stevan Markovic wrote a letter to his brother Aleksandar. In the letter he said that if I get killed it would be the fault of Alain Delon and Francois Marcantoni."

"And this Francois Marcantoni knew Alain Delon?"

"So who is this Francois Marcantoni?" Norris repeated.

"He is from Corsica, he also fought in the Resistance. Then became a gangster, spent time in prison. You name it, he has done it."

"Including murder?"

Lucile drew down her lips and rocked her head from side to side.

"And?" Norris said.

"And he's still alive. Although Julien says he's not in the best of health. He is living in Corsica for the time being, apparently he wants to return and spend his last days in Paris. I want to fly over and try and get an interview with him." She paused for a second. "Only thing is Norris, now I'm not working for the paper, money is not exactly falling from the trees." Her words coated with sugar.

"Wait until he comes back to Paris then."

"I haven't got time."

"And you say he's living in Corsica?"

"*Yes.*" she replied in French. "And if I can get him to...well you know, he might tell me what happened...a dying man's last confession and all that. How do you English say, 'It would be the icing on the...'"

Norris interrupted. "I know someone in Corsica."

Lucile searched for a reply. "I would rather go myself."

"Not if you can't afford it. You have already blown your budget on the photographs."

Lucile wasn't sure if he was joking. "What is his name?"

"Ah! That is where it gets a bit vague. Kevin has several names."

"He has several names! And what does Kevin do?"

"He's a writer."

"Oh." The cynicism now tinged with a mixture of surprise and approval. "What does he write?"

"Books."

Lucile sighed. "What type of book?"

"Novels."

She rolled her eyes. "Do you purposely act dumb? What type of novel?"

"War stories. Mainly about the French Foreign Legion. He's an ex-legionnaire."

Lucile thought for several seconds, her plan had worked. "He sounds perfect."

"You do realise Francois Marcantoni knowing Madam Veronique's father may just be a coincidence. You know it may have nothing to do with the murder of Markovic. She was just a kid in the war and if I remember correctly, she said they never saw their father again."

"Marcantoni survived though. If he and her father were friends in the Resistance he may have contacted the family after the war, they could have kept in touch Norris. This could be another reason why Madam Veronique is the woman in the photographs."

"Are you saying Francois Marcantoni had something to do with the pictures?"

"Come on Norris, think about it. This is not just a coincidence. Francois Marcantoni knew Alain Delon, Alain Delon knew Stevan Markovic."

"So how are you going to find out?"

"We'll just have to ask her..." She looked at him. "Won't we Monsieur Kinley." Her eyes doughy.

"Just like that."

"We stick to plan A, about me writing an article, getting justice for her family. Remember what she said about returning home after the war, how they were treated, that everything they owned had been plundered, and not just by the Germans." Lucile glared at Norris. "Remember she said write about that in your newspaper Mademoiselle Billet. I owe the people of Marseille nothing, she said." She paused for a second and sat forward on her seat. "Maybe I will do just that. I'm serious. Anyway I think she likes you." She placed her hand on Claude's door handle.

Norris remained sitting. "Haven't we forgotten something."

"Have we?"

"The Drowning Mary...The notebook."

"How do you English say." She leant towards him, her face only inches from his. "Watch this space mate!" she said in her best EastEnders voice. Then planted a kiss on his lips. They stepped out of Claude.

For the third time in as many weeks Norris lowered himself onto a chair in Madam Veronique's drawing room.

The old woman sat in her usual seat, studying her two guests in turn, hoping their faces would display the reason why they were there.

"*You do not wish to sit Mademoiselle Billet?*"

"*Sorry,*" Lucile replied. She had seen a brandy glass on top of the cabinet, a tiny glaze of liquid still at the bottom, another one had caught her eye, less than a metre away, also with a drop of liquid at the bottom, as if someone had left in a hurry. She perched herself on the edge of a chair, keeping her bag on her lap, the same way she liked to hug a cushion at home.

Madam Veronique noticed Norris had glanced sideways. He could see the painting was no longer where it usually hung, instead there was another painting, a second rate impressionist portrait of a man with a pipe, his skin heavily highlighted in blue. Norris scanned the entire room, The Drowning Mary had gone. He remained silent. She remained silent.

He looked at the old woman. "How are you?" As if he didn't really want to know.

"You English are so formal Monsieur Kinley. If you must know I am suffering from..." Madam Veronique looked at Lucile and spoke in French, so softly Norris couldn't hear, her smile flickering on and off with the words. Lucile leant forward to hear her, stopping when she got an overwhelming odour from the old woman's perfume. She whispered her reply. Madam Veronique returned her attention towards Norris. There was a glint in her eyes. "It appears I am suffering from old age, but that is not the answer you English expect is it Monsieur, to hear of someone's woes?" Her expression sobered. "But I am well enough Monsieur Kinley, thank you for asking. So are we to continue where we left off from your previous visit. Remind me, how did it end?"

Before either Norris or Lucile could answer.

"Oh yes. You persuade Matthieu to visit me, return what you stole and I will sell you the painting for one euro. It appears my old age doesn't seem to have played tricks with my memory."

"But I remember telling you the painting already belonged to my family. I am only taking back what belongs to me in the first place."

"How do you know your father didn't just return what rightfully belongs to my family?"

Norris knew how this woman thought, it reminded him of his own mother. "Because he didn't return it. You already had it. You had it on loan and refused to give it up."

"As I had his son." Madam Veronique smiled. "Then in that case, one of my demands has already been answered."

"I do not understand," asked Norris.

"Matthieu." Madam Veronique dropped her gaze to the floor, as if the carpet was transparent, like she was looking into the room below. "Just like the painting, he is back in his rightful place."

Lucile suddenly realised what the other glass was sitting on the cabinet. That is why someone had left in a hurry. She wondered if Helaine knew of Matthieu's return. It was only yesterday they had met him at the park. "*When?*" Lucile asked.

"You will have to ask him that Mademoiselle."

"*Is he here?*" asked Lucile, shooting a glance at the second brandy glass. She could imagine him scuttling back to his warren like a scared rabbit. She always had him down as a coward.

"How do you English say Monsieur. I am not his keeper," Turning her attention towards Norris "Have you brought a euro with you Monsieur?"

"Yes," he replied.

Madam Veronique looked at Lucile, but not directly at her, a smile spread across her face, her cheekbones became even more pronounced. "All we need now is the notebook."

"Where is the painting?" asked Norris.

"It is safe Monsieur."

Safe with Matthieu, thought Lucile. "I have decided to

write an article on the Second World War," she announced.

Madam Veronique stared at her.

"I thought I might write it from the perspective of a Jewish family living in Marseille. I remember what you said on our last visit. That you returned home from Switzerland to find your home plundered, and not by the Germans. Remember it was you that told me to write it." She repeated what the old woman had said on their last visit, the same words she had used in the car only moments ago. "Write about that in your newspaper Mademoiselle Billet, I owe the people of Marseille nothing. That is what you said. For what it is worth, I also believe your story should be told."

"What do you think I have been doing for the past forty years Mademoiselle Billet? Only for it to fall on deaf ears."

"Then this will be your time to tell it, and I am the person to write it." It was now Lucile could play her ace card. "I will return it if you give me the chance to write your story."

"Say it Mademoiselle, tell me what you are returning."

"I will return your notebook, *your notebook*, there, I have said it. But I will tell you now that I leave no stone unturned when I write an article. If I am satisfied you are just as serious as I am. If I feel you are telling me everything..."

"How will you know that?"

"I will ask you some questions, if you agree to answer them, then I will return the notebook."

"My notebook," Madam Veronique corrected. "The one you stole from me."

"It wasn't me who stole it, but I think you already know that."

"And you will return my painting," Norris threw in, placing a one euro coin on the table in front of him. "That is all three of your demands fulfilled."

Madam Veronique shot a glance towards him, then back to Lucile. "What are you up to Mademoiselle Billet?" Her words spoken through a sigh.

"The notebook and The Drowning Mary," Lucile said as if that was it, as if there was no more.

Madam Veronique rose from her seat and stepped over to the cabinet. She poured herself a large cognac, took a sip and returned to her seat, dabbing the corners of her mouth with a silk handkerchief, blotting up two stains of red lipstick as she did.

Lucile pulled out a pen and a notepad. "Tell me about your father," she said, writing as Madam Veronique spoke, sometimes verbatim. First page...

Nicolas Dennel, father, silversmith, wealthy, living, working Rue Sainte-Ascelina. Neighbours Jews. Susanne many friends, Hebrew school. Was she only survivor from class? Forty thousand Jews Marseille before war, one thousand remained. Jews taken death camps, some forests, dug pits, lined up, shot, buried alive, women and children. Nicolas sent family away, remained in France, fighting with Partisans. Secret rescue committee, escape line for Jews from Marseille. Susanne eleven, Bat Mitzvah one year, inform the world she was a woman, missed. December 1942, everything left behind. Susanne upset, rabbit with neighbour, hated, mistrusted. Two weeks Dennels slept in basement, farmhouse, Belcodene village, damp, starving and freezing. Owners risk death if discovered. Journey to Switzerland. Travelling night, trunks of cars, under bales of hay, farm trucks. Day, sleep, barns, attics, secret chambers. Susanne heard stories, folk dying, cold, decease, illness. Some caught, sent to death camps. Arrived Switzerland. Servants to a Jewish Swiss family. Constant fear of being thrown out of Switzerland. Nicolas knew expert counterfeiter, fake refugee registration forms. War over. Susanne, sister, mother return to Marseille. Susanne excited, see father after four years. Families living in house, none she knew. Woman told Dennel's home destroyed in bombing, not giving house up to Jews. Susanne, rabbit eaten, remember woman's smirk. Susanne noted name, woman now dead. A year later discovered fate of Nicolas. Comrade fought with Nicolas, found Dennel women in dilapidated room. Told Susanne Nicolas killed by German soldiers, four men ambushed. Susanne heard comrade tell mother Marseille resident informed on father to Nazis. Told Susanne name, name noted, crossed out. Comrade visit Rue Sainte-Ascelina. Dennel's return home.

A quiet fell over the room when Madam Veronique stopped talking. It was through this vacuum of silence that Lucile actually realised there was a story here, maybe something special. And if there was a connection with the Markovic affair? She felt an excitement surge through her.

Lucile put pen to paper again. "What happened to your mother?" She asked. Page two...

Ava-Marie Dennel, Ava. Family back in house. Life for Ava hard. Jews still blamed for hardship in Marseille. Daughters beautiful, Ava concerned Susanne. Pimps, streets, look for young Jewish girls. Susanne many lovers. Anti-semitism, Vichy Regime. Many Jews leave for new country. Residents of Marseille hostile. Ava made difficult decision. Leave everything behind again, meagre belongings. Arrive Paris. District where Jews live. Comrade help, Ava find accommodation, Le Marais in Paris. Susanne dancer, Moulin Rouge. Sister teacher art, local school. Dennel's life improve. Ava dream, see two daughters marry, want grandchildren, a boy, call him Nicolas. Sisters concerned for Ava, behaviour unpredictable, erratic. Flair up for no reason, angry, accuse Susanne cheap whore. Ava apologise, bad mother, her fault. Bed for days, not eating, drinking, cheap wine. Ava-Marie take own life, forty-nine. Susanne found hanging from hatch. Susanne twenty-two.

"*Oh,*" Lucile said, appearing truly sympathetic. It was also then she realised the true reason why the notebook was so important:

it had names, names from which she would exact her revenge.

"*I am sorry,*" Norris said, feeling an overwhelming empathy with her. He knew what it was like to lose a parent.

"*Ten years is all it took,*" was Madam Veronique's only response, void of emotion. It reminded Lucile of how Helaine always kept her true feelings to herself, Maybe it came with the profession.

It was when Susanne commented that all her mother wanted out of life was to have grandchildren. Lucile thought about Matthieu. Maybe that was why she felt so strongly about him. He was the closest she could get to giving her mother what she wanted. Maybe that was why she had thrown Helaine out so heartlessly; because Helaine had done what Susanne couldn't.

"*It must have been very hard for you,*" Lucile remarked.

"*No Mademoiselle Billet, on the contrary, it was the beginning.*" She reverted back to English. "I stayed on as a dancer at the theatre." Her face opened up, her eyes became wider, displaying a hint of a smile. "It was wonderful, I was free. I got to know rich businessmen and actors, artists and politicians, they all wanted part of me.

Lucile could guess what part.

"I was taken to the best restaurants, attended the most lavish parties. I was young and beautiful and I was available. I didn't need my Bat Mitzvah to become a woman." Suddenly her eyes became like daggers, her lips pinched, her face like stone; because she had shown little emotion before it seemed to make the reaction so much more powerful. "But I never forgot." She glanced down at Lucile's bag, as if she could see the notebook through the material. "I made sure of that Mademoiselle."

"What happened to your sister?" Lucile asked, trying to make the question flow with the conversation. "She was older wasn't she?"

Her pen started skating over the paper again. Page three...

Valeraine Dennel, beautiful. Personality opposite. Susanne extrovert, gregarious, fun-loving, clever. Valeraine, placid, respectable, loner. Worked hard at school, failed most subjects, good artist. Ava say make good wife, Susanne not. Valeraine married twenty-six. Still need to please Ava, even after death. Husband, Antoine Rousselle. Susanne hated. Handsome, Jewish, good artist. Knew painters. Valeraine friends Jean Dupuy, Lydia Corbett, Picasso. Valeraine and Antoine lease shop Montmartre, art gallery, Valeraine work. Hung Antoine's paintings. Valeraine run gallery, exhibitions, good business woman. Profit month, great success year. Friends contribute, famous artists. Valeraine powerful Paris art world. Susanne not welcome, sisters apart. Antoine named gallery Valeraine Rousselle Art Gallery, mistake, not see future. Marriage last seven years. Antoine painted models, slept with them. Told Valeraine just sex, loved her. He broke sacred vows, unforgivable Valeraine. Not allow destroy life, gallery. Bitter divorce, Valeraine told court gallery was hers. Many artists vouch. Lawyer said gallery had Valeraine Rousselle name. Court agreed. Valeraine wanted children, none. Not love another. Valeraine Rousselle Art Gallery famous in Paris. Claude Jacqueline Pompidou also visit.

When Norris and Lucile heard the name Rousselle they felt a surge of excitement, only to have it followed up with a bolt of electricity when Claude Jacqueline Pompidou was mentioned.

As soon as Madam Veronique had stopped talking, Norris rose from his chair and stepped over to where the large group of photographs hung on the wall. He tried to keep his movement composed, natural, like there was no other reason than wanting to stretch his legs. He recalled the Markovic photographs, the faces of the two women now embedded in his mind.

One by one Norris studied the black and white images, some orientated in portrait, some in landscape, all behind glass and set in expensive silver frames. He began scrutinizing every woman in every photograph, even the ones in the background, however many there were, however distant, Norris took a look at every single one of them. Some he would dismiss immediately, others he would take time over, spending a long time on one particular photograph. It was of a lavish dinner; set in a sumptuous and palatial room with chandeliers hanging from the ceiling and grand paintings on the walls. It was the one with Madam Veronique standing between the Pompidous.

Norris had met Valeraine Rousselle two years ago at her home in Montmartre. She was in her eighties, hunched, frail, as if her body had shrunk with time. He remembered her hair, wispy and grey, her face lined and creased, her eyes like two pools of water. But that was it, to him she was just an old woman with a sharp mind and a wise intellect.

He could feel the two women's gaze following his every move, their stare boring into the back of his head as he studied each photograph. He knew there was something wrong, something missing.

A voice came from behind. "Are you looking for someone Monsieur."

Norris remained silent.

"She is not in any of them Monsieur," Madam Veronique called out.

Still he remained silent.

"If it is my sister you are looking for, then you are in the wrong place."

Norris didn't reply. He remembered when Matthieu told him to look on the walls of her apartment, when he was looking for The Drowning Mary. There were photographs mixed in between the paintings, less formal than the others. All he could remember was that they were of the usual famous landmarks. He stepped to the side, following the wall. He stopped and looked up. That was when he saw it, above him, high up near the ceiling, a black and white photograph, it was like the Madam didn't want anyone else to see it. It was of three women, one middle aged, dark hair with even darker eyes, eyes that hid so much, a smile that was afraid to flower. The two either side of her were young women, similar in appearance, one slightly older than the other. Both had a natural beauty, fair hair, their eyes bright, full of the future, a wide smile beamed across both faces, but it was the younger one that looked the happiest, the freest.

Lucile rose and stepped over, standing close to Norris, her shoulder leaning into his. She wanted to slide the Markovic photographs from her bag, hold them up to head height, compare them with the older girl in the picture. She didn't have to.

"I have met your sister," Norris said with his gaze still hanging on the picture.

"*Ah yes,*" Madam Veronique replied.

"You know?"

"Yes Monsieur."

"You know where she lives?" Lucile whispered to him, her words hardly audible.

"Yes," Norris replied from the corner of his mouth, the word so small it nearly got lost.

"It was taken just after we moved to Paris," Madam Veronique said.

Norris and Lucile continued to look up. It was like the photo had a power over them, like they were being held in a trance, feeling sad and joyful rolled into one. They studied the faces, a contrast in personalities, a heavy weight carried by the mother, caution by the other, the youngest looking like the world was her oyster. As she looked at them Lucile felt her eyes well up. This street wise reporter who had been hardened by writing about children abused by their parents, penning articles on horrific murders and rapes, about the lives of drug dependant prostitutes, even living with them for a while to understand why. She had never been moved so much by one innocuous image.

Lucile wiped her eyes and pulled away from Norris, returning to her seat. He followed.

A long silence. Lucile spoke first. "Your father's friend. Would you tell me about him please?" Putting pen to paper once again. Page four...

Her father's comrade, name unknown. Susanne, sister, mother live fishing area of Le Vallon des Aauffes. Gutting and preparing fish for market, Jews only employment, wages paid in fish. Dennels stunk of fish, unable to wash out. Lived in one room. House more like wooden cabin. Gaps between planks, cold sea wind blowing through, wailing children. Amenities shared with other Jewish families. War not over for Susanne. Walk to Grande Synagogue to pray on day off. Check news of Nicolas. Monday afternoon, foreman called Ava, Man waiting their room. Ava thought husband. Susanne and Valeraine thought father. All recognise man from four years ago. Helped escape Switzerland. Told Nicolas is dead. Ava speak nonsense, hadn't heard, death of her husband not sunk in. Valeraine fall knees, crying. Susanne stood, felt nothing. Comrade explained details of death. Sorry own house bombed. Susanne explained. Father's comrade returned, told them they were going home. Susanne can still smell the fish now.

"Your father's friend, you never said his name," Lucile said.

"Francois, his name was Francois."

"Francois who?" Lucile asked.

The old woman thought for a moment. "Francois," she repeated.

Before Lucile had even entered the top apartment at Rue Sainte-Ascelina she had made a decision. She would return the notebook. Even if it wasn't her that stole it, nevertheless it had been stolen, she had it and it was not hers to keep. I must be getting soft, she had said to herself before leaving home.

Lucile also knew the Madam would have known it was

Matthieu who had taken it, she wondered if she had already confronted him about it, Lucile would like to have been a fly on the wall during that discussion.

After Madam Veronique had spoken about her father's comrade, the horrific ordeal her family had been through, every morsel of regret in returning the notebook had been wiped away. Through every bone in her entire body Lucile knew she was doing the right thing, of that she was in no doubt. If the Madam wanted her revenge then she will have it. Besides, Lucile had spent the night taking copies of every page.

Lucile dipped her hand into her bag, pulled out the notebook and stretched her arm at full length, dangling it in front of the old woman. Madam Veronique didn't take it immediately, remaining silent, her gaze dropped, just sat staring at it. She shook her head. "No Mademoiselle Billet, you must keep it, I want you to have it."

Lucile was taken aback at first, she then guessed why. The Madam had kept it for one reason and one reason alone — revenge. Now she had found her vehicle to fulfill that retribution. Many names in the book would have already died, but that was her intention; their families would know the wrongs of their ancestors.

Lucile knew by taking the recognition for exposing the hypocrisy of men who spout high morals and virtues, then do the exact opposite, she would be upsetting powerful people, feel the full blast from the French Establishment, every written word would be another bullet aimed her way. She thought about Stevan Markovic, maybe he was murdered for doing exactly that.

"*No Madam Veronique, you keep it,*" Lucile said. "*This is your retribution, not mine.*"

The old woman smiled, as if for the first time they had understood each other. She gently slid the notebook from her hand and placed it on the table beside her chair. Lucile already had what she had come for — the location of her sister, although not the way she expected. How was Norris to know Valeraine Rousselle was the Madam's sister? The icing on the cake was that she had found the identity of one of the women in the photograph.

"You once told me you knew the identity of the woman in the photograph," Lucile asked.

Madam Veronique sat, waiting.

"It was your sister?"

Lucile wondered if Madam Veronique had forgiven her for thinking it was her.

"If you say so Mademoiselle Billet." The old woman sighed. "Remember me to Valeraine when you see her."

Lucile smiled. "I will." Thinking anyone could have made the same mistake, they were sisters, one a copy of the other.

She could show Madam Veronique the three Markovic photos, have it confirmed there and then. Maybe she would be able to tell Lucile more about them, but she knew how Madam Veronique could play with people. Would she even tell the truth? Lucile would have to speak to Valeraine Rousselle first, find out why she was one of the women. There were so many questions to ask her. What had she to do with Stevan Markovic? Did she know who killed him? And that was only the start.

Norris had been waiting all this time, patiently listening to Madam Veronique speak about her family, soaking up the story about the terrible experiences she had endured. But that wasn't going to stop him. He picked up the euro from the table and placed it on the notebook. "You have the notebook. You have Matthieu. We made a deal Madame."

"You will get your painting back Monsieur, I promise. How do you English say, 'Patience is a virtue."

"I believe it was originally Latin." One thing Norris had learnt at that boarding school he so hated. "When will I get it back?"

"Good things come to those that wait. Is that also Latin Monsieur?" She soaked up Norris's stare. "You will get The

Drowning Mary soon. I promise."

A silence fell over the room, like everything had been agreed. No more would be gained if they stayed. They rose from their seats.

"One more thing," announced Lucile. "You said you lived in Rue Sainte-Ascelina before the war?"

"*Ah yes,*" Madam Veronique replied.

"And your father's friend returned the house to you."

"*Yes.*"

"Then you moved to Paris."

"*Yes.*"

"Now you are here, back in the same house. I do not understand."

"My mother tried to sell it before we left for Paris. If she had then our lives would have been very different. The authorities here in Marseille said they could find no proof of our ownership. We were Jewish. They were lying. Until we could get such proof it would stay empty. My mother never gave up. She was borrowing money to pay for lawyers, getting herself into a lot of debt. It was also our father's house, this made her even more determined. I think losing it played a big part in her suicide. I returned in 1970." She paused for a moment. "It was soon after that Susanne Dennel no longer existed, I became Madam Veronique." She placed a hand on the notebook. "It didn't take long before the authorities found proof of ownership." She looked at Norris with a glint in her eye. "How do you English say Monsieur? It is who you know."

Or who you sleep with he thought; but kept that to himself.

Norris and Lucile began the short walk back to the car. They had refrained from knocking on Matthieu's door. What would they say? They decided it would be best to speak to Helaine first.

"How did Madam Veronique know that you had met her sister?" asked Lucile as they stepped out onto the pavement.

She said they hadn't spoken for years.

Norris thought for a while. "Remi Cochet," he said.

More steps were taken in thoughtful silence.

"Did you notice she didn't offer us coffee?" Lucile asked.

"Not until you just mentioned it."

"I think she knew about you taking photos of her photos. I think she knows we have some of the Markovic pictures. I think she knows everything."

"You do a lot of thinking."

Lucile smiled. "It's the journalist in me."

"Anyway, how would she know about the Markovic photos."

Lucile thought for a moment. "Remi Cochet," she said.

More steps were taken in silence.

"You said later...remember. When we arrived. You said you would tell me why you met Teresa Flore."

Norris looked down at her. "Are you jealous?"

Lucile laughed and wrapped her arm around his, pushing into him, nearly knocking him into the wall. "She's a fine looking woman."

"A bit short for me," he remarked, then went on to tell her about Jamia and Ali's escape from Chad. About Crystal hoping to get them to Canada. That Teresa managed to get temporary travel documents. How she needed to borrow some money, although Teresa had never actually said 'borrow.' "Crystal is travelling to Paris with us to get the visas," were his last words.

"So Teresa came to see Monsieur money bags." Lucile remarked cynically.

Norris looked down at her. "It is my money."

"Sorry," Lucile replied.

Another period of silence as they strolled with her arm still coupled in his. Norris felt like they were a couple.

They arrived to where Claude was parked and opened both doors at the same time. It always made Norris nervous, climbing in together, at least with one door shut it felt there was a chance the vehicle would stay intact. He slammed his door shut with the sound of tinkling rust. Claude remained upright. He could breathe again.

"So you gave the notebook back?" he said.

"It's okay, Julien had already been through it, how do you English say? With a fine tooth comb." Lucile smiled at him. "Or is that Latin. Anyway I took copies, that was why I was up most of the night." She turned to look at him. "Do I have bags under my eyes?"

"Norris moved within centimetres of her face, as if he was a jeweller studying two gemstones. "No mate," he said, in his best East London accent, then planted a kiss on her lips.

Wednesday 30th June 2010
Rue Madeleine, Montmartre and
The Embassy of Canada,
Paris,
France

Squeezed between a biscuiterie and a Chinese restaurant, Lucile was staggered to see how diminutive the gallery looked, so insignificant, so mediocre. This bastion of French modern art, this renowned depository of anything abstract on canvas. The place where Dubuffets and Soulages could be found exchanging hands for a princely sum, where anyone could pick up a bargain from a lesser known artist — an investment for the future perhaps.

Lucile was expecting something much more impressive, if not, then maybe the gallery itself would be a piece of art, the outside splashed with paint like a Jackson Pollock or how she imagined Andy Warhol's Factory would have looked.

What Lucile saw on first sighting was the frontage shedding paint like old skin, its coating of deep burgundy now fading to brown and cracking like old bark, leaving bare patches of wood around the two bay windows, as though you could see into the raw flesh. It had greatly declined since Norris's visit two years earlier.

In fact, the only indication of it actually being the Valeraine Rousselle Art Gallery was the faded gold script fronting the awning, hardly distinguishable as the material flapped in the breeze. Only the two colourful paintings displayed on tabletop easels behind the bay windows suggested what was traded inside.

Norris and Lucile stepped in.

Less than two kilometres away was another awning, this one bright red, swaying above it was a flag displaying the maple leaf of Canada.

Crystal was sat on a padded chair in a long, plain room inside the Embassy, its walls adorned with large posters displaying pictures of calm lakes like mirrors reflecting the pine forests surrounding them. A robust wooden table with Canadian travel magazines splayed out on top in the shape of a Chinese fan. Some Embassy minion had gone to a lot of trouble and Crystal was not about to spoil its symmetry, neither were any of the half-a-dozen people also waiting in the room.

The door at the opposite end of the room opened and a man in an open neck shirt and rolled-up sleeves poked his head in, he called out a name that wasn't Crystal Bullion, although she felt a warm feeling of home on hearing the familiar accent.

A middle-aged woman, olive skinned, very French, rose and followed him through the door. As she sat waiting, three more people were called. With pen in hand Crystal dropped her head yet again, concentrating on the privately sponsored refugee application form she had been given at reception. She had already spent over twenty minutes completing the first portion and was now on the refugee section. The application would solely be a personal sponsorship, not involving either Amnesty International or Teresa's charity, The Way for Life. She knew first hand what the bureaucracy would be like.

The same door opened again, this time a woman, young,

very attractive, one that hadn't entered before, appearing just as informally dressed as the first gentleman. Crystal noticed her thick dark eyebrows turned down, as if in a permanent frown, undecided if she was a bird of paradise or a bird of prey. "Crystal Bullion," she called out, staring directly at Crystal as if she knew it was her.

Crystal rose and stepped forward, feeling disappointed that the young woman spoke in a French accent, realising she had spent far too long away from home.

As Lucile and Norris stepped into the gallery they noticed how empty it was of clientele, in fact there were none. A young woman sat on a chair behind a desk, slightly angled so she was facing the front door, as if she was watching the outside world like it was a television.

Norris remembered when he was inside the gallery two years ago, when there were a countless number of paintings hanging three or four deep, hardly a space between them. He recalled how in the centre of the room there were two large house plants, between them a gold legged baroque table with a porcelain lamp sat on top, casting a soft welcoming light, surrounded by champagne flutes ready to be filled for any potential client. He remembered the abundance of people leisurely roaming around as if they had all the time in the world, all with that same cerebral expression, studying each picture with a reverent smile, talking in words similar to Remi Cochet's tattle. He looked to the corner where he had sat on a comfortable leather chair, waiting for Valeraine Rousselle. The chair was gone.

No more than twenty paintings hung there now, all lined up in one row, a gaping space between each one.

The young woman stood. "*Hello,*" she said with a friendly smile. "*Please look around if you...*"

"*My name is Norris Kinley. This is Lucile Billet...*"

"*Norris Kinley!*"

"*Yes.*" Norris was taken aback by her reaction. "*Norris Kinley.*"

"*My name is Adalyn Petit.*"

Norris thought. "*Adalyn Petit...The letter.* The copy of the bill," he ended in English.

Adalyn frowned in confusion. "*Sorry Monsieur, I do not...*"

Lucile translated. "*The copy of the bill for The Drowning Mary.*"

"*Ah yes.*"

"*Thank you.*" Is all Norris could think to say.

"Adalyn smiled. "*Did you find out what happened to your father?*"

"*Yes, thanks to your letter we did,*" Norris tried to reply in broken French.

"*Oh, sorry. Does that mean he was the man at Toulon?*"

"*Yes.*" He paused for a second "But not how you think."

Lucile translated, adding. "*It's a long story. Too long to explain now.*" She waited, silence, relieved the conversation had run its course. "*We have come to see Madame Rousselle.*"

Adalyn glanced at her watch. "*Ah yes, of course Mademoiselle Billet. It was you who rang yesterday. Please, follow me.*"

Crystal sat in the small office, on one side of a desk, facing the woman with nothing between them, as if they were doctor and patient.

"My name is Christine Lamy," the young woman said. "I am a Resettlement Operations Officer for the Canadian Government." She paused for a moment, looking at the sheets of paper in Crystal's hand. "Are you happy you have filled out the forms correctly?"

"Yes honey."

"I'm afraid if the forms are incomplete then we will have to return them." The woman waited a second. "I'm sorry to say you will then need to submit entirely new ones if that is the case, then the whole process will start again." She paused, studying Crystal's reaction. "Sorry, but I don't make the rules," she added, which sounded nothing like an apology.

Crystal smiled. The woman politely took the forms and scanned downwards in a measured and unhurried manner, occasionally pausing for a short moment to look up. Crystal thought the doctor and patient had now become teacher and pupil.

"Where are the applicants now?" The young woman asked.

Crystal tilted her head as if in defiance. "Here in France sweetie."

After a short, hard glare. "You know if your application is successful we will have to interview them."

"I guessed that."

"We will also inform the sponsor when this will be scheduled."

By the blunt way she said it Crystal thought the woman was coming to an end. "Okay honey." The whole process felt far too quick, she had been there less than ten minutes. "What now?"

"You..." The woman looked down at the form. "You are Miss Bullion, the sponsor."

"Yes."

"If the application is correctly completed then the forms will be sent to the Resettlement Operations Centre in Ottawa. That is when the process begins. Both portions will be assessed before any refugee can be approved."

"How long will all this take?"

"On average about ten weeks."

"What!"

"We have thirty thousand waiting to be processed Miss Bullion. I'm afraid there is also an acceptance limit of twenty thousand for privately sponsored refugees."

Norris followed Adalyn through to the back of the gallery with

Lucile tailing behind. On the walls he saw several dark squares, where paint hadn't faded, he guessed that was all that remained of where some of the paintings had hung. He imagined the more saleable were put to the front of the gallery, replaced from one at the back once sold. "It has changed a lot since the last time I saw it," he remarked.

Lucile's translation stopped Adalyn in her tracks. "*Madame Rousselle is very old. I am sorry to say the gallery will die with her.*"

Norris held his hand up to stop Lucile from translating.

Adalyn continued. "*For two years she has not put any money back into the gallery.*"

"*What about the artists?*" Norris asked, attempting to speak in French again.

"*You have to attract wealthy clients to attract the best artists Monsieur. Then to attract the best artists you have to attract the richest clients.*"

Lucile explained.

"*Oh,okay,*"said Norris

"*The biggest spenders like to be indulged, pampered like spoilt children. They like to drink the most expensive champagne, eat the best food. Madame Rousselle was unrivaled at that, she knew the art world better than anyone.*"

Lucile translated, speaking quickly.

"*She would get great works of art from the best artists, organise the most lavish exhibitions, she would know who to invite, who was buying at the time. Madame could be very persuasive.*" Adalyn held her chin up as if she was proud to be part of the gallery. "*Madam Rousselle is very famous in the Parisian art world.*"

Adalyn waited while Lucile translated.

"*I was in Marseille when she began to lose interest, I first noticed it when she wasn't replacing paintings, refusing to sponsor exhibitions. That is why the Marseille gallery had to close, like she wanted it to happen. That is when I came here to*

Paris. I thought it would be different. Then I began seeing the same thing happening here. I love my job, I love art, I love the artists...some of them anyway, some clients too I like. I tried to talk to her. I tried to get her friends to talk to her, everyone that loved her tried to talk to her..."

Lucile interrupted with a fake cough, having to repeat Adalyn's words for Norris.

"*If the paintings you see here are not sold soon, they will be offered back to the artist. The gallery will close in one month.*"

Norris decided there was no time to waste. "Did Madame Rousselle ever mention Madame Pompidou?" he asked.

Lucile translated.

"*No, not to me.*" Adalyn said through a confused chuckle.

"*Maybe she visited the gallery?*" Norris asked, speaking in French this time.

Adalyn shook her head.

"*Did she ever mention anyone called Marcantoni?*" Lucile asked. "*Francois Marcantoni.*"

Adalyn frowned, then shook her head again.

"*What about Markovic?*"

"*Who?*"

"*Stevan Markovic?*"

"*No Mademoiselle. Like I said I arrived here in Paris from Marseille.*"

For several seconds the three stood in awkward silence.

"*The Madame is expecting you,*" Adalyn announced.

Crystal didn't know why she said what she was about to say. "I am a lawyer with Amnesty International." As soon as the words left her mouth she realised it sounded more like a threat than a plea for help.

Christine Lamy remained cool, her words calculated, she had heard it all before, although the actual words were new. "And how does that affect the application Miss Bullion?"

“I am sorry honey but these children have been through a war and have lost their entire family. They are both severely traumatised. To refuse them would be...”

Christine Lamy interrupted. “A Canadian migration officer will interview the refugees to check if they meet the eligibility criteria for resettlement. They will consider then if they have any special medical needs. Only then...”

Crystal interrupted the young woman again, raising her voice. “They have been living in a refugee camp for the past six years. Do you know what that is like?”

“I can assure you Miss Bullion the Canadian Government are not monsters, the asylum program works to provide protection for refugees, especially if they are in fear of persecution.”

Crystal continued. “The boy is in desperate need of expert help. Both will be coming to live with me in British Columbia. I can’t see the prob...” Crystal stopped mid-sentence, somehow it felt like they were holding two separate conversations.

The young woman softened her voice. “I wish there was more I can do, but we have our procedures. Your application will be put into the system,” she paused for a few seconds. “It will take its own course.”

“*The Madame is expecting you*,” Adalyn repeated as she pulled a door open, then waited while Lucile and Norris passed her, watching them disappear up the stairway.

The staircase was narrow with a long wooden bannister and stark white walls, the only light came from a single bulb covered by an oval-shaped paper shade hovering above their heads like a ghost. It all looked as though it had been built as an afterthought, like a secret passage only the chosen few knew about.

Norris tried to remember how he had entered her apartment two years ago — he knew it wasn’t this way. He recalled being led outside by a Frenchman, entering the apartment through a door in the street, between the gallery and the Chinese restaurant, then taken up two flights of stairs to the second floor: he even remembered his name, Louis Legay. He tried to think back to a few minutes ago, when he was approaching the gallery, he couldn't say for certain but he was sure the door wasn't there.

Lucile reached the top and stopped on the tiny landing, she stared back at Norris, even with him standing one step below their gaze still met eye to eye, only centimetres apart. Lucile turned and tapped lightly on the door.

"It is open." The words muffled.

Lucile turned the handle and stepped in. The hallway was square, also plain white like the staircase, with five doors set in the walls, four were closed, one open.

"In here Monsieur."

Norris led the way through the open door. If there was a room in contrast to Madam Veronique's then this was it. Even the sun that streamed through the windows appeared to do nothing to warm the place. The furniture looked as if it was from the seventies, a tall nondescript book cabinet, a glass topped coffee table ringed with coffee cup stains. Pushed up against the walls were two brown leather sofas covered with grey throws and a stack of randomly scattered cushions. A box television sat on a smaller table. What surprised Norris were the walls, they were bare, not a single painting, strange for an art gallery he thought. He felt they could only be like that on purpose. He spotted an easel in the corner of the room, unused, its wood pristine, clamped onto it was a virgin white canvas, maybe it was a work of art in itself.

"I am sorry I could not greet you in the gallery, I only go down there when I have to these days," she said, noticing Norris looking around. "It once belonged to the gallery Monsieur Kinley. It was where I could talk to guests in private." She paused for a second. "I live in it now."

Not only was the room in complete contrast to the

sumptuous surroundings of her sister's apartment, Valeraine Rousselle herself was also at the other end of the scale. Where Madam Veronique wore stylish suits and dyed her hair black, hiding behind that mask of thick make-up, Valeraine was at the other extreme, her hair was white, like it had already passed through the grey stage, untainted by chemicals; and although thinned with age it still cascaded down her back. When she spoke, the lines mapping her face moved naturally with every word, with every smile. She wore dark slacks and an oversized man's shirt with the sleeves rolled up to just below her elbow: her skin was like tissue paper, a grey veneer over bones. Norris thought she had aged a great deal over the past two years.

Valeraine looked across at Lucile. "*You are Lucile Billet?*"

"*Yes Madame.*"

She spoke in English. "You are a reporter and you want to write about my family." Her words cracking through a strong accent, even so her diction was clear, carrying a sure and confident flow, like she was used to speaking to people in other languages.

As she spoke, Norris tried to detect some resemblance to her sister, some mannerism, he even tried to imagine what Madam Veronique looked like under all that make-up and hair dye. He remembered the photograph taken when they were both young women, how they looked like two peas in a pod. Time changes people he thought.

"*Yes Madame, I work freelance.*" Lucile's answer spoken as though her mind was elsewhere.

"You have already spoken to Susanne."

"*Yes Madame.*" Lucile couldn't wait. "*Would you mind if I used your toilet.*"

Crystal was a lawyer, who achieved a First from The University of British Columbia. She was not one to give up. If anyone could, then she would find a way to persuade this young woman to speed up the resettlement process. "These are just children, they have lost their entire family, both have been traumatised by years of hardship. If the Canadian Government has any modicum of compassion they would find a way to help them now," Crystal announced, like she was pleading her case in a court of law.

Christine Lamy held a long glare on Crystal, but it wasn't hard or indignant, if anything it looked sympathetic. "What we can do straight away is check the sponsorship portion of the form. If the sponsor form is acceptable then we can proceed to the next stage."

"Thank you."

"And you say you are acting on behalf of Amnesty International."

"No sweetie, I never said that. I am an employee of Amnesty International. This is a private sponsorship, I will be sponsoring them myself."

"We will need to speak to your employer."

"Fine," Crystal answered, realising how flippant it sounded.

"Okay." Christine Lamy said, greatly protracting the first letter. "The sponsorship forms are usually straight forward, although I have to warn you that if we do find some discrepancy then they may be temporarily withdrawn or in some cases completely refused altogether. If it is all acceptable then we will look at the refugee portion, if that passes the eligibility criteria then the decision will be made to continue with the application. We will inform the refugee and the sponsor of the decision at the same time." Sounding as if she was reciting from a script. She looked down and studied both forms. "You have the same address...care of Teresa Flores in Marseille."

"Yes. We are moving around a lot at the moment, you can contact me on my cell phone." She needed to change the subject. "And what happens if the refugee form is refused? They are just children. If they are..."

"Have they been convicted of any serious crimes?"

Jamia had shot a man, but was never convicted of it. "No," Crystal replied.

"Have they had an application refused in the past."

"No honey they have not."

"Then they will not get an immediate refusal."

"Good. What happens after?"

"We will have to confirm their identity. Where they lived."

"They lived in a refugee camp."

"Before."

Crystal remembered Djamel telling her they lived in a small village called Tnyere. "How do you do that?"

"We collect biometric details, DNA samples if necessary, fingerprints, send digital images of the applicants, you know, anything that can identify them. We have to make sure they are who they say they are. You'll be surprised..."

"They have travel documents."

Christine Lamy's voice rose in anticipation. "Passports?"

"They are refugee travel documents."

"When were they issued?"

"About a week ago."

"Who applied for them?"

"Teresa Flores."

"The woman in Marseille?"

"Yes."

"The same woman you are staying with?"

"Yes."

Christine Lamy thought for a while. "The people in Quebec may need something else."

Crystal sighed. "What if they can't prove who they say they are?"

"We may have to send it to...You say they are Chadian citizens?"

Crystal didn't answer immediately. "Yes." she finally said, fearful of the young woman's next words.

"Then we may have to send their names and details to the

Chadian authorities, confirm their citizenship."

"And what if it is the Chadian authorities who they are running from?"

Another long and searching glare. "Don't worry. After the refugee form has been accepted we will schedule an interview with the refugees themselves, find out who their enemies are. If they are in fear of persecution then the officer will decide the degree of protection that is needed; and if that is not informing certain bodies, then that will be taken into consideration. Our officers are very skilled in finding the truth, if they are who they say they are and they have a legitimate case for applying for refugee status in Canada, they will pass the eligibility criteria. The Government call it admissibility screening." Christine Lamy struggled to smile. "They do like their word play...Anyway, I am afraid it has to be done." She looked directly at Crystal, trying to read her thoughts. "Is there a problem?"

"No...Sorry honey. I know they came from a remote village. I believe it was destroyed in the war. It would be..."

"You said they were in a refugee camp for six years."

"Yes."

"They would have been registered as refugees at the camp."

Crystal had underestimated Christine Lamy. "Maybe."

"But you were manager at...what was the camp's name?"

"Breidjing."

"You were the manager at Breidjing Refugee Camp?"

"Yes."

"Strange job for a lawyer working for Amnesty."

"What has that got to do with anything?"

"You are a sponsor Miss Bullion, everything has to do with everything."

A short pause. "I sort of fell into the job, plugging a gap so to speak sweetie. It was only temporary."

"The applicants would have been registered though?"

Crystal was trying to avoid revealing their identity. "Not

all get registered."

"But as manager you would have known, I mean if you were prepared to sponsor them. You are an intelligent woman Miss Bullion, a human rights lawyer, surely you would have known their refugee documents would have been useful for an application."

Crystal remained quiet.

"Don't worry, one of our officers can apply for them."

"Would it hold up the application process?"

"That is not my decision Miss Bullion."

Crystal had to think fast."I'll get them for you."

"Thank you." Christine Lamy said as if it was no surprise, like she knew Crystal had them all along.

"You know that Jamia and Ali were some of the first to arrive at the camp?" The calmness of her words gave no indication of what was about to follow.

Christine Lamy pulled her lips.

Crystal took a deep breath. "Well sweetie. At that time their priority was to find food and dodge bullets, try not to get dysentery or malaria." She lightened her voice, like she was about to tell a joke, but the words were far from it. "Do you know that when you get cholera you end up shitting and vomiting yourself to death? Imagine that honey, sixty toilets for thirty thousand people, sixty toilets full of shit and vomit." Her eyes pierced into the young woman. "Then the rains would come. That is when a sheet of canvas and old aid sacks would be sold for...well honey, whatever they had to give at the time. Worse still was when the aid trucks couldn't get through, vehicles would be attacked by rebels and food became even scarcer. Then everything becomes edible, and I mean everything. Roots and berries that were normally unpalatable, animals you wouldn't contemplate eating. They would have eaten grass, dug in termite mounds, food they were taught was poisonous would seem irresistible. But that's okay sweetie because after a time they wouldn't be able tell whether their stomach was empty or full. And then there are the girls, those pretty young innocent girls, just like Jamia. Every time they went out alone they would be in constant fear of being raped. That was the reason why I was sent there in the first place, to find out about the abuse. Do you know after a while I thought I wouldn't be able to find a girl that hadn't been abused one way or another." Crystal leant forward. "So Mademoiselle Lamy, do you think filling out refugee registration forms was the first thing on their minds."

Although Valeraine Rousselle told her the bathroom was the first door on the right, Lucile had deliberately opened the second door. It was strange though, because that actually was the bathroom. Confused, she swung left and opened the door next to it. Immediately in front of her were a large pile of brown cardboard boxes, all stacked up on top of each other, lots of them, the ones underneath collapsing under the weight and spilling sheets of paper over the floor. On the far wall was a desk with one of those old box like monitors sat on top, along with a toppled table lamp. Underneath, a computer lay with its cover off, its dusty guts open to the world, an office chair skulking alone in the other corner. Lucile knew the room was the wrong shape for it to be the one in the Markovic photos. She stepped to the left and opened the fourth door. It was a kitchen, long and narrow, lots of blues and greens, everything was over to the left, leaving the opposite wall bare. There was a sink, a two ringed cooker, a microwave, all sitting on a formica worktop with a curtain hiding what was underneath it. The light streamed in through a small window at the far end. Lucile shut that door and moved to the next, already knowing what was behind it, the staircase. There was only one door remaining, the one Valeraine Rousselle originally said was the bathroom. Lucile pushed it open.

For a second she froze in amazement. There it was, like seeing one of the wonders of the world for the first time. This was the same room as in the Markovic photographs, for Lucile there was no doubt, She stepped inside, becoming aware that she was now standing in the room from the most notorious photographs in French political history, excited that she was one of only a few people who knew it, maybe just one of four. Lucile took in a deep gulp of air, for some strange reason she was expecting it to taste of conspiracy or sex, or at least of something — there was nothing. To this day it had remained a bedroom. A bed was to her left, different to the one seen in the photos, this one had a plain wooden headboard and sturdy legs, not the wrought iron one as in the pictures. In the far corner stood a tall wardrobe, white with gold handles, again, not seen in the photos. A large window was behind the bed, two green curtains pulled open, one rippled from an open window, allowing sunlight to flood the room. But what eventually confirmed it for Lucile was the piece of furniture opposite, this was all Lucile needed to rid her of any tiny doubt she might have. It was the kidney shaped dressing table with the triptych mirror, still with the same glass top and ornate gold handles on the drawers, the same ones as on the wardrobe. Her eyes had become wide, staring at it like she had discovered some ancient artifact. She tried to imagine The Drowning Mary reflected in the mirror. Lucile took out her phone and began taking photographs, stopping when she realised it was from the wrong place. She had to think quickly, if the dressing table was in the same place, which she believed it was, then the original pictures must have been taken where the window was. She swiftly rounded the back of the bed and stood in front of it. She stared down at her phone, the dressing table was at the wrong angle, it would be impossible to see what was reflected in the mirror from where she was. Lucile moved to the corner of the room, this was the place, wondering if it was inside the wardrobe where the camera was hidden, or made to look hidden. She took more photos, checking the images again, thinking the Markovic photos were taken from a slightly higher position. She stretched her arms up just above her head and took a few more. One last look, she tried to visualise where The Drowning Mary would have hung, the top of the headboard was visible in the mirror, she stepped out into the room and looked at the empty space above it. Just like all the other rooms, the walls were bare.

Lucile returned to Valeraine and Norris.

"I am sorry Mademoiselle Billet. I have just realised, I told you wrong, it was the second door." Valeraine said. For the first time Norris had recognised some of Madam Veronique in Valeraine Rousselle, like she had told her the wrong room on purpose.

Crystal sat back in her seat and started to speak softly, she was now the teacher speaking to her pupil. "Do you know refugees are people who are forced to flee their country?" She raised her eyebrows. That was it, that was all she wanted to say, expecting Christine Lamy to read between the lines. A sharp nod. "That is what refugees are Miss Lamy."

"I..." Before the young woman even began she was interrupted.

"Then you know that these two children were forced to flee their country because they are refugees." She held her gaze on the woman opposite her. "And no lack of registration documents or proof of identity can force them to return."

"Tell me what is special about these two children Miss Bullion, there must be thousands in Breidjing camp in need of resettlement?"

Crystal thought this was the first time Christine Lamy had strayed from the usual text. How could she tell her that Jamia had shot a man, a Frenchman, an ex-officer in the French Foreign Legion? "Because two are better than none and I promised I would help them, I am certainly not going to break that trust now...If you wish to know the truth, it is because their father was a rebel commander, his gang fought against the Chadian government trying to protect his village, to stop his people from being murdered and raped. Ali has already been tortured, Jamia was accused of being connected with that same rebel group. If they are returned or if their location becomes known then their lives will be in great danger. Do you know they still have the death penalty in Chad?" Crystal stopped and waited.

Christine Lamy gazed down to the floor. "When we start processing the refugee portion we will schedule an interview with the refugee." It was like she hadn't heard a word Crystal had said. She looked up. "You can accompany them but you cannot be present during the interview."

Crystal felt she had wasted her breath. "Jamia only speaks Tama and Arabic. Ali is too traumatised to speak at all," She said wearily.

"We have officers who speak Arabic, we also have translators, child psychologists. They will not be the first we have interviewed who have been traumatised by war. Like you said so eloquently Miss Bullion, there is a reason why they have been forced from their own country." Christine Lamy took in a long breath. "If we approve the refugee for resettlement we will issue a visa. If we refuse the refugee, we send a letter to both the refugee and the sponsor with an explanation." Christine Lamy stood up, opened a filing cabinet drawer and pulled out two clean forms. "Let us do this properly, no mistakes this time."

Valeraine Rousselle took in a deep breath. "So Mademoiselle Billet, shall I confess all?"

An excitement shot through Lucile, she thought the old woman was genuinely wanting to reveal everything, that she was finally going to divulge all her secrets: until she saw the sarcasm in her smile, the mischievous glint in her eyes. Lucile played along. "Please Madame Rousselle, please do," she replied, returning an equally roguish smile.

Valeraine leant forward, huddled low in her chair, she

looked at Norris, then Lucile. "Are you lovers?"

"We are..."

"We are working together," Lucile interrupted before Norris could finish. She looked down at the old woman's hand. "I believe you were once married?"

Valeraine Rouselle's gaze returned to Norris. "Are you a journalist Monsieur Kinley?"

He thought for a moment. "Just a minder," he declared through a slight grin.

"I am sorry but I do not understand this word minder."

"I make sure Mademoiselle Billet stays out of trouble."

"*Ah yes.*" As if she sympathised. The old woman turned her attention back to Lucile. "Yes, I was married once. It was a long time ago."

"Is he still..."

Valeraine interrupted her. "Monsieur Kinley tells me you have spoken to my sister."

Lucile shot Norris a hard stare. "When?" she asked.

"While you were visiting the bathroom." The old woman said it like it was obvious.

Lucile was curious, had they talked about anything else while she was out of the room. "We have spoken to Susanne, yes," she admitted, then wondered if she knew of her sister's professional name. "Have you spoken to your sister?"

"Susanne was always the clever one, always the one with the wittiest answer. She could talk to anyone about anything. She got the highest marks at school, there was nothing she wasn't good at. All the other girls at school wanted to be friends with her. Do you know she could speak four languages by the age of eleven? When she grew up I thought she would make something of her life. All I was good at was art." She grinned — or was it a smirk. "Susanne became a dancer, all those brains and she became a dancer. Even then I think she knew."

"What do you mean she knew?"

"I think you already know the answer to that Mademoiselle

Billet."

"It would be better in your own words."

"I believe it would be better in my sisters own words."

"You didn't answer my question Madame, have you spoken to your sister?"

"No Mademoiselle, I haven't."

Lucile saw Norris looking at her, also knowing why. "When did you receive The Drowning Mary?" she said, just like that.

"Ah, The Drowning Mary." as if she had been waiting. "We had an inclusive deal with the artist, all his works would be given to Remi Cochet. How he got them I do not know. I never met Francois Degarmo personally."

"But the Paris gallery kept it for a while?" Norris asked.

"I asked Remi for it. I asked him to send two Degarmo works up here."

"And The Drowning Mary was one of them?"

"Yes, The Foundering of Death was the other. Strangely beautiful. You should see it."

"I have," replied Norris, although he would have described it as strange rather than beautiful. "I believe it is in the Pompidou Centre now."

"*Yes Monsieur.*"

"Who bought it?" asked Lucile.

"Mademoiselle Billet, you know I could never divulge my clientele."

Lucile remembered Remi saying those exact same words. "It was Madame Pompidou herself, wasn't it."

"If you say so Mademoiselle."

The more she spoke the more Lucile and Norris could see her sister in her. The answers were calculated, calm, as if she had nothing to hide. Exactly like Madam Veronique.

"So what happened to The Drowning Mary?" Lucile asked.

"I was surprised we didn't sell it. After the Pompidou Centre bought The Foundering of Death I thought it would have been snapped up. So I sent it back down to Remi. I thought you knew all this. Why all this interest in one painting?"

Lucile glanced towards Norris. It was then she realised he hadn't told the old woman what happened to his father — or Matthieu. "What happened to it while it was here?"

"It was a long time ago. I can only guess we hung it in the gallery. Like I said, it was a very long time ago, I have had many paintings here Mademoiselle. If we cannot sell them after a period of time we offer them back to the artist, some we may keep in storage, bring them out again when that artist is back in vogue. Remi Cochet would have made that decision after we returned it to Marseille. I thought you wanted to write about my..."

"Do you know how long it was here in Paris?" Norris asked, his tone soft, sympathetic.

"I cannot remember."

"Would you have had it hanging somewhere else in the apartment?" Lucile asked, feeling she was getting within touching distance.

Valeraine looked around at the bare walls, as though that was answer enough. "The gallery downstairs was for the paintings. Upstairs, Antoine...

Lucile interrupted."Antoine?"

"Yes, my husband at the time. He insisted that only his paintings hung in our apartment."

"What about this floor."

"This floor belonged to the gallery. It was where the staff could make coffee and use the bathroom, where I had the office. In this room we would entertain..."

"Entertain?!"

"Yes." Valeraine replied, appearing not to notice Lucile's eagerness. "Where we could discuss a potential sale in private, maybe over a bottle of champagne...or two"

"And the bedroom? I saw a room with a bed when I was looking for the bathroom."

"*Ah yes, the bedroom.* The bedroom was for friends, artists, sometimes a client would stay. Now I use it. Are these questions relevant to my family?"

"No, sorry, of course not. It's just the journalist in me. Snooping where I shouldn't."

Valeraine sunk back into her chair. "So where would you like me to start Mademoiselle Billet?"

Lucile wanted to say... 'Firstly you can tell me why you were in the Markovic photographs, why the bedroom in those pictures happened to be the room next to this one?'... "Tell me what you remember about the war," she said.

The answer was immediate. "Everything, I remember everything, every small detail. When you lose a mother and father you never forget."

"You were living in Marseille?" Norris asked.

"I was born in the house we were living in at the time. It was on Rue Sainte-Ascelina." She held a long gaze on Norris. "*Yes Monsieur*, the same one my sister is living in now, but I think you already know that." She waited for a reaction, none came. "I was a young girl when the war started, fourteen years old, an age when I thought I knew it all, I think all children of that age do. How wrong could I be, I soon discovered I knew nothing. Susanne was three years younger than me." Maybe it was the slight pause, hardly noticeable, but both Lucile and Norris knew why it was there. "An innocent young girl at that time." A sharp breath of air confirmed it. "My father had a workshop on the ground floor where he made trophies, he used to joke that he made the best in France, that he was famous amongst trophy makers, that people used to come from all over the world just to see him at work. My father was always joking with us. We were surrounded by all kinds of businesses. I remember Mr Nachman who lived opposite us, a kind old man who sold books, he was one of the first to go. Next to him were Mr and Mrs Clouatre, they were jewellers, I always used to think they thought they were better than us, they always looked down on Susanne and myself, Papa was friendly with them though, I think it was because they gave him a lot of work. They went not long after Mr Nachman." Her gaze fell onto empty space. "And my Maman, I believe all she wanted in life was to love and be loved. To see her two daughters become women, find good husbands, to grow old surrounded by lots of grandchildren. She always made sure we had the best of everything, food, clothes, education, everything. She used to tell us, 'Why walk in the gutter when with one small step you can walk on the pavement."

"Sorry Madame, I can't help but notice your English is very good," remarked Norris

"We had an English nanny for five years when we were in Marseille. Maman was finding it difficult after Susanne was born. She was young, in her twenties, to be honest I can't really remember much about her: she was very strict, I remember that. How do you say? Regimented, everything had to be done at the exact time. Some of my clients were English, they like to speak in their own language."

"Yes," Norris agreed, thinking they probably had no choice.

"You see Monsieur, I have never played with dolls or drawn trees with pink leaves or run around wearing fairy wings. To her we were just little adults and had to act as such. Papa told her that she must only speak English to us at all times, he knew that would be the quickest way for us to learn. So Susanne and myself were brought up with both French and English. I was fluent in a year." The old woman stopped talking.

"What happened to her?" asked Norris.

Valeraine shrugged. "I remember her leaving a few years before the war." She puffed out another breath of air. "I suppose that was one good thing about it. I think she must have returned to England. Then we were taught English at school. After that we listened to the BBC on the radio, until it was mostly about the rise of Hitler, that was when Maman stopped us listening."

"Tell me about the war," Lucile said, this time she left the notepad in her bag and just listened.

"The war changed everything. Everything my Father and Mother had worked for was taken away, leaving us nothing. I think that was what hurt my mother the most, that we were never given them back, even when they could have been. Even our house was stolen from us; and the authorities did nothing to help." Valeraine paused for a moment, her eyes flicking from Lucile to Norris, like she was going to say something, but didn't. "Marseille was in the *zone libre*, the free zone, it was run by the Vichy regime. The Minister and the Chief of Police were both puppets of the Nazis. All you need is a common enemy to unite an entire city. But it is not the fascists I am talking about, it was not the Nazis that were the enemy." Madam Rousselle placed a hand high up on her chest, gently patting herself. "We were the enemy, it was us, my father, my mother, Susanne and myself, all the Jews of Marseille, we were the common enemy. At first it wasn't too bad, I think my father must have bribed a few officials, hoping it would soon blow over. Then stories of what was happening to Jews in other countries began to trickle through, creep into our conversations. Firstly about Jews being moved into ghettos where they were given very little food or water. Families crammed into tiny apartments. We heard many were dying of disease and starvation. Then they would be taken to camps." Her eyes glassed over. "I need not tell either of you what it meant for the poor souls who were taken there. Then it came to Marseille, we had heard of friends taken from their homes and forced to live in the old port. My best friend at the time was Denise, her father was an important official in the synagogue. She had overheard him talking to her mother. He was saying a boy had escaped from a truck and hid in a forest. The boy told stories of how German and Polish Jews were being rounded up and taken to pits where they would be shot. Denise said her father was weeping as he was telling her mother. He said the pit became full of bodies screaming and crying, the boy even saw a mother with a baby laying in the pit, alive, slowly being buried. I remember it well because Denise also began crying as she told me. At first I thought she was play-acting, just to scare me, then she pleaded with me to believe it, that it was the truth. I began arguing with her, saying that they were just rumours. I couldn't believe another human could be so evil. How could people do that to others? I mean fellow countrymen, whatever their religion, we are still human, is that not more important. Then my father began going out late in the evenings. My father never went out, he would never leave us alone. My mother never said why, not to me or Susanne, even when we asked. That was when I knew something was wrong. Then one evening I saw him return, he must have thought I was asleep, but I saw him from the top of the stairs: he was dressed in dark clothing and was breathing heavily, as if he had been running, he looked scared. I heard him tell my mother that the soldiers were so drunk they didn't even feel it, that he and his comrades could pick them off one by one, as easy as plucking feathers from a chicken he told her. I remember my mother didn't even look shocked, she just helped him off with his coat, telling him she would make him something to eat. Then a week later I saw him pull a long gun out from under his coat, he looked dirty, especially his face, like he had been out of the city. My mother took the weapon from him and disappeared into the workshop, returning empty handed. It was about that time my father had also lost his sense of humour, he began to grow distant from us, turning inward. This is when I knew." Valeraine stopped talking.

For a moment Lucile and Norris remained silent, waiting for the old woman to continue. "*Knew what Madame?*" Lucile finally asked.

"We knew our lives were about to change forever, that terrible times were to follow, I knew the forces of evil were coming. We were made to wear yellow stars on our coats so people could identify us as Jews. They began to stare, horrible stares, like a bad smell had crept under their noses, like we had done something terrible, when we had done nothing. After a while I began to think I had done something, something awful. How could so many people be wrong? My Maman said it wasn't us that were evil, it was them, that me and my sister were too young to have done anything bad. As the days passed, friends went missing, more and more chairs were becoming empty in our classroom." She took a deep breath. "Then one morning Denise wasn't sat on the wall where we would meet before walking to school, I can picture her face now, that beaming smile when she saw me coming." The old woman's eyes stared into empty space. "I can even see it now, seventy years later." She then looked at Norris, her gaze hanging on him. "As clear as I can see you Monsieur. Denise also had a sister, much younger than herself, I think she was about three or four at the time, lovely little thing she was, beautiful hair with flowing golden locks." She paused for a second and slowly shook her head. "I can't remember her name." It looked as though she was fighting back a tear. "It was over a week later when I went around to Denise's house to see if there was any news of her. Two men were carrying out something on an old door, like they were using it as a makeshift stretcher. I could see there was a tiny body under a blanket. I asked one of the men who it was, he told me it was the little girl who lived there. They said they had found her body under a bed, that her mother must have hidden her there. She must have been waiting for her family to return, only they never did. The man told me she had died from starvation...or a broken heart." Valeraine took a deep breath. "When I asked him about the rest of the family he said he didn't know, that they were probably taken to one of the camps." She paused, lowering her eyes. "I never saw Denise again. It was not long after that my father sat us all down in the drawing room; I had never seen him so sad, like a dark cloud was hovering over him. It was the 17th of December 1942, I will never forget that date. He told us we had to go away, that it was far too dangerous for us to stay in Marseille. But it was what he said next, I felt like his hand had plunged into my chest and ripped out my heart. He told us he was going to stay, that he needed to protect our house. I remember he told us that all this fighting was just nonsense and it would be over in a few months, that we would be able to come back and start from where we left off. But I knew the world had gone mad. He told us we were going on a journey and it wouldn't be easy, that some bad men wanted to hurt us if we stayed here, he said that my mother would look after us. I cried for the entire week. All Susanne was concerned about was her rabbit, she insisted she take it with her and threw a tantrum when told she couldn't. My father said he had already spoken to our neighbours and they would look after it; I knew then it would end up in a stew."

"How did you get on with Susanne at the time?" asked Lucile.

"We were never close, even after everything we had been through. Did it draw us closer? I thought she was too young at the time to understand, I was wrong, she understood everything. When you have everything taken away from you, including your childhood, you grow up quickly Mademoiselle."

"And now?" Lucile asked.

"I love my sister." Is all Valeraine said in reply.

"Yes, of course."

The old woman continued. "We left Marseille a week later, I remember the date, it was Christmas Day. We put all our lives into two small suitcases. I wanted to take my best dress, my church shoes, both wholly inappropriate for the journey, especially in winter. In the end it was my mother who chose my clothes, my warmest coat and dresses, many changes of underwear, the fur lined mittens I hated, a hat, a scarf. Now I can look back and realise she probably saved my...our lives. The only item she allowed me to take was my sketchpad and pencil."

"Oh." Lucile's face opened up. "You wouldn't still have it would you?"

Madame Rousselle appeared not to hear. "I drew in it everyday, I drew everything. It was one of the few things that stopped me from going crazy."

"What happened to it?" asked Norris.

"It kept us warm one cold night...along with the pencil."

Norris pulled in his lips.

"It was after the war when I heard the Vichy regime had helped the Nazis round up thousands of Jews in Marseille, sending them to extermination camps. Many were my friends. I found out later Denise was one of them. I found out she was sent to Royallieu-Compiegne Internment Camp from the Old Port, then onto several other camps. I heard she died in Auschwitz." Madame Rousselle rubbed her hands together. "If we had waited another two weeks then I wouldn't be here talking to you. Please put that in your story Mademoiselle."

Lucile remembered Madam Veronique saying something similar. She looked up and saw a tear in Valeraine's eye. "Would you like a rest. I could make you a coffee Madame."

Valeraine replied in French. "*No, I will finish. I am sorry but it is important for me to tell you.*" She took another deep breath. "We were taken to a farmhouse just outside the village of Belcodene. The first thing we did was to tear the yellow stars from our coats and burn them in the kitchen stove. I felt free again. I thought at least staying on a farm we would get decent food. *No!* We were fed garbage and old scraps, leftovers. Food was scarce, even for the farmer and his wife; it was mid-winter. On the day we arrived we were led down to a secret room next to the basement. All it had in it was a mattress and a bucket. I remember it being very cold and damp, everything I touched felt wet, it wasn't even fit for an animal, but that's all we were, animals burrowing underground. We used to huddle up together under mangy old blankets soaked from the damp. Myself and my mother used to lie either side of Susanne, using our bodies to keep her warm. I remember listening to her teeth chattering, feeling her body shivering, at least then I knew she was alive.

Sometimes it was so cold I couldn't sleep, and if I did I thought I would never wake up again. I remember one morning the frost had matted my hair. I was convinced we were going to die there." She took another deep breath, as if she was trying to gain strength from the air. "The room was concealed behind a false wall, an old wooden cabinet had to be pulled back and pushed over a small hole every time we entered or left it. We could hear the farmer sweeping the dirt to cover where the cabinet legs had marked the floor. I thought we would all die behind that hole, that the farmer and his wife would get caught and taken away, and we wouldn't have the strength to push the cabinet away; just three skeletons discovered many years later. For the first few days the farmer used to make us practice crawling into the room, in and out, over and over again. Susanne was always first, then me, Maman last. He used to quietly snap at us, telling us we had to be faster, until we were able to scuttle through like rats, and sometimes I used to think that's all we were, rats in a sewer. Other times we were able to go up into the house itself, if we were lucky we were allowed outside so we could use the toilet and get some exercise. That was when I used to see the old couple at their most nervous, they never smiled or spoke much, even to each other. I think the wife would have been very kind under normal circumstances. We all had lice in our hair, Maman said we would have to cut it all off, right down to the scalp, which sent Susanne crazy. She told me later it wasn't the lice that upset her, but Maman saying she needed to cut all her beautiful hair off. The lice were annoying though. Anyway, the wife took Susanne under her wing and helped us get rid of them with a concoction of plants and bark crushed up with tractor fuel. She rubbed it into our heads and had to keep it there for three days. It worked, even if it did stink. Sometimes when I looked at the farmer and his wife I thought they knew what was coming, that they had already accepted their fate. After the war my mother went back to the farm to thank them. She learnt they had been caught hiding another family, all of them were killed.

She then found out they had been tortured before being strung up in the village square as an example, hung like old carcases. Two weeks after we arrived at the farm a man came to collect us. It was such a relief to see and speak to another human again, especially someone so fresh faced. He was young and thin, quite short, his stature made him look even younger. At first I didn't think he was much older than me, although he told me he was twenty-five, but that is what teenagers do, isn't it, lie about their age, I did. He carried a large backpack, so tightly packed it was near breaking point. He had a rifle pushed through one of the straps and a bullet holster under his jacket. But it was his humour I remember best, trying to make us laugh all the time with his stupid jokes. Susanne always found them funny. Not me though, I don't think I laughed once. Maman just placated him with a forced grin that made her look like she was about to cry. He told me his name was Francois. That was all he said at the time, just Francois."

Lucile used all her willpower to remain silent.

"When the sun went down he led us away from the farm. I was not sorry to leave but sad to say goodbye to the farmer and his wife. They were good people. Sometimes we travelled in the day, always staying under the cover of trees, sometimes at night. I soon found out what was in the backpack: two large sheets of canvas so we could fashion a tent using branches, the four of us huddled together to keep the cold out. Francois was always next to me." The old woman looked at Lucile. "I suppose you could say he was the first boy I had slept with. Occasionally we would find a derelict building to sleep in, or a hayloft, he always seemed to know where they were. I had learnt to take catnaps, even if it was for only a few minutes, I was always tired, always hungry. Francois used to leave us sometimes, hidden away, building a small fire to keep us warm, then he would disappear. We must have looked quite a sight on our own, like three witches we would huddle around a fire in the middle of the woods or in a shallow cave. Francois would return with food, usually milk and cheese, one time he came back with a shoulder of ham. I think he must have known a lot of people or he was an expert thief. I remember he always took his gun with him. Maman tried to keep up standards, cleaning our teeth using the spit on a finger, always combing our hair, although I think that was more to keep the lice away. Sometimes when we came to a stream she would make us strip naked and wash, always making Francois turn the other way. I kept a close eye on him, seeing if he would steal a quick glance, he never did, not once." An impish grin came to Valeraine's face. "Although I think I would have liked him to. Susanne always wondered why I took a long time washing, especially since the water was freezing. It woke me up though. We always remained close to the country roads, staying on the other side of the hedgerow or in the trees. Sometimes we had no choice but to walk on the tracks. Francois said he had a sixth sense, he would know if someone was close by. We were still in Vichy France so there were a lot less German soldiers than in the north. A couple of times a convoy passed us on the road, always appearing to be in a hurry. Francois said they were in a rush to get to the south coast, he had heard the allies were having great victories in North Africa. We also had a lot of luck. At one time when we were in a country lane, we were stopped by a policeman on a bicycle. Francois said his sixth sense appeared to have let him down that time, that was the trouble with bicycles he told us, you couldn't hear them. He had taken the policeman out of earshot and had a quiet word with him. I thought he must have been a sympathiser or Francois had bribed him or something because he let us continue. It was later Francois told us he told the policeman that when the Germans are defeated, which they will be, he would be the first person he would come looking for if he told anyone about us. I think Francois could be quite scary when he wanted to be. Another time when we were crossing a field of cabbages, he suddenly shouted for us to drop. I remember Francois got up slowly, his rifle pointing at someone in the distance. I think it must have been the farmer, he had his arms in the air. We continued on into the woods." Another playful grin came to the old woman's face. "There was one cabbage in that field that had a bite size chunk out of it."

"I didn't know cabbage grew in winter," Lucile remarked.

"Neither did I Mademoiselle Billet. Maybe it was divine intervention." The old woman blew out a sarcastic breath. "What is good belongs to God and what is bad belongs to the Devil." She looked at Lucile, then Norris. "That is far too convenient isn't it Monsieur."

Norris raised his hands. "You're speaking to an atheist Madame Rousselle."

"Then we are of the same mind."

"But you are Jewish," said Lucile.

"I was born into a Jewish family, yes, that is true. But just because my parents are Jews that does not make me one, I will not be labelled like that. I am not my mother or my father."

Lucile was taken back by the forceful way in which she said it.

"What if I was born a Muslim or Catholic, a Hindu, maybe a Buddhist, I wouldn't be Jewish but I would still be me. We have no choice what religion we are indoctrinated into. Then to have others attack me for something I had no choice in. What if Hitler said he was a prophet? What if he said he had spoken to God? Would the German people have believed him? That is what you have to ask yourself. It is all far too convenient. I just know you don't have to be religious to know what is right and what is good, what is wrong and what is bad. Neither will religion stop you from doing either." Valeraine sat forward in her chair, staring at Lucile. "Now I don't have to answer to God Mademoiselle. I only have to answer to myself."

"And do you answer to yourself?" Lucile asked. " Isn't that also far too convenient.

The old woman thought for a moment. "If you expect

anything then the only person that suffers is yourself. Believe me Mademoiselle I know. Now I expect nothing. Now I am not disappointed."

"And then?" asked Norris.

"Many times I used to ask myself why God had abandoned us. Now I know Monsieur, it was because he was never there."

A short silence followed.

Norris spoke first. "Please go on Madame, you were trying to get to Switzerland."

"We managed to get to a small fishing village called Nernier, it is on Lake Geneva. Francois said we had to stay outsidc and hid us in some trees beside the bank. The sun was beginning to fall below the horizon, I remember the yellow light sparkling on the water, I remember thinking it looked like liquid gold. There was a silhouette of a chateau sitting high on a rock out in the lake as if it was floating on the water. It was strange because I felt at peace there, I thought this would be a nice place to die. I was thinking about death all the time in those days, even more than I do now. I also remember thinking those awful midges would kill me before the Gestapo did. Then Francois left us, saying he would return in a short while. He had done it so many times before, I was always scared when he did. He told us if he didn't come back then one of us would have to go to a village called Yvoire and find a fisherman named Leonard the Ear. When he said the name I thought it was one of his stupid jokes. He didn't laugh though, he always laughed at his own jokes. He also said it would have to be me, that Susanne was too young and she needed to have her mother with her. I think he was testing me, even back then."

"What do you mean even back then?" Lucile asked.

"We were in the middle of escaping a war. Everything was a test back then, I think he was seeing if I could take charge of the situation if anything happened to him." Her glare still hung on Lucile. "He also left the gun, the first time he had. I started to feel really scared then, it was getting dark, I began imagining the trees were soldiers, the branches were their guns. I remember the breeze rustling through the leaves sounded like people whispering, that they were soldiers looking for us. Francois was away for hours. I began to miss him, I thought something had happened. He had been our strength, telling us where to go, when to go, when to eat, what to eat, when to breath, he was our lifeblood Mademoiselle." She looked at Norris. "If he didn't return Monsieur what would have become of us, we were like lost children. I would have to go and find this man with the stupid name. It was then we heard this strange sound." Valeraine's cheeks blew out. "Pop, pop, pop."

Norris thought she was making the sound of a gun firing.

"It was coming from the lake and getting closer. Maman pulled us behind a tree. Then the noise died down until it was just a gurgling sound. The black outline of a small boat appeared, I could see it was only slightly larger than a rowing boat, the front half was covered, a tiny round window in the side, a smoking chimney poked up above it. It was quite close, no more than a couple of metres away. I saw Francois and another man sitting at the rear, the man said something. I think it must have been that he couldn't get any closer because Francois jumped from the boat and into the water, his legs disappeared up to the middle of his thighs. He began wading towards us. I remember feeling so pleased to see him again. He stopped in the water, beckoning for us to go to him. Francois carried Susanne like she was a baby, handing her up to the man. Maman followed them. I was last into the water, my feet getting stuck in the mud, it felt like someone was trying to hold onto me, pull me down. I could see the name of the boat painted on the side, I remember it even to this day, the Azur Olage. Francois helped me through the water, his arm around my waist, his grip strong but gentle at the same time, I didn't want him to let go, but the other man pulled me up. Then Francois said the words I had been dreading ever since we left the farm. He said it was now he would have to leave us. I knew this time would come, I just hoped that it never would. I remember him leaning on the side of the boat, telling us Leonard the Ear would take us halfway across the lake where we would be met by another boat. He told us that once we stepped onto that boat we would be in Switzerland, we would be safe. Saying goodbye to Francois was like leaving my father all over again, without the kiss, although I wanted him to. I also remember the sickness of not having him there, like a knot in the pit of my stomach, we had become so close. Then we set off. At one time Leonard the Ear must have seen me staring at the side of his head, because he leant over until he was only centimetres from my face, I remember his breath, it was horrible, like stale tobacco."

Norris sat back, feeling glad he had given up smoking.

"He said he lost his ear when he was casting his fishing line out into the lake. He told me the hook had ripped it from the side of his head. He said he didn't mind because his ear was such good bait that a few seconds later he caught the biggest fish he had ever done in his life, that it kept him and his family fed for a whole month." Valeraine shook her head slowly. "And I believed him. I was so gullible back then. I don't know exactly how many, but we must have spent several hours on the Azur Olage. Leonard the Ear told us to sit under the cover and keep out of sight; but I sat near the entrance so I could still see out. It wasn't long before the sun had completely sunk below the horizon. The water was so calm and dark, it reminded me of the bowls of indigo ink we used at school, it was strange the things that reminded me of home. When I glanced behind me I saw a line of moonlight rippling on the water, always appearing to be aimed towards us, like it wanted to point us out to any Nazi patrol boat. I remember sitting back and staring up to the night sky, I had never seen so many stars. When we bobbed on a wave it felt as if I was being lifted high up into the sky, as if it wanted me to become a star as well, sparkling like a jewel, like they were all the souls of the dead, and if that happens to me when I die then I have nothing to be afraid of. There were so many of them, more than I could count. It felt as if they were sparkling just for me, as if they were trying to tell me something. Then there was one like none of the others, it was larger, brighter, its sparkle was like a bright flash, two flashes, then it disappeared altogether. I saw Leonard the Ear pick up his torch, flicking the switch on and off in the direction of the light, two short, and one long, the same was returned. He then slowed the engine until the boat was like a piece of deadwood bobbing on the water. Another boat began to emerge out of the darkness, much larger than the Azur Olage, the hull loomed high above us as it drew alongside. There was a shout from above. I remember being told to stretch up my arms, then being hauled onto a wet deck." Valeraine paused for a second, then her voice softened. "The next thing I remember was being gently shook by a huge man with a ginger beard. I must have fallen asleep. With my eyes not yet focused I hadn't seen his finger over his lips. I must have gone to say something because his hand smothered my mouth, the smell of rotting fish filled my nostrils and I could see the remnants of guts and scales smeared on his fingers. I had no idea who he was at the time, I just lived with the hope that every stranger we met would take some sort of pity on us, that they weren't going to hand us over to the Gestapo. I quickly wiped my mouth after he took his hand away and threw myself into Maman's arms. Then I realised it wasn't only his hand that stank, the whole place had a horrible stench of engine oil and fish, we all did, even me. I also realised the boat wasn't moving, not even bobbing up and down. I could hear men shouting, their voices mixed with a loud booming sound. Eventually my eyes adjusted. It was odd because we were hidden in a tiny space with walls made of strange baskets, they were even above us, seaweed hanging off them, dripping water onto our heads. Then the noise stopped. A few minutes later another man came to see us, he was older than the first, his face full of deep wrinkles, like his eyes were set inside cracked glass. He was wearing large gum boots and had a kind face. Without saying anything he indicated for us to follow. He led us up a ladder and through a small hatchway onto the deck. I remember it was such a relief to breath in the cold, crisp air again, even if there was still a stink of fish. He kept waving his hand back and forth, like it wanted to pull us along without touching us. We followed him over a short plank and back onto firm land. It felt like ages since I had stepped on something that wasn't moving under my feet. We just blindly followed him towards a small truck parked on the quay. Again our lives were placed in the hands of a complete stranger, and if it meant climbing into the back of a van to be taken away and shot by the Gestapo, then we did it without protest. But we had little choice, I mean friends you can pick, can't you Monsieur, Mademoiselle? Families, they are there, part of you, they have your blood in their veins; but strangers that appear out of the darkness, for them you can only have trust. The driver was the huge man with the ginger beard, the older man sat in the passenger seat. As the vehicle drove away he pulled out three envelopes from under his seat. He turned around and handed them over to Maman, she pulled out a sheet from one, it looked like it could disintegrate in her hands. He told us they were Refugee Registration papers, that they were drawn up by a very skillful Catholic priest who wanted to help Jews. He said they were issued in Geneva and the date was July 1938, that is why they looked so old. 'Four years,' he said with a smile as if he had just done the arithmetic. He said it was because the Swiss Government had made a deal with Hitler; if we stopped accepting Jews after that date then they wouldn't invade. More importantly we had to keep them with us at all times and if we were caught without them we would be arrested, if lucky, interned...if not, we would be sent back to France, then who knows where. He didn't say the death camps, but I knew what he meant. He told us lots of things, firstly why we were in a van stinking of fish. He said it was called the fish wagon, that they used it to deliver the night's catch to cafes and homes. He told us that we were in Switzerland, that we were safe from the

Nazi's but not from the Swiss police, although many were on our side. I remember he told us that we were not to trust anyone, unless we had been told to do so, most Swiss citizens hated the Germans, but they would also blame us for using up their dwindling supplies. He said we would still have to survive without being able to work for money, although it was possible for us to work for food and shelter. The Jewish Refugee Assistance Organisation had found us somewhere to live with a good Jewish family. He said we would earn our keep by working around the house and garden. I was just relieved it wasn't gutting fish. He told us his name was Lucas and the driver was his son Samuel and that they were Swiss Jews working for the same organisation; that we would stay the night in their house where we could wash, eat and be given a change of clothes. What he said next sent a shudder through me. He said he would put us on a train in the morning, one going to Domdidier. He told us we had our papers and we would be given tickets, that we would have to change trains at Lausanne, then board one to Avenches, get off at the stop before Avenches, a place called Domdidier, from there we could walk to Oleyres. The entire journey would take about five hours, and we would have to do it...alone. If anyone asks you tell them you have been staying with your uncle and cousin at Nyo; but you never got on with us." A smile brushed past Valeraine's lips. "Then he said, you then tell them the truth, that you couldn't stand the stench of fish anymore. You tell them the IF have found you a good family in Oleyres and that is where you are going. After all my concern, Lucas and Samuel were very kind, both worked hard to get us ready for the journey, trying not to make us look like the three Jewish refugees we obviously were. I suppose I should have been thankful, I was going to be sitting on a train, not trudging through muddy forests and cabbage fields. They washed our clothes and hung them above the stove. Then we had a stand-in bath using a saucepan to pour lukewarm water over our heads. I remember splashing each other and laughing.

It was the first time I had seen a bar of soap in ages. Lucas and Samuel left in the fish wagon to do some deliveries. When they returned they fed us on a potato stew mixed with crab and six fried eggs on top with a whole loaf of bread. At least it wasn't fish." The old woman stopped, sounding like she was trying to steady her voice. "Then I cried. I hadn't cried since my Papa told us he was staying in Marseille, not a single tear had left my eyes since then. After everything we had been through it was over something so trivial. Samuel gave myself and Susanne a chocolate drink, the tears just flooded out. In truth I don't think it was the chocolate drink. I think it was everything: his and Lucas's kindness, Leonard the Ear and Francois risking their lives just for us, people we had never met before, the farmer and his wife paying the ultimate sacrifice. We were alive, safe in a country that was not at war. I can remember the surprise on Susanne's face, I mean seeing her older sister like this. Maman had pulled me towards her, cuddling me like a baby until all my tears had been drained away. I had always been the strong one, the one who didn't complain, the one that just got on with it." She looked at Norris "But you can never tell what goes on in people's minds can you Monsieur?"

Norris thought she was trying to tell him something.

"Their kindness didn't stop there either. Lucas allowed Maman to sleep in his bed, with Susanne and myself sharing Samuel's. I remember the sheets, they felt crisp and fresh, I thought I was sleeping in heaven. That is what our lives had become, how the smallest of things could make us feel so grateful. Lucas and Samuel had stayed downstairs. They must have slept on the wooden chairs or stayed up all night, that is how we found them, wide awake, puffing on clay pipes. I remember the thick fog in the room stinging my eyes."

Norris thought about all the cigarettes he had smoked, how he regretted ruining his health; then wondered what a clay pipe was like to smoke.

"In the morning we dressed in clean clothes. Our battered

old suitcases were replaced with one large one, at least it made us look respectable. After breakfast of more fried eggs and bread, Lucas and Samuel drove us to the station, they even allowed Maman to sit at the front with Susanne on her lap. I sat at the back with Lucas. I had the feeling this man and his son had never been apart in their entire lives. I remember thinking that I wanted to stay with my Maman and Papa for the rest of my life. To this day I still wonder what happened to Lucas's wife, Samuel's mother. We never asked and they never told us. It was strange sat in the back of the fish wagon. This man sitting opposite me had done so much for us and I still couldn't talk to him. I remember him asking me questions about what I wanted to do when I grew up? What was my school like? Did I have lots of boys chasing me? It was as if my mind had gone blank, all I could do was answer with a stupid grin and a nod or shake of the head. Lucas just smiled back, just like my Papa would have done. Ten minutes later we had parked outside the railway station and were waiting for the train. It wasn't long before we said our goodbyes and were heading for Lausanne. Samuel had handed us a piece of paper with instructions. I still have it Mademoiselle. I will always have it."

"Maybe I could take a picture of it for the article?" Lucile remarked.

Valeraine replied with a single nod. "Maman, Susanne and myself were now on our own. For the first time we were not relying on the guidance of others. It was strange because I remember feeling naked, as if everyone was staring at us. For a country not at war I was surprised how many soldiers were in our carriage, I remember their metal helmets and grey trench coats, a rifle over their shoulder, it seemed as if half the passengers had a uniform of some kind. We sat in seats facing each other, Susanne with Maman, and me on the other side beside the window, trying our hardest to look like the respectable Swiss French family we obviously were not. I don't think anyone could have guessed what we had been through though. Everyone looked so sad, lost in their own thoughts. I looked at Maman and Susanne, I saw they also had the same expression. A very tall man with a pencil moustache sat down next to me, he was wearing an expensive coat and shiny shoes. I can remember his black leather gloves clutching a book, like his life depended on it, but he didn't look at it though. Then it happened. I think it was only about fifteen minutes into the journey when a train guard entered our carriage, but he wasn't on his own, a man with a stern face and a grey suit was following him. Maman must have seen the look on my face because she glanced around, quickly turning back when she saw them. She became rigid, scared, she pulled out the tickets from her coat and held them tightly, too tightly, I could see the white of her knuckles. Her head remained down, trying to hide the fear in her eyes. She began to make me feel nervous. I tried to take a peep at the man sitting next to me, wondering if he had noticed anything, luckily his eyes had remained forward, like he was looking through her. The guard began walking down the aisle, the man following him, rocking from side to side, using the sides of the seats to balance themselves, checking and clipping the passenger's tickets, completely ignoring the soldiers. Then it was our turn. Maman quickly raised her hand, giving him the three tickets, like she wanted to get this over and done with as quickly as possible. He held one on top of the other and clipped one hole, then handed them back to her. As the guard was about to move away, the man in the suit stopped and glared into Maman's eyes, as if he could detect something was wrong. 'Papers.' he snapped. I can hear the word now, like a gunshot. Maman looked at me, 'papers Maman," I said as cool as you like, Francois would have been proud of me. I then drew mine out of my pocket and was just about to pass it over when the strangest thing happened. A large hand blocked me, it was the man sitting next to me. Then I saw him flick a finger up, as if he was dismissing the man. He didn't look at anyone, his gaze just remained fixed forward the entire time. The man in the suit continued down the aisle as if none of us existed, it was like he had been hypnotised. Even to this day I can't explain it."

"Did he not speak to you afterwards?" asked Lucile.

"Maman tried to thank him. But he just ignored her. His eyes were fixed ahead for the entire journey, like he was looking into empty space, like he was in a trance, I'm sure I didn't see him blink, not once. He left the train at the station before Lausanne. He just got off his seat without even acknowledging us. If I was a believer I would say he was our Guardian Angel: that he never actually left us, that he had been with us all the time since leaving Marseille, keeping us safe: and that he only showed himself at that time because he knew something bad was going to happen."

"But you are not a believer," remarked Norris.

"No Monsieur I am not. I believe there is an explanation for everything. All we need to do is look at ourselves, wait, just say we do not know, then it will be answered eventually."

"Or we can create a guardian angel," he said.

"From a child's imagination," added Lucile.

"*Yes Mademoiselle, a child's imagination*," she said in French. "I even started to think that Francois was also a manifestation of him. Until..." Valeraine suddenly stopped herself.

"Until what?" Lucile asked.

"Nothing." She quickly started the story again. A half smile appeared. "Fortunately there was no need for this Guardian Angel to show his face again. We changed trains at Lausanne, Maman even had the courage to ask a guard if this was the right train to Avenches. We got off at Domdidier. That was when we began looking at Samuel's instructions. I think he and Lucas must have travelled the route themselves, and quite recently. He had written everything down, what the houses looked like, sometimes describing their roofs, their colour, even their windows. And if there wasn't a house, he would point out a distinguishing feature, like a large tree or barn. What he didn't describe was the mud sodden tracks. Each step glued our feet to the ground, after a while it felt like I was wearing concrete blocks, having to stop and scrape the mud off the soles every few minutes. Sometimes Samuel had written a description of the view, the shape of a distant hill. For myself and Susanne it had become like a game, like a treasure hunt. I wondered if he had done it on purpose. It is the quiet ones who surprise us the most, isn't it Monsieur?"

Norris wondered why she was addressing him again. Maybe his father had spoken to her about him.

"Samuel hardly said two words to us the entire time we were at Nyon; but in the instructions he would make a joke about what he had written, like he wanted us to forget about the horrors in the world. We even managed to laugh out loud when he wrote that one hill looked like a Chinaman's hat, and it was probably from the Ming Dynasty. Neither Susanne or myself could see it at first, then we all decided it was the one ahead of us in the far distance, the one that was more like a pregnant lady laying down. When I think back now we were like drunks, only our bottle had the sweet taste of freedom." Valeraine paused, like she was feeling guilty for the way they had felt. "Through all this I still had this tight knot deep in my guts, a sick feeling that would stay with me until I saw him again, although I didn't know it would be one I would carry for the rest of my life." She looked at Lucile.

Lucile closed her eyes, a simple acknowledgement that she understood, that she already knew.

"We passed through a small village called Pra Gaud. Several minutes later we entered Oleyres. Lucas had told us it would be far too dangerous to write down the address or even the names of the couple we were staying with. All he said was to keep walking when we reached the village, so we did. Apart from the odd dog sniffing around, the streets were empty and silent, until we turned a corner, a soldier was stood ahead of us, wearing a long trench coat and holding a rifle in his hands, he was waiting at the end of the road. Maman told us to keep walking, not to draw suspicion on ourselves. 'Remember what Uncle Lucas told us, we were registered as refugees four years ago and have been living with him and our cousin Samuel in Nyon. We hated them and fish, so the Jewish Refugee Assistance Organisation have found us a family here in Oleyres.' As we approached him I could feel my knees turn to rubber, I think Susanne must have felt the same because she had grabbed Maman's arm with both hands and buried her head below her shoulder. As we got closer I saw the face of an old man under the helmet. His flabby, grey skin had several days of white stubble, he was wearing round glasses that made him look like an old professor. He didn't see us at us first, he just kept gazing up the road. I can remember his face when he turned to look at us, it was as if he was expecting us. I will never forget his first words. 'Did you have a pleasant journey?" he asked, which shocked me. How could he ask such a thing? Now I think back it wasn't such a ridiculous thing to say after all. How would he have known what we had been through, holed up in his safe little village playing soldiers. What he saw was a mother and her two rosy cheeked children wearing clean clothes and carrying a new suitcase. He probably thought we had caught the train all the way from Marseille, slept like babies the entire journey, after a pleasant meal in the dining car. He spoke French with a German accent, told us his name was Albert Dreifuss and his wife was called Eveline. Maman didn't say one word in return, she just smiled every time he said something. He led us down a road with houses on one side and fields on the other. He told us he was in the Home Guard of the Swiss Reserve Army, 'I alone will stop the German Army invading Oleyres' he proudly joked with a thrust of his gun. I remember thinking he seemed nice. When we came to the end of the road, when I thought it must be the last house, we didn't stop, instead we carried on for about another hundred metres. He finally halted beside some tall trees. As we followed him between two a chalet became visible in front of us, all made of wood, it made the road look like an afterthought, there to pull the house into the twentieth century, like a hand reaching out to grab someone drowning, then having to let it go. A beautiful wooden balcony completely surrounded the first floor. I remember the ornate window shutters, all painted with swirling red patterns. Above our heads were plate size wooden spearheads hanging from the roof eaves, as if one could easily snap off and impale the top of your head. I always made a point of never standing underneath them. As he took us around the back I remember hearing a thud and a crack as we approached a door. His wife was inside a small room piled high with chopped wood, there were splinters all over the floor. I can remember her face to this day, intense, she looked angry." Valeraine stared at Norris. "I think you English would say she was a woman who would tell you how it is."

"I know the type." Norris replied, thinking of his mother.

"It was like she knew more about you than you ever did about yourself, even in that first moment. She seemed a lot younger than the old man, maybe by twenty years. She rested a large axe on her shoulder and took a scarf off her head, displaying short unruly dark hair and sharp features. I remember the introduction felt very formal, she spoke in German, prompting Susanne to translate. Insisting we call her Frau Dreifuss and her husband Herr Dreifuss, her manner was very stiff, wooden, like she had become part of the house herself. I guessed it was Herr Dreifuss's idea to give a home to refugees, to help fellow Jews fallen on hard times, saving them from the extermination camps. I can recall her looking down at our feet and telling us to take off our shoes outside before we went in. The way she said it made me feel like I was intruding." Valeraine stopped for a second and looked at Lucile. "Although I didn't know it then Mademoiselle, this woman was going to change my life forever."

Lucile wanted to ask how; but chose to remain silent. She

would wait, enquire later.

"We were given one room, on the ground floor. It was comfortable, it had a fire, a bed each, that is all I can say about it, in truth a bed each is saying a great deal. I think one of the conditions Frau Dreifuss had put on her husband was that he found a family that could look after the house and garden." Valeraine released a long sigh. "Being the oldest daughter I was chosen to do the hardest work, the work a man would have done. I soon found out why Frau Dreifuss wanted to hand over the chore of chopping the wood, it seemed to be a never ending task in winter. Herr Dreifuss had terrible arthritis in his hands and wasn't able to hold the axe, the poor man wasn't able to do much at all, his knuckles had swollen to the size of golf balls. I think they must have given him a great deal of pain, although I never heard him complain. When he had said 'he alone will stop the German Army invading Oleyre,' I now doubted if he could even pull the trigger. Before I forget Mademoiselle. The strange thing is, those first words about him fighting the German Army was the only time the war was mentioned. It felt as if Herr Dreifuss wanted to get the discussion over with there and then, as if it wasn't happening. Frau Dreifuss didn't mention it either, so neither did we, not even amongst ourselves." Valeraine's gaze dropped. "We only spoke about Papa in our prayers, although we felt he was always with us. We all missed him, like there was a huge Papa size hole in our lives. Frau and Herr Drefuss never asked about him, I think they knew though." She looked up. "I remember thinking chopping wood was probably worse than gutting fish. At the beginning my fingers had become sore with deep calluses and blisters, wearing gloves didn't help much. The day would start early and finish late, much of it under a hand-held lantern. Then by the end of winter the skin on my hands had become so hard it felt as if I could grate cheese on them. When the summer months came, when I thought I would get a rest from all that chopping, it was me who had to collect the water. There was no running water in the house, instead it had to be drawn up by a hand pump in the yard. Herr Drefuss told me when they laid the water pipe it was such a misty day they didn't see their house in the distance. Like I said, I was very gullible."

"But not now?" asked Lucile.

"I have lived for many years Mademoiselle." She looked at Norris. "How do you English say? I have picked up a few tips along the way."

Norris smiled.

Valeraine took a deep breath. "In the hot months I could be there for ages, forcing the handle of that stupid pump up and down, praying for that gush of water to come spurting out into the bucket, then only managing to get a dribble. I used to close my eyes and dream of being back home, imagining my father coming up from the workshop, his face covered in metal dust. We had electricity though, Herr Dreifuss called it hydropower and said that it came from the lakes. I remember thinking why the water couldn't come from the lakes. He told me it must have been a clear day when they laid those cables! He was very funny, funnier than Francois. Maman spent most of her time in the kitchen, it was on the ground floor next to our bedroom. She was in her element, cooking and baking; although food was scarce she always seemed to scrape enough to feed the five of us. I remember Maman used to make rosti's from the previous nights boiled potatoes, always topped with fried eggs. There were always eggs, I don't think the Swiss could live without their fried eggs, everyone in the village had hens. That was one of Susanne's jobs, feeding the hens and collecting the eggs. There was powdered milk and margarine when we couldn't get cows milk or butter. Frau and Herr Dreifuss always ate upstairs, sometimes listening to the radio at the same time. We used to freeze like little mice when they did, holding our breath, trying to listen to what was being said. All we got was a muffled voice in German, Susanne occasionally caught the odd word, whispering it back to us in French when she did. Most of it was propaganda about how the Nazi's were defeating the Allies, which greatly worried us. It was at the end of the first year when things began to change. Herr Dreifuss had been told by Maman how clever Susanne was, how she always got top grades at school, that given half a chance she could become a teacher or doctor, maybe a lawyer. The other villagers had also got used to seeing us, like we had come part of the community. We even helped sow the seeds for vegetables when they ploughed up the local football field. Maman had made friends with a few of the other mothers from the village and she began visiting their houses, leaving me to my chores. It appeared Herr Dreifuss had a lot of influence because he managed to get Susanne a place at the local school. I say it like that because although many of the villagers put up with us, many still frowned upon our presence. Some thought we would take their jobs, eat their food, take their children's places at school, so it was no easy feat what Herr Dreifuss had done. The only difference to the other children was she had to wear her owen clothes and walk home every lunchtime to eat with us. God forbid another child might see her actually eating food or wearing their clothes; but that's how it was then, we had to be careful of things like that. Jewish refugees were second class citizens and we had to know our place. But rather that than a death camp Mademoiselle, Monsieur."

"What about you?" Norris asked. "Weren't you allowed to go to school?"

"*No Monsieur*, the kids my age went to a school in Domdidier, Herr Dreifuss had no influence there. I remember seeing the school bus pass by a couple of times. In some ways I was glad, the children never looked happy."

Both Lucile and Norris noticed how her words faded away, like she was trying to hide the truth, as if she would have liked some children of her own age to mix with.

"You said Frau Dreifuss would change your life forever." Lucile remarked.

"*Ah yes.* It was one morning, when Susanne was at school and Maman was at one of her...Maman's mornings. The first time I had not been in the company of at least one of them. Maman said I was now old enough to look after myself. Herr Dreifuss was also out of the house, probably on one of his patrols, stopping the German Army single handed. We were never allowed upstairs, I think it was a way for Frau Dreifuss to shut us out of her life, to have her own space. How do you English say Monsieur, out of sight out of mind.

Norris replied with a sharp nod.

"Even after a year I still think she thought of us as strangers, like three annoying rats scuttling around her house. Sometimes I could go for weeks without seeing her, a woman we hardly saw was controlling our lives, passing on her commands through her husband. I didn't mind that though, I mean not seeing her. It was Herr Dreifuss who used to come downstairs to collect their meals." Valeraine sat back in her chair and took a deep breath. "Every second of every minute of every day all I wanted was for Papa to contact us, to see him walk down that road, to tell us we could go home. Only on this day I heard something else. '*Fräulein, Fräulein.*' It was Frau Dreifuss. I waited, thinking she must be calling for someone else, but she kept repeating it over and over again. I ran upstairs and waited by the door, like it would have been a crime to enter the room. I didn't see her at first, it was only when I eventually stepped in that I saw her feet poking out from behind a chair, I moved further in and saw her laid out on the floor. *'Where have you been girl?'* She snapped at me. I told her I would go and find Herr Dreifuss or Maman. '*No no girl, help me up, I'll be fine'* she said. That is when I realised she had said it in perfect French; all this time only speaking German...and she could actually speak French. She told me she had fainted, that is all, as though it was no big deal. I was to help her up into the chair and get her some water, then she would be fine. So I did. After I fetched the water, just as she was sipping from the cup, I began looking around the room, at the carved wooden furniture, the ornaments, the shelves full of books. But it was what I saw on her wall."

Both Norris and Lucile could see Valeraine staring downward, silent, like her mind had been transported back to that time.

"Never in my life have I seen anything so beautiful." She then raised her eyes, they had come alive. "It was then I realised, at that exact time, through all the bad that was happening, through all the evil in the world; there was still great beauty. Frau Dreifuss saw me looking at it. "*Landschaft mit gelben Vögeln*," she said in German. I was spellbound, just standing there like some idiot girl. It was like I had been put into a trance. Frau Dreifuss repeated it in French." So Madame Rousselle also did. "*Landscape with Yellow Birds*." And again in English. "It is by Paul Klee. Frau Dreifuss then began to speak to me in French, without the hint of an accent. Why she had only spoken German all this time I would never know. All I could think about at that time was the painting. She said he was a Swiss artist, born in Münchenbuchsee, and that it was not very far from where we were. Then she said something that meant nothing to me at the time, but if I knew then what I know now." Madame Rousselle paused, as if she was making space for her next words. "Frau Dreifuss said she too had also come from Münchenbuchsee and had known him." Valeraine's eyes widened. "She knew Paul Klee Mademoiselle, Monsieur. Imagine that, knowing Paul Klee."

Lucile guessed he was some kind of famous artist, she just hoped his paintings were better than those of Francois Degarmo.

"She said even as a boy he was different to all the other children. That he once said to her, 'a line is just a dot that went for a walk.' It was the first time I had seen Frau Dreifuss smile." Valeraine then made a strange gesture with her hand, like a puppet having its arm string pulled up. "I remember lifting my finger, pointing like an imbecile to another painting. *That is called The Tree of Life,* she said." Again, Valeraine had reverted to French, "*It is by Gustav Klimt,* she said. At the time they were just names, no more than people's names. I could see she was looking at a small sculpture on a cabinet, like a stick man, as if it had been stripped of its flesh, like it was baring its soul to the world. She went on to tell me that it was an original bronze by Giacometti. She said many were copies, but not that one. She said I could hold it if I wanted. So I did. It felt incredible, like I was touching the soul of the artist himself. It was then she turned her head around to look behind her." Madame Rousselle had put a hand to her chest. "I can tell you Monsieur, Mademoiselle, it was me that nearly fainted. What she was looking at must have been at least a metre and a half high and a metre wide. If I was in a trance from the Paul Klee then this nearly put me in a permanent coma. It appeared to be glowing yellow, like I could see an aura around the painting. Frau Dreifuss told me it was also by Gustav Klimt and was called Portrait of Adele Bloch-Bauer."

"Yes I know the one," said Norris.

"But she liked to call it The Lady in the Gold Dress...So I did too." A half smile brushed her lips. "I still do."

"Is it that one with..." Lucile began, proud that she knew at least one painting, two if you included The Drowning Mary.

Valeraine interrupted. "*Yes yes Mademoiselle Billet, it is that one.* Do you know Gustav Klimt had actually used gold and silver leaf. She told me her print was very special, a limited edition of fifty, because it also had gold and silver leaf. I remember the woman's face in the painting, I said she was like a queen surrounded by treasure. It made me think that Frau Dreifuss would have looked like Adele Bloch-Bauer when she was younger. Then I remember scanning the walls, feeling her eyes on mine, in some places the paintings were two or three deep. She told me each one's title, then who the artist was, sometimes a brief description and if they were originals or not. Some were by local artists. I found out later she was a great exponent for modern painters in the region, helping to promote their work, organising exhibitions. Now I knew where she went to when she used to leave the house; I think she was trying to keep the legacy of Paul Klee alive. There was also another print by him which she said was called Senecio, that it was of the face of an old man with two expressions, one reflecting his happy past, the other angry about his future. All I remember is the simplicity, like a child's painting, and the colour. In my naivety I thought I could do something just as good, how little I knew. I remember telling her it looked more like a woman because it had blushing pink cheeks and a thin neck. I remember feeling proud when she agreed with me, she appeared pleased that I had an opinion, that I could think for myself; but she said the title was Latin and it meant old man. She was very knowledgable about art. There was another painting. It was of a naked woman with a grotesque body, like she was deformed, her legs wide apart showing the world what shouldn't be seen. I remember screwing up my face in disgust, then feeling bad when Frau Dreifuss told me off. I felt I had shrunk down to nothing. She told me never to dismiss any artist or their paintings." Valeraine glared at Norris. "That is why I saw something in Francois Degarmo Monsieur. Even the ugly can be beautiful Frau Dreifuss said. Eventually I had run out of wall, arriving at the last painting. She told me this painter was the one she had most respect for. That his paintings could talk to you, like words moving on the canvas. It was the first Kandinsky I had seen."

Both Norris and Lucile noticed she said it like it was a great milestone in her life.

"She told me he was the purest of all abstract artists. That the painting was called Yellow-Red-Blue and there was no reason on earth to call it anything but that, any other words would not have been enough. That was when I blurted out to her that I was an artist. The words just came out, like I had no control over them. I felt like I was putting myself on the same level as the paintings on her wall. This stupid teenage girl trying to make out she was something she wasn't. It was then I saw her smile again, I remember her exact words. She said, 'we are all artists.' The next day, after Herr Dreifuss saw the doctor out, she came downstairs and gave me several sheets of paper, brushes and paint. She taught me how to stretch the paper, also the different techniques, like using a toothbrush to splatter the paint, dropping wet paint on top of wet paint; but most of all she taught me to follow my feelings, to be spontaneous and courageous. She told me to paint with my eyes closed, 'see with your soul' she said. I remember her telling me to use the paint like a dancer uses the stage. She told me that some days I would feel inept, that I would think of myself as the worst artist ever to have existed, and other days I would think I was going to be the future Picasso. She said that many paintings would end up in the wastebasket. I might get one acceptable painting out of ten, one good painting out of a hundred, one great painting out of a thousand; but I must never lose confidence, never give up hope. She told me painting is just an extension of yourself. Frau Dreifuss began taking me to meet other artists and poets, also writers. We had to be careful, there were many fascists about: like the Nazis, they saw it as degenerate art, that we were trying to corrupt society." Valeraine blew out a puff of air.

Norris thought she did that a lot; as if she had been doing it all her life.

"I sometimes wondered if that was why Frau Dreifuss did it, that it was her way of fighting the war. I learnt to talk with these people about art and literature. I remember listening to a disagreement about how cobalt blue could fill a space better than French ultramarine, how one word could sound better than another with the same meaning. They also drank too much wine, sometimes the discussions would get very heated. Another artist told me how to balance a picture, how to leave an area for the eye to rest: 'look at a Piet Mondrian,' he said, then you will understand. Some of the younger artists began to flirt with me, fight for my attention, some asked me to model for them, wanting to paint me naked. When I told Frau Dreifuss she said it was natural but I would have to ask Maman first. So I did. Maman refused."

"And would you if she had said yes?" asked Lucile.

Norris saw creases appear around her lips as her smile widened.

"I was sixteen at the time, and all I wanted was to paint and talk with artists, intellectuals. What Maman didn't know, wouldn't hurt her."

Lucile wanted to ask her if she had modelled naked since then, maybe with another woman, maybe in a photograph. It was too soon. Later.

Valeraine continued. "Chopping wood and pumping water had become less of a chore, I just did them quicker so I could get back to painting. Even the air became clearer, warmer, I began to smell the sweetness of the pine trees. I started helping Frau Dreifuss organise exhibitions, she even included some of my works. Some sold but Maman told me I couldn't keep the money, 'we were not allowed to work for money,' she said. That we were taking money away from other artists and we would get into trouble if we were ever found out. I don't think she really believed it herself. I tried telling her that painting was not work." Valeraine paused for a second. "You see Monsieur, Mademoiselle, when I saw the pictures on her wall that day, I saw the power of art, I felt the effect it had on me, on other people. It was then I thought I could change the world with my paintings. But every generation thinks they are the ones to save the world, don't they."

"Or destroy it," replied Norris.

"Yes Monsieur, or destroy it. We are all drawn to the horror are we not Mademoiselle Billet? That is why you are writing this story."

Lucile couldn't argue with that. "So what did you do with the money?"

“Maman told Herr Dreifuss to have it for our keep, although I’m sure his wife spent it on art materials for me.” Valeraine held her gaze on Lucile for several seconds. “So you see Mademoiselle, that is how Frau Dreifuss changed my life. Without her I would not be here sitting with you now.”

“Tell me what happened when you returned to France?” asked Lucile.

“It started when we were eating in the kitchen. I remember Herr Dreifuss running down the stairs.” Valeraine’s eyes looked to the side, a smile came to her face. “I can see him now, he was very excited, he began dancing on the spot with his hands in the air, going round in circles. He was shouting that Marseille had been liberated, that he had just heard it on the radio. The Allies had taken Marseille and all of France would soon be free, he couldn’t get the words out fast enough. I remember him squeezing Maman’s shoulders, lifting her up from the seat and dancing with her. I remember Maman also looking happy. ‘The War will soon be over,’ he cried, ‘you will be able to go home to your husband.’ It was the first time he had mentioned Papa. After the excitement, after he stopped dancing he sat down, a sadness had come over him. He said he would miss us, that he we had become the children they had never had. Then the day came for us to return home. It was about a week after Herr Dreifuss gave us the news. We were to leave Frau and Herr Dreifuss. I was very sad, if he said we had become the children they never had then they had become like grandparents to me. I remember there were lots of hugs and tears., not Frau Dreifuss though, she remained impassive the entire time. I was so grateful to this woman. I was no longer a girl anymore, I had become a woman, but mostly I had become an artist.”

Lucile wondered what she meant when she said she had become a woman. She didn’t pursue it.

“Frau Dreifuss had given me my destiny. She even packed all my art materials for me, adding more brushes, paper and paint, this woman who herself had just enough to eat. She told me to draw at every opportunity." The old woman paused for a second. "But I only had one thought on my mind, we were going home to see my Papa, the one thought that always gave me strength, the one hope I had always kept with me. If you think it was difficult for us entering Switzerland, then leaving was something else, bureaucracy had replaced the Nazis. We were immediately taken to an intern camp at Saint-Julien-en-Genevois. Even after France was liberated, even though we had a house and Papa to go home to, we still had to live in squalid and overcrowded conditions while we waited to be processed. The problem was we had no passports and the only papers we had to prove our identity were forged. It was one interview after another, held in separate rooms with questions continuously fired at us, not giving us time to think. I think they must have thought we were Nazis, imagine how that made us feel. They asked about our life before the war, our escape with Francois. What do you say Monsieur? No stone was left unturned."

Norris didn't answer.

"Who did they think we were, we were Jews for God's sake, couldn't they see that? Eventually they believed us and we were put on a train. Three years after leaving France we finally arrived back in Marseille. The first thing I noticed were the soldiers, there were so many on the streets. Most spoke English with strange accents. I remember one had smiled at me and tipped his helmet, he called me M'am. I remember being frightened by the roar of army vehicles trundling along our roads, the ground vibrating under our feet. We passed tanks that had become burnt out shells, you could still see the swastikas on some, the dried blood on the road. Many houses were reduced to rubble, whatever contents could be salvaged were piled high in the road. Bed sheets and clothes were strewn around the pavements. We passed a group of men in civilian clothes carrying rifles, they were leading four women with shaven heads and wearing only underwear. I saw another woman on her own, also with a shaven head, wearing dirty clothes and unwashed, she was carrying a baby." Valeraine shook her head." In my naivety I thought she was bald because she had head lice, until I saw people spitting at her and the baby." Valeraine looked up, looking first at Lucile, then Norris, as if her eyes were telling the story. "Then I discovered the truth, about them being collaborators, how they were being humiliated. But it doesn't make it right does it? We did what we had to do to stay alive. I learnt later some had no choice, sleep with German officers or risk being sent to a death camp, or being shot there and then: some were. Then we turned into our street and saw our house for the first time in three years. I remember thinking I will be seeing Papa in a few minutes, I was so happy. I remember Maman rummaging about in the hem of her dress I wondered what she was doing until she pulled out a key and held it high in front of her face, that is why she had insisted on wearing that old dress. She was beaming out this wide smile, the first time I had seen her like that since she had danced with Herr Dreifuss. We had come home, all we had been through and we had finally come home. I watched as she tried putting it into the lock, trying several times. Papa has changed the lock, she said. She banged on the door and waited for him to answer. Only it was a woman that opened it. Maman tried to step past her, I remember this man appeared, he pushed her back. The woman said this was her house. Maman argued with her, saying it was ours and we had to leave it to escape the death camps, that we wanted back what was rightfully ours. She argued for ages. When they didn't back down Maman became very angry, shouting at them to get out, telling them they were trespassing and when Papa returned he would kill them. That was when the woman disappeared, returning with another man. He was a horrible brute, smelling of sweat and alcohol. He became aggressive and shoved Maman to the ground, slamming the door shut. We went to our neighbours and asked for their help. I remember the look on their faces when they saw us, like they had seen three ghosts. Maman asked if they would tell these people that it was our house.They refused, everything my Papa had done for them and they refused, not even giving us food and water. And when we asked about Papa, they told us they hadn't seen him since the day we left. Susanne asked about her rabbit. Without any thought the woman bluntly told her she had been eaten, that she had made a fine stew for such a scrawny animal. Then she said, 'don't worry your pretty head little girl. I slit its throat just the way you people like it.' I can remember being surprised by the look on Susanne's face. There were no tears, no fit of temper, not her usual wild tantrum we were used to; but I could see it in her eyes, I could see the hatred. It was then I knew this woman would not die a natural death." Valeraine fell into silence, staring straight at Lucile. It was then, at that exact moment; the old woman knew about the notebook. "We went to the Grande Synagogue. Maman spoke to a woman outside, the woman told her she had lost her entire family in the death camps. She said we should go to Le Vallon des Auffes, that a lot of Jews had already gone there. I remember shuddering when I heard the words. I knew Le Vallon des Auffes was a fishing village, flashbacks of Nyon came back to me; so you can imagine my relief when Maman said we should go inside instead. If Papa was looking for us then this is the place he would go. But we weren't prepared for what awaited us. It was overrun with hundreds of people, all trying to find information about missing relatives. They were yelling out names and shouting that they too had lost their homes. It appeared everyone was in the same situation as us. We managed to squeeze through, only to hear the workers telling people to come back when it was quieter. No one did. We tried pushing through the crowd, shouting out Papa's name, hoping to see his face emerge. I looked at every man, wanting the next one to be him. I saw one man, he was the same height, his thick dark hair the same as Papa's, his face hidden behind stubble, for a brief moment our eyes met, then parted. My heart sank several times on that day. We dragged our suitcase to Le Vallon des Auffes. I tried to plead with Maman not to go there, remember Lucas and Samuel I said, remember the fish wagon, remember that disgusting smell. She told me we had little choice, that I was a woman now, that I could do it. I could see the desperation in her eyes. On the way she would stop strangers and ask if they knew the whereabouts of Nicolas Dennel, most ignored us, others just shook their heads. When we arrived, all I could see were fishing boats bobbing in the harbour and tiers of wooden houses piled on top of each other like boxes ready to collapse. We were met by an old woman with a voice as deep as a mans. She told us to work hard and everything would be fine, then led us to a small room in a cabin teetering precariously on a steep slope. I felt the cold sea air roar through gaps between the planks, carrying the horrid smell of fish, even inside there was no escape from the stench. After only a few days I could tell you exactly which way the wind was blowing. For a month we gutted and boned fish, then returned to the room we shared with rats. The three of us would continually wash, trying to rid ourselves of the smell, scrubbing away the fish scales stuck to our skin like glue. On Sunday Maman walked us to the Grande Synagogue to check if there was any news of Papa. There wasn't. Afterwards we sat and prayed, just to be away from that horrible place. I had never prayed so much." Valeraine looked at Norris. "I thought God had deserted us Monsieur, that I had done something terrible to upset him, that the three of us had done something awful and we were being punished. Then one day Maman was called out by the foreman. People were always being called out, for the smallest reason, for something they had done wrong, maybe an argument with another worker or just for looking at him the wrong way. There was a rumour why women got called out by him. I just hoped he didn't want Maman for that. If you refused him then you were no longer needed, your entire family would be thrown out onto the streets; then the woman would have no choice but to find the only employment she could. While the soldiers where still in

Marseille there would be no shortage of that type of work. Maman returned a few minutes later, I remember the foreman standing behind her, his head was down, his face and neck covered in red blotches, he looked agitated, his demeanor docile, like a wild dog who had just been tamed. But it was the expression on Maman's face I remember the most, she was so excited. She told us a man was waiting in our room. Only one word entered my mind, all our minds...Papa. The three of us threw away our aprons and ran. Maman was the first to enter, flinging the door open. I pushed in front of Susanne, ready to throw my arms around him. Then I saw someone else sat in the chair, his legs outstretched in front of him like he owned the place. His mouth was tight, held in a near permanent grin, I recognised him immediately. For a moment he just sat there, staring at us, his eyes were cold, like death itself, the eyes of someone that had seen too much in their young life. This was not the Francois I remembered, the Francois I had loved. I wanted him to tell one of his stupid jokes, make us all laugh. Instead he looked at us one by one, slowly nodding as he said our names, like he was pleased to see we were still alive, or maybe he was surprised that we still were. 'Ava,' he said, then 'Valeraine,' last was 'Susanne,' staring at her the longest. He turned back to Maman. 'He is dead,' was all he said." Valeraine leant forward, her elbows resting on her knees, rubbing her hands together, like they had a mind of their own. Norris saw her eyes glaze over, she closed them, the tears seeping through her eyelids.

"I am sorry," Norris said.

"No Monsieur, Mademoiselle, it is me that is sorry because I cannot remember what happened next. When I try it feels like someone has disturbed a wasps nest in my head. I remember Francois stepping over to the door, he turned and looked around at our tiny room, the dismal way we were living. He said he was sorry the magnificent house my Papa described to him had been bombed. It was Susanne who explained, only because she was the one that still had the capacity to do so. Francois returned the next day and told us to collect all our belongings, he said we were going home. When I asked him about the families living there, 'I hope they like fish,' he said, the first recognition that his humour hadn't deserted him. I then asked about the brute living on the top floor, 'I hope the fish like him', but this time there was no smile. When we returned we discovered our home had been ransacked, there was nothing left. We learnt the Nazi's would have had everything first, taking anything that was valuable, what remained the people of Marseille had. I remember Francois telling me afterwards that it was only people involved with the Vichy regime who were allowed to live in the larger houses, that it was well known Jews had money hidden away, ready for their return. As soon as Maman had entered she went straight to her bedroom. I saw her fall to the floor, crying. There was a hole in the wall, all Papa's silver trophies had gone. Now we had a large house with no money and no means to stay alive.

Maman told Francois he could come and live with us, after all the house was large enough. He did for a short while, only to make sure we were safe. I think he did it for Papa's sake. He knew no one would touch us while he was there. Sometimes I had him all to myself when the two of us went out at night, stealing furniture left on the streets. We got stopped many times, he always managed to talk his way out of it, like he could diffuse any situation with one of his stupid jokes, in truth I think they took pity on him. We were carrying a mattress one night when I heard him telling a policeman that we had a baby at home with nothing to sleep on. I remember wishing that was true."

Norris looked around the room. He wondered if the lack of personal possessions and furniture was a throwback to that time.

"When I was alone with Francois I used to ask him about Papa. How well did he get to know him? Did he like Papa?" Valeraine paused for a short moment. "How did he die?

Francois told me they were members of the Francs-Tireurs et Partisans and they were a resistance group made up from members of the communist party. Francois said he was a communist. I asked if Papa was too. He wasn't a fascist, is all he said. He told me how they used to ambush Nazi convoys heading south; and that was how Papa died, the Nazis were forewarned of one ambush. Francois managed to escape but Papa was captured along with three others. But it was his last words I will never forget Monsieur. He said it was a Frenchman from Marseille that told the Nazis about the ambush. It was only later I found out what the Nazis did to resistance fighters."

She looked at Norris. He lowered his head.

"He also told me that Papa had paid a lot of money to get us into Switzerland. Francois admitted to not wanting to take us but Papa had said he trusted no one else. Then one evening after returning from one of our evening excursions, he told me it was time for him to see his own family in Corsica. I think he knew it was the one reason I could not argue with. I had to say goodbye to him a second time. It brought back memories of Lake Geneva; but this time I could say goodbye properly.

The pause that followed said everything.

"It was not my first time Mademoiselle."

Lucile thought back to when Valeraine had left Switzerland, when she said she had become a woman. She remembered how she implied that she had posed naked for artists. Maybe she would ask about it later.

"I missed Francois so much. Everyday I hoped he would return and everyday I felt a great sadness when he didn't."

Lucile looked up, wanting to ask Valeraine if she ever saw him again.

The old woman started talking again. "For two years we managed to survive in that house. Maman had a job working nights in a bakery owned by a Jewish family, although she was paid very little she could bring home bread and cakes left over from the previous day, even if much of it was stale. Maman had always been able to bake, her fruit challah on the Sabbath was the best in Marseille. When she wasn't working she would go to her bedroom to sleep. But I knew otherwise. It was then..." Her words stumbled. "It was then I knew something was wrong. Sometimes I would stand outside her door and hear her cry. I think this was the beginning..." Valeraine stopped mid-sentence.

"The beginning?" Norris asked.

"Her illness Monsieur." Valeraine said it with a tilt of her head, as if Norris already knew.

"I still had the painting materials Frau Dreifuss had given me, so I spent a lot of time in the house drawing and painting. Sometimes I would go out onto the streets and sketch the ruins, sometimes the soldiers. I always chose the Americans because most would pay me if I gave them the picture, sometimes offering me extra if I went for a drink with them. I think Frau Dreifuss must have known I would run out of paint at some point because she had tied a bundle of pencils together over a small sketchbook.

"*And did you?*" asked Lucile in French.

"*Run out of paint?*"

"*No, did you go for a drink with the American soldiers?*"

"*Of course,*" she replied, also in French.

Lucile wanted to ask more, but didn't. "Tell me about Susanne."

"Susanne was seventeen and had grown into a very beautiful girl. I knew Maman had become concerned about her because she would go out in the day smelling of expensive cologne and wearing nice clothes, not knowing where she had got the money to buy them. Then she wouldn't return home until late. Maman knew she had already taken lovers and was concerned that she might be enticed by the pimps patrolling the streets looking for young attractive women. I too had been propositioned several times."

"What did you do?"

"*Sorry Mademoiselle.*"

"When you were propositioned?"

"*I am not a whore Mademoiselle.*"

"*Sorry,*" Lucile replied.

The words were spoken too quickly for Norris. But somehow he understood.

"People were becoming hostile as more and more Jews began pouring back into the city. Without work and no money, crime increased, the streets became too dangerous to go out. Then we heard of a land where all Jews would be welcome, many families had already begun fleeing there. Maman had started to rent out rooms just to earn some extra cash, all to Jewish families in need of shelter; but she started arguing with them when they couldn't pay us and refused to leave the house. Everyday I prayed Francois would return, take me away from all this. Then out of the blue Maman said she was going to sell the house. I thought we were going to board one of those overcrowded boats to this new country; but instead she said we were going to Paris. I don't know who was the most excited, me or Susanne. This was the place where Picasso and other artists hung out, where I could discuss art with painters and poets as I had in Switzerland. Then Maman returned from the town hall, she had been told the proof she needed for ownership of the house no longer existed. All the paperwork had been burnt by the Nazis. They said we couldn't sell it, no one could, we couldn't even rent it out."

"But Madam Veron..." Lucile stopped. "But Susanne lives there now."

"For Susanne the proof was found." Was all Valeraine said. "It was the next morning, Maman's day off from the bakery when Susanne walked into the drawing room. I remember it because of the stupid look she had on her face. She had a hand hidden behind her back, she pulled it from behind her and held it over the table in a fist, her fingers sprung open. A roll of banknotes dropped to the table, some falling in front of me. I don't know what Susanne was expecting, all I could see was this expression on her face, like we should be grateful. Maman had remained quiet, I could see her eyes were wide, frozen, just staring down at the money. Then her lips became pinched, like she was holding back the words. It was Susanne who spoke first. I can't remember the exact words, something like, Paris here we come. She said it as if we should all be happy. I would have been if Maman hadn't done what she did next. She shot up from her chair and started screaming at Susanne."

Valeraine looked across at Norris. "When you asked me about Maman, when you asked what the beginning was, I think this was all part of it. I had seen Maman and Susanne have some heated arguments before, but not like this one. Maman called her a whore, saying she had dishonoured the name of our family. That she could have been anything she wanted. It was when she said Papa would have been ashamed of her, that was when Susanne started screaming back at her. She said she was a dancer in a club, no more than that. She said she danced for the soldiers, that she was just thanking them for liberating us, and that was it, she was not a whore. The argument only stopped when Maman curled up in a ball in the corner of the room, sobbing like a baby. I crouched down in front of her. I told her what Susanne said was true, that she was not a prostitute, she was a dancer. That she didn't tell her because she knew this would have been the response. I said we should be grateful she was giving us this money. I said this was our chance to get out of Marseille, away from the people who betrayed us, from the people who betrayed Papa. In truth Mademoiselle, I didn't know what Susanne did, she may very well have been a whore at that time. I just wanted to go to Paris. I couldn't really care less where Susanne got the money. Then I had an idea. I told her to wait while I went to my room. I returned with the money I had made from the sketches I had sold to the soldiers, showing it to Maman, it was nothing to what Susanne had dropped on the table, just a few francs. I was going to buy paints and brushes with it. What happened next surprised me; after all that shouting

I thought Maman was going to start on me, saying I was in it with my sister. But Maman just looked up to me and nodded, like she had accepted everything I had said. After she had sat curled up on the floor for over two hours I realised she was suffering more than I could have ever thought. I was scared, fearful of what was happening to her. I just hoped Paris would be the cure. We never mentioned the money again, mine or Susannes. We both knew how selfish we had been, keeping it for ourselves, especially when we knew the little Maman made from the bakery was used to feed and clothe us.

We boarded up the house the best we could and arrived in the Le Marais district of Paris one month later. Le Marais was an area where Jews had congregated." Valeraine puffed out one of her cynical breaths. "If there is one thing that Jews are good at, that is congregating. Susanne's money had paid for everything, the train tickets, the first three months rent on the apartment, everything until we could get our feet back on the ground again; and then there was still some left over. I knew then it wasn't only dancing. She told me to keep my money, to spend it on art materials, to keep painting, that I was good at it. I managed to get a job at the local school teaching art. Susanne rose to the top, a dancer at the Moulin Rouge, I had never seen her so driven, so ambitious, as if she...'Valeraine stopped herself. "And Maman, all Maman wanted was for me to settle down, find a good husband and give her grandchildren."

"Neither you or your sister had children?" Norris asked.

Valeraine lowered her gaze. "No," she said flatly. "Maybe that would have saved her." She paused for a second. "We will never know."

"But would you have liked children?" asked Lucile.

"It was too late. Maman took her own life a year later."

Lucile was startled by the calm way she said it.

Norris knew exactly how she would have felt.

"I sometimes think Maman had waited. I mean not for us to marry, but for us to be at a place where we could look after ourselves, where she thought we didn't need her anymore. For the last ten years it was only us she had to think about. Never knowing if your children were going to be taken away from you and sent to a death camp. When we were in Le Vallon des Auffes we were told stories about families separated from each other, their children dying alone, relatives not knowing if they were alive or dead. Then to find your home and possessions, everything you've worked for; taken by the people you trusted. Sometimes I used to watch her hug herself, trying to fight the devil inside, I felt helpless. Her face began to change, her eyes darkened, her behaviour became more unpredictable, erratic, vicious. It was Susanne who always got the brunt of it, never me. Her mood would suddenly flair up for the slightest reason, accusing her of all kinds of wrongdoings, mostly about relationships with men, that she was a cheap whore: I think she knew the truth. Then she would start apologising, saying it was her that was a bad mother, that it was all her fault. She would take to her bed for days on end, hardly eating or drinking. I think she knew then what she had to do to be free from the torment. She had lost control of her life, all she wanted now was to be in control of her death. It was Susanne who found her, hanging from the open hatch in the attic, a rope around her neck. I remember returning home from school and finding the police at our apartment, Maman's body had already been taken. I was twenty-five Monsieur, Susanne twenty-two. Maman was forty-nine. Suicide was not uncommon in our community, people had been through so much."

"Your sister has a photograph of the three of you together." said Norris. "It has the Eiffel Tower in the background."

"*Ah yes.*" The thought of it brought a smile to the old woman's face. "Both Susanne and myself have copies. It was the last picture of Maman, taken about a month before she died. I remember she had stopped a stranger and asked him to take it."

"But you all looked so happy," remarked Lucile.

"Maman had good days, but it was there, believe me Mademoiselle it was there." She looked at Norris first, then Lucile. "I remember her telling us to smile. I think that is how she wanted us to remember her, happy together."

"What happened after?" Lucile asked.

"We both stayed on at the apartment. I continued teaching, Susanne kept dancing. How do you say Monsieur, we were like ships passing in the night."

Norris nodded.

A half-grin brushed by Valeraine's lips. "Only with Susanne it was usually two ships." The smile dissolved. "Then I met someone, Antoine. It was a year after Maman's death. She would have been pleased, he was a good Jewish boy, very desirable. He was also a gifted artist and knew the cream of the Parisian art world. We spent half our life in the Dome Cafe, drinking and talking to the great in the Paris art world. I once met Ernest Hemingway, he tried to flirt with me, telling me he was writing a book called, 'Across the River and into the Trees.' I remember telling him it was a good title. Then he told me it wasn't a good title...it was a great title!" Valeraine blew out another sigh. "So I married Antoine. After Maman's death I still felt she had influence over me, that I still needed to please her, that she could now have her grandchildren. I should have known then it was a mistake, apart from art we had nothing in common. It appeared my schoolgirl naivety and gullibility had never left me. Susanne hated him, I should have listened to her, if there was one person in this world who knew about men then it was my sister. The wedding was a grand affair, traditionally Jewish. The ceremony was held under a chuppah made of..."

"Chuppah?" asked Lucile.

"It is a canopy, beneath it is where the ceremony is held. Ours were canvases stitched together, splashed with paint, held up by four easels. Jean Dubuffet took the place of my father, escorting me in. Many great artists attended. In the centre of the banqueting hall we had a fountain of wine, people could fill up their glasses to their hearts content, and they did, especially Antoine. I came up with this idea of having a large canvas placed on an easel with brushes and paint laid out on a table next to it. Every artist there would make a mark on it. Lydia managed to persuade Picasso to go first, then she second..."

"Lydia?" asked Norris.

"Lydia Corbett. She was a friend of Picasso, very beautiful. She became a very good friend of mine."

"Marcel Duchamp painted an exquisite chess king and queen, telling us it was me and Antoine, he added that in chess it is the queen that protects the king, I think he was trying to tell me something. Jean Dupuy was thc last one to draw on it, he wrote our names, mine at the top, Antoines at the bottom, connecting them with black lines, only some of the lines from Antoine's name drifted over the edge of the canvas, many thought it was his genius. I think he and Marcel knew what Antoine was like, that they were trying to tell me something: in my stupidity I never saw it. How do you say Monsieur? I was looking at him through rose tinted glasses."

Norris nodded.

"Can you imagine what that canvas would be worth now."

"What happened to it?" asked Norris.

"It was burnt by Antoine, he said it was an artist's way of breaking the glass." Valeraine could see Lucile and Norris's confusion. "It's a Jewish tradition where everyone shouts *mazel tov!* Except no one did. Antoine was very drunk at that stage. He staggered over to me and said it was a demonstration of forgetting what was in the past and welcoming in a new life. Only I didn't want to forget my past, and I was very far from welcoming in my new life."

"For years I put up with his drinking and staying out late with his friends, a lot longer than I should have. We both still painted, although he didn't really notice mine anymore. I had managed to lease a shop in Montmartre, converting it into a gallery. We both moved into the rooms on the top floor."

Norris raised his eyebrows and pointed to the ceiling.

"Yes Monsieur. I was hoping things would get better." She blew out another one of her breaths. "At first it was Antoine's paintings we displayed, only a few were mine. Then we began selling more and more works by other artists. Not that he noticed, I was sneaking more of them in and a lot less of his. It was easy, Antoine left the day-to-day running of the gallery to me, only so he could paint...and drink...and..." Valeraine stopped for a moment. "His work was beginning to suffer, it became erratic, I couldn't even say it was original, it was just plain bad. Sometimes I would lie to him, I would say a piece of his had been sold, when really I had thrown it out with the rubbish. I began staying downstairs in the gallery for hours, just not to be with him, sometimes late into the evening, organising exhibitions, talking to dealers and artists, learning what paintings were popular at the time, trying to guess what the next trend would be, which artist would become popular. I even learnt how to influence the market, just hints. I believe you English would say, 'sow the seeds' Monsieur."

Norris nodded again. Realising he was doing it as much as the old woman was puffing out her cynical breaths.

"The gallery began to specialise in abstract paintings. I can thank Frau Dreifuss for that, she had taught me well. Within a couple of months the gallery started to make a profit, a year later it had become a great success. Many of our friends contributed works, established artists and unknown ones. I had become one of the most powerful women in the Parisian art world."

"And your sister, did you see much of her?" asked Lucile.

"Susanne stayed on at the apartment, we hardly saw each other. Occasionally I might meet a customer who knew her, telling me she was mixing with the rich and powerful, although I doubt if many of my married clients would admit to it. I heard she was a hostess, another way of saying..." Valeraine stopped mid-sentence.

"Thank you Madame," is all Lucile said, like a reassurance.

Valeriane returned a smile. "It was Antoine who insisted we should call it the Valeraine Rousselle Art Gallery, he joked that half the name was his anyway, and by rights I should take the other half. That was his first mistake Monsieur."

Lucile remembered what Madam Veronique had told her.

"He should have called it the Antoine Dennel Art Gallery. I discovered that it was not only art that he had learnt from Picasso.

"*Sorry Madame*," Lucile said.

"Antoine was not only painting his models Mademoiselle, he was also sleeping with them."

"Oh. *Sorry Madame,*" This time the apology sounded different.

"I learnt afterwards that no woman was safe in the same room as him." She exhaled another one of her sharp breaths. "Except me apparently. But mostly he had broken the sacred vows of our religion, for that I could not forgive him. He tried telling me that the affairs had meant nothing to him, that it was only me he loved. In other words he knew it was the gallery that paid for everything and he was about to lose it. Valeriane prodded herself several times. "I was the gallery. The divorce that followed was not..shall we say friendly. Susanne introduced me to a lawyer, she said he was the best, one of the most respected and expensive in Paris. She also told me he wanted to keep his reputation, so not to worry about paying him. Antoine wanted half of the gallery, telling the court it was only his paintings we sold. You should have seen his face when my lawyer revealed to the magistrate the bill of sales for the last six months, not one was his. Then my lawyer said that everything was in my name, including the gallery, he showed the magistrate a picture of the board outside. I can remember how he had walked over to me and swept his hand in front of us like a bad amateur actor. The Valeraine Rousselle Art Gallery, he roared, saying my first name the loudest, like he was introducing the next act in a show. Susanne joked with me afterwards that she expected me to get up and start singing. Then he told the court it was actually Antoine's suggestion to name it that, like he had given me the gallery." Valeraine blew another one of her sharp breaths. "Antoine even admitted it. Many artists stood up in court and vouched for me, most had no choice, because they knew it was me who sold their paintings. Lydia charmed the magistrate so much I'm sure I saw him melt in his chair. She was one of the few women who hadn't slept with my husband. In the end the court agreed, the gallery belonged to me." Valeraine stared at Norris. "I was no longer that gullible young girl Monsieur."

"And Susanne, was she happy?" asked Lucile.

"*Ah yes.*" Valeraine held her gaze. "Susanne told me afterwards the verdict was a foregone conclusion anyway, that she made sure the magistrate had seen her in court, ensuring he knew I was her sister. Susanne got what she wanted, not only from seeing me divorce Antoine, but also from Paris. Not only did she know magistrates and lawyers but many people in power, like politicians. The last time I saw her she told me she was making plans to move back to Marseille. I think she knew exactly what she was doing. I think she knew right from the beginning when she dropped all that money in front of Maman. She also told me she had a weapon worse than any Hitler had, and the people of Marseille would know about it."

"What did she mean by that?" Norris wanted to hear her say it.

"Please Monsieur, I just told you I am not that gullible young girl anymore."

"I mean did you know what this weapon was at that time?"

"No Monsieur, not then."

"Do you know now?"

"Do you Monsieur?"

"*Ah yes.*" he replied, like a Frenchman would.

Lucile didn't know if she should say what she was about to say, she did anyway. "How about you Madame, were you also part of it?"

"Susanne and myself are not the same Mademoiselle."

Lucile thought it was a strange answer. "When did she leave Paris?"

Valeraine drew up her bottom lip up and shrugged. "Late sixties. I can't remember exactly."

Lucile nodded slowly. "What happened after the divorce?"

"The gallery continued making money Mademoiselle. Something else Frau Dreifuss taught me, she said always put the art first and how important it was to promote new artists. 'Keep the market fresh and the dealers will stay interested,' she said. 'Choose artists that will push the boundaries.'" Valeraine glanced over to Norris. "Maybe like Francois Degarmo, Monsieur."

Norris wondered why she had used the word, maybe.

"That way the public will keep talking, nothing sells a painting faster than the public hating it. The more they criticised, the more the dealers would think themselves one step ahead, that they saw something others didn't. Then I opened another gallery in Marseille, in my home city. My Papa had sold trophies there, now I was selling art.

"*And Susanne?*" asked Lucile.

"*Retribution Mademoiselle, Susanne sold retribution.*" Valeraine waited for a response, none came. "Susanne had already moved there, she said she knew someone that would make an excellent gallery manager, someone that was very knowledgeable about abstract art. His name is Remi Cochet." Her gaze wandered between Lucile and Norris. "But it was an encounter two years later that would put the Valeraine Rousselle Art Gallery on the highest level of the Parisian art world. A woman had entered the gallery. I knew immediately she was different as soon as she walked through the door. It was the way she carried herself, like she floated. Her face hidden behind the largest and blackest sunglasses, her head covered by a silk scarf. As she spoke a flick of golden hair dropped onto her forehead, it was as she removed the scarf and sunglasses I saw who it was. I remained behind my desk, just watching her stroll around my gallery as if she had all the time in the world, studying each painting in turn. Then she turned to me and spoke." Valeraine's expression turned inward. "This woman was very knowledgable about art, she knew many of the artists I had on display. She asked lots of questions, and when I answered them she listened intensively, like she wanted to learn, like she knew I was one of the most authoritative experts on modern art in Paris. Then she introduced herself, not that she had to. She said her name was Claude Jacqueline Pompidou, the wife of the French Prime Minister."

Lucile guessed it was about the same time as when the Markovic photographs were taken. Her heart began thumping harder, her mind began racing, thoughts falling over each other. She looked over towards Norris. He stared back. No words needed be said.

Valeraine continued. "She said she was opening an art centre in her husband's name, that it would be the greatest building for culture in Europe. It was being designed by Renzo Piano and Richard Rogers and it would be a legacy for the people of France. Then she asked how my sister was, but she didn't say it in a vindictive way, not like she knew who Susanne was, I mean her... It was as though there was a warmth in their friendship. She told me both her and her husband had met Susanne at many events, how well connected she was, how impressed she was with her intellect and knowledge. Susanne must have told her that she could speak four languages by the age of ten because I had to confirm it for her. She then told me it was through Susanne she had learned my name. I had a feeling she knew more about me than she would admit. What she said next that took my breath away. She wanted me to recommend a painting that could be included in the museum, an abstract work, but not by a known artist. There were two conditions: he or she had to be French but not a Parisian artist.

She said she wanted to reflect the quality of work from the provinces, the grass roots of French art. So I contacted Remi. He sent me two paintings, The Drowning Mary and The Foundering of Death. I gave Madame Pompidou the choice."

"And she chose the The Foundering of Death," said Norris.

"*Yes Monsieur.*"

"Why not The Drowning Mary?"

Valeraine tilted her head. "Indeed Monsieur, why not?"

Lucile didn't think about her next words or the consequences. The first time she heard them was when they left her mouth. "So when you couldn't sell The Drowning Mary, you hung it in the bedroom next door." Her eyes remained on the old woman.

For a moment Valeraine just stared back at her. "How did you know that?"

Again, Lucile couldn't stop herself, it was like someone had control over her. She slid her hands into her bag and pulled out one of the photographs. "There is a painting reflected in the mirror of the dressing table." As if she should disregard the two women lying naked on the bed."

"*So me talking to you has nothing to do with you writing about my family?*"

"*Has this painting nothing to do with your family?*"

Valeraine held out her hand. "*Let me see it.*"

Lucile leant forward and passed it to her. She then sat back in her chair and waited. "The photograph is one of several found in Stevan Markovic's car at the same time he was murdered."

A quiet smile came to Valeraine, like she hadn't heard Lucile. "I was very beautiful."

"So it is you in the picture?"

Valeraine angled her head to one side, her eyes had become wide. "I look younger than I was."

"You had black hair."

"A wig."

“So who is the other woman?”

“Rumours were it was Madame Pompidou.”

“Was it?” Lucile snapped. “If you were the other woman then you would know?”

Valeraine thought for a moment. “I didn’t tell you, before Madame Pompidou came to the gallery I had another visitor, someone I hadn’t seen for twenty years.” She leant forward and spoke quietly, not quite a whisper, but close. “It was Francois, I was so happy to see him again. Even in his mid-forties he still had that youthful look, that roguish grin, like he was seeing the world through a joke. The only obvious change was that his thick mane of unruly hair had gone, the hair I once ran my fingers through. It had been plastered back, its wildness tamed with grease, like a man wanting to hide his baldness.” Her eyes dropped, her body hunched over nervous hands. “Strangely there was no warm hug. I felt as if I was still that little girl to him, we kissed each others cheeks, it was cold, like we had met for the first time.” Valeraine puffed out a sharp breath. “Everything we had been through together and I still felt I was invisible to him. Then I wondered why he had come to see me, I could feel then there was something suspicious about it. I took him up to my apartment. Firstly he wanted to know about mine and Susanne’s lives. I had this feeling he knew everything already. After I finished I remember him saying Papa would have been proud of us. That was it, that was all he said. When I told him about Maman’s suicide it was obvious he already knew. Then he started reminding me of how he had saved my life. That he only did it because my Papa asked him and if I had stayed in Marseille I would have been sent to a death camp. It was like he was saying I owed him my life. It was what he said next that explained why here was there. He said he needed my help. I could tell by his eyes that he wasn’t just asking; but that it was a threat. He then started talking about his life. He told me after he left me in Marseille he had returned to Corsica to see his family. He said his island had been ravaged by the War, that his people were finding it hard to survive. He told me he had reverted to the only thing he knew, how to use a weapon, he said it was not to kill the fascists this time, although it would be a bonus if he did. He said he was withdrawing money from banks." Valeraine puffed out one of her sharp breaths. "He said only when they were closed though. His jokes hadn't improved. He then tried to justify it by saying it was the fascists who owned the banks, so nothing had changed anyway. And for me to remember that Papa had also fought the fascists and like Papa he had been caught and sent to prison. I remember hating the way he was comparing himself with my Papa. He said two policemen came to visit him while in prison. He joked that they were like the Gestapo, that they were in fact the French Secret Police, the Espionage Police, he said."

Lucile raised her eyes. "Louis Wallon and Henri Capitant?"

"*You are well informed Mademoiselle.*"

"Do you know who they were working for?"

Valeraine thought. "*No, Mademoiselle,* Francois didn't tell me."

"Did Francois mention a Luicien Aimé-Blanc?"

"Like I said, he didn't say. He told me he was serving a long sentence, that he had a good life before then and had even become friends with Alain Delon. He said the two policemen had made him an offer. They told him he could be released immediately if he did what they asked." She paused for a moment, like the silence was wanting to say something else. "That meeting had taken place two weeks before he came to see me."

Lucile could feel her hand becoming clammy, her mouth dry.

"Francois told me that the two policemen wanted Georges Pompidou's reputation...how do you English say Monsieur? 'Dragged through the mud'."

Norris returned a sharp nod.

"That they needed to stop his campaign for Presidency.

They said it was a matter of national security."

"Why?" asked Norris.

"Francois didn't..."

Lucile interrupted. "Because he was threatening to dissolve the SDECE."

"SDECE?" asked Norris.

"The French espionage service. The organisation where Louis Wallon and Henri Capitant worked."

"Now you know Monsieur," said Valeraine.

"So Francois asked you to be in these photographs?" asked Lucile.

"How can you refuse someone that had risked their life to save yours and your families? He promised me my face would be hidden, that I would wear a wig, no one would know."

"You still haven't said who the older woman was," remarked Lucile.

"Francois said he knew someone."

"But who was she?" Lucile had raised her voice slightly.

"I do not know, she hardly spoke, she just followed instructions. When she did speak it was always in French but with an accent, she wasn't French, maybe German." She glanced towards Norris. "Maybe English Monsieur. I think she looked older than her actual age. What I can tell you, she was made up to look exactly like Claude Pompidou. I know because I helped her."

"What was her name?" asked Lucile.

"I do not know. She didn't say, and we didn't use names. She was very nervous though, I think like me she had no choice."

Norris spoke next. "You said Francois visited you before you met Claude Pompidou."

"He came to the gallery a week before her visit. It only occurred to me later why Susanne had told Madame Pompidou about me; because it was Francois who had asked her. I remember Susanne being excited one day, telling me how she had met Alain Delon. Then it all began to add up: meeting the actor at a party, Francois saying he was his friend."

"I still don't understand. If he promised to hide your face then why ask you anyway. Why involve you at all? Why just not use...well, you know, any woman that was willing to do it for money." Norris made rabbit's ears with his fingers. "Like actresses?"

"I think it was because he could trust me. He knew I would stay quiet if the truth came out. The women you are talking about would probably sell their grandmother to the highest bidder. " She paused for a second. "And the painting Monsieur. It was Francois who asked me to hang The Drowning Mary in the room, also saying where to hang it. It was only by coincidence he saw the painting here in this room, he just happened to see it. It was going to be the..."

"The clue to validate the photographs, stop forgeries." Norris smiled. "Forgeries of forgeries. Very subtle though."

"It had to be Monsieur. That is how Louis Wallon and Henri Capitant would know, like an artist's signature."

"But you agreed to be in the photographs," said Lucile.

"*No,*" she barked. "Not at first. You underestimate me Mademoiselle Billet. I do not obey any..."

Lucile interrupted. "So why did you accept?"

"It was on Claude Pompidou's third visit, after Remi had sent me the two paintings. She had chosen The Foundering of Death, she took it that same day, carrying it out under her arm, telling me she would pay me the next week. Normally, I would never let a painting out the door without having the money first; but you do not refuse France's First Lady. Only she never turned up when she said she would. You see Mademoiselle, Monsieur, I never saw her again. I was angry. She made me feel as if I was still that gullible young girl. That was when I told him I would do it." An impish grin brushed passed her lips. "To be honest with you I quite enjoyed being naked in front of him, under his control, knowing he was watching me with another woman."

Lucile cleared her throat. “So where does Stevan Markovic’s murder come into all this?”

“*Ah yes,* Stevan Markovic. I think his...how do you say Monsieur, his days were numbered anyway.

Norris nodded yet again.

“When the news broke about his murder it was all over the newspapers. I read that he was known for throwing parties, secretly taking photographs of his guests. Then a rumour was put around that the Pompidou’s also attended these parties. I do not know if it was true.”

“And Francois knew Markovic.” Lucile asked. “After all, he was Alain Delon’s bodyguard?”

“*Yes,* but Francois never mentioned him to me, why should he, his murder came after. Before that I had never heard his name, not until the whole affair became public. But if you think about it Mademoiselle, it was perfect. Francois had discovered Markovic approached newspapers with other photographs, probably ones taken of people who refused to pay up. He knew these newspapers would vouch for his illicit dealings. Also, half the dignitaries in Paris wanted him dead. Then the rumours about The Pompidou’s attending his parties, finding the photographs in Markovic’s car, the secret police saying Madame Pompidou was one of the women. Sorry Monsieur, how do you English say? ‘Kill two birds with one stone’.”

“Not a saying we should be proud of Madame,” replied Norris.

“So Francois did kill him,” announced Lucile.

“Stevan Markovic wouldn’t be the first person Francois had killed,” replied Valeraine.

“So are you saying...”

“No Mademoiselle. I do not know who killed Stevan Markovic. I have never seen Francois since the photographs were taken. I heard he was arrested for it, then released, although I think that was all for show.”

“What happened to the rest of the photographs.”

Valeraine shrugged. "The Chief of Police was thought to have taken them. It is said he handed them over to Georges Pompidou after he became President." Valeraine stared down at the photograph still in Lucile's hand. "This is the first time I have ever seen one."

"I have another two." Lucile pulled them out of her bag. "These are all I have Madame."

The old woman's eyes darted around the pictures. She handed them back. "What are you going to do with them?"

"What would you like me to do with them?"

Valeraine thought for a while. "Desperate people will do things that most people couldn't even imagine, most only stopping when they have succeeded. I have seen it many times Mademoiselle. I learnt revenge and hate you can blame on others, just ask Susanne; but guilt, guilt is yours alone to keep." She took a deep breath. "Three weeks after the photographs were taken, Madame Pompidou sent one of her staff to the gallery, a young man. He said she apologised for not returning when she promised. He then paid me the money I was owed for The Foundering of Death. He said she would have come herself if it wasn't for the recent publicity she was getting."

"You mean the photographs?"

"*Yes.*" Valeraine looked at Lucile. "You asked me what I would like you to do with the photographs?" Her eyes had become as still as a millpond. "You must publish them, tell everyone what I have told you Mademoiselle Billet. Everything, leave nothing out. Tell them it was not Madame Pompidou in the pictures. I will vouch for it."

"What about your reputation? asked Norris. "What about the gallery?"

"I am an old woman, soon I won't even be that. When I die, my gallery will die with me. I care nothing about reputation. But you Mademoiselle, you will tell my story to the world, my family's story, everything, leave nothing out." Valeraine glared long and hard at her. "I have told you everything. Everything I know. Now I am tired."

Crystal signed and dated both forms, handing them back as if they were rare parchments. She rose from her chair and stretched out her arm. "Thank you honey," is all she said, knowing no more could be done, it was now out of her hands.

Christine Lamy stood and accepted their parting with a warm grip and a reassuring smile. "We will have the papers ready on the 4th July," she said. "You will stay in our lovely capital until then?"

Crystal departed the Embassy knowing her life was about to start a whole new chapter: she had passed the point of no return, there was no turning back.

Norris and Lucile stepped out of the gallery and crossed the road, he stopped and glanced back, only to look at the gallery one last time. But instead, what drew his attention was what was beside it, an irregular shape of different coloured bricks. It was where the door leading up to the second floor apartment had once been, the one he had stepped through two years ago. He wondered how anyone could get up there now.

Lucile released a long sigh. "And I still don't know who murdered Stevan Markovic," she said.

Norris thought for a while. "I believe there is only one man who could tell us that," he replied.

Tuesday 17th May 1983
Boulevard Vigouroux,
Marseille,
France

Dark eyed, unshaven with sunken cheeks, his skin sallow, Irene Kinley hardly recognised her husband. He was standing on one side of the doorway, she on the other; and that's how it was for the next half-a-minute. The two of them just staring at each other, both waiting for the other to speak. Their silence driven by different reasons. His was shame, guilt, remorse, self-delusion, greed, the list was endless. Her feelings could be summed up in just a couple of words — pure loathing. He moved out of the way and waited for her to enter. She stepped in, never once breaking eye contact, not wanting him to think he had defeated her. For her that was important, it had been for the past few years, even more so now.

Irene turned and glared at him with an expression of cold steel. "You said you wanted to discuss a divorce."

He remained silent.

She could see he had the demeanor of a man that had lost everything.

"How is Norris?" he finally asked, his words heavy.

"He has just gone back to school. He hates...." She stopped, before she arrived she had told herself to say the least possible. From experience she knew how he would only listen to the words he wanted to hear, replying with what suited his objective, an intent that was not usually a favourable outcome for her. "You said you wanted to discuss the terms for a divorce," she repeated. Irene knew he would want money, lots of it, probably most of it. She was willing to listen — to start with.

He sat on a chair and beckoned for her to sit opposite.

"Yes," he finally replied.

Irene Kinley felt a half smirk brush past her lips, she tried to stop it, but couldn't. She thought back to all those years he ruled their marriage, like a dictator drunk on power, controlling her every move, manipulating her every thought, abusing her mentally and sexually. Irene thought marriage was about love — he wanted it to be about fear. She was naive at the beginning, inexperienced, hating every second of his cravings, thinking every act was abhorrent, how dirty she felt afterwards, always anxious to wash his smell off. She thought it was normal to start with, that his repugnant requests were the same as in every other marriage. Then on a visit to her doctor she discovered different: the doctor told Irene sodomy and the wanton infliction of pain was very far from the norm.

Irene began making excuses — a headache, an infection, it hurt too much. Then she began to blatantly refuse him, knowing how she would suffer the consequences afterwards. That was when the abuse was at its worst, when he began forcing himself onto her, into her. But she never gave in, Irene Kinley needed to have her self-respect back. Then it suddenly stopped, for her it was a relief, she thought he had just got tired of her — maybe she had won, maybe he just got bored. To her relief he began spending more time away, she found out why, discovering he was going elsewhere for his needs, using the only way he knew how — money, her money. It was worth every penny.

She gazed at her husband with unseeing eyes, trying to think if there was anything in their marriage that made her happy, there was nothing. Norris was the only good to come out of it, but even that had been a hardship.

Then one day Joseph Kinley made one of his many trips to Paris, only this time it was different, he never returned. As the weeks drifted by she hoped it was the end, that she would never see him again. But she knew there was only one way she would feel completely free. Then several months later and out of the blue she got a phone call from him. He said if she came to Marseille that he would grant her the divorce she so desired. At first she thought it was one of his games, one of his many deceptions to dupe more money from her. Part of her wanted to ignore him, deep down she knew it would have nothing to do with a divorce. But he had said something to her which gave her an idea, something he wanted, something he couldn't get in France. Don't look a gift horse in the mouth she thought.

"You told me you have changed your name."

"My life is in danger." he said.

Was this the start of his pretence, his trickery? She had heard it so many times before. He had always been a fantasist, believing he was someone he wasn't. This was different though, he sounded paranoid, anxious, like a man that had lost his grip on reality. She knew whatever he said would make no difference, purposely shrugging, knowing he would hate her lack of concern, something she had learnt over the years.

His expression changed. She recognised the bloodshot rage in his eyes, the tightening of his lips, the pulsating temples, the grinding of his teeth — but she refused to be afraid.

"My name is Jean-Paul Karel," he said through gritted teeth.

"Probably wise dear," she said. "I mean if you think people are trying to kill you." Her words thick with sarcasm. "So no one knows you as Joseph Kinley?"

"No.."

"And everything referring to Joseph Kinley has been destroyed?"

"Everything, I am now officially Jean-Paul Karel." He sounded proud.

"You have always been very thorough dear."

"Joseph Kinley is now dead."

That is all she wanted to hear. She remained silent.

"The divorce money is for my son."

She played the game. "Norris is well taken care..."

He interrupted. "No, I have another son."

"Someone wants to kill you and you have a son." She paused for a second. "Oh Joseph dear, you have been busy."

"His name is Matthieu."

"Yes dear." The words dismissive.

"No!" his irritation returned. "It is true."

She remained cool, knowing how to react, never look submissive. She knew deep down he was a coward. "So who is the mother, some backstreet whore?" She wondered if she might have pushed him it too far, it wouldn't be the first time. She waited, her expression displaying nothing but calmness. "I am pleased for you," she said. " I hope you will be very happy." She stood. "Do try to keep this one dear. Goodbye." She took a step towards the door, playing him at his own game, anticipating his next move, like a game, one she had played many times before. He was far too transparent to be any good at it.

He shouted back at her. "Remember the house is half mine, everything in our marriage is half mine, including Norris."

It was what she expected, she turned. "Norris is not a commodity to be half owned. And it was you who left us." She threw a fake smile at him. "Remember dear?"

"Don't kid yourself, you wanted me to go," he spat.

She closed her eyes and sighed. "The only reason I am here is to hear you say that you want a divorce and to give you what you have asked for. But I know that is not all you want. I will give you money if you like, a lot more than you deserve."

His eyes widened in disbelief. "I will pay it back." Sounding more like an eager schoolboy.

Irene smiled. "Good." She didn't believe a word of it. "Then we must celebrate, here, I have brought it for you." She sat back down and pulled out a half-bottle of whisky from her bag. She was expecting him to be angry about it not being a full-size bottle, but that would have meant more dilution. Normally she hated it when he drank, knowing he would drop the little inhibitions he had, always to her detriment. "It is your favourite," she said, turning the label towards him. "I hope it is the right one, I remember how you used to drink it before..." She wanted to say, before you used to rape me, but didn't. Instead, she held it in one hand and hovered the other hand around its neck. She then threw her arm out. "You open it dear," before handing it over to him. He gripped the neck and paused. For a split second horror surged through her as he looked down at the cap. The tiny syringe hole was virtually invisible, just a dot in a single letter. She breathed a sigh of relief as he broke the seal with a series of clicks.

Irene pulled out a pen and cheque book, watching as he poured himself a drink. She had always been teetotal, he knew that. "You can have all the money you want," she said, her eyes fixed on his. She waited. "How much dear, ten thousand, twenty thousand?"

He took a gulp from the glass. A warmth spread through his body.

Irene waited. It had worked, her last two words had taken his mind away from any unusual taste, although she had hoped there was none. How would she know?

He ran his tongue along his top lip. "Then I will leave you alone," he said.

She had heard those same words before — so many times before.

"Have another drink while I write it out." The point of the pen hovered over the book.

"Its been a long time." His words had become slurred. "It is a long time since..." He stopped, his eyelids felt heavy. "Since I have...I feel..." He looked down, she still hadn't written it out.

"Take another sip dear."

He put the glass to mouth. "You haven't...I feel..."

"Enjoy it dear. It has probably been a while."

"Yes, you are right." He put a hand on his stomach. "Maybe it's something I have eaten."

Irene could see his eyes glazing over. "Have another sip dear, take a good, long one. It is the best single malt." She stretched her arm out, placing the tip of one finger under the glass, guiding it up to his mouth. She was hoping it wasn't too obvious. "It will take the pain away, make you feel so much better. That's it." She slowed her words and looked down her nose. "A nice long sip dear. See, see how good it makes you feel."

He gulped down another mouthful. She poured some more into the glass. Another guzzle. He coughed, not realising some of the liquid had trickled down his chin. He began gazing around the room, his eyes rolling in their sockets, his mouth open. Irene knew he was starting to hallucinate. He began mumbling, saying things that made no sense at first. She thought it was the poison talking. She asked him questions. He answered them.

"The money," he slurred.

She began asking him more questions, especially about a certain day fifteen years ago. He answered them all. She stopped and looked down. The pen touched the paper. She looked up.

His eyes began to roll back into his head. "I don't feel..." He placed a hand on his stomach again. "My stomach is hurting..." He began to grimace.

The pen lifted from the paper. Irene leant over towards him, her face only centimetres from his. His eyes became motionless, gazing directly at her. Her smile widened, she wanted him to see she had won.

"You have put something..."

"It is just whisky dear, your favourite, you asked me to get it for you. Drink some more, it will make you feel better."

She held the glass at an angle, forcing more of the liquid down his throat, watching him gulp the contents. He began to splutter. She kept the glass at the same angle, studying his eyes, watching as he finished. Waiting for his life to ebb away.

His chin dropped, a low groan, then silence.

Irene Kinley took a make-up mirror out of her bag and held it in front of his face, a slight mist appeared. She waited. He had remained still, she prodded his arm. She held the mirror in front of his nose and mouth again, for an entire minute. She turned it towards her, it was clear. She puckered her lips and stroked a flick of her hair from her forehead. Irene then took a new whisky bottle cap from her purse and placed it on the table, putting the old one in her bag. She rose and walked over to the door, stopped and turned. "You were not wrong when you said someone wanted to kill you dear."

Irene put a scarf over her head, a pair of sunglasses over her eyes, unfolded a walking stick, arched her back, opened the door, shuffled out of the apartment and slid her gloves off.

Saturday 2nd July 2010
Hotel Manon,
Paris,
France

Interview spoken in French: 30th June 2010
Kevin (aka Tim Borrin, aka Toby Brown)
talking to Francois Marcantoni in his
home at Ajaccio, Corsica.

Norris slotted the tape cassette into the machine, pushed the flap shut and shoved the red play button down. A noisy crackle came through the speaker, it was loud, too loud, if it remained throughout the entire recording it would drown out everything he or Lucile needed to hear. Both breathed a sigh of relief as a click was followed by near silence, then...

Presumably Francois: (A gruff sound).
Kevin: (In a warm but serious tone). "*Thank you for talking to me Monsieur, especially at such short notice.*"
Francois: (His voice strained). "*Ah yes. In my health it will have to be at short notice.*"
Kevin: "*Do you mind if I take notes.*"

Francois: (With a throaty chuckle). "*I hope you are a fast writer?*"

"He sounds very old," remarked Norris.

"That's because he is," replied Lucile, before loudly shushing him.

Kevin: (A hesitant laugh).
Francois: "*You are English Monsieur?*"
Kevin: "*Yes, but I live in Calvi now.*"
Francois: "*You cannot leave our beautiful island?*" (Difficult to tell if it was a statement or question).
Kevin: "*No.*" (Changing to a lighthearted note). "*Some of us feel we have nowhere else to go.*"
Francois: "*Ah yes. I know the feeling.*" (A pause). "*You told me on the telephone you were once a legionnaire? Is that why, because you have nowhere else to go?*"
Kevin: "*Amongst other things.*"
Francois: "*We all have something or someone to hide from Monsieur.*"
Kevin: "*Do you Monsieur?*"
Francois: "*Maybe we are just hiding from ourselves.*"
Kevin: "*Ah.*" (Extending the word). "*Then that freedom usually comes at a higher cost.*"
Francois: "*Ah yes.*" (Muffled, like he was chewing on something). "*Very true.*"
Kevin: "*We all have our weaknesses Monsieur.*"
Francois: (A sarcastic laugh). "*Some may call it a strength.*"

Silence.
The click of a lighter.
Followed by a long wheezy breath.

Francois: "*Do you know I gave these things up many years ago.*" (Like he wanted to change the subject). "*Then I found out*

it was too late, they had already beaten me. So now I have joined forces with them, now we work together." (It sounded like there was a hidden meaning). "*Would you like one Monsieur?*"
Kevin: "*No thank you.*"
Francois: (A long release of air — or smoke). "*Do you know I once met Remy Raffalli during the war?*"
Kevin: (No reply, like he was waiting).

Norris turned to Lucile. "Camp Raffalli was where Kevin was stationed in Corsica, the camp was named after Remy Raffalli. Kevin told me this himself." He spoke quickly, feeling pleased with himself for keeping up with the conversation. His French had greatly improved since his time in France.

Lucile returned an impatient nod and shushed him again.

Francois: "*Charles Tillon had organised a meeting with the FTPF and...*"
Kevin: (Interrupting). "*Sorry Monsieur, I do not understand. What is the FTPF? Who is Charles Tillon?*"
Francois: "*Charles Tillon was leader of Francs-Tireurs et Partisans. We were resistance fighters in the war. We were also communists.*"
Kevin: (No comment, like he was waiting again, nor did he question Francois's use of the word 'we').
Francois: "*A secret meeting was held in the hills at Ardeche. That is when I met Raffalli. He was an officer in the Free French Army. Charles Tillon and another FTPF leader called Albert Ouzoulias were also there. Albert Ouzoulias especially asked for me, because I was Corsican.*"

A clunking noise, like a heavy door handle?
Then different sounds: a motorcycle engine,
a dog barking, a child screaming, a bicycle bell;
as if the outside world
had been let into the room.

Amongst all this was an indistinct woman's voice.

Francois: (Softly) "*Ah Yes. Thank you Alice. Would you like a drink Monsieur?*"
Kevin: "*Yes please.*"
Francois: "*Coffee? Beer? Maybe you would like a cognac?*"

Lucile overplayed a roll of her eyes and tutted. "Get on with it Kevin or whatever your name is."

Kevin: "*Coffee please.*"
Francois: (Muted, like his head had turned away). "*Coffee and a...*" (Indistinct).
The woman's voice: (Angry). "*You know Doctor Aravena said not to smoke those things and not to drink this early.*"
Francois: (Also angry). "*Doctor Aravena will be glad to see the back of...*"

A click and a loud thud.
The outside noise shut out again.
Silence.

Francois: "*Alice.*" (A faint tut). "*Half my age and she thinks she is my mother.*"
Kevin: "*Please continue Monsieur Marcantoni. This man said he knew you were from Corsica.*"
Francois: "*Ah yes, Albert Ouzoulias. He knew I came from Corsica. Remy Raffalli was going to fight a campaign in Italy with the French Expeditionary Corps. They wanted to ask me about Corsica.*"
Kevin: "*What sort of questions?*"
Francois: "*Mainly about the Corsican people.*" (His voice became tetchy). "*He asked if I knew people that he could rely on.*"
Kevin: "*Did you?*"

Francois: (No reply).
Kevin: "*Sorry Monsieur, of course. Was Nicolas...*"

A click of the door lock again.
Followed by the sounds of the
street again.

A woman's voice: "*Monsieur.*"

A tap and a rattle,
then the clink of a spoon.

Kevin: (Quietly). "*Thank you Madame.*"

A chink, like glass on glass.

A woman's voice: (Still angry). "*Your cognac. And it will not be me carrying you out.*"

Lucile leant over the tape machine. "Ask him about Markovic," she said, her voice raised.

Francois: "*Thank you Alice.*"

Silence, followed by another thud.
The outside world quiet again,
as if someone had flicked a switch off.

Kevin: "*Was Nicolas Dennel at this meeting?*"
Francois: "*No Monsieur.*"
Kevin: "*But you knew Nicolas Dennel?*"
Francois: "*Ah yes, I remember on the telephone you said you were going to write about the Dennel family.*"
Kevin: "*I am researching the possibility.*" (Choosing his words

carefully).
Francois: "*Ah yes.*" (A pause, as if in thought). "*Why?*"
Kevin: "*Try something new? Get away from the usual crap.*"
Francois: "*Ah yes.*" (Another short pause). "*I am also a writer Monsieur.*"
Kevin: "*Yes I know.*" (Unconvincingly). "*I will try and read them one day.*" (Even more unconvincing)

Lucile slapped her hands on the table. "Now!" she shouted at the tape machine. "Marcantoni wrote a book about the Markovic affair." Her eyes became round. "Ask him about it."

Kevin: "*My friend said you fought alongside Nicolas Dennel?*"

"No!" Lucile cried out. "He's missed it." Protracting the word and dropping her elbows onto the table, her chin cupped in her hands. "I should have gone to interview him," she said softly in defeat.

Francois: "*You have experienced armed conflict Monsieur?*"

"I take it you have read this book?" Norris asked, not knowing if she had.

Lucile shushed him again, waving her hand in the air, then spoke anyway. "There was nothing in it that I didn't know already."

Kevin: "*Yes, In Africa. But it was mostly humanitarian.*"

Francois: "*Ah yes. Saving lives is always preferential to taking them.*"
Kevin: "*I agree.*" (A long silence).
Francois: "*You wish to tell me Monsieur.*"

"Who is fucking interviewing who?" Lucile yelled at the

machine.

Kevin: "*A man decided to go on a Sunday stroll; in Chad; in the midday heat. When we...my fellow soldiers and myself found him he was nearly a Sunday roast. He later told us his older brother had gone to join the Chadian army, leaving him to protect his younger family. He told us the rebels came to his town, they killed his youngest brother and raped his sister. This man managed to escape, deciding his life wasn't worth living anymore he...let us say found a nice warm spot and waited to die, that was when we found him. He told me his name was Marcel Nkusi, we kept in touch. Then for some reason he went back to his home town. That was when the rebels finally caught up with him. The poor sod was tortured to find out the whereabouts of his brother.*" (A short pause). "*If you can't change the world then you just hope it doesn't change you, he once told me. His brother wanted revenge for Marcel's death, no matter how he got it. He went looking for the rebels, eventually wiping out the entire gang, including the leader.*" (Another short pause). "*This was a man that gave killing a bad name Monsieur. This Captain also had a vendetta on the rest of his family, every single member, not resting until he had killed them all. So the rebels dispatched an assassin to kill this Captain. She...*"
Francois: "*She! A woman?*"

"What's wrong with that." Lucile said, unsmiling. Norris wondered if she had heard herself.

Kevin: "*She is the daughter of the rebel leader. Only she shot the wrong man.*"
Francois: (After a long silence). "*Unfortunate.*" (A shorter silence). "*I can see why your books are about your experiences.*"
Kevin: "*In a way, but they are mostly about the Legion, fiction,*

nothing like real life. Everyone loves a hero."
Francois: "*But not a dead hero Monsieur, only dead enemies.*"
Kevin: (Seemingly waiting).
Francois: "*But in real life it is always the hero who gets killed.*"
Kevin: "*Is Nicolas Dennel a dead hero?*"
Francois: (No words, just the rasp of a strained breath)
Kevin: "*I believe you also knew Nicolas Dennel's wife and two daughters?*"
Francois: "*Nicolas asked me to help them escape to France, get them into Switzerland. The Spanish route was becoming far too risky, too many people were being caught.*" (A long pause). "*At first I refused, I wanted to stay and kill Nazis. Then I was captured, my comrades had left me to my fate. But not Nicolas, he followed us through the woods until the time was right. Then single handed he killed four Nazi soldiers and helped me escape. How could I refuse him after that.*" (Another pause). "*When I first met his family I remember thinking they were all very attractive, even the mother, but especially Susanne, the youngest daughter, I knew then she was going to grow up and have any man she wanted.*" (The inference obvious).
Kevin: "*And Valeraine?*"
Francois: (A deep sigh) "*I would say pretty, more than beautiful. I think she had a crush on me so I tried to spend more time with her sister and mother. They used to laugh at my jokes.*" (A short pause). "*Valeraine was always wanting to be with me, following me around like a puppy, her eyes on me all the time. When we slept in the tent she was always watching me. It was creepy Monsieur.*"

Lucile yelled at the machine. "Markovic! Markovic! Markovic!" Slapping her hands down on the table with each shout. "Ask him if he killed Markovic."

"Calm down." Norris said. "Kevin knows what he's doing. He's just loosening up Marcantoni's tongue."

"He might not live that fucking long!"

Francois: "*Then after the war I went searching for them. I wanted to give them news of their father, they had a right to know, to start a new life. I knew they would have left their names at the synagogue, everyone did, hoping their loved ones would return one day. I found them in a tiny fishing village called Le Vallon des Auffes. I went there to tell them the truth, that Nicolas had been captured in an ambush, that he would have been tortured by the Gestapo for days, maybe weeks. He would have been kept in solitary confinement, made to listen to the screams from the other prisoners. Then they would have executed him and dumped him in a mass grave. I went to tell them Nicolas Dennel was the bravest man I knew, that he didn't talk.*" (A short pause). "*But I am a coward Monsieur.*" (Another short pause). "*I lied. I told them he was killed outright, a bullet to the heart, that he didn't suffer, that we buried him in the woods just outside Marseille, that a Jewish comrade conducted the ceremony. I told them our ambush plan had been disclosed by an informer, that he was from Marseille; and that was the truth. It was strange because I had thought it would be Susanne who wouldn't be able to take the news, instead she just remained quiet, her eyes fixed in front of her, not even a squeak. It was Valeraine who lost control, throwing herself at me, shouting that I was lying, that it was my fault. When I was leaving I told them I was sorry their house had been bombed. It was Susanne who told me what had happened, how it had been occupied by strangers. I knew immediately the Germans would only allow a particular type of Frenchman to live in a large house like that, a Nazi sympathiser, maybe an informer. That was when I helped them get it back, but not for them Monsieur, for me. For me the war was not over.*"

Kevin: "*How did you get the house back?*"

Francois: "*I asked her to describe the man living on the top floor. She told me how he had shoved her mother to the ground. I knew the type, a coward. I might not be a large man Monsieur,*

but the hate in my heart was greater then anyone elses. A woman opened the door, I pushed her out of the way, the woman screamed. When I got to the top floor he had already come out of his apartment. He was big, but not fit, he didn't have a chance, he fell with one punch. As he was falling I kicked him, that was when I heard the first snap. It sent him rolling down the first flight of stairs." (The tone in his voice was one of pride). "*Then I kicked him all the way down the next flight, then four more, stopping on each landing while I knocked on the occupants door, making sure they saw him, telling them this would be their fate if they didn't move out immediately. By the time we reached the ground floor every bone in his body was broken, there wasn't a part of him not covered in blood.*"
Kevin: "*Was he dead?*"
Francois: (Ignoring the question). "*The people in the other apartments packed up on that same day. After that, I stayed in Marseille for a while, with the three of them, helping them build their lives again. Valeraine insisted she came with me when I went out on the streets at night, stealing whatever we could, mostly furniture recovered from bombed houses. I think she liked the excitement. She was always asking me questions about her Papa, how he died? Ones I couldn't answer. Then the night before I left for Corsica, she wanted to say goodbye to me, she wanted to give me something to remember her by.*" (A short pause). "*I said no at first, but she became persistent, she insisted, wouldn't take no for an answer.*" (Another short pause). "*I did it for her Monsieur. I can tell you now, it wasn't her first time.*"
Kevin: "*Apart from that man in the house have you killed anyone else?*"
Francois: "*I never said I killed him Monsieur.*"
Kevin: "*Have you killed anyone?*"
Francois: "*Many Nazi's.*"
Kevin: "*Anyone else?*"
Francois: (A long pause) "*You are asking me if I am a*

murderer."

Lucile froze, her mouth open, her eyes wide. Even Norris angled his head so his ear was closer to the speaker.

Kevin: "*Something like that.*"
Francois: "*I am ninety Monsieur. Do you know the doctor has given me one month to live, two at the most? If I keep smoking these things and drinking cognac like you English drink tea then hopefully it will be sooner.*"
Kevin: "*I am sure some people care. Alice certainly does.*"
Francois: "*Yes, but she is my daughter. Many wouldn't though, including Valeraine.*"
Kevin: "*Why Valeraine?*"
Francois: "*You said earlier that freeing yourself comes at a higher cost.*"
Kevin: "*I remember.*"
Francois: "*My freedom came at a very high price.*"
Kevin: "*How much?*"
Francois: "*The future President of France. The price for my freedom was be to bring down Georges Pompidou.*"
Kevin: "*That is a high price Monsieur.*"
Francois: "*I knew what would hurt him the most.*"
Kevin: "*Madame Pompidou?*"
Francois: "*Ah yes, but how? I had a friend who was a very famous actor.*" (A pause, like he was waiting). "*He knew someone who arranged parties. Many important people attended these parties Monsieur at which this person used to take secret photographs and blackmail his victims afterwards.*" (Another pause). "*My friend knew this.*" (A deep sigh). "*Then I think the Gods must have been looking down on me Monsieur. I met Susanne Dennel again at a party, shortly after I was released; thinking back it wasn't really such a coincidence. She told me most of the girls there worked for her. I couldn't believe it at first, she had changed in so many ways. I was right about*

her becoming a great beauty Monsieur. We talked for a long while, mostly about our memories from the War, and her family, but also about politics and Georges Pompidou's campaign for Presidency. It was then Susanne told me she knew the Pompidous." (A long pause followed, like he was saying something without actually speaking). "*She said that Madame Pompidou was going to build a museum for modern art, it would be in her husband's name. I noticed how everyone treated Susanne with respect, like they wouldn't want to cross her. She told me about Valeraine's marriage, how it broke down, that she now owned an art gallery in Montmartre. As she spoke I could see the plan falling into place. All she had to do was introduce Claude Pompidou to her sister, persuade her that the art centre should not only be for famous artists, that she should have one work by a good provincial artist as well, for the people of France, think how that would look for the Pompidous; that Valeraine could help her find a painting like that for the museum; and that Madam Pompidou herself should go and talk to her. All I had to do after that was to try and persuade Valeraine to be in the photographs.*"
Kevin: "*What about the other woman?*"

"At last!" Lucile cried.

Francois: "*I knew someone who owed me, he said he could get a woman, an older woman. He knew nothing of what it was about.*"
Kevin: "*Who was he?*"
Francois: "*A nobody.*"
Kevin: "*Did he have a name?*"
Francois: "*Everyone has a name Monsieur. Even the person who organised those parties. But you know that already.*"
Kevin: "*Did you know who the woman was?*"
Francois: "*I did not ask Monsieur.*"
Kevin: (He knew the code, never give names). "*So you took the*

photographs?"
Francois: "*What you are really asking Monsieur is if it was me who killed Stevan Markovic and planted the photographs?*"
Kevin: "*And did you?*"

Lucile and Norris had frozen, only breathing when they had to.

Francois: (A throaty sigh, then silence).
Kevin: "*It was you who took them.*" (The 'was' was greatly emphasised)
Francois: (Another grating sigh, followed by a short pause) "*I have very little time to live Monsieur. I could own up to killing your Queen of England and it would make no difference.*"
Kevin: (Sarcastically) "*And have you killed the Queen of England?*"
Francois: (A loud laugh, followed by a spluttering cough).
Kevin: "*So did you kill Stevan Markovic?*"
Francois: "*Someone was in the wrong place at the wrong time or the right place at the right time. It wasn't looking good for Markovic whichever way you look at.*" (Another long silence).
Kevin: "*And that place was the rubbish dump at Elancourt.*"
Francois: "*A rubbish dump was where he belonged Monsieur.*"
Kevin: "*Did you kill Markovic for your actor friend?*"
Francois: (A loud laugh).
Kevin: (Forceful) "*Did he ask you to murder Stevan Markovic?*"
Francois: "*Before his murder Stevan Markovic sent a letter to his brother. It said if he is murdered then it would be at the hands of myself and...*" (A short pause) "*Alain.*"
Kevin: "*Inconvenient.*"
Francois: "*I would have done society a favour Monsieur. Markovic was a boil that needed to be lanced. People would have thanked me, including many in high places.*"
Kevin: "*The Pompidous?*"
Francois: (No reply).
Kevin: "*The police?*"

Francois: (A puff of air, then silence)
Kevin: "*Do the words The Drowning Mary have any meaning to you?*"
Francois: "*Switch that machine off and I will tell you every thing.*"
Kevin: "*I'm afraid I can't do that.*"
Francois: "*Because your friend needs to hear?*"
Kevin: "*Something like that.*"
Francois: "*Monsieur...?*" (Stretching the word).
Kevin: (A short silence). "*Kevin Brown, Monsieur Marcantoni.*"
Francois: "*Monsieur Brown, the world is made of few masters and many slaves. What are you Monsieur?*"
Kevin: (Silence).
Francois: "*I thought not. Then if you wish to know the truth, you must switch that machine off.*"
Kevin: (Silence).

A click

The same loud crackle fizzled through the speaker. Norris and Lucile waited for a long while. Norris pushed the red button down, the noise stopped. He pressed on the tape flap, it popped open. He slid out the cassette and placed it on the table next to the machine. Each movement was calculated and precise, each movement watched attentively by Lucile. Norris waited for her reaction.

"He switched it off," Lucile said.

Norris was surprised by her calmness. "Apparently."

"That means Marcantoni must have told him."

Norris raised his eyebrows and drew down his lips. "Maybe."

"You must speak to him, find out what was said."

"You don't know Kevin, he is an ex-soldier, thay have a code..."

"Phone your friend." Lucile interrupted, her words

assertive.

Norris took out his phone and prodded the screen, put it to his ear and waited. His grip became tighter. "Kevin, it's Norris..." He stopped and listened. "Yes I have." He looked at Lucile. "Yes she is." He waited again. "Oh okay, phone me when you get here." He poked the screen once again and returned it to his pocket. "He won't talk about it on the phone, he's coming to Marseille."

"Is that all he said?"

"He's not a man to mince his words."

"Shame he didn't do that with Marcantoni."

Sunday 4th July 2010
Gare de Marseille-Saint-Charles,
Marseille,
France

The African man stepped through the station door and watched as the three descended the steps, until they had dropped out of sight, the clomping of a suitcase the only indication of their existence.

The woman pulling the case had the appearance of someone entering middle-age, neatly styled blonde hair, perfect make-up, wearing a floral summer dress and carrying a bag over her shoulder. The African man thought she looked American. The other woman was younger, late twenties, she was short with dark shoulder length hair and a rucksack hanging from her back. She was wearing an oversized black t-shirt and jeans, attempting to conceal her plumpness under loose clothing. French, he guessed. The man accompanying them was tall, very tall, pale skinned, a slightly curved spine made it appear as if his head was leading his body. He was wearing light summer trousers and a beige, short sleeved shirt, a sports like holdall bag hung from one hand. He could have been from any Western European country.

The man following them had taken a mental note of their appearance — just in case, having nearly lost them on several occasions already. To do so would be more than his life's worth.

He himself was Central African with shiny black skin, his bloodshot eyes set deep in a heavily lined skeletal face. He waited for a few seconds before taking several cautious strides forward, halting when he could see to the bottom of the steps. He caught sight of them again, they had veered to the right and stopped on the pavement. He started his descent on the left, just one of many using the steps. He began slowly at first, staring directly ahead but managing to keep them in his peripheral vision. He quickened as he saw the tall man hail a taxi, a few seconds later a white saloon stopped. Cheek to cheek kisses were exchanged and the blonde woman climbed into the back, leaving the tall man to stow her suitcase in the boot.

The African man swiftly skipped to the bottom of the steps and waited. A dark Peugeot pulled in front of him, he just managed to miss the door as it opened while still on the move. Inside was the driver and two men sat at the back, all were Central African. The man threw himself onto the front passenger seat and the car sped away.

Crystal, Lucile and Norris arrived at the Gare de Marseille-Saint-Charles four hours after leaving Paris. The time on the train was filled with Crystal telling them about her experiences with Christine Lamy, how the young woman had helped her fill out the form a second time, advising her on the correct wording to use. 'She was a complete honey' was how Crystal described her. She told Lucile and Norris the whole process of getting Jamia and Ali into Canada would hopefully take no more than a month or two. Crystal then added that in the meantime they will have to find somewhere else to live, somewhere cheaper, somewhere safe. Where? That didn't matter. Also she would have no choice but to stay with them. Crystal then listened as Lucile told her about Valeraine Rousselle, how she told them about her horrific experiences in the war, how she was one of the women in the Markovic photographs. At the end Lucile voiced her disappointment in still not knowing the identity of the older woman, other than she was a foreigner. She said she will ask Julien to look into it, see if he could identify her, but doubted if even Julien could manage that. She knew these small details were important in corroborating the authenticity of her story, although she had misgivings about the other woman still being alive. More importantly, who the actual murderer was had still evaded her, although she told both Crystal and Norris her money was still on Francois Marcantoni. Norris told Lucile he would contact his friend in Corsica, see if he could make contact with Marcantoni, find out the truth.

It was just past lunchtime when the train pulled into the station, the three exited through the main doors and descended the steps.

"Allow me," Norris said, in true English gentlemanly style as he offered to carry Crystal's suitcase.

"I'm fine honey," she replied, choosing to drag it behind her, cursing as it smacked against her calf every time it dropped down a step, feminism comes at a high price she thought to herself. They finally arrived at the pavement with Crystal announcing she would need a taxi to get to the hotel. Norris looked along the road and waited, he lifted his hand. A large white saloon pulled up beside them. They exchanged farewell kisses and Norris lifted the suitcase into the boot. The taxi pulled away.

Seconds later a dark blue Peugeot passed close by him and stopped abruptly in front of a black man about twenty metres away. It shot away. Neither Lucile or Norris thought anything of it.

The dark Peugeot slowed as they saw the taxi pull up outside the Hotel Abella. The four occupants watched as the door opened and the blonde woman stepped onto the pavement, walking around the back to retrieve her suitcase. The Chadian army captain recognised her immediately. "*Turn left and stop,*" he told the driver.

The driver opened the boot and handed her the suitcase. She paid him, he looked irritated. Crystal doesn't do tips: no one had tipped her for trying to feed thirty thousand starving people in the middle of a drought, no one had tipped her for trying to save the lives of children racked with cholera and dysentery, no one had tipped her for stopping a young girl from being raped. She never expected one, so no one else should.

She entered the hotel and immediately headed for the elevator. Less than a minute later she stepped out onto the fourth floor, dragging her case behind her. She reached the door, knocked three times and waited. Another two knocks, more silence. She knocked once again. "It's Crystal sweetie," she whispered.

Teresa opened the door, her face impassive. Crystal stepped in and saw Jamia and Ali sitting on the bed, pillows tucked behind their backs, mesmerised by a pop video playing on the television, the sound on mute. Teresa had insisted, she would go crazy if she heard Jessy Matador singing Allez Ola Olé one more time. Jamia swung her legs over the side of the bed as soon as she saw Crystal.

"How's it been honey?" Crystal asked.

Teresa returned an unconvincing smile. "How was it in Paris?"

Jamia stood. "*Did you see the Eiffel Tower?*" she asked.

"*Yes,*" she replied in Arabic. "*So will you soon.*" Her gaze hanging on Jamia for a short while. "I need a shower sweetie," she said just as the phone rang. She looked at Teresa, then the phone, then shrugged. "I need a shower." Heading straight for the bathroom. "*I'll tell you later,*" calling back to Jamia.

Jamia sat back on the bed, wrapping an arm around Ali, her attention absorbed by the television again.

Teresa picked up the phone.

A second African man stepped through the hotel door and into the foyer, he was not the same man as the one at the railway station, this one was much younger, fresh faced, chubby cheeked. He sauntered up to the reception desk with a warm, wide smile. "*I have just dropped a passenger off at this hotel, she had blonde hair, I think she was American. I found this on the seat,*" he said, holding up a pen.

The receptionist took it from him.

"*It looks expensive,*" he said, continuing to beam out his pristine, white-toothed smile.

"*Does it?*" Her reply was blunt, discourteous even, thinking it looked like any other cheap pen, he probably doesn't know any different she thought. To her he was just a taxi driver, there was no reason to be polite. She stared at the computer screen and tapped on the keyboard.

The African Man waited.

She then wrote on a tag and tied it to the pen. "*I will make sure she gets it,*" the receptionist said without looking at him, continuing with her duties as if she had dismissed him.

He remained rooted to the spot.

The receptionist looked up. "*Thank you,*" she said coldly.

He waited.

"*Thank you Monsieur. I'm sure she will appreciate how kind you have been,*" she said with a fake smile. "*I will inform her it was you.*"

He leant over the desk and picked up the pen by the tag. "*Maybe I could take it up to her.*"

She snatched it back. "*Thank you Monsieur, but only residents and members of staff are allowed upstairs.*"

The African man beamed out his warm smile again, turned and left the hotel.

The receptionist picked up the phone.

Crystal stepped out of the steamy bathroom in a soft white

dressing gown, her face flushed with a pink glow. "Who was on the phone?" she asked Teresa.

"Just the receptionist. Nothing important. You left a pen on the backseat of a taxi. Do you know she speaks perfect Span..."

"A pen?"

"Did you get a taxi here?"

"Yes."

"Then you left it on the backseat. The driver gave it to her. She said the porter will bring it up when he comes back from his coffee break." Teresa's words tailing away as she saw Crystal pick up her bag and rummage around inside. After several seconds of searching she pulled out a pen, holding it up for all to see. "This is my pen." Her frown deepened. "Phone the receptionist back, tell her the driver must have been..." She paused. "No honey, first ask her what the taxi driver looked like."

Teresa lifted the receiver and dialed for the receptionist. After a short wait she spoke in Spanish. "*It is...*" She stopped herself. "*It is me again. You just told me a pen belonging to my friend was left on the backseat of a taxi. Yes..thank...No no...I will collect it. What did the taxi driver look like?*" A few seconds of silence. "*Wait please.*" Teresa held a hand over the mouth piece. "He was black, short, stocky, about thirty..."

Crystal interrupted. "It must have been another..." Her words came to an abrupt halt. Her expression darkened.

Teresa glared at her, she put the receiver back to her ear. "*Please do not send the porter up, keep it there and do not let anyone know this room number.*" A short pause as Teresa listened. "*He may have seen...*" She closed her eyes. "*No, everything is fine.*" Teresa calmed her voice. "*Someone will come down and collect it.*" She waited for a second, placed the receiver back down and looked at Crystal. "You had better get dressed."

"*408,*" is all the second African man said as he returned to the

Peugeot.

The Captain pulled a small pistol from under the seat, checked the magazine with a clunk of metal, screwed a silencer onto the end of the barrel and rested it on his lap, his hand remained wrapped around the grip. "*My family's revenge will soon be complete,*" he said under his breath.

Same day
L'Autre Cafe,
Marseille,
France

Norris's Great British self-consciousness had kicked in long ago. For the past ten minutes he couldn't help but notice the waiter's behaviour: a stony glare, a deep sigh, another wipe of the table. Norris knew that he and Lucile had already made their coffees last much longer than the acceptable given time — even for a French cafe, even if the table was outside and the furthermost one away, even if some of the other tables were unoccupied.

On the other hand, Lucile appeared not to have noticed; which came as no surprise to Norris. From the day he had met her he had learnt that she had very little conscience whatsoever, no moral compass, he always thought it was just the attributes of a hard-nosed journalist. It became obvious her patience was wearing thin: that annoying finger tapping, the incessant glances at her watch, a look his way followed by an exaggerated roll of her eyes. Sometimes he tried to make a playful comment about the situation, sarcastically saying it was her eye make-up that was making her look sad, which usually prompted a long hard glare, followed by an even more pronounced roll of her eyes. Norris also knew there was only one reason she had remained at the cafe; the man they were waiting for had information far too important to miss. If everything went to plan then the last two pieces of the jigsaw would finally be placed in position: she would know who the other woman was and who killed Stevan Markovic.

Norris's mind wandered, he knew a month ago he would have puffed his way through at least half a dozen cigarettes by now, knowing the satisfaction would have far outweighed the guilt. The craving hadn't abandoned him, the willpower he needed to stop himself from entering the cafe to buy a packet was as strong as ever. Not helping him were the three overly made-up, middle-aged women sipping on their espressos at the table next to them, theatrically holding their white sticks between two bony fingers, a cloud of smoke drifting above them, or more annoyingly, towards Norris.

So it was a great relief when a taxi stopped outside the cafe only a few metres away and Kevin stepped out. Norris remembered that meeting in the tukul, the one with the blue door, when Major Guerrette was present, just the three of them in the round hut. How Kevin looked then, in one of the harshest countries in the world. Hair virtually cut to the scalp, perfectly ironed summer trousers, shiny brown leather shoes, a chequered shirt, its short sleeves tight with muscle, tattoos running up and down both arms, shoulders back, his spine as straight as a rod. That was not a forced gait, it was as if he had been born like it. Even at his age he was still a formidable man. His spell in the French Foreign Legion would remain with him forever. Norris also thought he was the male equivalent of Crystal, maybe they would make a good couple, like he and Lucile hopefully would. Kevin's handshake was firm but brief.

The waiter appeared out of nowhere.

"*Beer,*" Kevin said flatly, without raising his eyes.

"*Coffee with milk please,*" Norris said, gazing up with a

smile.

Lucile shook her head quickly, like it had shuddered, continuing to stare at Kevin. “Did you get held up? It’s been well over an hour.”

“Unfinished business,” he replied.

Lucile waited for an explanation. None came. “We listened to your tape,” she said.

Kevin turned towards Norris. “So your father topped himself?”

Norris was surprised he had completely ignored Lucile, knowing she would have loathed that. “That is what the police said. He poisoned himself.”

Kevin nodded slowly, like he approved. “At least he wasn’t a jumper, that really pisses me off.” He paused for a second. “Why?”

“Why what?”

“Was he down in the dumps or something?”

“I don’t know. He...” Norris stopped talking as he saw the waiter return with the beer and coffee.

“We listened to your tape.” Lucile repeated, taking advantage of the break in conversation.

“I got to Marcantoni just in time, you could say he was knockin’ on heaven’s door...or damnation’s is more to the truth,” he added.

Lucile turned to Norris as if Kevin wasn’t there. In a way it was revenge for ignoring her a few seconds ago. “Does he always speak in riddles.”

Norris laughed, so did Kevin.

Lucile thought Kevin was straight from the set of EastEnders, wasting so much of her life watching every episode was now justified. She continued. “I want to talk to you about what he said after the tape was turned off.”

Kevin turned his attention back to Norris. “Was it to do with his son?...What’s his name?”

“Matthieu.” Norris shook his head, he felt uneasy, knowing

Lucile would be hating being spurned once again. "I don't know. My father..."

Kevin turned back to Lucile, stopping Norris in his tracks. "You want to know who knocked-off Stevan Markovic?"

Lucile's eyes widened in anticipation. "Yes I do."

Kevin ignored her again. "How well did you know your old man?"

Norris was surprised how effortlessly Kevin could swap from one conversation to the other, he wasn't sure if it was a strategy or he just didn't want to disappoint either. He finally answered. "It was a long time ago, I was in my early teens. Neither of my parents were close. I mean we weren't exactly a loving family. To be honest I didn't really know my father that well, he spent a long time away in France, on..."

Lucile interrupted, raising her voice. "Francois Marcantoni said if you turned the tape off then he would tell you the truth."

Kevin's eyes narrowed, he answered in French. "*He did Mademoiselle.*"

"*So he told you who killed Markovic Monsieur?*"

"*He did.*"

Lucile waited. "*Who?*"

For several seconds Kevin's gaze was fixed on hers. "*We will have to discuss something first.*"

Nine out of ten times Lucile knew that would be the reply, information came at a cost, she had hoped this man might have been different. "*Did he also tell you who the older woman was?*"

"*No, just that somebody he knew managed to locate a lookalike.*"

She waited. "*How much do you...?*"

Just as Lucile spoke there was a sound not unlike a snake charmer coming from Norris's groin region, he shifted on his seat and slid his phone from his pocket, prodded the screen and placed it to his ear. "Norris." As he listened his body became tense, his back straightened, he put one hand on the armrest, ready to push himself up. "Then phone the police," he said as he stood.

Kevin and Lucile broke eye contact, their attention now firmly on Norris.

Norris stood. "Oh...Okay...Are you sure?" He waited. "And you are still at the hotel? What is...?" He waited again. "I'll come now." He looked at Lucile, then Kevin. "Sorry, I have to go."

"What is it?" She asked.

"Crystal and Teresa, they think the Chadian army officer knows where they are. I need to get a taxi."

"Where are they?" asked Kevin.

"In a hotel. They've managed to change rooms. I have to find them somewhere else to stay, somewhere safe."

"So why didn't they phone the old bill?"

Norris knew it was Jamia who had shot Major Guerrette. Kevin was an ex-legionnaire, as was the Major, that made them virtually brothers. How would Kevin react if he knew the person he was helping was the assassin. "She said they couldn't."

Lucile also rose from her seat, the anticipation of another story started the adrenalin pumping once again. Now a freelance journalist she had to take everything she could get. She knew this had annoyingly taken priority over finding out who Markovic's killer was, and there was nothing she could do about it, just stay with Kevin, that is all, he would have to tell her eventually. "Claude is round the corner," she said.

Norris sighed and dropped a fifty euro note on the table, more than double the amount on the bill. Neither his coffee or Kevin's beer had been touched, much to the waiters bewilderment. The three strode away.

"So why couldn't they phone the rozzers?" repeated Kevin.

"Crystal is trying to help some people."

"Who?"

"That's not important. What is important is that I have to help them."

"Who is Crystal?"

"She was the Camp Manager at Breidjing."

The next few steps were taken in silence. "Who is Claude?"

This was a question Norris was glad to answer. "More like what is Claude," he replied. "It's a car or it could be two by the time we've turned the first corner." Saying it loud enough for Lucile to hear. She slapped him high up on the arm — which Norris took as a sign of affection.

Less then a minute later they arrived at the Citroen 2CV: it was parked a metre from the curb, like it had just been dumped there, flaking paint like old wallpaper, displaying patches of rust like they were open wounds. It was so heavily dented it looked like someone had crumpled it up and let it spring back into shape.

Norris instructed Kevin to sit in the back, saying that it was probably better for his health. The three climbed in and after a loud pop the car shot off from standstill to top speed with nothing in between.

"Crystal said she thought she was followed from the railway station," Norris announced.

Lucile stared at him for an uncomfortable amount of time. A right corner approached, she crunched into a higher gear before flinging Claude around with only one hand on the wheel, forcing the gear back up again. "Do you remember that large dark car at the railway station. The one that drew up at the bottom of the steps after Crystal left us?" she asked.

"Vaguely."

"Three men were in it, I remember they were wearing hoodies. I thought it was strange at the time." Lucile turned again. "A fourth jumped into it, I think he was African."

"That was very observant," Kevin replied.

Lucile gazed at him in the mirror. "It's what I do," she remarked, a smugness in her tone.

"Why didn't you say something?" asked Norris.

"Why? Because they were black and wearing hoodies! I

thought it was only the French who were racist."

"It was you who said it was strange."

"Yes, strange that it was a hot day and they were wearing..."

"Not that they were black and they were wearing..."

"What has their colour got to do it? I never mentioned they were black."

"You said one was African."

"I said I think...and that doesn't mean..."

The argument finished five minutes later with Lucile slowing Claude as they approached the Hotel Abella. She crooked her neck to look at any parked cars close by. They passed the hotel, then a side street. Claude was now down to near walking pace, she quickly sped up again. "Did you see it?" Pulling into the next road and slinging Claude into a empty space and turning the engine off in one single action. "What now?" She said to Norris just catching Kevin putting his phone away.

"Someone will have to go and check out the hotel," Kevin replied.

"I'll go," said Norris.

"No. I think Mademoiselle Billet will be best."

"*Why me!? Let Norris, he doesn't like the company anyway.*"

"Me and your old man have been to that area in Chad, we might..."

"He's not my old man!"

"You could have fooled me...and we both look English. Anyway, it will be too risky for us," said Kevin.

"For you! I was at the station, you weren't there so that makes you the obvious choice."

"I thought you wanted Norris to go? And I have met Captain Nkusi."

Norris wondered when, then thought no more of it.

"Norris then," Lucile suggested.

"He was also in Chad...and at the station. *I am sorry*

Mademoiselle."

"Lucile, my fucking name is Lucile!"

"All you have to do *Lucile* is book into a room, then get out."

Lucile turned to look Kevin directly in the eye. "Who is going to pay for this room?"

"I'll pay you back later," Norris said, not knowing why.

"And what about the Peugeot? What if someone is in it? How am I going to pass the car without being seen?"

"Go round the block so you enter the hotel from the other direction." He looked at Norris. "What room number?"

"Sorry."

"The room they are in?" Kevin waited. What's the bloody room number!?" he repeated.

"She didn't say," Norris lied.

"What was the number of their first room?"

Norris answered without hesitation. "408."

Kevin looked back at Lucile. "Tell the receptionist you would like a room on the top floor, say you prefer to be away from the noise...or you like the view. There are six floors to the hotel, our friends are probably on the fifth. Use the stairs, go to the fifth floor, if a member of staff gets suspicious, tell them you're lost. Note any exit doors. Also take note of anyone you see, use your intuition, note their appearance..." He paused for a second. "If they are black. Then go to your own room. Here is my phone number, once there phone me." Kevin held his gaze on her, like he was trying to read her thoughts. "Any questions?"

"I thought you said all I had to do was book a room," she remarked as she stepped onto the pavement with her rucksack over one shoulder. With one hand on the roof she bent down to look at Kevin. "Think of this as payment for the information Marcantoni gave you." She slammed the door with an unnerving rattle of the window.

"I pity any man that gets involved with that lady," Kevin said as they watched her walk away.

Lucile arrived at the end of the road and turned left, she knew if she was going to enter the hotel from the other direction then she would have to continue on that same road. She stopped, good stories don't write themselves she thought and turned left. The Peugeot instantly became visible in the distance, like a sinister assassin waiting in the shadows. She remained on the left of the pavement, trying to look like a casual shopper, occasionally stopping to look through a window. She continued, wondering if she could be seen in the car's rearview mirrors. The road was clear. Lucile was now opposite the car behind the Peugeot, she began crossing the road, keeping her eyes ahead. She was over halfway when a car turned into the road, heading in her direction. She had no choice, Marseille drivers like nothing better than to honk their horn for no reason, she knew it would draw unnecessary attention to her. She stepped between the car directly behind the Peugeot and the one behind that. Lucile was now on the pavement on the same side as the car, she moved over towards the buildings. To see inside the car she would have to crouch down, turn her head, blatantly look in. She was now beside it, a quick glimpse over her shoulder. In that fraction of a second Lucile saw the bottom of a blue striped shirt, then dusty, dark trousers stretched out, one leg over the gear stick, the knee was high, a sandal resting on the edge of the passenger seat with dirty black toes poking out, she saw an arm hanging down, but not in a natural position: the man looked asleep.

She turned the corner onto the main road. About fifty metres away was an ornate stone porch held up by stumpy Roman style pillars, a dark blue flag hung above it, the gold words of Hotel Abella just visible as it flapped lazily in the breeze.

"What is the plan?" asked Norris.

"Rescue the damsel in distress," replied Kevin.

"Is that it!"

"Is there another way?"

Norris didn't answer.

Both men stepped out of the car and headed away from the main road on the same route Lucile had taken. Once they got to the road where the Peugeot was parked they immediately crossed over to the other side. When they were virtually on top of it Kevin veered away from Norris and into the road, quickly opening the driver's door, not once showing the slightest hint of hesitation. The driver, who had his back against the door fell backward, his torso hanging out of the car. Kevin held the door with his leg, stopping the driver from falling out altogether. He quickly sat him back up, looked around the car's interior and pulled out a dusty baseball cap from inside the door and placed it on the driver's head, pulling the peak down over his face. He shut the door, wiped the handle and returned to an ashen faced Norris. They continued on in silence.

The reception desk ran along the length of the back wall, behind it was a young man in his early twenties with a perfectly trimmed beard, Arabic in appearance, hair like sprayed velvet. Other than him, the lobby was empty. "*May I be of assistance Madame?*"

"*Double room on the top floor please,*" Lucile said.

His eyes fell on the computer "*Just...let me...check what we have...available,*" he said in short bursts. "*How long for Madame?*"

"*One night.*"

"*Ah yes Madame. We have the Courtois suite. Very nice Madame. It has two double bedrooms. Very nice Madame.*"

Lucile had had these conversations many times before, the hotel charging double for a space not much larger than a normal room. "*No thank you. Just a double please,*" she said bluntly.

"*It has a very nice view of the courtyard.*"

"*Have you a double room on the top floor available?*"

He looked down at the computer screen again. "*Yes Madame. A very nice room.*"

"*Then I will take that one.*"

"*Very good Madame. If I may have your card.*"

The young man swiped the card and looked in the direction of two metal doors. "*I will call the porter to carry your bag.*"

"*No thank you and where are the stairs?*" she paused for a moment, soaking up another one of his robotic looks. "*I don't do elevators,*" she said.

The blank gaze remained, like someone had flicked off his switch.

"*Bad experience,*" she added, irritated that she had to explain herself..

"*Ah yes.*" Like he had just woken up. "*Very wise Madame. The stairs door is on the right of the elevator.*"

Lucile thanked him, threw the rucksack over her shoulder, walked through the door and began the climb upwards. She could feel her heart thumping, scary thoughts began to enter her mind, what if she bumped into them and they recognised her? They could kill her there and then, dump her body in a chambermaid's cupboard.

She reached the fourth floor, encountering a small space just before the corridor. Just as she stepped into the corridor, a light streamed from an open door. She waited, a man stepped out, a black man, African looking. Lucile quickly took a step back. Had he seen her? She hadn't seen him look her way. She ran up the stairs to the sixth floor. Now what should she do? If the man had seen her he could be hunting her down now, she could be trapped with nowhere to run. There was a sign opposite, an arrow pointed to the left, 621- 640. Another sign, an arrow to the right 601-621. She turned right, striding down the corridor; there it was, 617. She slid the card into the slot and shoved the handle down. The door remained shut. Every fucking time she thought to herself; and her heart started thumping harder. She took the card out, turned it the other way and tried again: the door opened. A sigh of relief before a quick glance back, the corridor was clear, she stepped into the room.

"Was he shot?" Norris finally said, as if he needed the time to grasp what he had just seen.

"He's having a long nap." Kevin stopped and turned, his eyes intense. "If you want you can walk away now."

Norris wanted to say he would like just that, to step away from it all, that he was no hero, a natural born coward in fact. Then he thought of Lucile, he thought of Crystal and Teresa, how they had helped him when he was looking for his father. He thought of the two Chadian children, both caught up in a brutal civil war, the same war that took their family. He thought of how all their lives were in danger because of him. "No, I'm coming with you," he said.

Lucile remembered Kevin's words, 'Once there, phone me.'

He answered immediately. "Are you in your room?"

"*Yes*," she replied, too nervous to have noticed she had said it in French.

"*What's the number?*" Kevin asked, also in French.

"*617.*"

"*Top floor?*"

"*Yes.*"

"*Did you see any of our friends?*"

Lucile wondered who he was talking about. "*Which ones?*"

"Speak English. The ones we don't want to see."

"In that case yes...well...I think so. An African man was coming out of a room on the fourth floor," she sounded nervous.

"Where? What number?"

"I don't know the number. Left at the top of the stairs, it was near the end on the right."

"Did he see you?"

"I don't know...I don't think so. I didn't wait to find out."

"What about exit doors, fire escapes?"

"There is one at the end of each corridor, towards the back of the building."

"Good. Now ring down to reception. Tell them you are expecting company. Go down to the first floor and leave through the fire exit. Do not take any other route. Do you hear me? *Do not take any other route.*" The last words spoken clear and precise in her native tongue.

After Kevin hung up, he keyed a short text into his phone then tapped the send button. "Okay, let's go."

"So the driver of that car was tranquilised?" asked Norris.

"Out like a baby."

"Not dead?"

"No."

"Who did it?"

"Did you?"

"No."

"Then I would be suspicious of everyone else if I was you."

"Everyone?"

"Everyone."

Norris looked at him. "Including you?"

Kevin stopped and looked at him again, the intensity still there. "Everyone," he repeated.

Norris followed Kevin through the glass door of the hotel and into the lobby, watching as he marched straight up to the reception desk in the same blatant way he had the car.

"*We have come to visit someone,*" he said.

"*Name of the guest Monsieur?*"

"*Billet, room 617.*"

The young man studied the computer screen.

"*If you would be so kind as to sign the visitors book,*" he said, glancing towards Norris with a forced smile as if to say this included him. Kevin signed in as Toby Brown along with the time and date, also who he was visiting and the room number. Norris began to sign in with his own name, raising the pen after only a few letters, he had to think quick, Norman Wisdom he wrote, jotting down ditto marks under everything else. The receptionist nodded towards the elevator, "*It is on the sixth floor.*"

"*Where are the stairs?*" Kevin asked.

The receptionist glanced up. "*Bad experience Monsieur?*" he said.

"*What!?*"

"*Bad experience Monsieur?*"

"*What!?*"

The receptionist pointed towards the stairwell door.

Lucile exited room 617 and took the elevator, nervously having to share it with a tired looking man wearing a cheap suit, he kept lifting his arm and glancing impatiently at his watch, causing Lucile to nervously stiffen every time he did. It was several seconds later when she heard a dong above her head, the number three button had lit up, with a clunk and a sigh the elevator nudged itself into position on the third floor. The metallic doors slid open leaving an empty space in front. Lucile waited, she was feared the worst. A sheepish looking woman clutching a young boy's hand appeared. Lucile breathed a sigh of relief. Both remained in the corridor. "*Sorry,*" the woman said. "*He likes to push the buttons.*" Lucile quickly prodded the close-doors button, poking her tongue out at the boy before they completely shut.

Finally the number one button lit up and the doors opened. Lucile hesitantly stepped half into the corridor, looking both ways, leaving the man to shuffle forward, pulling his small suitcase with short tugs like it was a pet dog. The doors began to shut, forcing her out into the corridor. Without waiting she began striding in the direction of the fire exit, then it became a trot, virtually a sprint. She slammed the escape bar forward with all her body weight, flying out as it flung open, nearly head butting a large African looking man in the chest. She stepped back and stared at him in horror.

Just as Kevin was leaving the reception desk he stopped mid-turn. "*What is your name?*" he asked, looking back over his shoulder.

"*Salim Lahsaini Monsieur.*"

The hotel door swung open and a young couple stepped into the lobby from the street, together they waited behind Norris.

"*Where are you from Salim?*"

"*Morocco.*"

"*Where in Morocco?*"

"*Tangiers.*"

"*Ah yes, Tangiers.*" Kevin's manner changed, like Salim had suddenly become his friend. "*Caid's Bar?*"

The young man wondered what Caid's Bar had to do with anything. "*Yes monsieur...It is now The Piano Bar. It is very nice...very nice monsieur.*" His voice was beginning to crack. Norris had learnt that Kevin could have this effect on people.

A whirring noise came from the left, then a clunk. The elevator door opened. A tired looking man with dark eyes and wearing a cheap suit stepped out rolling a disobedient suitcase behind him, hesitating before joining the queue behind the young couple.

"*Your visa has run out,*" Kevin said softly.

The young man's eyes widened.

Kevin leant forward, resting his elbows on the counter. "*Are you here illegally Salim?*"

A voice came from behind the young couple. "*Excuse me but I have a plane to catch.*"

"*Which one is it Salim?*" Kevin repeated.

Another shout from behind. "*If I could just pay...*"

Kevin turned, took a step to the side and glared at the man. "*If you don't shut the fuck up it won't be a sodding plane you'll be needing.*"

The young woman from the couple turned and spoke to the man behind her. Through the stutter in her voice Norris could just about make out what was said. Something about credit card numbers, which resulted in the cheap suited man leaving the hotel, quickly followed by the young woman dragging her boyfriend with her.

Kevin raised his eyebrows, waiting for the answer. His voice became calm, as if his show of anger was no more than just that. "*Show me the names of the guests in the hotel Salim.*"

The receptionist tapped the keyboard then turned the computer screen. Kevin leant over the desk, he was only interested in one name, Flores, after that was the number 513.'

As Norris stepped onto the stairs he wondered what he would do if one of Captain Nkusi's men came down at the same time, just as Lucile had. Would he know how to react? Would he be able to stay natural? Not look scared? They might recognise him, he could be staring down the end of a barrel. He looked down at his hands, they were shaking. He recalled a recurring nightmare, one he had as a boy, in his early teens. He was climbing a flight of stairs, on and on they went, higher and higher, not going anywhere, when he wanted to turn and go back the steps behind him were no longer there, just — nothing. It was exactly how he felt now, there was no going back. Maybe that was what the dream was about, maybe it was a prophesy foreseeing his own death. He reached the first landing and turned, the steps were still there.

"How did you know he didn't have a visa?" Norris asked.

"He smelt of fear. The rest was guesswork."

Norris continued to climb, passing the first floor entrance, then the second; when he got to the third he was startled by the door flying open with a loud thud. He stepped back startled. A young boy came running through, about four or five years of age, bounding down the stairs as if he was on a mission, dragging his mother behind him. "*He likes stairs,*" she said as they passed Norris.

Kevin waited until they were gone. "Your Spanish friend, is her name Flores?" he asked abruptly.

"How did you know that?"

"I take that as a yes."

Norris thought. "She was my boss at the charity," he waited for a response. "Why?"

"No reason." Kevin began taking two steps at a time, sometimes three, he was virtually one flight ahead. Norris could feel beads of sweat dripping down his cheeks and his neck, soaking into his collar, his breathing became deeper. He chastised himself for those thousands of cigarettes he had smoked, tens of thousands. He felt as if he could do with one now.

Kevin stopped on the fifth floor landing. "513," he said.

Before Norris could ask how he knew, Kevin had stepped through the door and into the small space before the corridor. "You go to the room. I'll follow."

"Aren't you coming?"

"The receptionist said only two men entered the hotel. There were four, one is napping, so one is missing. He could be following us. We can't allow anyone to see you go into that room. Remember it was only you she told."

Norris didn't question him. He looked at the plaque: 501-521, next to the numbers was an arrow pointing to the right.

"Wait for me there," said Kevin.

Lucile looked up at the man, he was large, barrel chested, wearing clothes as black as his skin, a roll-neck sweater and neatly creased trousers over tree trunk thighs. He was just standing there like a silhouette against the glow of the afternoon sun, staring down at her. But it was his eyes that shocked her the most, soulless, dark, as cold as stone.

Lucile began to feel sick, she wanted to cry, to plead with him that she still had the rest of her life in front of her, to scream for help but no words came, it was like she had been paralysed. This was it she thought, there was nothing she could do, her life would soon be snuffed out by a man who thought nothing of killing another human being. She closed her eyes as he stuck out a strong arm, expecting to feel his fingers wrapped around her neck. When she opened them again she saw the palm of a flat hand in front of her. "*Key,*" he said.

Lucile continued to stare up.

With the other hand he put a black baseball cap on his head. The one word written above the peak as clear as daylight, 'POLICE'. "*Key to room 617.*" He waited. "*If you wouldn't mind Mademoiselle Billet.*"

Lucile wondered how he knew her name. She carefully placed the key into his hand.

He crossed his arms and leant back against the iron railing, he looked down the fire escape and gave the faintest of nods.

It was the noise she heard first, like a drum roll. Then she saw them, also in dark clothing, uniforms, heavy with equipment. They were wearing balaclavas, some carrying weapons, like a line of shadows running up the iron steps, only to pass her and into the hotel corridor. The first few had their guns at eye level, sweeping them from side to side, slinking forward with bent knees. She wasn't counting but there must have been at least twenty, maybe more, they just kept coming, one after another. One word on their backs, 'POLICE.' As soon as the last man disappeared, the large African man followed them in, his nonchalant swagger displaying his irrefutable authority. It was all over in less than a minute.

Lucile stood on the fire-escape landing, very alone but very alive, with the feeling it had all been one surreal dream, until she heard the steady clomp of more footsteps rising up the iron stairwell, this time a lot slower. An older man in civilian clothes with thick, iron grey hair, unshaven, skin like a stewed prune and near invisible glasses plodded upward as if it was all an unnecessary chore. He stopped and faced her, catching his breath. "*Thank you Mademoiselle Billet. Your timing was impeccable.*" He held out his hand and spoke through a long breath. "*I am Commissaire Rougier.*"

She shook his hand, feeling relieved it was as clammy as hers, thinking he smelt of cheap aftershave and stale tobacco. "*Have you come to save us?*" Was Lucile's immediate response, annoyed with herself for sounding like a helpless woman.

"*Ah yes.*" Stretching the word. "*But this has nothing to do with you or your friends Mademoiselle, although I think the outcome will be just as favourable.*" He stretched his arm out like a waiter showing her to a table. "*Please, follow me.*"

Lucile hesitated.

"*Please Mademoiselle. I am on your side.*"

She followed him in. "*Who was that man?*" she asked.

"*His name is Marius Guerrette. Maybe you know him better as Alain Serre.*"

Lucile stopped. "*But he is dead.*" Causing the Commissaire to do the same. "*I thought he had been killed in Chad.*"

He turned. "*Whoever pulled the trigger was not used to firing a gun. The bullet grazed his head, that is all.*"

So that was Alain Serre Lucile thought, feeling like he had some kind of celebrity status. "*So where are you taking me?*"

"*Where you have just come from.*"

She stopped again. "*Sorry, I don't understand.*"

"*Room 617.*" Commissaire Rougier said it like it was obvious, he began walking again, quickening his pace.

Lucile followed, catching him up just as he reached the elevator. "*There is nothing in room 617 monsieur. Like you said, I have just come from there.*" She heard the muted sound of her phone buzzing in her bag.

"*Don't worry, we waited until you left.*"

A whirring sound came from below them, then a clunk. In front of them the doors to the elevator slid open.

"*What do you mean you waited until I left? I don't understand?*"

Commissaire Rougier stepped into the elevator and kept his finger on the open doors button. "*So we could plant the bait.*"

"*What bait? I don't understand. Who are you trying to catch?*"

"*Someone we have been after for a long time. Join me, you might get a good story out of it, I have heard that being a journalist is not much different than being a detective.*"

"*How do you know I am a reporter?*"

"*Mademoiselle Billet, please, give me some credit. Now will you step in.*"

Lucile joined him in the lift and the Commissaire took his finger off the button.

"*It was important we arrested him outside of Chad. When you and your friends came to Marseille we hoped he would follow the two Chadian children.*"

"*Captain Nkusi?*"

"*It was your friend Norris Kinley that gave us the idea. When he contacted the other Englishman...*"

"*The Englishman, you mean Kevin?*"

"*I do not know his name Mademoiselle. I believe he is like that cowboy.*"

Lucile had to think. "*The one with no name.*"

"*Yes.*"

"*Clint Eastwood.*"

"*Ah yes. Clint Eastwood. The Good, the Bad and the Ugly. I like a cowboy film where the good nearly always...*"

"*And who is the good in all...*" Stopping mid-sentence when she heard her phone buzz, again she ignored it.

"*All this man needed was someone he could trust. Someone that helped save his brother's life would be perfect. Someone that could give him the information he has been longing for.*"

"Where the Chadian girl is."

Commissaire Rougier raised his hands to waist height. "*And here we are.*"

"*You mean Captain Nkusi.*"

The lift slowed, nudging itself to a halt. The doors opened.

Crystal opened the door. Norris thought she looked as if she was dressed for a summer garden party, although her expression said something different. She stood back, allowing him to enter, quickly shutting the door.

As he entered Norris saw Teresa sat on the bed, her back against the headboard, her legs pulled up to her chest as if she was hugging herself. Jamia and Ali were sharing a single armchair, Jamia's arm around her brother, like they could never be parted.

"Are you on your own?" Crystal asked.

"No."

"Who else is with you?"

"Kevin. Lucile is also here, but hopefully she has left the hotel."

"Kevin, you mean Tim Borrin?"

"Or Toby Brown. Pity there's not three of him." Crystal stepped forward and peered through the eyehole.

"They won't be out there," Norris told her.

"I'm not looking for them," she replied. "And who is Lucile?"

"A friend. She is a journalist."

"Helpful sweetie. So where is this Kevin now?"

"I don't know. He said to wait for him here."

Teresa's sharp Spanish accent sliced through the air. "An African man came into the hotel pretending to be Crystal's taxi driver. We think he found out their room number." She quickly added. "Not this one, this is my room."

"And the receptionist doesn't know you are connected?"

"No honey," replied Crystal. "We are not complete idiots."

Norris slid his phone out of his pocket and tapped in a message and sent it to Lucile.

He waited. No answer. "So they don't know you are in this

room."

"So what do we do?" asked Crystal.

"We wait." He looked over to Jamia and Ali. "How are they bearing up?"

Crystal answered, her voice raised. "They've been living in a refugee camp for the last six years. This is just a stroll in the..."

"They are well." Teresa interrupted. "Thank you for helping us Norris."

"Sorry sweetie," said Crystal. "I'm a bit on edge." She took another step forward and looked through the eyehole. "Can't we just go?"

"No it's too dangerous. You are safer here for the time being." He could see by Crystal's expression he hadn't convinced her. "Kevin will come and get us when it is safe." He patted his pocket, wishing he could stop doing that.

A heavy silence fell over the room. Even Norris began nervously peeping through the eyehole. He sent another text to Lucile. Again he waited, again there was no reply.

"Have you got food and drink?" he asked.

"Are you hungry?" replied Crystal.

"No, I was thinking..."

"We only have what is in the mini bar."

"Good." Norris repeated it. "Good." The second time lost in thought. Lucile hadn't answered his texts. He was becoming concerned. "I'll give it a minute, then go and see what is happening," he said.

Neither Crystal or Teresa responded.

Half-a-minute later Norris stood in front of the door, checked his phone once more, peeped through the eyehole and took a deep breath.

The first sound he heard as he stepped into the corridor was the click of the door closing behind him. He now knew there was no escape, he would be like an animal caught in a trap. Then he thought why he was there, if something had happened to Lucile he would never forgive himself. As he reached the staircase landing he realised he was still holding his breath. To his right the flight of steps fell below him, he turned and started the climb to the sixth floor. As he reached the top he was startled by a man in a black balaclava stepping out in front of him. A semi-automatic gun held up head high, pointing at Norris.

Norris knew he was dead. It was the man's eyes that told him, intense, threatening. He shouted one word, it was in French. Norris understood.

Lucile and Commissaire Rougier were not alone as they stepped out of the lift. The corridor was crowded with men in dark uniforms, some standing in a circle listening to another giving orders. It was then they heard a shout come from behind the door. Just a single word in French. "*Stop!*"

"*Ah yes. I believe your friend has lost his patience. Maybe you should have answered your phone Mademoiselle Billet.*" Commissaire Rougier remarked as he stepped into the corridor.

Norris glanced over the gunman's shoulder to see a face, one he thought he recognised. That was when he heard his own name being spoken, like when it is whispered in a passing conversation, and that is all you hear, just your own name. The gun continued to be aimed between his eyes, a tense finger wrapped around the trigger, the white of a knuckle worryingly giving his intention away. Norris then saw a flicker of movement, a man stepped in front of the gunman, thankfully the weapon was lowered. "We seem to meet under unusual circumstances Monsieur Kinley." The French accent belonged to someone he knew. "He will not shoot you now." Sounding as if it could have been a strong possibility. "Not unless you upset him Monsieur Kinley."

Norris studied the face. "Commissaire Rougier."

"I hope your friends are safe. I believe you have just come from there?"

Norris returned a sharp nod.

"Please...phone them, tell them I am sending a police officer down to stand guard outside their room, tell them it is only precautionary. Please tell them they are safe."

The Commissaire waited while Norris finished the phone call. "Did you find out who drew those sketches Monsieur Kinley?"

Norris was surprised to hear that question at this time. "No, unfortunately I didn't."

"Neither did we. After you left I looked into it. Do you know we had the best experts look at them?"

"Was Remi Cochet one of them?"

"The name is familiar. Come Monsieur Kinley, there is someone you will be pleased to see."

The first person Norris saw as he entered the corridor was Lucile standing in front of the lift. He smiled, pleased to see her response was the same. Even under these circumstances he wondered if she felt something for him. He stepped closer, wanting to give her a hug, waiting for her to make a move towards him — she didn't. "I was worried about you," he said.

"Why?"

The Commissaire stepped past them.

Norris didn't answer, instead he placed a soft hand on her back, it felt good just to touch her again. "We should follow."

Lucile tried to recall what room 617 was like, she remembered the carpet was a kind of non-colour, grey she thought, soft under foot. She remembered sitting on the edge of the bed and making the phone call to Kevin, then using the hotel phone to speak to the receptionist. That was it though, that was all she could recall. Now she could see it was more spacious than she had thought, even if it was crawling with police officers. There were at least a dozen of them, some were smaller, women she thought, two were standing close to a man in handcuffs, one was holding onto the metal band between the wrists. They all stared at the Commissaire when he entered, as though they were waiting for him to speak.

Norris immediately knew who the man was, he could even see a slight resemblance to his brother Marcel. There was another man, larger, dressed in dark clothing and a baseball cap, he had his back to Norris.

Kevin was also in the room, standing slightly back. When Lucile and Norris entered he had given them a single nod, not like a greeting, but as if to say mission successfully completed, a military nod. Another man in worn clothing was being hurriedly led away by two police officers. When Norris looked again, the large man had turned so he was side on. Norris recognised him instantly, his disbelief followed by overwhelming relief: he had always felt responsible for the shooting of this man.

The Commissaire stepped over to the handcuffed man and held up a sheet of paper. "*Captain Neo Nkusi. I have a...*"

The Captain interrupted. "*Who are you?*"

The Commissaire paused. "*I am Commissaire Rougier, Marseille Police.*"

"*I will remember that name Commissaire Rougier.*"

"*I don't think you are in a position to threaten me Captain Nkusi.*" The Commissaire cleared his throat."*Captain Neo Nkusi, I have a European Warrant for your arrest. You are to be taken to the Examining Magistrate where you will be charged and granted a lawyer if you so wish. Then you wil be read your rights. If the Examining Magistrate finds the evidence satisfactory you will be extradited to the International Court of Justice in Hague at a later date. There you will stand trial.*" His words calm, like he had read them from a script.

The Captain sounded and looked defiant. "*What are you charging me with Commissaire Rougier?*"

"*The Examining Magistrate will...*"

Major Guerrette butted in. "*You tortured and murdered innocent people in cold blood, you enlisted child soldiers, the list goes on Captain.*"

"*And your witnesses Major, where are they now?*"

"*The boy is still alive.*"

"*The boy!*" Captain Nkusi released a loud laugh. "*I doubt if he even knows his own name. Yes yes Major, let him be your witness.*"

Major Guerrette took his baseball cap off and wiped a hand over the top of his head. Norris could remember him doing the same in the tukul with the blue door, like everything was such an unnecessary chore. The bullet wound was now clear to see, a couple of centimetres above his left ear, still black and matted. He replaced the cap. "*There was another boy, the one you captured with the rebel leader's son. You thought you had killed him at Scorpion Rock. Even a boy was too clever for you Captain Nkusi, you should have checked to see if he was dead. It was he who led us to the bodies of the men you butchered.*"

The Captain's stare hung on the Major for several seconds, his smile twisted into a sneer. "*There was a war on Major. You want to arrest me for killing the men who murdered my brothers, the men who raped my sister. You tell me you wouldn't have done the same, that anyone wouldn't have done the same?*" He looked around the room. "*You are all hypocrites,*" he hissed. "*Believe me Major Guerrette there are many who have done far worse than...*"

"*Enough!*" Commissaire Rougier shouted. "*You will have your say in court.*"

The Captain ignored him. "*In court!*" His eyes had become fierce, threatening. "*You French are still telling us how to run our lives, trial by white men with their white laws.*"

"*Enough!*" The Commissaire repeated louder. He nodded once to the police officers and stepped aside. The Captain was hauled away.

As he passed Kevin, the Captain glared at him, a look so evil he would have butchered him there and then if he could. "*When I am free Englishman, I will find you and kill you, cut you down like the dog you are.*"

Captain Nkusi was led out of the room, followed closely by Commissaire Rougier and Major Guerrette. Norris looked at the Major as he passed, waiting for any sign of recognition, none came. "What was that all about?" he asked.

"The Captain has been arrested for crimes against..."

"No, about him wanting to kill you." Norris only understood some of the last bit. "He said something about you being a dog."

Kevin grinned. "I knew his brother Marcel, I saw what the rebels had done to his family."

"Yes, I remember, then surely the Captain should thank you?"

"I said I would help him get his revenge. Do you know when a man is that obsessed he will believe anything...and pay anything." Kevin puffed out his bottom lip and slowly shook his head. "He wasn't happy to find out I was not his friend."

"No, I didn't expect he would be."

"But I find its better to be pissing out of the tent than into it."

"Its according to who's inside." Norris thought some more. "So where does the Major come into all of this?"

"After he left the Legion he worked for Interpol. His job in Chad as a security advisor was not, well, let us say not all that it was made out to be, the ICC needed someone to get closer to the enemy."

"A Major in the Legion with a ruthless reputation, central African origin, who better?" said Lucile.

"He was sent there to hunt war criminals, as was your Crystal Bullion."

Norris's mouth fell open. "Crystal?"

"In a small way."

"How small?"

Kevin thought for a moment. "Hardly noticeable. Captain Nkusi was one of the most brutal of the war criminals; but he was protected in Chad, we had to get him out of the country.

Then you phoned me, wanting me to speak to Francois Marcantoni. That is when it all fell into place. That was when we decided to bring the mountain to Mohammad."

"You lied to us," said Lucile.

"Never let the truth get in the way of a good lie," Kevin remarked.

"So Crystal was made to think that is why they had to escape Chad" said Norris. "Like you said, get him out of the country. So the Major asked you to become a friend of the Captain, feed him the information."

"Yeah," Kevin stretched the word, angling his head like he was feigning surprise. "Fucked up world we live in isn't it?"

"You used us!" Lucile said.

"You were never in danger."

"But it was me that led them to this room."

"No, I did." Kevin replied. "They didn't know the room number until I told them...and by then you had gone."

"But it was you who told me what to do, even when to open the fire door."

"Like I said Mademoiselle Billet, you were never in danger."

"So this was all an elaborate set-up!" Norris added.

"It was necessary. The ICC had tried to have him arrested before, through the proper route, only the Captain had too many friends in Chad. We had to get him out of the country."

"You used the two Chadian children as the bait," Norris said. "And Crystal was all part of this."

"Only up to a certain point."

"What point?"

"A very blunt one: she was working for Amnesty International in Eastern Chad, investigating the abuse of young girls. The ICC were able to help by arranging for her to stay on as the Breidjing Camp Manager. You scratch mine and..." Kevin paused for a second, his stare hanging on Norris. "She knew nothing of why we wanted the two children here. All she needed to know was that they were safe. All's well that ends well."

Norris remained silent.

"I thought you would understand," remarked Kevin. "Shall we go and give them the good news?"

"No!" Lucile snapped. "First you need to tell me what Francois Marcantoni said."

"You already have a story here," Kevin told her. "Notorious war criminal caught in refugee trap. Think of it, you can describe how you were part of the operation." He widened his eyes. "Even better, female reporter helps catch ruthless war criminal."

Lucile thought he was playing games again, using delaying tactics, maybe still angling for some kind of payment. Her patience had become stretched to the limit. "No!" she snapped. "I need to know what Marcantoni told you. I have helped you, I have put my life on the line, now it is your turn."

To her surprise Kevin had walked back into the room, only stopping when he got to the window, remaining with his back to them, as though he was enjoying the view. "Susanne Dennel," he said gazing down at the courtyard.

"Susanne Dennel!"

Kevin turned. "Susanne Dennel," he repeated.

"Marcantoni said it was Madam Veronique."

"No, he actually said it was Susanne Dennel."

"So you are saying it was Susanne Dennel who killed Markovic?" Norris asked.

"Someone else pulled the trigger but it was her name on the bullet."

"She paid someone, a hit man. Who?"

"Marcantoni told Susanne Dennel something, something that would seal Markovic's fate."

"Yes I know. Stevan Markovic used to throw parties where..." Lucile stopped, she felt a surge of excitement. "I know he used to take secret photographs and blackmail the victims afterwards." Although it was forty-two years ago, she knew the unsolved scandal was still fresh in the French public's minds. This would also be sweet revenge for the way La Provence had treated her: she would sell the story to a competitor, rub dirt into her old editor's eyes.

"But did you know it was Susanne Dennel who used to supply the girls for these parties?" Kevin asked.

"It wouldn't surprise me," replied Lucile.

"And did you know Marcantoni told her Markovic was spreading a rumour that she was involved in the blackmail?"

"And was she?" Lucile asked.

Kevin shrugged. "But it wasn't that that sealed Markovic's fate. Marcantoni knew there would be something else that would put the final nail in the coffin."

"What?" she asked flatly.

"He told her Markovic had a brother and he..."

Lucile interrupted. "Yes yes, Alexandra. He wrote a letter stating it would be Delon or Marcantoni's fault..."

"No, an older brother. His name was Marko. He was much older than Stevan, fifteen years to be exact."

"Having an older brother is not a crime." Norris remarked, maybe he was biased.

"No, but for Susanne Dennel being a collaborator for the Wehrmacht was."

"The Wehrmacht?" asked Norris,he had heard of the name but never knew what it meant.

"They were the combined forces on the Nazi side controlling the occupation of Serbia and..." Kevin paused for a second. "Vichy France if the truth be known."

"Oh, I can see how that must have upset her." Norris remarked." But was it true?"

Kevin shrugged. "Does it matter?"

"Did Marcantoni say who the actual killer was?" Lucile finally asked.

"Marcontoni told me he knew someone, a nobody, a maverick, someone not on the police radar. He said this man was owing to him, big time. It was he who also planted the photographs in Markovic's car."

"Did he say his name?"

"I asked but he wouldn't tell me."

Lucile didn't believe him.

Norris thought about The Drowning Mary. He didn't know why but for some reason he knew the painting had to be the missing link in all this. But where? How? He could only think of one person who could answer some of these questions.

"Your friends will be wondering where you are," Kevin said. "Let us give them the good news."

Wednesday 7th July 2010
Windyridge House,
Thame,
England

Irene Kinley knew this day would come, she didn't know exactly when, but she knew it would come all the same.

She knew it when that strange foreign woman came to visit her, the one with a voice like scratched glass, who didn't like tea for God's sake. Having to listen to her prying into her life, nosing around this very same room, telling her that her son was missing and had she heard from him. His own mother? Her own son? Irene tried to think what her name was, Flores? That was it, Teresa Flores, her memory hasn't failed her yet. But it was later, when she turned up with that pretend American woman, too much mascara and hair-lacquer for Irene's liking. Along with all that fake friendliness: who calls people honey and sweetie these days anyway? Far too many foreigners in this country, Irene thought; but it was when they started asking those questions about her husband, that was when she knew for certain, she knew then it would only be a matter of time.

Norris sat facing her, a mother and son sitting either side of the hearth in two Georgian chairs, like an old married couple.

She could see streaks of grey hair had begun to sprout above his ears and in his sideburns. "You are looking older dear," she remarked.

He didn't reply.

"It is strange how time flies with age." She waited. More silence. "I should know."

His gaze slid away from her.

She wondered how much he knew? There was so much of it, so much to tell. Whenever she thought about it, which was every day, probably every hour of every day, she told herself she would tell him the whole truth, the entire story, she would leave no stone unturned. She knew he would hate her afterwards, that he would probably never want to see her again.

Norris finally spoke. "Do you know Dad..." He stopped after the word Dad, it was like it had got caught in his throat. "Do you know father..." That was better, his father didn't deserve to be called Dad, not since the day he upped and left him without even a goodbye. "Do you know father is dead?"

"Is he dear?"

For a fleeting moment Norris was stunned by the answer, even her expression had remained unchanged. More surprising, she didn't even want to know how.

"He is buried in Marseille. The police think he committed suicide."

Irene remained silent, just staring at him through those old woman's eyes, like two damp marbles.

"Do you also know he had a son...I mean another son, not me?" He took a deep breath. "I have a half-brother." Just as Irene opened her mouth to answer, Norris continued. "His name is Matthieu, he is French, he lives in Marseille." His gaze unwavering. "He is one of those foreigners mother."

Irene replied immediately. "Yes dear." Just like that, as if Norris had just asked her if they were having peas with their roast dinner.

She always had this ability to intimidate him, make him

uneasy without actually doing or saying anything; just by the uncaring coldness in her manner. He looked up at the ceiling, then side to side, finally his eyes rested down on to the carpet, anything so as not to face his mother at that moment — or was it he didn't want her looking at him. "Yes mother." Not Mum, it hadn't been Mum for a very long time, and it has never been Mummy, even when he was a young child.

Irene had never been a loving mother, no tender cuddles or kisses, in fact it was the reverse, always disciplining him for the slightest misdemeanor, packing him off to that school at the earliest opportunity, not appearing to care when she discovered he was being bullied, telling the teacher it would be character building. And it didn't stop there: when he was older, past schoolboy age, whenever he stayed in the house, he always remained in his bedroom, not wanting to be near her, especially in the same room as her, thinking of excuses to go out, to be as far away from her as possible. Probably the reason he had started the search for his father.

"Do you know who the mother of Matthieu was?" Norris asked.

"Yes dear, she was one of those women, a lady of the night I believe they are called. I do not know her name if that is what you are asking."

"Did you know father wanted to bring Matthieu back to England?"

Irene leant forward, resting her elbows on her legs. Norris noticed the curvature of her spine had become even more pronounced over the past few years, the bones protruding through her thin cardigan. Along with her sagging neck and long knobbly fingers he thought she had become even more reptile like. Norris waited for an answer.

"I told him he was a grown man and could do whatever he wanted as long..."

Norris quickly interrupted."As long as it didn't involve you." He looked away and blew out a scornful breath.

"Something like that dear."

"Did you know that Matthieu's mother didn't raise him, that he was brought up in a brothel by a madam and the other..." He paused for a short moment. "Women." He said the word like his mother was deaf. He waited, staring at her with open eyes, wondering if she understood what he meant. "Did you know he was only a baby when his mother handed him over to them?"

Irene shifted in her seat. "No dear, I didn't."

"Nor did you care."

"Why should I Norris?" Her tone assertive.

Irene rarely called her son by his name, usually it was dear, the same as she called everyone else. He remembered years ago when he was just a child, whenever she did say his name it was usually the sign of bad times ahead: then she would punish him with some prolonged menial and degrading household chore, probably for the most petty of misdemeanors.

She continued. "But he was not my baby. I expect you saw many a child in a worse situation in that refugee camp you went to visit. Why don't you tell me about them dear?"

"Because this one is my brother."

"Is he though? Is he really?" Irene tilted her head. "Are you sure? The mother was one of 'those women' as you put it."

Norris had no riposte, how could he prove otherwise. A long uncomfortable silence followed.

"How did you meet father?" he finally asked.

"You know that already dear."

"No, I want the truth mother. You are the only one on this planet who can tell me." Norris realised he had raised his voice, this was how the quarrels began when he was a teenager, when he began to argue back, usually finishing with him stomping off in a tantrum, slamming every door in the house; when he wasn't scared anymore.

"What is the truth dear? The world is flat. There is a God. Maybe everything is just an illusion to us mere mortals."

Norris thought she was playing with him. "Have you heard

of a Jean-Paul Karel?" he said calmly, like he had just thrown it into the conversation.

This was it, this was all Irene Kinley needed. It was at that exact moment, just as the name departed her son's mouth that she knew the time had come. She took a long, slow breath. "Yes dear I have heard of Jean-Paul Karel." Dismissing it as if it wasn't important, just like Norris had done only seconds before. "Do you know when I met your father he was just a furniture salesman? Selling overpriced foreign rubbish, not even the quality of a Sheraton dear. He couldn't even get that right." She stopped.

Norris waited.

"Do you know your Grandparents knew each other before we met? The first time I met his parents I could see they were embarrassed by him, couldn't wait to get rid of him. And when I found out why...well dear, it was far too late, not that I had any choice. Your Grandpa couldn't get me to tie the knot fast enough, in his eyes I was not getting any younger. He even told me I was past that desirable age." She looked away. "Not that I thought I was desirable at any age dear. But he was desperate for a grandson, someone that could carry on the family line, an heir to the throne like it was some great estate. Your Grandpa was a man used to getting his own way, even threatening to cut me out of his will. Do you know your father and I had absolutely nothing in common; and I certainly didn't love him dear, to be honest with you I didn't even like him, in fact I despised him. The feeling was mutual you know, but your father had the gift of the gab, moreso when he saw my parents had money. Not that your Grandpa or even your Gran cared, in fact I think they knew what he was like. Your father wasn't a looker, but he was nine years younger, so in their eyes that balanced it out, made it all acceptable, as though age could make someone compatible. They told me I would be stupid not to accept his hand." She paused for a second and took in a deep breath. "So we married in 1968, a year before you were born."

Hearing 1968 he immediately thought of another event that happened the same year. He knew what Lucile's reaction would have been if she had heard it. Norris decided to dive straight in. "Do you know there was a scandal in France that involved the murder of a man called Stevan Markovic? Do you know that was also in 1968?" He waited, her face remained impassive. "But it wasn't the murder that shocked most people, it was photographs found in his car." He waited again, again nothing. "They were reported to be of Georges Pompidou's wife with another woman."

Irene was shocked he knew so much. "The world is full of photographs with two women dear."

"Not like these." He waited for her to question him, she remained silent.

Irene continued as if she hadn't heard. "Neither of us wanted children you know."

"Are you saying I was a mistake?"

"No dear, you were wanted, but not by me."

Norris had known it all along, maybe he just wanted to hear her say it.

"The truth is I never wanted children. It is not a crime you know." Her palms turned upward. "And yet you are here."

"And father, did he want me?"

Irene thought for a moment. "You were the key to my family's wealth. So yes dear, I suppose he did."

"But did he really want me?" he repeated.

"After you were born your father started spending more time in France. I never went with him, not that I wanted to, not that he asked me. In truth I was just glad to see the back of him. He became an art dealer you know, using my money to buy and sell paintings. I had no choice but to stay at home and look after you. Do you know you were hard work as a baby Norris? A real crier, lungs like a foghorn." She blew out a fake laugh. "Sometimes you just wouldn't stop, on and on you would howl. Sometimes I thought you would cry yourself to death."

Norris thought she said it like that wouldn't have been a bad thing.

"Even when you were in my womb it felt like you were trying to kick yourself out. Do you know I had no help from anyone, not a single person, not your father, not your Grandpa, not even your Gran, nobody dear. Not that your Grandpa would have allowed your Gran. My money was held in a trust, released only by your Grandpa when he saw fit; so when I asked for some to pay for a nanny, he flatly refused. He was happy to release money to finance your father's art deals, but to save my sanity. 'A child needs his own mother,' he would say. The truth is dear, the people who wanted you, deserted me...deserted us." Irene raised her eyes. "But instead of growing to love you, I grew to despise you. I wanted to love you dear, I wanted it so much...so much."

Norris could see his mother's eyes had become like small pools, he could see teardrops forming in the corners, dampness seeping through her eyelids, ready to spill down her cheeks. That was when he realised how much she had been through.

"But I couldn't you see. You had always been a difficult child." The slightest of smiles brushed past her lips. "Stubborn as a mule."

"I remember the stringent set of rules I had to abide to, without fail...otherwise...There were so many, no young child could..."

"No dear, that's why it wasn't surprising when at the age of four or five you turned to your father for love. Not that I blame you now, but how do you think that made me feel? I mean I was the one raising you." She studied Norris's reaction. "But it was not your fault dear, it was mine, I blame myself you know. Every time he came home he would have a gift for you. You couldn't wait to see him, always so excited to see what he had brought you." Irene stared straight into his eyes. "Do you know the affection you have for your father was only gained through blackmail?"

Norris didn't answer, he didn't think it was a question. He recalled the earliest memories he had of his father, when he used to return home from his trips, how excited he woud be to see what he had brought him. He remembered once getting a miniature car, a vintage Bentley in racing green, so perfect in every detail it looked as if it had been shrunk down from a full size version; but instead of playing with it he kept it on show, sitting proudly on top of its box high up on a shelf. He remembered it because it was the one he had given to Marcel no more than a month ago. Norris wondered what had happened to it. He could also remember a model soldier wearing combat gear and carrying a gun, that would speak when a button on his back was pushed, even if the words were said in a strange language. Norris then realised the first words he learnt in French were '*Surrender or die.*'

"But did he love me mother?" he asked.

"From a distance."

Norris's next question was immediate, like he wanted to catch her off guard. "Did you ever love me?"

Her answer was just as instant. "You just said it dear."

"Said what?"

"I am your mother. A mother would give their life a thousand times for her son."

"And would you?"

"Of course dear."

"But did you ever..." He stopped himself. "Do you love me?"

"Yes dear, very much."

A silence came between them, but not a heavy one, it was like a great weight had been lifted. If only she had said those same words many years ago.

"Maybe it is because I didn't know how to show it, maybe I still don't. It is not your fault I am a terrible mother; but you had no one else dear, every child needs someone to look after them, to make them feel safe. It was me who was left to do that,

I had no choice, there was no one else." She stopped talking and sat back in the chair, she needed to leave him with his own thoughts.

Norris finally raised his chin and spoke. "You said you had heard of Jean-Paul Karel?"

Irene sat motionless. She knew if he had the minutest slice of love for her now then that would soon be snatched away forever. She took a deep breath. "Grandpa and Grandma had an apartment in Paris; it was in the same building where your other grandparents also had one. Both were very grand, just like the inside of a palace, a bit garish for my liking dear, far too foreign.

Norris looked around the room they were in.

"Your Grandad on your father's side was a high ranking diplomat, a very important man in Paris. Their home belonged to the British Embassy you know?"

Norris didn't answer. He wondered if his Grandad was around during the Markovic affair, maybe he knew the Pompidou's, maybe Madam Veronique. "Yes I remember meeting him once, they came to this house, I must have been around six or seven. I remember he spoke very softly, he asked me lots of questions which made me very nervous; other than that I can't remember much about him." Norris turned his head to the side. "I can't remember my Grandmother at all."

"He died in his sixties. She turned to drink and died not long after. That happens a lot dear, couples who have been deeply in love dropping dead within months of each other."

"Not you and father though."

"No dear, we never did anything together," she said softly, as if she regretted it. "Do you know your father was adopted?" she threw in, knowing this would be the first time Norris had heard this. She waited.

"No," he replied after several seconds.

"Just like when you looked for your father, he had also looked for his real mother. It was before I met him. His parents had told him he was adopted at a time when they thought he would understand. They said he was only a baby when they took him on, that his biological mother couldn't afford to keep him, that she already had five children; and his father had long gone. Her surname was Karel and..."

Norris interrupted. "And she had named him Jean-Paul."

"Yes dear. That is why they named him Joseph Peter, keeping the same initials would be like a testimony to his ancestral past."

Norris thought about the initials on his gravestone. "You said he went searching for her."

"I think his adoptive parents wanted to explain why he was nothing like them. They were good people, a rotten apple like him couldn't have possibly come from their bloodline."

"Did they actually say that?"

A smile brushed over her lips. "No dear."

She tried to change the subject. "Do you know I had met your father..."

"But he used the name Jean-Paul Karel?"

"He used both names dear. For different reasons."

"What reasons?"

Irene searched for the answer. "Good and bad, although I think they crossed over sometimes." She waited. "Do you know I had met your father before? Only on a couple of occasions though, at functions in your Grandad's apartment, and then we only talked briefly. Even then I thought he was an arrogant little shit."

Norris was surprised to hear her swear, even during their lowest times she never swore. He remembered she always said swearing was for people who had little command of the English language.

"Modesty was not his strong point you know." She puffed out a long, weary breath. "Your father was...how do those public bar types say dear? A chancer. He liked to mix with low-lifes, petty criminals, gangsters, frequent the same bars and cafes as them. That was when he called himself Jean-Paul Karel." She stared long and hard into her son's eyes. "And yes dear, I did know about his sordid little habits. He thought mixing with these people made him look important. What he didn't realise, those types probably stood on bugs more important to them than he was. Isn't it strange dear, the closer you want something the further away it appears." She sat back up. "Anyway, your Grandpa insisted we get married. He said it had all been arranged. I thought he was sending me to hell." She said it so matter-of-factly that Norris wondered if all the emotion had been sucked out of her. " I didn't dismiss the idea of going to hell...or heaven if God would have me, if you know what I mean? At the time I thought it was my only way out. If only I had the courage dear; which I didn't."

"You could have refused."

She thought for a while. "I had lived my entire life in comfort; with nothing to worry about, I was given the best of everything, toys, nannies...yes dear, I had a nanny even if your Grandpa didn't think it fit I should have one for you. Anyway, I had everything. You should have seen the doll's house I was given, it was bigger than the houses most common people lived in. I was sent to the most expensive girls' school, one that would mould me into a dutiful wife, one where I would leave with the savoir faire to attract a rich husband...with the priority being on wealth dear. But I didn't, nor did I want to. Your Grandpa made it very clear that if I didn't go ahead with the marriage then I would be left penniless, I would be thrown onto the streets. You see dear, like you were with me, your Grandma and Grandpa were all I had, without them I was nothing. I suppose they thought when they left this world I would at least have someone to look after me. In some ways I found that quite comforting...If only they knew."

"Was it that bad?"

"You have no idea dear. Right from the beginning I had made it clear to your father that I had no intention of marrying him." She glanced away for a second. "But like everything else he turned it to his own advantage. Do you know your father would sell his own Grandmother for a fast buck...or me as I was about to find out. He told me that one of his so called friends wanted a woman to pose for some photographs. He said they needed someone slightly older and not to worry because I would be made-up so no one would recognise me. And when I asked what they were for he refused to tell me. He knew I was desperate, that I would do anything to get out of this marriage. Your father told me if I agreed to it; he would tell my parents that he would refuse to marry me. He said he would make up some excuse, one that nobody could put the fault on me."

"When was this?"

"September 1968. It was just before we were to be married."

Norris's gaze fell to the carpet. He couldn't believe what he was hearing, could she be talking about the Markovic photographs. An image of them entered his mind, a picture of a woman naked on the bed with the young Valeraine Rousselle. He tried to recall if there was any resemblance. His eyes began flicking manically from side to side, recalling photographs of his mother when she was younger, not that there were many. He felt his throat tighten, a nauseous feeling rising up from his stomach. It could well be her, he was sure there was a likeness. He tried to find reasons why it couldn't be. He could find none.

Norris then thought of the favourable light that he could be held in Lucile's eyes, he had found out who the other woman was. Another thought entered his head, not a good one, he then realised how much like his father he was.

Irene continued. "The day came. Joseph drove, which I found strange because he hated driving in Paris. I soon found out why when he stopped the car and pulled a blindfold over my eyes, covering it with sunglasses. He gave me a scarf and told me to wrap it over my head. He said I looked like Audrey Hepburn, which was probably the nicest thing he had ever said. Not being able to see made me very scared, I had to trust this man." She lowered her eyes with a slow shake of the head. "Trust him." The words come out with a puff of air. "He drove for a short while before stopping the car again. I remember sitting there for a long time, I don't know why, maybe he was waiting for the road to clear, maybe we were too early." She looked up, but not towards Norris. "He then opened the car door and led me through a doorway into a room. I remember him telling me to take two steps forward and to wait there. I had never been more frightened, I couldn't see anything. I wanted to take the blindfold off, I knew that would probably seal my fate though, so I kept it on. The next sound I heard was the car door slamming and the noise of the engine speeding off into the distance. I was alone."

Norris could see her gazing to one side, as if she was trying to recall the moment.

"I heard footsteps, heavy like a mans, they seemed to echo off the walls, as if the room was large and empty. He spoke French, not harshly though, a kind voice, saying things that he hoped would calm me. I think he could see how scared I was. He said no harm would come to me and I was perfect." She turned her gaze towards Norris. "Which didn't exactly reassure me dear. We then climbed some stairs, I remember how gently he held onto my arm, giving me instructions as we walked, cupping my elbows in his hands as he led me upwards. He then took me into a room and untied the blindfold. I saw another woman, I remember she was wearing a silk dressing gown, her arms wrapped around her waist. She was very beautiful, slender, jet black hair, I think it was a wig because her skin was very pale. Her eyes were fixed on mine, stopping me from looking around, but I could sense a large bed to my side. It was then my suspicions were confirmed."

You don't know the half of it Norris thought to himself. He knew there were so many questions he should ask. He missed Lucile being there, she would know what to say. "Did you know who the man was?" he asked.

"No dear. He was older, that is all I can say. I got the impression the other woman knew him, although she was very careful not to say his name. I remember he had a nice face, he had a small mouth that looked as if it was held in a permanent grin, he kept cracking stupid jokes. I was very nervous dear, I just wanted to get it over with. I kept telling myself this is going to get me out of marrying your father, over and over again, like a mantra."

"Did you know who the other woman was?"

"No, other than she was very beautiful, a lovely slim figure, and her skin felt so soft, like yours when you were a baby."

Norris was feeling uncomfortable. Lucile was still in the forethought of his mind, he couldn't let her down, not now. He let his mother continue.

"Although she looked younger, she came across as being of a similar age to me. I could tell she was also nervous...but determined. She kept instructing me what to do, controlling my every move. She told me not to tell anyone else what was going to happen, nor where I was or who I met, not that I knew dear. I was very careful not to look at the man for too long, or ask questions. She told me if any of this got out I would be in great danger, but she didn't say it in a threatening way, she didn't have to. She said it like my fate would be out of her hands. I remember beginning to regret being there, thinking marrying your father would have been preferable. Before we...you know, began, the man left the room. The woman told me to undress and gave me a blonde wig and a dressing gown. She told me to sit at a dressing table in the corner of the room where she would help me make-up."

Norris remembered the same table in the pictures, the reflection of The Drowning Mary in the mirror. He then imagined his mother's face also being there.

"I remember she was very kind, very gentle when she touched my face; but she only spoke the bare minimum, just the odd command. Strangely dear I wanted to ask her about herself, about her life. How did she get into this situation? I wondered if she was being blackmailed like me, if we were comrades in arms, if she too was trying to get out of a marriage. I also wondered what she would be like as a friend." She paused for a second. "That is how lonely I was."

Norris realised he could answer all of those questions. Maybe he would tell her later. He could take her to France, introduce her to Valeraine Rousselle. Lucile could take photographs of the two women meeting. What a story that would make. The two women involved in the most notorious photographs in French political history meeting for the first time after forty two years. Norris could feel his skin tingle, how could Lucile refuse him after that.

Irene continued. "I remember the woman kept looking at a page from a newspaper, she was very careful I didn't see it. After each glance she would make a slight adjustment to my make-up or hair. When she had finished she called the man back in. I remember his smile as soon as he saw me, he seemed to be very pleased with the result. We took off our dressing gowns and got onto the bed. The actual business of taking the photographs only took a few minutes, it was very..."

Norris needed to change the subject. "Did you find out who the other woman was?"

"No dear."

"Did they tell you what the photographs were going to be used for?"

"No, and I didn't want to know. I thought it was for a smutty magazine, I believe they do things like that don't they, pretend to look like someone famous, an actress or someone well known. A celebrity; I believe you call them dear. I just hoped when the next issue was published this one would soon be forgotten about. I knew no one would recognise me, the woman had done a very good job. I think the man wanted us to feel as if we were on our own because he hid behind a curtain to take the photographs. Do you know I found the entire episode quite exciting, you could say exhilarating dear, even when I was on the bed with her. In some ways I quite enjoyed it, I mean being close to someone else, having them touch me like they loved me. She gazed at Norris. "Oh dear. Have I embarrassed you?"

"You always embarrass me mother."

"Maybe that was why I didn't want to get married, maybe I preferred women."

Norris didn't want to give her the satisfaction of looking shocked. He shrugged apathetically.

A playful grin came to her face. "Don't worry dear, I am not a lesbian."

"I wasn't worried."

"I was a victim, that is all, one orchestrated by your father. It is not me you should blame dear."

"I'm not. But you still married him?"

"Luckily for you." A pretend smile came to her face. "Think of all the babies who weren't born because people didn't get together."

Norris thought she was trying to make him feel grateful.

"Do you know I believed what he had said. I actually thought that your father would keep to his word, that he would call the wedding off. But instead he told me my life was not my own anymore, that he was now in control of me. He then threatened to tell a newspaper who the actual woman in the photographs was, that he would name me."

"So he told you what the photographs were about."

"Yes dear. He said if the French public ever found out then I would be the most hated person in France. He said from now on I would do as I was told. We were still going to get married and I was going to fund his lifestyle. The only good thing he said was that he would spend most of his time in France, only so he could continue with his dirty little pursuits. He said all I had to do was have a child to please my parents."

Not for the first time Norris felt worthless.

"He had it all worked out. I sometimes think it was him who organised the whole sordid business on that day." She blew out another disparaging breath. "Your father was never that clever though. He said that once we had a child my parents would leave me alone, then he would too; and thankfully that is what happened dear. He only returned to this country occasionally, just on a pretence to satisfy your Grandpa and Grandma, and of course to give you your gifts. Then one day he said he needed a large amount of money, he told me it was to buy a painting. Of course I didn't believe him."

"The Drowning Mary," Norris said more to himself.

"Sorry dear."

"The Drowning Mary, that was the name of the painting. But you still gave him the money."

"Yes dear. What choice did I have? What choice have I had?"

"Did you know that same painting was in the room when those photos were taken?"

Irene's eyebrows turned downward, deep furrows appeared in her forehead. "How did you know that?" she asked.

"I have three of the photographs."

A long thoughtful silence.

"Do you have them now?" Her words soft.

"A friend does." His eyes clung to hers. "Don't worry, they are safe."

Another long silence. "Where did you get them?"

Norris remembered how he promised never to divulge Monsieur Bret's name. "It is not important." He could see she was shaken by his admission. It felt like bittersweet revenge for all those years void of love. "Do you know why father wanted that painting?" he finally asked.

"Is that what all this is about?"

"Not all, no."

"He wanted it for someone else."

"Who?"

"I do not know, neither did I care about his sordid little dealings."

Norris thought it was about time to tell her the truth. "It was a woman called Susanne Dennel who had Markovic murdered." He didn't tell her Madam Veronique and Susanne Dennel were the same woman. "Did you know her sister was the other woman in the photograph?"

"No I didn't. Your father said he dropped me outside a house in Montmartre, that is all. I went in with a blindfold and I came out with a blindfold."

"That house was an art gallery. The Valeraine Rousselle Art Gallery. Valeraine Rousselle was the other woman. Her maiden name was Dennel. She told me this herself; and before you ask mother, no she doesn't know who you are."

"You have met her?"

"Yes, twice." He waited a moment. "Once when I was trying to find father. The second time was only a few days ago, with a friend."

"Is this the friend with the photographs?"

"Yes."

"Is she your girlfriend dear?"

Norris was surprised by the question, he wanted to say yes. "I am not sure," he replied.

"Never mind dear."

He thought she sounded patronising. "Do you know the pictures were a setup?"

"A setup. Is that what you call it?"

"So you found out who you were made-up to look like?"

"It wasn't difficult dear. It was all over the French newspapers. I read a man had been murdered; that he was once a bodyguard for a famous French actor. It said that photographs were found in his car and the President's wife was photographed having sex with another woman. The report said the photographs were taken by a man called Markovic. I knew immediately dear; it was the ones from that day. I became very frightened, I thought they were going to find out it was me. I immediately returned to England. Do you know dear I have only left this country once since? I even began telling people I had never travelled abroad!"

"It was when that foreign looking woman knocked on my door, the one with that horrible scratchy voice."

"Teresa Flores."

"Yes dear. Do you know she gave me a migraine?"

Norris didn't answer.

"She told me she was looking for you, that you were missing in Chad and may have been kidnapped. But I knew otherwise dear. I do feel sorry for that Mr Markovic though, he seemed to be such a pleasant fellow for a foreigner."

"Sorry...Oh...It wasn't Markovic who took the photographs."

"Was it not dear?" She sounded genuinely surprised. "That is a relief."

"It was a man called Francois Marcantoni."

"Was it dear?"

"Do you know who murdered Markovic?"

A moments silence. "Yes."

"Who?"

"He did, Jean-Paul Karel...Your father"

Norris wondered if she was telling the truth. The words hanging in the air like a question mark.

"Not Joseph Kinley?"

"No dear, I just said, Jean-Paul Karel."

"Why?"

"Why did he kill this Markovic fellow?

"Yes mother," he said through a sigh.

"Because your grandfather, your father's father...because..." She paused for a second. "Because your grandfather knew that woman."

"Madam Veronique is that woman's name."

"Is that so."

"Actually Susanne Dennel and Madam Veronique are one and the same."

"Is that so dear?"

"Your Grandfather was a very important man in the Embassy. If news got out...well, I think it was made clear; Marcantoni blackmailed your father into doing whatever he wanted, including murder, including using you."

"I don't understand, how do you know all this?"

"He told me."

"He told you he killed Markovic. When did he tell you?"

This was it. The time had finally come, when she would probably lose her only child. "He asked me for more money. I agreed, but only if I could go to Marseille, give it to him face to face. When I arrived he looked half the man he was, I hardly recognised him dear. It was then I realised he was all alone, that I was the only friend he had left in the world. Isn't it strange dear how life can change."

"Why?"

"Why? I have already told you dear."

"Why did you go? It is not as if you wanted to...I mean you didn't want to leave the..." The words slowly tailed away. "I told you earlier that father had died."

"Yes dear, I heard you."

"But you knew already didn't you?"

"Yes dear."

"An old woman was seen entering the block around the same time. That was you wasn't it?"

"Yes dear."

"I don't understand." Norris tried to think. "You were there when he took his own..." Norris suddenly stopped, his eyes widened. "It was you. It was you who killed him. Wasn't it?"

"Of course dear. What did you expect?"

"You killed my father."

"Your father killed me long before that." Her voice hardened. "Have you not been listening dear?"

"And you thought you got away with it."

"But you decided to go searching for him. It was then I knew you would discover the truth. You were always a tenacious little fellow."

"I don't understand. It was then he told you everything?"

"I thought it was the poison at first, like it was acting as a truth drug. I asked him a question and he answered it, like a confession, much like you are doing now. Then I realised he knew he was about to die. He was quite brave really, wanting to tell me everything, the truth dear , get it all off his chest you could say."

"I don't understand."

"Put old ghosts to rest. I know of no other way to say it dear."

Monday 2nd August 2010
Cafe de la Fontaine,
Marseille
France

Julien was sat in the corner of the cafe, sipping lazely on his double espresso, beside him a large window bathed him in warmth from the midday sun. The location purposely chosen, not only so he could look cool donning his recently purchased Ray-Bans, but also to ogle at the young women passing by on the pavement outside; and if the truth be known, the not so young. Annoyingly for Julien, his time was cut short when Remi arrived less than a minute later.

Cheek to cheek air kisses were exchanged, polite greetings traded, small talk swapped. Julien gossiped mainly about the newspaper, telling Remi the story of Angelique and her footballers, how it fizzled out after the paper discovered Angelique herself was sleeping with the centre forward. He joked about Henri, the flustered editor forever trying to wield his authority over him. Then they got onto the subject of art, which they always did. Julien knew it was an excuse for Remi to fulfill his quota of artspeak, convinced the old gallery manager rehearsed it at home before he left for the cafe, probably in front of a mirror, like learning lines in a play. Julien listened with his usual pretend enthusiasm, only today his attentiveness was harder to fake, other matters dominated his mind.

Remi stopped talking, followed by silence.

"*It has been a long time since we spoke like this,*" Julien finally remarked.

"*It has. We should do this more often my friend.*"

"*The last time was before my colleague Lucile Billet came to visit you.*"

Remi had hoped that meeting wouldn't be mentioned.

"*Although Lucile is not my colleague anymore.*" Julien added. Not wanting to disclose how much he knew about Remi's meeting with her; which was everything.

"*Ah yes. She came to see me with the Englishman. He was very tall, not my type I'm afraid.*"

"*Sorry Remi, Mademoiselle Billet asked me if I knew where you lived. She wanted advice on an artist...I hope you didn't...*"

"*No, not at all Julien,*" Remi lied, the last thing he wanted was someone asking him about those sketches again. He also wondered how much his friend knew about the meeting, probably everything knowing Julien. But did he know when and where the sketches were found? Did he know about the three Markovic photographs? Many of their conversations were like a game of chess. What did he know? Who could outsmart the other. "*Glad to be of help, or not help in this case. They wanted my expert opinion on some drawings; but they were very small photocopies, not good quality at all. It was impossible for me to tell them anything I'm afraid.*"

"*Lucile thought they may have been by one particular artist?*" Julien asked, wanting Remi to say who it was.

Remi wanted to avoid saying the name but knew it would look more suspicious if he didn't. "*Ah yes, Francois Degarmo.*"

"*And you said they were definitely not by him?*"

Remi had to be careful, he knew what a wily old fox Julien

could be. "*I told them Francois Degarmo's touch was more sophisticated, he painted from the soul, from the heart, his expression of colour was more complex...*" He stopped, noticing how bored Julien looked. "*It was not Francois Degarmo's work.*"

"*I believe the police also spoke to you about those same sketches?*" Julien asked in a very matter-of-fact manner, trying to make the question flow with the conversation.

Remi knew Julien was very well informed, after all that was his job. But he wasn't expecting that. He even knew Julien wasn't living in Marseille at the time of the prostitute's death. Why would he ask though? "*Did they? I remember they asked me about some drawings. It was such a long time ago. Were they the same? My memory is not as it used to be.*" Remi tried to play ignorant, looking to the side, pretending to think back. "*Ah yes, I think they may well have been.*" He added, hiding his discomfort. "*You always surprise me with how much you know my friend. What did I tell them?*" he asked, even if he knew the answer.

"*The same as you told Mademoiselle Billet and the Englishman.*"

Remi blew out an unconvincing laugh. "*At least I am consistent.*"

Julien turned both his palms upward. "*And if the great art expert Remi Cochet does not recognise the painting then the artist is a nobody?*" His smile lacked humour.

"*Ah yes Julien they are.*"

"*And it was your gallery that sold paintings by Francois Degarmo, so if anybody knew the artist, then you would Remi.*" Julien paused a second. "*Did you sell many?*"

Remi looked down at his coffee cup, but not actually focusing on it. "*We sent two up to the Paris gallery, they only sold one though, it was called The Foundering of Death. The Pompidou Centre bought it, although they didn't pay as much as they should have.*"

Julien thought he sounded bitter. "*That must have been quite an achievement, I mean an unknown artist selling a painting to the Pompidou Centre.*"

Remi felt like their conversation had gone past being just their usual shallow afternoon chat. "*The gallery owner was very astute.*"

"*And the other?*"

"*Sorry?*"

"*The other Degarmo you sent up there.*"

"*Ah yes. It was called The Drowning Mary. They didn't sell it.*" Remi's words sounded hesitant. "*Forgive me Julien but what is this all about?*"

Remi watched as his friend crouched down and picked up a small leather case off the floor, placing it on his lap. He saw him pull a newsletter out, trying to catch the heading on the front: but even before Julien had sat back up he began flicking through the pages, stopping at one, folding it back so it was facing outward. Julien slid it in front of his friend and waited while Remi digested the pictures.

"*It was Lucile Billet who told me the police had also asked you about the sketches, that you told them the same as you told her, that you said you didn't know the artist. So I decided to do a bit of investigating myself. I knew Francois Degarmo was from Marseille, he was an artist, we both know that much. The strange thing was Remi, I could find out nothing about him, it was like he didn't exist. Something always exists.*" Julien leant forward, his elbows on the table, speaking so softly his words could hardly be heard. "*Until I went to the École Supérieure des Beaux-arts that is, just on the off chance. I asked about students enrolling between the end of the war and 1960. The lady in the office took me into a small room and pulled four boxes off the shelf, all packed with registration cards. It took me three hours Remi.*" Julien feigned surprise. "*Then guess what?*"

Remi didn't answer.

"*I came across one with Francois Degarmo's name on it,*

it said he had enrolled in 1953, then left the school three months later. It said the reason was for misconduct..."

"*He left on his own accord Monsieur.*"

Julien was surprised Remi had called him Monsieur. "*I just assumed...*"

"*Don't assume. He was misunderstood, many great artists are.*"

Julien took a deep breath. "*Anyway, old Julien Caron was not one to give up, so I delved deeper. The woman at the college was very obliging, very knowledgable, and luckily for me, very, very well organised. We like that in a person, don't we Remi?*" Julien held up the palms of his hands. "*And what woman can ignore Julien Caron's charm. She told me the college published a newsletter every month, that they began printing it after the War. She said an issue had only been missed on a few occasions.*" Julien paused for a second. "*But not the one with a picture of Francois Degarmo. And not only that, beside it there was a picture of one of his paintings, and under that was the name of the painting.*" Julien was talking as if each sentence was a surprise. "*The Drowning Mary, Remi. The painting is called The Drowning Mary.*" Julien waited. "*They always kept a dozen file copies of the newsletter. So guess what? They were kind enough to let me have one. This one.*"

"*One day The Drowning Mary will be recognised as a great work of art,*" Remi remarked.

"*I hope you are right my friend.*"

Remi gazed down at the newsletter. "*What are you going to do?*" The words calm, as if he had been expecting this moment.

"*I think we should straighten out some facts first.*" Julien waited, he had never seen his friend so lost for words.

"*The sketches shown to you by Lucile Billet and the police, are they by the hand of Francois Degarmo?*"

"*What if I said no?*"

Julien leant even more forward, his words hardly audible.

"They have fingerprints my friend. They have the wallet, the money, the sketchbook. They all have fingerprints on them." Julien didn't know that for certain, he just knew Remi would think he did. *"All they would have to do is test them against his prints. But let us hope it doesn't come to that Remi."* Julien studied Remi's reaction. The chess match of words had now entered its endgame. *"The sketches Remi, were they drawn by Francois Degarmo?"*

"Yes."

"The picture in that newsletter." Julien's finger hung above the headshot, prodding downward. *"The one with the words Francois Degarmo underneath it. The one in the column headed 'Artist smashes up studio'."* Julien took his sunglasses off, his eyes looked down at the picture, then up towards Remi, they were unblinking, narrow, the skin around them heavily creased, like holes in a spiders web. *"The picture was taken a long time ago. Is that you Remi?"* Julien feigned surprise. *"It looks like you."*

Remi looked down, too ashamed to face his old friend eye to eye. *"Yes,"* he puffed out.

"Are you Francois Degarmo, Remi?"

"Yes."

Julien took in a deep breath. *"Did you kill that prostitute?"*

Remi didn't answer immediately, he knew this was one checkmate he couldn't avoid. His stare shot up. *"It was an accident Julien, I didn't mean to do it, she stole my wallet, I just wanted her to give..."*

Julien's words fell over Remi's. *"Yes or no Remi?"*

"Yes," he finally said.

A long silence followed.

"If you hadn't smashed up that studio then you wouldn't have been in that newsletter. I wouldn't have known, no one would have."

"No one understood the meaning of true art Julien."

"You mean your art Remi."

"I painted from the soul, from my heart. They used to criticise me all the time, find fault with everything..."

"It was a school Remi. That is what they do."

"Even the other students." Remi gazed up, in the short time they had been at the cafe his eyes had darkened. *"My art explored the emotive quality of colour, defeating the oppression of bourgeois attitudes..."* he stopped when he saw Julien's apathy. *"I was hotheaded in those days, a bit of a rebel."* He stopped again. *"Then I grew up."*

"And you got a job managing the Valeraine Rousselle gallery?"

"Ah yes. It was Susanne Dennel who helped. I knew her from.... She knew I was very knowledgable on modern art, she was the one that suggested I could sell my paintings through the gallery. All I had to do was change my name. Only no one bought them. Then Madame Rousselle asked me to send some works up by an unknown artist, one from the grass roots of the art world."

"I sent a recent work, 'The Foundering of Death'." Remi paused for a moment. *"And an older piece, 'The Drowning Mary,' I thought they were my best work. She didn't know they were by me. The Pompidou Centre bought 'The Foundering of Death.' There was much criticism over the purchase, not only because it was by an unknown artist, but because they said it was poor quality, like a child's painting: they said it looked as if a monkey had painted it, that it didn't deserve to be hung in such a great bastion of modern art. I have been to the Pompidou Centre many times, stood in front of my own painting, having to listen to the rubbish people said about it. On a couple of occasions I told them they knew nothing, that they did not understand true art, that the artist has questioned the identity of chaos against the structured and tedious uniformity of life."* Remi paused for a moment. *"Madam Rousselle kept 'The Drowning Mary' for a while, but couldn't sell it, even after the Pompidou Centre bought 'The Foundering of Death'."*

"So when Valeraine Rousselle thought she was returning 'The Drowning Mary' to the Marseille gallery, she was in fact returning it to you. It was the same."

"Yes Monsieur."

"So you also used the gallery to sell your paintings?"

Remi rolled his eyes. *"Sell. Not one sold Monsieur, not even 'The Drowning Mary.' Sometimes I had to stand there and listen to these idiots criticise my own work, can you imagine what that was like. So I stopped painting. Francois Degarmo stopped painting."*

"You stopped because you killed that girl. That was when you decided to kill Francois Degarmo at the same time. If you could wipe Francois Degarmo off the face of this planet then you would be removing the killer."

"Then Madame Rousselle told me an Englishman was coming to Marseille to buy 'The Drowning Mary.' She had mentioned there was a painting by Francois Degarmo for sale, and that he had a work hanging in the Pompidou Centre. Like I said Julien, Madame Rousselle was very astute."

"So you sold 'The Drowning Mary' to the Englishman's father."

Remi forced a smile. *"He recognised a great piece of work Julien."*

Julien smiled with him. *"You mean you bamboozled him with those words of yours. I remember you said to me once that it is always about the money, never about the painting. But 'The Drowning Mary' wasn't even worth anything close to the amount you sold it to him for."*

"He was a fool, worse than that, he was a fool with money. He thought he knew about art."

"The space on the ground floor, the one you never let anyone see, that was your studio wasn't it Remi? That is where you painted."

"Ah yes. But not now. Not for a very long time."

"What are you going to do Julien?"

"*Shouldn't the question be...What are you going to do Remi?*"

"*I didn't mean to kill her Julien, she wouldn't stop struggling, all I wanted was my wallet back, then I would have let her go.*" Remi glared at Julien, his voice hardened. "*It was over twenty years ago and who cares about the death of a prostitute anyway?*"

"*Me...I do Remi. There is one thing I don't understand, I thought you preferred boys rather...*" Julien stopped. "*Ah.*" Stretching the word in realisation. "*Just in case. No one would think an old homosexual would have even gone anywhere close to a girl prostitute.*" He nodded slowly. "*People who get close to other people think they know them...but they don't. That one even fooled me.*"

Remi gazed down at the newsletter. "*Does Mademoiselle Billet know you have this?*"

"*No one does. First you tell me what you are going to do.*"

Remi raised his hands in a futile gesture. "*What if I do nothing?*"

Julien's tone was harsh, accusing. "*You killed someone Remi, an innocent girl. I'm afraid that is not an option.*"

"*What is it you want me to do Julien?*"

"*It is not me you should be asking my friend.*"

Thursday 9th September 2010
Charles de Gaulle Airport,
Paris,
France

Norris sat back in his seat, stretched out his legs, folded his arms and stared up into empty space. His mind began to wander as aimlessly as the people trundling around the terminal with their trolleys and suitcases.

He thought about the last few months. How it started at an airport in one country and finished at an airport in another country. Never in his wildest dreams did he think it would have taken him to the places it had or the people he had encountered. Then to top it all, to find out it was his father who killed Markovic and his mother was the other woman in the photographs. Norris smiled to himself, he could write a book about it: deciding he would leave that to Lucile — or would he? Would anyone believe them anyway?

He then thought about how the journey began, the job interview with Teresa at the charity, an underhand ploy to get into Chad — his guilt still remained. Then how they had returned to England in June, the day before he had that conversation with his mother, saying their farewells at

Aylesbury railway station with a formal handshake, taking separate taxis to their final destinations. Both promising to keep in touch, a promise which had yet to be kept.

Norris's mind wandered back to an hour ago, when he was in the terminal cafe with Crystal, Jamia, Ali and Lucile. Crystal was surprised when Jamia had said she wanted to return to Chad; after being told Captain Nkusi had been charged with war crimes and taken to The Hague. She said it was the land of her mother and father, of her brothers, the place where their spirits could be free.

Crystal added that the Canadian authorities had finally granted Jamia and Ali refugee status. With the help of Christine Lamy her sponsorship had been fast-tracked. She also knew that once in her home country the adoption process would just be a formality. She would try and be a mother to them, hopefully return to practising law again, maybe specialise in immigration, helping other refugees needing to escape their country. After all she had first hand experience.

In the end Crystal said she had managed to convince Jamia that her and Ali would live a comfortable life in Canada. They would never again have to worry about where their next mouthful of food would come from, their next mug of clean water: they would be free from the threat of disease, but most importantly they would be safe. She had also told Jamia that it was not a foregone conclusion Captain Nkusi would be found guilty. She was a bright girl and this would be her chance in life. She would receive the education she so desired, maybe become a lawyer like herself, a teacher, a doctor, fulfill her greatest desire and travel the world. She told Jamia after she had graduated she could make the decision herself to return to Chad. Then she would be armed with the most powerful weapon she could ever hope to possess, the ability to help her own people.

Norris had asked Crystal to translate that they would be welcome to stay with him in England anytime they wished. Jamia's thanks were in Arabic, but the words 'Buckingham

Palace' were somewhere there, if only just audible. He was also delighted to see he had drawn a smile from Ali.

Crystal said the clincher was when she described what snow was like to Ali. How excited he became, discovering something so white and cold could exist in this world — when all he had known was heat and dust.

She explained to Jamia how Ali would get the care he needed in Canada. It was obvious his experiences at Scorpion Rock still remained in the deepest recesses of his mind, and with expert psychological support those demons could be exorcised. Jamia agreed. It was settled, Canada it is. Everyone was happy with the decision.

Norris unfolded his arms and placed them behind his head. He thought back to the last time he had seen Crystal, Jamia and Ali, when they had passed through the check-in desk ten minutes earlier. He wondered if it would be the last time he would see them — thinking it probably would.

He peered through the crowd, hoping to see Lucile return with the coffees. She was nowhere to be seen.

Norris sank back into his own thoughts again. An image of 'The Drowning Mary' came to mind. Madam Veronique, as promised, had handed over the painting to him, telling Norris she didn't like it anyway. It was strange because he told her exactly the same, that he had never liked it. And for both, the memories it conjured up were not good ones. Norris decided to give it to Helaine, after all, she seemed to be the only person on this earth that actually liked it. He also gave her the copies from the sketchbook, telling her how an expert had told him they were not from the same hand, even they could make mistakes. Norris was still not convinced.

It made him think about the journey to find his father; remembering a novel he once read. It was called 'The Road.' A father and son relationship, both trying to survive the horrifying circumstances they were thrown into after the near annihilation of humanity. He recalled the ending, not knowing if the son survived with his new found family after his father died. It made him think about his own mother, how she had killed his father. It was strange because after that conversation their relationship had taken a whole new turn, surprisingly one for the better. Maybe religion has a point he thought, forgiveness will always triumph over revenge.

Norris felt something nudge his foot, he opened his eyes to see Lucile handing him a coffee. She sat.

"You were asleep," she said.

"I was thinking," he replied, shaking his head in disbelief, as he had done many times over the last few weeks, the same unanswered questions ploughing through his mind, one after another, over and over again. "I still can't get over what Helaine told you."

"It's true Norris. I really don't know why you keep asking. A man turned up at Helaine's doorstep and confessed to killing Nicole."

"Just like that?"

"Yes, just like that."

"And he said his name was Francois Degarmo?"

"Yes."

"Why?"

"Why what?"

"Why did he turn up; just like that?"

"He told her he had served a life sentence and wanted her to release him."

"That is what Helaine said."

"Was it because he knew she had 'The Drowning Mary'?"

"She said he didn't know about that. She said he was stunned to see it hanging in her room; and that he nearly dropped to the floor. But he was pleased someone liked it."

"Wasn't she scared, I mean he had already killed once."

"She said not. He was old and weak and this is Helaine we are talking about."

"And is she going to release him from his life sentence."

"No, not yet."

"Oh...So why did he kill Nicole?"

"I've asked. She won't say anymore."

"But there must be...You must speak with her."

"Don't you think I've tried Norris."

"And she won't go to the police about Nicole's murder?"

"No."

"Why?"

Lucilc's glarc was answer in itself.

"I would like to meet him." Norris said flatly.

"Well you can't." The reply just as blunt.

A short pause.

"What is she going to do?"

"She said he was going to make the world a better place."

"What!? That's it?"

"Yes Norris."

"What does she mean by that?"

Lucile shrugged. Both fell into a long thoughtful silence, Norris continued to slowly shake his head in disbelief.

"*We need to talk,*" Lucile finally said in French.

He looked around. "*Here?*"

"*Yes.*" The word like a puff of air. "*You have been avoiding me. And please don't tell me you haven't.*" She repeated it in English. "Don't lie and say you haven't."

"I won't."

"Kevin told us that Marcantoni said he knew who the murderer was."

"He did. I remember."

Lucile released a long sigh."I think Kevin knew who the killer was. I think Marcantoni told him."

"Apparently."

Lucile widened her eyes. "Apparently!?" she cried. "What is going on Norris? Your father wanted to give Madam Veronique 'The Drowning Mary' so he could have Matthieu. That same painting was in the photographs. Is this not an unbelievable coincidence Norris? You are keeping something from me."

Norris remained silent.

"Norris." Lucile said quietly. "Could you go into a relationship knowing you are keeping secrets from your partner?"

Norris thought she was taking him for granted, he had feelings, didn't she realise that. Apart from that time in Beaune when they had made what Norris thought was wonderful love, every other time after that she had blatantly shrugged off his advances. It had slowly ground him down, he was too weary to try anymore. "What relationship?"

"Would you want your own child to be raised by both their mother and father?"

"If I had a..." Norris stopped, was she trying to make some poignant comment about his relationship with his parents. Maybe she just wanted his opinion. He repeated the words in his mind. The hustle and bustle of the terminal gradually faded into oblivion. The realisation slowly rising in his body. "Are you saying..."

"Yes." She interrupted. Then for some odd reason she needed to say it in French. "*I am pregnant.*" Maybe it was too important to use any other language except her native tongue. She repeated it in English. "Yes Norris, I'm expecting a baby...our baby."

Norris thought of his own upbringing, the father who was never there, the mother void of love. "Yes I would very much like to be involved in raising my..." He smiled. "Our child."

"Then I repeat Norris. Could you go into a relationship knowing you are keeping secrets from your partner?"

For a split second Norris thought she was playing games, he knew how her journalistic mind worked, but even for Lucile this would be far too low. "No secrets," he said. "I promise to tell you everything if you promise me one thing." He stared long and hard at her. "Could you go into a relationship without trusting that person?"

She ignored the question. "What do you want me to promise you Norris?"

"I repeat Lucile. Could you go into a relationship without trusting someone?"

"*Non,* I could not go into a relationship without trusting him." Bobbing her head from side to side with each word. "Neither could I promise you something if I do not know what it is," she quickly added.

"I want you to promise me that you will not publish what I am about to tell you."

"Then you will have to say what it is you are about to tell me."

Norris paused for a moment. "We have a saying in England; 'what came first, the chicken or the egg'?"

"Sorry, I do not understand."

He raised his eyebrows. "You have to promise not to publish first, before I tell you what I know."

"But I cannot promise until..." She broke into a smile. "The chicken or the egg. Now I understand....You tell me what you know then I promise not to publish whatever it is." Lucile waited.

"Okay, I'll give you a clue." he finally said. "I know who the other woman is. I also know who murdered Markovic."

Lucile laughed out loud, causing people to look at them again. "And you want me to promise not to publish that!"

"Yes Lucile, that is exactly what I want."

"And if I can't promise."

"Then I can't tell you."

"The chicken or the egg," she repeated.

"The trust or the secret," Norris added.

ALSO BY
THE SAME AUTHOR

The Unfortunate Basil Albright

Baz's life is like a jigsaw puzzle, once connected every piece has an effect on the other, however distant. As the picture evolves his life becomes increasingly tortuous.

This is the unlikely story of Basil Albright's life from his earliest memory to the tragic consequences of his death.

A loner, a father, a one-time lover and a killer. Baz brushes shoulders with gangsters, tackles the most uninhabitable airfield of the Second World War and joins a drug-fuelled hippy commune. He questions beliefs and searches for answers. But most of all, Basil Albright is a victim of unfortunate events.

"Do you believe in the Virgin Birth?"

"Yes of course, I am a Christian."

"Well, you could be from a virgin birth then?"

"That's ridiculous!"

"You believed in one Virgin Birth, why not another?"

The prequel to The Drowning Mary

THE TUKUL with the BLUE DOOR

Recently employed by The Way for Life charity, Norris Kinley has been sent to Breidjing Refugee Camp in war-torn Chad to organise the transportation of food aid. But is this the true reason why he is there? Five days after his expected return to the UK and no one has heard from him.

For Teresa Flores the Operations Director at the charity and Crystal Bullion the Camp Manager at Breidjing, one word instantly comes to mind — kidnapping.

Spanning four weeks and three countries, the truth of what happened to Norris slowly unravels.

42089967R00223

Printed in Poland
by Amazon Fulfillment
Poland Sp. z o.o., Wrocław